The

INFINITE

PLAN

Praise for *The Infinite Plan*, a *New York Times Book Review*
Notable Book of 1993

"Allende writes with passion and conviction. . . . Her new novel is ambitious in scope."

—Merle Rubin, *Christian Science Monitor*

"Written in the spare and simple, virtually reportorial style favored by classic American writers such as Theodore Dreiser and Sinclair Lewis. . . . Allende's approach enables her to take a vast amount of America's collective experience and reduce it to human scale via the personal narratives of her characters.

—Ron Grossman, *Chicago Tribune*

"An ironic and romantic comedy, a compendium of American culture, family life, and war and love between the sexes."

—Anne Whitehouse, *Atlanta Journal-Constitution*

"Allende is a genius. . . . [She] has chosen a literary road closer to Theodore Dreiser or James T. Farrell."

—Carolyn See, *Los Angeles Times Book Review*

"Stunning. . . . [Allende] draws on her keen powers of observation and insight to make this new California milieu vivid. . . . It's a confident artist who is willing to experiment and change, while maintaining the highest standards. The result is rewarding, for Allende and her readers."

—Diana Penner, *Indianapolis Star*

"A beautifully told tragedy"   —*Mademoiselle* magazine

"A richly embroidered, ambitious tale . . . intensely imagined."

—*Publishers Weekly*

"An artful blend of aching realism and provocative meditation."

—*Booklist*

4 sophia

Books by Isabel Allende

THE HOUSE OF THE SPIRITS

OF LOVE AND SHADOWS

EVA LUNA

THE STORIES OF EVA LUNA

PAULA

APHRODITE: A MEMOIR OF THE SENSES

DAUGHTER OF FORTUNE

PORTRAIT IN SEPIA

MY INVENTED COUNTRY

ZORRO

INÉS OF MY SOUL

THE SUM OF OUR DAYS

ISLAND BENEATH THE SEA

FOR YOUNG ADULTS

CITY OF THE BEASTS

KINGDOM OF THE GOLDEN DRAGON

FOREST OF THE PYGMIES

Isabel Allende

The

INFINITE

PLAN

a   n o v e l

Translated from the Spanish
by Margaret Sayers Peden

HARPER ⬤ PERENNIAL

NEW YORK • LONDON • TORONTO • SYDNEY • NEW DELHI • AUCKLAND

HARPER ● PERENNIAL

Originally published in Spain as *El Plan Infinito* by Plaza y Janés Editores, S.A., Barcelona.

A hardcover edition of this book was published in 1993 by HarperCollins Publishers.

A signed first edition of this book has been privately printed by The Franklin Library.

P.S.™ is a trademark of HarperCollins Publishers.

HarperCollins books may be purchased for educational, business, or sales promotional use. For information please write: Special Markets Department, HarperCollins Publishers, 10 East 53rd Street, New York, NY 10022.

First HarperPerennial edition published 1994. Reissued in Perennial 2002.
First Harper Perennial edition published 2010.

Designed by Claudyne Bianco

The Library of Congress has catalogued the hardcover edition as follows:

Allende, Isabel.
    [Plan infinito. English]
        The infinite plan : a novel / Isabel Allende ; translated from the Spanish by Margaret Sayers Peden.—1st U.S. ed.
            p. cm.
        ISBN 0-06-017016-6
        I. Title.
PQ8098.I.L54P5713 1993
863—dc20   92-54741

ISBN 978-0-06-197682-7 (P.S. edition)

11 12 13 14 RRD 10 9 8 7 6 5 4 3 2

My thanks to life, for all it has given,

for all the laughter and tears I have lived....

Violeta Parra, Chile

I am alone, at dawn, on the mountaintop. Below, through the milky mist, I see the bodies of my friends. Some that have rolled down the slopes lie like disjointed red dolls; others are ashen statues surprised by the eternity of death. Stealthy shadows are climbing toward me. Silence. I wait. They approach. I fire against dark silhouettes in black pajamas, faceless ghosts. I feel the recoil of the machine gun; I grip it so tightly my hands burn as incandescent lines of fire cross through the sky, but there is no sound. The attackers have become transparent; they are not stopped by the bullets that pass right through them, they continue their implacable advance. I am surrounded. . . . Silence. . . .

My own scream wakes me, and I keep screaming, screaming. . . .

Gregory Reeves

PART ONE

PART ONE

They traveled the roads and byways of the West, unhurriedly and with no set itinerary, changing their route according to the whim of the moment, the premonitory sign of a flock of birds, the lure of an unknown name. The Reeveses interrupted their erratic pilgrimage wherever they were overcome by weariness or wherever they found someone disposed to buy their intangible merchandise. They sold hope. In this way they traveled up and down the desert, they crossed mountains, and one early morning they saw day break over a beach on the Pacific coast. Forty-some years later, during a long confession in which he reviewed his life and drew up an accounting of his errors and achievements, Gregory Reeves told me of his earliest memory: a boy of four, himself, urinating on a hilltop at sunset, the horizon stained red and amber by the last rays of the sun; at his back were the sharp peaks of the hills, and, below, a plain stretched farther than the eye could see. The warm liquid flows like some essence of body and spirit, each drop, as it sinks into the dirt, marking the territory with his signature. He prolongs the pleasure, playing with the stream, tracing a topaz-colored circle on the dust. He feels the perfect peace of the late afternoon; he is moved by the enormity of the world, pervaded with a sense of euphoria because he is part of this unblemished landscape filled with marvels, a boundless geography to be explored. Not far away, his family is waiting. All is well; for the first time he is aware of happiness: it is a moment he will never forget. At other times in his life, when confronted by the world's surprises, Gregory Reeves felt that wonder, that sensation of belonging to a splendid place where everything is possible and where each thing, from the most sublime to the most horrendous, has a reason for being, where nothing happens by chance and nothing is without purpose—a message his father, blazing with messianic fervor as a snake coiled about his feet, used to preach at the top of his lungs. And every time he had felt that glint of understanding, he remembered the sunset on the hill. His childhood had been an overly long period of confusion and darkness, except for those years of traveling with his family. His father, Charles Reeves, guided his small tribe by employing severe but clear-cut rules; all of them worked together, each fulfilling his duties: reward and punishment, cause and effect, a discipline based on a scale of immutable values. The father's eye was upon them like the eye of God. Their travels determined the fate of the Reeveses without altering their stability, because routines and standards were fixed. That was the only time in his life that Gregory had felt secure. The rage began later, after his father was gone and reality began, irreparably, to deteriorate.

The soldier had begun the march in the morning, with his knapsack on his back, but by early afternoon he was already sorry he had not taken the bus. He had set out whistling contentedly, but as the hours passed he felt the strain in his back, and his song became sprinkled with curses. It was his first furlough following a year of service in the Pacific, and he was returning home with the aftereffects of a bout with malaria, a scar on his belly, and as poor as he had always been. He had draped his shirt over a branch to improvise some shade; he was sweating, and his skin gleamed like a dark mirror. He intended to take advantage of every second of his two weeks' liberty and spend the nights playing pool with his friends and dancing with the girls who had answered his letters, then sleep like a log and wake to the smell of freshly brewed coffee and his mother's pancakes, the only appetizing dish from her kitchen—everything else smelled like burned rubber, but who was going to complain about the culinary abilities of the most beautiful woman for a hundred miles around, a living legend, with the elongated bones of a fine sculpture and the yellow eyes of a leopard. After hours without sign of a soul in this lonely countryside, he heard a motor coughing behind him; in the distance he could just make out the hazy outlines of a truck shuddering like an animated mirage in the reverberating light. He waited for it to come closer, hoping to hitch a ride, but as it approached he changed his mind; he was startled by the eccentric apparition, a pile of tin painted in insolent colors and loaded to overflowing with household goods crowned with a chicken coop, a dog tied with a rope, and, attached to the roof of the cab, a loudspeaker and a sign in large letters, reading THE INFINITE PLAN. He stepped back to let it pass, then watched it come to a halt a few meters farther on, where a woman with tomato-red hair leaned from a window and beckoned him to join them. He was hesitant to take this as a blessing; cautiously, he walked toward the truck, calculating that he could not possibly ride in the cab, which already contained three adults and two children, and would require an acrobat's skill to clamber onto the load in the rear. The door opened and the driver jumped out.

"Charles Reeves," he announced with courtesy, but also with unmistakable authority.

"Benedict, sir . . . King Benedict," the young man replied, wiping the sweat from his forehead.

"We're a little crowded, as you can see, but if five can fit, so can six."

The other passengers had also jumped down. The woman with the red curls started off in the direction of some bushes, followed by a little girl of about six, who to save time was pulling down her underpants as she went, while her younger brother, half hidden behind the second woman, stuck out his tongue at the stranger. Charles Reeves lowered a ladder from the side of the truck, scrambled over the bundles with agility, and untied the dog, who leapt fearlessly from the top and began to run around, sniffing at weeds.

"The children like to ride behind, but it's dangerous; they can't stay there alone. Olga and you can go with them. We'll put Oliver up front so he doesn't bother you; he's still a pup, but he's as snappish as an old dog," and Charles Reeves signaled the soldier to climb aboard.

King Benedict tossed his knapsack atop the mound of goods and utensils and followed it up, then held out his arms to receive the boy, whom Reeves had lifted above his head, a skinny child with prominent ears and an irresistible smile that made his face seem all teeth. When the woman and the girl returned, they, too, climbed on the back; the man and the other woman got into the cab, and the truck started off again.

"My name is Olga, and these two are Judy and Gregory," said the woman with the impossible hair, settling her skirts as she divided apples and crackers. "Don't sit on that box. The boa's in there, and we don't want to block the air holes," she added.

Young Gregory had stopped sticking out his tongue as soon as he realized that the traveler was fresh from the war. A reverent expression replaced the impudent faces, and he besieged the passenger with questions about combat airplanes until he fell victim to drowsiness. The soldier then attempted a conversation with the redhead, but she replied with monosyllables, and he didn't want to press her. He began to hum an old song, darting glances from the corner of his eye at the mysterious box until everyone else had fallen asleep on the pile of bundles; then he could observe them at will. The children's hair was so blond it was nearly white, and in profile their pale eyes appeared sightless; in contrast, the woman had the olive complexion of some Mediterranean peoples. The top buttons of her blouse were unfastened; drops of sweat dampened the neckline and then trickled in a slow thread down the crevice between her breasts. She had lifted one arm to cradle her head on a large box, revealing dark hair in her armpit and a wet stain on the cloth. Benedict looked away, fearful of being caught staring and having his curiosity misinterpreted; until now these folks had been friendly, overly friendly, he thought, but you never could be sure with whites. He deduced that the two children belonged to the couple, although, judging from their apparent ages, the Reeveses could as easily be the grandparents. He reinspected the contents of the load and concluded that the strange entourage was not moving, as he had first thought, but lived permanently in this house-on-wheels. He observed that they were carrying one drum containing several gallons of water and another with fuel, and he wondered how they obtained gasoline, which had been rationed for some time now because of the war. Everything was in meticulous order: utensils and tools hung from pegs and hooks; suitcases were contained in precisely dimensioned compartments; nothing was loose, every bundle was marked, and there were several boxes filled with books. Soon the heat and rocking of the journey overcame him, and he fell asleep against the chicken coop. He awakened at midafternoon as he felt the truck come to a stop. The boy's body across his legs weighed almost nothing, but immobility had cramped his muscles, and his throat felt dry. For a few moments he did not know where he was. He pulled his flask of whiskey from his pocket and took a long pull to clear his mind. The woman and the two children were covered with dust, and sweat carved furrows down their cheeks and neck. Charles Reeves had pulled off the road beneath a grove of trees, the only shade in all this desolation. They would camp there to let the motor cool, he explained to the soldier, who by this time was feeling more at ease, and the next day they would take him home. Benedict was beginning to like this strange family. Reeves and Olga lowered a couple of rolls of canvas from the truck and set up two ragged campaign tents, while the other woman, who introduced herself as Nora Reeves, started a meal on a cumbersome kerosene stove; her daughter, Judy, helped her, while the boy, with the dog at his heels, looked for firewood.

"Are we going to hunt rabbit, Papa?" he asked, tugging at his father's pants leg.

"There's no time for that today, Greg," Charles Reeves replied, pulling a chicken from the coop and breaking its neck with a firm snap.

"You can't get meat. We keep the chickens for special occasions," Nora explained, as if apologizing.

"Is this a special day, Mama?" Judy asked.

"Yes, child. Mr. King Benedict is our guest."

By dusk the campsite was in order: the chicken was boiling in a pot, and each person was following his own interests in the light of carbide lamps and the warmth of the fire. Nora and the children were doing lessons, Charles Reeves was leafing through a worn copy of *National Geographic,* and Olga was stringing necklaces with colored beads.

"They're for good luck," she told their guest.

"And invisibility too," the little girl added.

"How is that?"

"If you begin to turn invisible, you put on one of these necklaces, and then everyone can see you," Judy clarified.

"Don't pay any attention to her; those are children's tales." Nora Reeves laughed.

"It's true, Mama!"

"Don't contradict your mother," was Charles Reeves's sharp reprimand.

The women set the table—a large board—with a cloth, china plates, glasses, and spotless napkins. The soldier felt that such a display was not very practical for camping—in his own home they used tin utensils—but he refrained from comment. He took some canned meat from his pack and timidly offered it to his host; he did not want to appear to be paying for his dinner, but neither did he want to accept their hospitality without contributing something. Charles Reeves placed the can in the center of the table, alongside beans, rice, and the platter with the chicken. They all held hands while the father blessed the earth that gave them shelter and the gift of their food. There was no alcohol to be seen, and King Benedict did not dare show his whiskey flask, thinking that maybe the Reeveses abstained for religious reasons. He had been struck by the fact that in his brief prayer the father had not mentioned God's name. He noticed how daintily they all ate, holding their silverware in their fingertips, although there was nothing affected about their manners. After they ate they carried the tableware to a water-filled dishpan, to be washed the next morning; they closed up the cook stove and gave the scraps to Oliver. By then the night was so dark it had obscured the light of the lamps, so the family settled around the fire that illuminated the center of the camp. Nora Reeves picked up a book and began reading aloud a tangled tale about Egyptians; apparently the children were already familiar with the story, because Gregory interrupted, saying:

"I don't want Aïda to die sealed in the tomb, Mama."

"It's only an opera, son."

"I don't want her to die!"

"She won't die this time, Greg," Olga said with conviction.

"How do you know?"

"I saw it in my ball."

"Are you sure?"

"Absolutely sure."

Nora Reeves sat staring at the book with vague dismay, as if changing the ending would be more than she could manage.

"What ball is that?" the soldier asked.

"The crystal ball where Olga sees all the things nobody else can see," Judy explained, in the tone of someone speaking to a retarded person.

"Not everything; just some things," Olga corrected.

"Can you see my future?" Benedict asked, with such anxiety that even Charles Reeves looked up from his magazine.

"What do you want to know."

"Will I live to the end of the war? Will I come home all in one piece?"

Olga walked to the truck and in a few moments returned with a glass orb and a faded cloth of cut velvet, which she spread over the table. King Benedict felt a shiver of superstition and wondered whether he had chanced into an evil sect, people who kidnapped babies—especially black babies, according to the old women where he lived—to tear out their hearts in their satanic masses. Judy and Gregory were curious and hovered near, but Nora and Charles Reeves returned to their reading. Olga indicated to the soldier that he should sit facing her; she grasped the ball in fingers tipped with peeling nail polish, stared for a long time into the sphere, then took her client's hands and intently examined the light palms creased with dark lines.

"You will live twice," she said finally.

"What do you mean, twice?"

"I don't know. I only know you will live twice or live two lives."

"Maybe that means I won't die in the war."

"If you die, you'll surely come back to life," said Judy.

"Will I die or not!"

"I guess not," said Olga.

"Thank you, ma'am, thanks a lot." Benedict's face lighted up as if she had just handed him a certificate guaranteeing permanent life in this world.

"All right," Charles Reeves interrupted. "It's time for bed. We'll be leaving early tomorrow morning."

Olga helped the children put on their pajamas and almost immediately retired with them to the smaller tent, followed by Oliver. Shortly thereafter Nora Reeves crouched down at the tent flap for a last look at her children before going to bed. Lying near the fire, King Benedict heard their voices.

"Mama, that man scares me," Judy whispered.

"Why, daughter?"

"Because he's as black as my shoe."

"He isn't the first black man you've seen, Judy. You already know there are people of many colors, and that's the way it should be. We whites are in the minority."

"I see more white people than black ones, Mama."

"This is only one corner of the world, Judy. In Africa there are more blacks than whites. In China people have yellow skin. If we lived farther south, across the border, we would be exotic creatures; people would stop in the street and stare at your white skin."

"Just the same, he scares me."

"Skin doesn't matter. Look into his eyes. He seems to be a good man."

"He has eyes just like Oliver's," Greg noted with a yawn.

Toward the end of the Second World War, life was hard. Men were still leaving for the front with a certain adventurous enthusiasm, but the patriotic propaganda had not made solitude any more bearable for the women; for them, Europe was a distant nightmare. They were tired of rationing, of keeping the house in good repair, and of bringing up the children by themselves. The widespread poverty of the preceding decade was not to be seen, but neither was there prosperity, and farmers were still roaming the highways in search of good land—white trash, as they were called to differentiate them from others who were as poor as they were but even lower on the social scale: blacks, Indians, and Mexican *braceros*. Although the Reeveses' only earthly possessions were the truck and its contents, they were better off than many; they seemed more refined, less desperate; their hands were free of calluses, and their skin, although tanned by life in the outdoors, was not, like the farm laborers', as tough as a boot sole. When they crossed a state line, the police, experienced in distinguishing subtle levels of poverty, treated them respectfully; they detected no trace of humility in these travelers. They did not force them to unload their truck or open their bundles, as they did farmers run off their land by dust storms, droughts, or the machinery of progress, nor did they insult them, looking for a pretext to use force, as they did with Latinos, blacks, and the few Indians who had survived massacres and alcohol; they merely asked questions about where they were headed. Charles Reeves, a man with the face of an ascetic, burning eyes, and an imposing presence, would reply that he was an artist and was taking his paintings to be sold in some nearby city. He did not mention his less tangible merchandise, in order not to create confusion or find himself forced to provide long

explanations. Charles Reeves had been born in Australia and had
shipped half around the world in boats captained by smugglers
and drug dealers. One night he had disembarked in San Francisco. This is as far as I go, he had decided, but his wanderlust
would not allow him to stay long in one spot, and as soon as he
had exhausted the city's surprises he began his peregrinations
through the rest of the country. His own father, a horse thief who
had been shipped to a penal colony in Sydney, had passed on to his
son his passion for that animal and for open spaces: the outdoors is
in my blood, he had always said. Enamored of the wide-open
country and of the heroic legend of the winning of the West,
Reeves painted its vast panoramas, its Indians and cowboys. With
his small trade in paintings and Olga's fortune-telling, the family
scratched out a living.

Charles Reeves, Doctor in Divine Sciences, as he always introduced himself, had discovered the meaning of life during a mystic
revelation. He would tell how he had found himself alone in the
desert, like Jesus of Nazareth, when a Master materialized in the
form of a snake and bit him on the ankle—look, here's the scar.
For two days he lay in agony, and just when he felt the icy clutch
of death rising from his belly toward his heart, his intellect had
abruptly expanded: before his feverish eyes appeared the perfect
map of the universe, with all its laws and secrets. When he awakened, there was no trace of the venom, and his mind had entered a
superior plane from which he never intended to descend. During
that radiant delirium, the Master had commanded him to divulge
the Unique Truth of *The Infinite Plan,* and he had done so with
discipline and dedication, despite, as he never failed to inform his
listeners, the grave impediments that mission entailed. Reeves had
repeated the story so many times that in the end he believed it and
had completely forgotten that the scar had been acquired in a
bicycle accident. His sermons and books brought in very little
money, barely enough to pay for renting the meeting sites and for
publishing his works in inexpensive pocket-size editions. He did
not taint his spiritual labors with gross schemes for financial gain,
as was the case with many of the charlatans traveling around the

nation in those days, terrorizing people with the threat of God's wrath in order to swindle them out of their pitiful savings. Nor did he resort to the offensive practice of whipping his audience into a frenzy of hysteria and then exhorting the foaming-mouthed participants rolling on the ground to cast out the Evil One—primarily because he denied the existence of Satan and was repelled by such performances. He charged a dollar to come in to hear his sermons and another two to leave: Nora and Olga stood guard at the door with a pile of his books, and no one dared pass by without purchasing a copy. Three dollars was not an outrageous sum, considering the benefits his listeners received; they went home comforted by the certainty that their misfortunes were part of a divine plan, just as their souls were particles of universal energy; they were not abandoned, nor was the cosmos a black space in which chaos prevailed: there was a Great Unifying Spirit that gave meaning to life. To prepare his sermons, Reeves used any source of information at hand: his experience and his unfailing intuition, things his wife had read, and gems from his own perusal of the Bible and the *Reader's Digest*.

During the Great Depression, Reeves earned a living by painting murals in post offices; in that way he had come to know almost the entire country, from the humid, sweltering lands where echoes of weeping slaves still reverberated to icy mountains and tall forests. But he always returned to the West. He had promised his wife that their pilgrimage would end in San Francisco, where one luminous summer day in a hypothetical future they would unload the truck for the last time and settle down forever. Even after the jobs painting post office murals had dried up, he still occasionally painted a commercial sign for a store or an allegorical canvas for a parish church. At those times the travelers would stay in one place for a while and the children would have the opportunity to make friends. They would brag and boast to their playmates, spinning a web of such yarns and fibs that they themselves would tremble at the terrifying visions: bears and coyotes that attacked by night, Indians that chased them to rip off their scalps, and outlaws their father fought off with his shotgun. Scenes flowed from Charles Reeves's brushes with astounding facility, from curvaceous blondes holding a bottle of beer to an awesome Moses clutching the Tablets of the Law. Such major commissions, however, came infrequently; it was more usual to sell only the smaller canvases Olga helped him paint. Reeves's own choice was to reproduce the nature he found so enthralling: red cathedrals of living stone, sere desert flats, and abrupt shorelines, but no one bought what they could see with their own eyes, things that reminded them of the harshness of their fate; why hang on the wall the very thing they could see out their window? So from a *National Geographic* clients would select the landscape closest to their fantasies, or the picture whose colors went with the worn furniture in their living room. Another four dollars bought them an Indian or a cowboy, and the result might be a war-bonneted redskin on the icy peaks of Tibet or a pair of cowboys in ten-gallon hats and cowboy boots shooting it out on the pearly sands of a Polynesian beach. Olga could quickly copy the landscape from the magazine, then, in only a few minutes, Reeves would draw the human figures from memory and the clients would pay their bill and leave, carrying a canvas whose paint was still wet.

Gregory Reeves would have sworn that Olga had been with them always. Much later he would ask what her role in the family had been, but no one could answer, because by that time his father was dead and she was a forbidden subject. Nora and Olga had met on a boatload of refugees from Odessa crossing the Atlantic to North America. They had lost touch with each other for many years but were reunited by chance after Nora was married and Olga's career as a midwife, healer, and fortune-teller was well established. When the two of them were together they always spoke in Russian. They were totally different, one as introverted and shy as the other was exuberant. Nora, long-boned and deliberate of gesture, had a face like a cat and combed her long, colorless hair back in a bun; she never used makeup or wore jewelry, but always looked freshly groomed. On dusty travels where water for bathing was scarce and it was impossible to iron a dress, she was somehow able to keep herself as neat and tidy as the starched white cloth on her table. Her natural reserve increased with the years; little by little she became detached from the earth and ascended to a dimension no one could reach. Olga, several years younger, was a short, sturdy brunette with full bust and hips, a narrow waist, and short but shapely legs. A wild head of henna-dyed hair, in shades of vermilion, fell over her shoulders like an outlandish wig. She was draped in so many strands of beads that she might have been an idol loaded down with baubles, a look that lent authority when it came time to tell fortunes; the crystal ball and the tarot cards budded like natural extensions of her beringed fingers. She hadn't a trace of intellectual curiosity; she read nothing but the crime reports in the sensationalist press and an occasional romantic novel. She had never cultivated her gift of clairvoyance through any systemized course of study, because she believed it was a visceral talent. You either have it or you don't, she always said, it's no use to try to acquire it from books. She knew nothing about magic, astrology, cabala, or other facets of her calling. She barely knew the names of the signs of the zodiac, but when the moment came to peer into her crystal-gazer's ball or lay out her marked cards, a prediction was always forthcoming. Hers was not an occult science but an art of fantasy composed princi-pally of intuition and shrewdness. She was genuinely convinced of her supernatural powers; she would have bet her life in defense of one of her predictions, and if they sometimes failed she always had a reasonable explanation on the tip of her tongue—usually that what she had said had been misinterpreted. She charged a dollar to divine the sex of a child in its mother's womb. She would lay the woman on the floor with her head pointing north, place a coin on her navel, and dangle a lead weight tied to a length of fishing line above her belly. If the improvised pendulum swung clockwise the child would be a boy; if the reverse, it was a girl. The same sys-tem could be applied to cows and pregnant mares by swinging the weight above the animal's hindquarters. She gave her verdict, wrote it on a piece of paper, and kept it as irrefutable proof. Once, they returned to a hamlet they had visited several months before and a woman accompanied by an ill-tempered parade of curious onlookers came out to demand her dollar back.

"You told me I was going to have a boy, and look what I got! Another girl! I have three already!"

"That can't be. Are you sure I predicted a boy?"

"Of course I'm sure. Don't you think I know what you told me? That's what I paid you for."

"You must have misunderstood me," Olga replied, unfazed.

She climbed onto the truck, rummaged through her trunk, and produced a slip of paper she showed to everyone present; a single word was written there: *girl*. An admiring sigh swept through the crowd, including the mother, who scratched her head with perplexity. Olga did not have to return the dollar but in fact reinforced her reputation as a prophetess. There were not enough hours in what was left of the afternoon and part of the night for her to attend to the line of clients waiting to have their fortunes told. Among the amulets and potions she offered, the most requested was her "magnetized water," a miraculous liquid bottled in crude green-glass vials. She always explained that it was ordinary, everyday water but that it had curative powers because of being infused with psychic fluids. She carried out her bottling operation on nights of the full moon, when, as Judy and Gregory had witnessed, she merely filled the containers, sealed them with a cork, and pasted on labels—but she guaranteed that in the process the water was charged with positive force, and that must have been the case, because her products sold like hotcakes and the users never complained of the results. According to how the water was used, it provided various benefits: drinking it cleansed the kidneys, rubbing it on relieved the pain of arthritis, and massaging it into the scalp improved mental concentration—but it had no effect on affairs of the heart, including jealousy, adultery, and involuntary spinsterhood. On this point the healer was very clear, and she advised every purchaser of that fact. She was as scrupulous about her nostrums as she was in charging for them. She maintained that there is no such thing as a good remedy that is free; she never charged, nonetheless, for assisting at a birth. She enjoyed bringing babies into the world: nothing could compare to the moment when the infant's head emerged from between its mother's bloodied legs. She offered her services as midwife on isolated farms and in the poor areas of small towns, especially Negro neighborhoods where the idea of having a baby in a hospital was still a novelty. While she waited beside the mother-to-be, she hemmed diapers and knit booties for the baby; it was only on those infrequent occasions that her boldly painted sorceress's face grew soft. The tone of her voice changed as she lent support to her patient during the most difficult hours and as she sang the first cradle song heard by the babe she had helped into the world. After a few days, when mother and child were well acquainted, she would rejoin the Reeveses, who were camped nearby. As she said goodbye, she wrote the child's name in a notebook; it was a long list, but she called them all her godchildren. Births bring good luck, was her brusque explanation for not charging for her services. She was like a sister to Nora and like a grumbling aunt to Judy and Gregory, whom she thought of as her niece and nephew. Charles Reeves she treated like a colleague, with a mixture of petulance and good humor; they never touched, they seemed scarcely to exchange glances, but they acted in tandem not only in the work of the paintings but in everything they did together. It was they who handled the family's money and resources, they who consulted maps and decided which roads to take; together they went out hunting, disappearing for hours in the deep woods. They respected each other and laughed at the same things. Olga was independent, adventurous, and as resolute as the preacher; she was forged from the same steel. For that very reason she was not impressed by either the man's charisma or his artistic talent. It was only Charles Reeves's masculine vigor—which later would also characterize his son, Gregory—that on occasion could subdue her.

Nora, Charles Reeves's wife, was a being destined to silence. Her parents, Russian Jews, gave her the best education they could afford. She graduated with a teaching certificate, and although she left the profession when she married, she kept up-to-date by studying history, geography, and mathematics in order to teach her children, because the bohemian life they led made it impossible to send them to school. During their travels she read magazines and esoteric books, with no presumption of analyzing what she had read, content to pass on the information to the Doctor in Divine Sciences for his use. She hadn't the least doubt that her husband was gifted with psychic powers that enabled him to see beyond the veil and discover truth where others saw only shadows. They had met when they were no longer young, and their relationship had always been characterized by a certain decorum and maturity. Nora was not suited for the practicalities of life; her mind floated in otherworldly dreams, more preoccupied with the potential of the spirit than with everyday vicissitudes. She loved music, and the most splendid moments of her uneventful existence had been the few operas she had attended as a girl. She treasured every detail of those spectacles; she could close her eyes and hear the brilliant voices, suffer the tragic passions of the performers, and luxuriate in the color and richness of the sets and costumes. She read the librettos, imagining every scene as part of her own life; the first stories her children heard were of the star-crossed loves and inevitable deaths of the world of opera. She took refuge in this extravagant, romantic atmosphere when she felt weighed down by the vulgarity of real life. For his part, Charles Reeves was a man who had sailed the seven seas, earning a livelihood as a jack-of-all-trades. He had in his seabag more adventures than he could ever tell; he had left behind him a trail of broken love affairs and a few offspring he never heard of again. When Nora had first seen him haranguing a crowd of amazed churchgoers, she was immediately infatuated. She had become resigned to her spinster's fate, like many women of her generation whom chance had not gifted with a sweetheart and who lacked the courage to go out and look for one. Having been suddenly, and tardily, smitten, however, gave her the courage to overcome her natural shyness. The preacher had rented a hall near the school where Nora taught and was distributing handbills announcing his lecture when Nora caught her first glimpse of him. She was impressed by his noble face and determined air and out of curiosity went to hear him, expecting to find a charlatan like so many that passed through, leaving no trace of their passing but a few faded posters peeling from the walls; she was, however, in for a surprise. Standing before his audience, aided by an orange suspended from the ceiling, Reeves explained man's place in the universe according to *The Infinite Plan.* He did not threaten punishment or promise eternal salvation; he limited himself to practical solutions for bettering one's life, for soothing anguish, and for saving the resources of the planet. All creatures can and must live in harmony, he argued, and to prove it he opened the lid of the boa's box and let it coil around his body like a fireman's hose, to the amazement of his listeners, who had never seen a snake so long or so fat. That night Charles Reeves put into words the confused feelings Nora had not known how to express. She had discovered the teachings of Baha Ullah and had adopted the Bahai religion. Those Eastern concepts of loving tolerance, of the unity of mankind, of the search for truth and the rejection of prejudice, had clashed with her rigid Jewish background and the provincialism of her milieu, but listening to Reeves made everything seem simple; now, knowing that this man had the answers and could serve as her guide, she had no need to worry about such fundamental contradictions. Dazzled by the eloquence of the delivery, she overlooked the vagueness of the content. She was so moved that she found the courage to go up to him at a moment when he was alone, with the intention of asking whether he was familiar with the Bahai faith and, in the case that he was not, meaning to offer him the works of Shogi Effendi. The Doctor in Divine Sciences was aware that some of his sermons excited certain women, and never hesitated to seize the advantage of such bonanzas; the schoolteacher, however, attracted him in a different way. There was something pure about her, a transparent quality—true rectitude, not just innocence, a luminosity as cold and uncontaminated as ice. He not only wished to take her in his arms—his first impulse on seeing her strange triangular face and freckled skin— he also longed to penetrate the crystalline surface of this stranger and light the banked fires of her spirit. He proposed that she join him in his travels, and she immediately accepted, with the sensation of having been taken by the hand once and for all time. At that moment, as she envisioned the possibility of surrendering her soul to him, the process of disengagement that would mark her destiny was begun. She left without a single goodbye, with a pouch of books as her only baggage. Months later, when she discovered she was pregnant, they were married. If it was true that a raging fire burned beneath her phlegmatic appearance, only her husband knew. Gregory himself spent his life captivated by the same curiosity that had attracted Charles Reeves in that rented hall in a godforsaken town in the Midwest; a thousand times he attempted to breach the walls that isolated his mother and reach her inner feelings, but as he had never succeeded, he decided that she had none, that she was hollow and incapable of truly loving anyone; at most, she manifested an undefined sympathy toward humanity in general.

Nora grew accustomed to depending on her husband, more and more becoming a passive creature who fulfilled her duties by reflex as her soul escaped worldly concerns. So strong was Reeves's personality that to make space for him, she herself gradually faded from the world, turning into a shadow. She participated in the routines of their communal life, but she brought little to the energy of the small group; her only contributions were the children's studies and matters of hygiene and good health. She had come to the United States with a boatload of immigrants, and during her first years in the country—until her family had worked their way out of adversity—she was minimally and poorly nourished. That period of poverty had burned the pangs of hunger into her memory for all time; she had a mania for nutritious food and vitamin pills. She communicated some aspects of Bahaism to her children in the same tone she used for teaching them to read or to name the stars, without the least spirit of conviction. Only when she spoke of music did she grow passionate; those were the only times her voice was vibrant and color lighted her cheeks. Later she would agree to raise her children in the

THE INFINITE PLAN · 23

Catholic Church, which was the standard in the Hispanic barrio where they were to live. She understood the need for Judy and Gregory to blend into their surroundings; they had enough to bear with differences of race and custom without being further mortified by unknown beliefs like her Bahai faith. Besides, to Nora all religions were basically the same. She was concerned only with morality, and anyway, God was beyond human comprehension. It was enough to know that heaven and hell are symbols of the soul's relation to God: proximity to the Creator leads to good and to gentle pleasures, while distance produces evil and suffering. In contrast to her religious tolerance, she would yield not an inch in principles of decency and courtesy; she washed out her children's mouths with soap if they used profanity, and she curtailed their food if they did not hold their fork properly. All other punishments were the father's responsibility; she merely identified the offense. One day she caught Gregory stealing a pencil from a store and informed her husband, who made the boy return it with apologies and then, before Nora's impassive gaze, burned the palm of his hand over a blazing match. For a week Gregory had an open sore. He soon forgot the reason for the lesson and the person who had inflicted it; all that stayed in his mind was his rage against his mother. Many decades later, when he was at peace with his memory of her, he could be quietly grateful to her for the three major gifts she had given him: love for music, tolerance, and a sense of honor.

The heat is unrelenting, the ground is parched; it has not rained since the beginning of time, and the world seems to be covered with a fine reddish powder. A harsh light distorts the outlines of things; the horizon is lost in a haze of dust. It is one of those nameless towns like so many others: one long street, a café, a solitary filling station, a jail, the same wretched shops and wood houses, and a schoolhouse with a sun-faded flag drooping overhead. Dust and more dust. My parents have gone to the general store to buy the week's supplies; Olga has been left to look after Judy and me. No one is in the street; the shutters are closed: people are waiting for it to cool down before they return to life. My sister and Olga are drowsing on a bench on the porch of the store, dazed by the heat; they have given up brushing away the annoying flies and are letting them crawl over their faces. The unexpected smell of burnt sugar floats on the air. Large blue-and-green lizards lie motionless in the sun, but when I try to catch them they dart away and hide beneath the houses. I am barefoot, and the earth is hot on the soles of my feet. I am playing with Oliver; I throw him a worn rag ball, he fetches it, I throw it again, and in this game I wander away from the store. I turn a corner and find myself in a narrow alley, partly shaded by the unpainted eaves of the houses. I see two men. One is heavyset, with bright pink skin; the other has yellow hair. They are wearing work overalls; they are sweating, their shirts and hair are soaking wet. The fat one has cornered a young black girl; she must be no more than ten or twelve. He is holding her off the ground in the crook of one arm, and he has clamped his free hand over her mouth. She kicks once or twice and then falls limp; her eyes are red from her effort to breathe through the hand that is suffocating her. The second man has his back to me and is struggling with his overalls. Both are very serious, focused, tense, panting. Silence. I hear the men's puffing and the beating of my own heart. Oliver has disappeared, along with the houses; there is nothing but the threesome suspended in the dust, moving in slow motion, and me, paralyzed in my tracks. The man with the yellow hair spits twice in his hand, moves closer to the girl, and parts her legs, two dark toothpicks, dangling limply. Now I can't see the girl; she is crushed between the heavy bodies of the rapists. I want to run; I am terrified, but I also want to watch. I know that something fundamental and forbidden is happening, I am a participant in a violent secret. I can't breathe, I try to call my father, I open my mouth but nothing comes out; I swallow fire, a scream fills me inside, I am choking. I must do something, it is in my hands, the right action will save us both, the black girl and me; I am dying but I can't think of anything to do, I can't move a muscle, I have turned to stone. At that instant I hear my name in the distance—Greg, Greg!—and Olga appears at the mouth of the alley. There is a long pause, an eternal minute in which nothing at all happens; all is still. Then the air is vibrating with a long scream, Olga's hoarse and terrible cry, followed by Oliver's barking and the voice of my sister, like the shrill of a rat, and finally I am able to draw a breath and I begin to scream too, desperately. Surprised, the men drop the girl, who as her feet touch the ground darts away like a frightened rabbit. We stare at one another; the man with the yellow hair is holding something purple in his hand, something that seems detached from his body, something he is trying to force inside his overalls. Finally they turn and walk away. They are not perturbed; they laugh and make obscene gestures. How would you like a little yourself, you dumb bitch? they yell to Olga. Come here and we'll give you a sample. The girl's underpants are lying in the street. Olga grabs Judy and me by the hand, calls the dog, and we hurry, no, we run, toward the truck. The town is waking up, and people are looking at us.

The Doctor in Divine Sciences was resigned to disclosing his ideas to uncouth farmers and poor laborers, who were not always capable of following the thread of his complicated lecture; he did not, nonetheless, lack for followers. Very few attended his sermons for reasons of faith. Most came out of simple curiosity; there were few diversions in those parts, and the arrival of *The Infinite Plan* did not pass unnoticed. After setting up camp, Reeves would go out to look for a place to speak. It was free only if he knew someone; if not, he had to rent a hall or clean out a place in a tavern or barn. As he had no money, he used Nora's pearl necklace with the diamond clasp, her only legacy from her mother, as security, with a promise to pay at the end of each meeting. In the meanwhile, his wife would starch her husband's shirtfront and collar, press out his black suit—shiny from wear—polish his shoes, brush his top hat, and set out the books, while Olga and the children went from house to house distributing handbills inviting everyone to "The Course That Will Change Your Life: Charles Reeves, Doctor in Divine Sciences, Will Help You Find Happiness and Win Prosperity."

Olga would bathe the children and dress them in their Sunday best, while Nora dressed in her blue dress with the lace collar, severe and out of style, but still decent. War had changed how women dressed; now they wore tight knee-length skirts, jackets with shoulder pads, platform shoes, elaborate pompadours, and hats trimmed with feathers and veils. In her nunnish dress, Nora looked as prim as someone's grandmother from the first years of the century. Olga, for her part, was not one to follow fashion, but prim is not a word anyone would ever use in regard to her clothes: she was flamboyant as a parrot. In any case, people in those small towns knew nothing about the niceties of fashion; they worked from sunup to sunset, drew pleasure from a drink or two of whiskey—still prohibited in some states—a rodeo, the movies, a dance from time to time, and listening to war reports and baseball games over the radio; it was easy to see why they were attracted by a novelty. Charles Reeves had to compete with revivalists preaching the new awakening of Christianity, a return to the fundamental principles of the twelve apostles and a literal reading of the Bible, evangelists who crisscrossed the country with their tents, bands, fireworks, gigantic illuminated crosses, choirs of brothers and sisters decked out like angels, and loudspeakers that bruited to the four winds the name of the Nazarene, exhorting sinners to repent because Jesus was coming whip in hand to drive the Pharisees from the temple, and calling upon them to combat satanic doctrines such as the theory of evolution, the evil invention of a heretic named Darwin. Sacrilege! Man is made in the image and likeness of God, not monkeys! Buy a bond for Jesus! Hallelujah! Hallelujah! blared the loudspeakers. Churchgoers flocked to the tents, looking for redemption and entertainment, all of them singing, many dancing, and from time to time someone writhing and gasping in ecstasy, while the collection trays filled to overflowing with the gifts of those hoping to buy a ticket to heaven. Charles Reeves offered nothing so grand, but his charisma, the strength of his conviction, and the fire of his discourse were persuasive. It was impossible to ignore him. Occasionally someone would walk forward to the platform, begging to be freed from pain or unbearable remorse; then Reeves, without the least trace of hypocrisy, simply, but with great authority, would lay his hands on the head of the penitent and concentrate on easing his suffering. Many thought they saw sparks shooting from his palms, and those who had benefited from his treatment swore they had been shaken by an electric shock to the brain. For most in the audience, it was enough to hear him once to want to sign up for his classes, to buy his books, and become a follower.

"Creation is governed according to the rules of *The Infinite Plan*. Nothing happens by chance. We human beings are a fundamental part of that plan because we are located on the scale of evolution between the Masters and the rest of the creatures; we are intermediaries. We must know our place in the cosmos." So Charles Reeves would begin, galvanizing his audience with his deep voice, standing solemnly beneath the orange strung from the ceiling, garbed from head to toe in black and with the boa curled around his feet like a thick coil of ship's rope. The creature was totally apathetic and unless directly provoked never moved. "Listen closely, so you can understand the principles of the *The Infinite Plan*. Even if you don't understand, it won't matter; all you have to do is follow my commandments. The entire universe belongs to a Supreme Intelligence; that Intelligence created it and is so immense and perfect that no human being can ever comprehend it. Beneath the Supreme Intelligence are the Logi, representatives of the light who are charged with carrying particles of the Supreme Intelligence to all the galaxies. The Logi communicate with the Master Functionaries, through whom they send the messages and rules of *The Infinite Plan* to man. The human being is composed of the Physical Body, the Mental Body, and the Soul. Most important is the Soul, which is not present in the earthly atmosphere but operates at some distance from it; it is not within us, but it dominates our lives."

At this point, when his listeners, somewhat bewildered by his rhetoric, began to exchange glances of fear or mockery, Reeves would electrify his audience anew by pointing to the orange to explain the nature of the Soul floating in the ether like a cloudy ectoplasm that could be seen only by those expert in the occult. To prove it, he would invite several persons from the crowd to study the orange and describe its appearance. Invariably, they would describe a yellow sphere, that is, a common orange, whereas Reeves saw the Soul. Then he would introduce the Logi, which were in the hall in a gaseous state and therefore invisible, and explain that it was they who kept the precise machinery of the universe in working order. In every age and every region the Logi elected Master Functionaries to communicate with man and divulge the plans of the Supreme Intelligence. He, Charles Reeves, Doctor in Divine Sciences, was one of those men. His mission consisted of teaching the guidelines to mere mortals; once he had completed that stage, he would pass on to become part of the privileged contingent of the Logi. He stated that every human act and thought is important because it has weight in the perfect balance of the universe and that therefore each person is responsible for fulfilling the commandments of *The Infinite Plan* to the letter. He then enumerated the rules of minimal wisdom, through which the monstrous errors capable of derailing the project of the Supreme Intelligence could be avoided. Those who did not capture all this in a single conference could take the course of six sessions, in which they would learn the rules of a good life, including diet, physical and mental exercises, controlled dreams, and several systems for charging the batteries of the Physical Body and the Mental Body, thus assuring themselves of a dignified life and peace of Soul after death.

Charles Reeves was a man ahead of his time. Twenty years later several of his ideas would be predicated by various spiritualists up and down California, the last frontier, the goal of adventurers, desperadoes, nonconformists, fugitives from justice, undiscovered geniuses, impenitent sinners, and hopeless lunatics, a place where even today every possible formula for avoiding the anguish of living proliferates. It is not Charles Reeves, however, who must bear the blame for having initiated bizarre movements. There is something in the air of the place that agitates the spirit. Or maybe those who came to populate the region were in such a hurry to find their fortune—or easy oblivion—that their soul lagged behind, and they are still looking for it. Uncounted charlatans have profited from this phenomenon, offering magic formulas to fill the painful void left by the absent spirit. At the time Reeves was preaching, many in that land had already found a way to get rich by selling intangible benefits for the health of the body and solace of the soul, but he was not among them; he honored austerity and decorum, and thereby earned the respect of his followers. It was Olga who had glimpsed the possibilities for turning the Logi and the Master Functionaries to more commercial ends, perhaps by acquiring a site and starting their own church, but neither Charles nor Nora ever evinced any enthusiasm for that covetous idea; for them, divulging their truth was quite simply a heavy and inescapable moral burden, and never an excuse to peddle cheap merchandise.

Nora Reeves could point to the exact day she lost faith in human goodness, the day her unspoken doubts about the meaning of life had begun. She was one of those people who are able to remember meaningless dates, so with even more reason the event of dropping two cataclysmic bombs, signaling an end to the war with Japan, was burned into her brain. In years to come she dressed in mourning for that anniversary, just when the rest of the country was throwing itself into celebrations. She lost interest even in those closest to her; it is true that maternal affection had never been one of her principal characteristics, but from that moment on she seemed to divorce herself entirely from her two children. She also withdrew from her husband, but so discreetly that he found nothing to reproach her for. She isolated herself in a secret cloister, where she remained untouched by reality until the end of her days; forty-some years later, without ever having participated in life, she died convinced that she was a princess of the Urals. On that fateful day, people celebrated the final defeat of the enemy with slant eyes and yellow skin, as months earlier they had rejoiced at the defeat of the Germans. It was the end of a long combat; the Japanese had been vanquished by the most powerful weapon in history, one that in only a few minutes killed one hundred thirty thousand human beings and condemned that many more to a drawn-out agony. The news of what had happened produced a horrified silence through the world, but the victors blocked out visions of charred bodies and pulverized cities in a tumult of flags, parades, and marching bands, anticipating the return of their fighting men.

"Do you remember that black soldier we picked up on the road? Do you suppose he's still alive? Will he be coming home too?" Gregory asked his mother before they left to watch the fireworks display.

Nora did not answer. They were in a city like many other cities, and while her family danced in the crowd, Nora sat alone in the cab of the truck. In recent months the news from Europe had strained her nerves, and the devastation of the atom bomb had been the last straw, plunging her into doubt. There was nothing else on the radio, and the newspapers and movies featured Dantesque images of concentration camps. Step by step, she followed every detail of the atrocities and accumulated suffering, obsessed by trains in Europe that made no stops but carried their cargo straight to the ovens, and by the hundreds of thousands cremated in Japan in the name of a different ideology. I should never have brought children into this world, she murmured in her horror. When a euphoric Charles Reeves brought home the news of the bomb, she had thought it obscene to rejoice over a massacre of such dimensions; her husband seemed to have lost his sanity along with everyone else.

"Nothing will ever be the same again, Charles. Humanity has committed something worse than original sin. This is the end of the world," she lamented, terribly distraught but maintaining the facade of her customary good manners.

"Don't be silly. We should applaud the progress of science. It's a good thing the bomb is in our hands, not the enemy's. No one can stand up to us now."

"They will use them again and wipe out life on this earth!"

"The war is over, and we've been spared even worse. Many more would have died if we hadn't dropped the bombs."

"But, Charles, hundreds of thousands did die."

"They don't count; they were all Japs." He laughed.

For the first time, Nora had doubts about the quality of her husband's soul and asked herself whether he was a true Master, as he claimed. It was late at night when her family returned. Gregory was asleep in his father's arms, and Judy held a balloon painted with stars and stripes.

"The war is over at last. Now we'll have butter and meat and gasoline," Olga announced, radiant, waving a tattered paper flag.

Although nearly a year passed between the time of his mother's depression over the inhumanity of war and his father's death, Gregory remembered the events as one; in his memory, they would forever be related: it was the beginning of the end of the happy days of his childhood. A short time later, when Nora seemed to have recovered and was no longer talking about concentration camps and bombs, Charles Reeves fell ill. From the very first, his symptoms were alarming, but he was proud of his strength and refused to believe that his body could betray him. He felt young; he could still change a truck tire in a couple of minutes or spend hours on a ladder painting a mural without getting a cramp in his shoulder. When his mouth filled with blood he attributed it to a fishbone stuck in his throat; the second time it happened he said nothing to anyone but bought a bottle of Milk of Magnesia and took a spoonful whenever he felt his stomach in flames. Soon he lost his appetite and survived on milk toast, broths, and baby food. He lost weight, and his eyes clouded over; he could not see the road clearly, and Olga had to take over the wheel. She realized when he was too tired to travel any farther, and stopped so they could set up camp. As the hours dragged by, the children entertained themselves running around the campsite, because their mother had packed away their books and was not giving them lessons. Nora had not accepted the fact that Charles Reeves might be mortal; she could not understand why his strength was flagging—his energy was hers as well. For years her husband had controlled every aspect of her life and that of her children; the detailed rules of *The Infinite Plan,* which he administered as he pleased, left no room for doubts. With him she had no freedom, but neither was she besieged by uneasiness or apprehension. There was no reason to be alarmed, she told herself; after all, Charles has never had much hair, and those deep wrinkles aren't new, they were carved by the sun long ago; he's thinner, that's true, but he'll snap back in a few days, just as soon as he begins to eat like he used to; this is nothing but indigestion. "Don't you think he's much better today?" she would say to no one in particular. Olga watched without comment. She did not attempt to treat Reeves with her potions and poultices but limited her care to holding wet cloths to his forehead to lower the fever. As the invalid declined, fear inexorably infected the rest of the family; for the first time they felt they were drifting and realized the extent of their poverty and vulnerability. Nora retreated like a whipped dog, unable to put her mind to finding solutions; she sought consolation in her Bahai faith and left all problems to Olga—including her husband's care. She could not bring herself to touch that sick old man; he was a stranger: how could she possibly recognize him as the man who had charmed her with his vitality? Her admiration and reliance, the bases for her love, disintegrated, and as she did not know how to construct new ones, respect turned to repugnance. As soon as she found a good excuse, she moved into the children's tent, and Olga went to sleep with Charles Reeves—to nurse him through the night, she said. Gregory and Judy became accustomed to seeing her half naked in their father's bed; Nora ignored the situation, preferring to pretend that nothing had changed.

For a while the unveiling of *The Infinite Plan* was suspended, because the Doctor in Divine Sciences lacked the fortitude to instill hope in others when he was beginning to lose his own and secretly wonder whether the spirit truly transcends or whether it can be dashed to smithereens by a bellyache. He did not even feel like painting. Their travels continued, with tightened purse strings and with no perceptible purpose, as if they were looking for something that was always a little farther down the road. It seemed quite natural for Olga to assume the place of the father, and the others never questioned whether that was the best solution; she set the itinerary, drove the truck, hoisted the heaviest bundles, repaired the engine when it wouldn't start, hunted rabbits and birds, and with the same note of authority issued orders to Nora and paddled the children when they got out of hand. She avoided large cities because of the merciless competition and the eagle eye of the police, except when they could camp in industrial zones or near the docks, where she could always find a client. She would leave the Reeveses installed in the tents, gather up her necromancer's trappings, and go out to sell her arts. For traveling she wore rough workman's pants, an undershirt, and a cap, but to ply her trade as fortune-teller she pulled a gaudy flower-printed skirt from her trunk, a low-cut blouse, jangling necklaces, and yellow boots. She brushed on makeup with a free hand—cheeks like a clown, red mouth, blue eyelids—and the effect of that mask, her clothes, and the fiery hair was so intimidating that few dared turn her away for fear that with a flourish she would turn them into a pillar of salt. When they opened the door and found a grotesque apparition standing before them with a crystal ball in one hand, their jaws dropped, a moment of hesitation that Olga seized upon to get into the house. She could be very charming when the occasion demanded, and often returned to the camp with a piece of pie or some meat, gifts from clients satisfied not only with the future promised in the magical cards but even more with the spark of good humor she had injected into the uninterrupted boredom of their lives. During that period of great uncertainty, the sibyl fine-tuned her talents and, spurred on by circumstances, developed unknown strengths, ripening into the larger-than-life woman who was such an influence in Gregory's childhood. When she walked into a house she had only to sniff the air for a few seconds to absorb the climate, feel the invisible presences, capture the signs of misfortune, divine the dreams, hear the whispers of the dead, and comprehend the needs of the living. She soon learned that life stories repeat themselves over and over, with very few variations; people are all very much alike, they experience love, hatred, greed, suffering, happiness, and fear in the same ways. Black, white, yellow, as Nora Reeves used to say, we are all the same under the skin; the crystal ball is blind to color, but not to pain. Everyone wanted to hear the same good fortune, not because they thought it was possible but because by merely imagining it they felt better. Olga also discovered that there are only two kinds of illness: those that are fatal and those that heal themselves in their proper time. She would pull out her vials of many-colored sugar pills, her bag of herbs, and her box of amulets to sell health to those who could be cured, convinced that if the patient set his mind to getting well, most likely that was what would happen. People had more confidence in her than in the impersonal surgeons in the hospitals. She was not legally qualified for most of the operations she performed—abortions, tooth extractions, stitching up wounds—but she had a good eye and good hand, so that she never got in serious trouble. One glance was all she needed to see the signs of death, and in that case she never prescribed a treatment, partly because of scruples and partly not to damage her reputation as a healer. Her experience in treating the infirm did not help in the case of Charles Reeves; she was too close to him, and if she saw fatal symptoms, she did not want to admit it.

Whether out of pride or fear, the preacher refused to see a doctor, prepared to overcome his suffering by pure obstinacy; after the day he fainted, however, what little authority he could claim passed into Olga's hands. They were on the eastern edge of Los Angeles, where there was a large Latin population, and Olga made the decision to drive Reeves to the hospital. In those days the atmosphere of the city already radiated a certain Mexican flavor despite its uniquely American obsession with living in perfect health, beauty, and happiness. Hundreds of thousands of immigrants were putting their stamp on the place: their scorn for pain and death, their poverty, fatalism, and distrust, their violent passions, but also their music, highly spiced food, and exuberant sense of color. Hispanics were banished to a ghetto, but their influence was borne on the air; they did not belong to the country and, superficially at least, seemed not to want to belong, but secretly they hoped their sons and daughters would be integrated. They half-learned English and transformed it into a Spanglish so deeply rooted that with time it became accepted as the Chicano tongue. Bound to their Catholic tradition and cult of the soul, to a musty patriotism and machismo, they did not assimilate; they were doomed for two or three generations to the most humble service jobs. North Americans thought of them as undesirable people, unpredictable and dangerous, and many protested—Why the hell can't they stop them from crossing the border? What are the damn police for?—but they hired them as cheap labor and kept a sharp eye on them. The immigrants assumed their marginal role in the society with a measure of pride: bowed, yes, but never broken, *hermano*. Olga had visited the barrio more than once and felt at home there. Brazenly she rattled off Spanish, scarcely aware that half her vocabulary was formed of invented words. She felt the barrio was a place where she could earn a living from her art.

They drove the truck to the door of the hospital, and while Nora and Olga helped the sick man from the cab, the terrified children met the curious gaze of people peering out to observe the bizarre conveyance with all its brightly painted esoteric symbols.

"What in the world is that?" one inquired.

"*The Infinite Plan*, can't you see?" Judy replied, pointing to the letters on the top of the truck. That was the end of the questions.

Charles Reeves was admitted to the hospital, where a few days later they removed half his stomach and sutured the holes in the remaining half. While he was there, Nora and Olga, with children, dog, boa, and bundles, moved into temporary quarters in the patio of Pedro Morales, a generous Mexican who years before had completed the entire course of Charles Reeves's doctrines and to prove it had on his wall a diploma acknowledging him to be a superior soul. Morales was as solid as a brick wall, with strong mestizo features and a proud mask that melted into geniality when he was in a good humor. Several gold teeth sparked from his smile, set in for elegance after his healthy ones had been pulled. He would not think of allowing the family of his Maestro to wander any farther—women need protection, there are bandits everywhere, he said. There was no room in his house for so many guests, because he already had under his roof six children, a slightly mad mother-in-law, and assorted relatives. He helped the women set up the tents and install their kerosene stove in his patio, and set about coming to their rescue without offending their dignity. He always addressed Nora as *doña,* with great deference, but Olga, whom he considered much closer to his own level, he called *señorita.* Inmaculada Morales, his wife, was totally impervious to the ways of foreigners and, unlike many of her compatriots in this alien land, who trotted around balancing on stiletto heels, with their faces painted and their hair frizzled by permanents and hydrogen peroxide, was faithful to her native traditions. She was small, slender, and strong, with a placid, unwrinkled face; she wore her hair in a long braid that hung below her waist and dressed in simple aprons and espadrilles, except on days of religious festivals, when she showed off her black dress and gold earrings. Inmaculada was the pillar of the household and the soul of the Morales family. When her patio filled up with guests, she did not blink an eye; she merely stretched the food with the tricks of any hospitable woman—stirring a little more water in the beans, she called it—and then every evening invited the Reeveses to eat with them. "Here, *comadre,* come, bring the young ones and try these burritos," she would offer timidly. "We don't want the chiles to go to waste; just look how much there is, thanks to God's grace," and somewhat embarrassed guests would take their seats at the welcoming Morales table.

It took Judy and Gregory several months to learn the rules of a sedentary life. They found themselves surrounded by a warm tribe of dark-skinned children who spoke rapid-fire English and wasted no time teaching the Reeveses their language, beginning with *chingada,* the most ringing and useful word in their vocabulary, even if not one to say within earshot of Inmaculada. Led by the Morales children, they learned to find their way through the labyrinth of streets, to bargain, to recognize at a glance enemy gangs to be avoided, and to know where to hide and how to escape. With the Moraleses, too, they went to play in the cemetery and observe the prostitutes from afar and victims of fatal accidents at close hand. Juan José, who was the same age as Gregory, had an unfailing nose for tragedy; he always knew where the automobile accidents occurred, the assaults and knife fights and murders. He made it his business to find within a few minutes the exact place where a husband whose wife had run off with a traveling salesman had committed suicide by standing in front of a train because he could not bear the shame of having the world know he wore the horns. Someone saw him smoking calmly, standing between the rails, and shouted at him to jump off the track because the locomotive was coming, but he stood right where he was. Juan José had heard the gossip before the tragedy occurred. The Morales and Reeves children were the first to show up at the death scene, and once they had overcome their initial fear, they helped pick up the pieces—until the police ran them off. Juan José had kept a finger as a souvenir, but when he began to see the dead man everywhere he realized he had to give up his trophy. It was too late to return it to any of the kin, because all the other bits and pieces of the suicide had been buried some days before. The boy, frightened by the soul in pain, did not know how to dispose of the finger: throwing it on the trash heap or feeding it to the Reeveses' boa did not seem a very respectful way to atone for his affront. Secretly, Gregory consulted Olga, and she suggested the perfect solution: very quietly to leave it on the church altar, a consecrated place where no soul in its right mind could feel offended. Padre Larraguibel, whom everyone simply called "Padre" because of the difficulty of pronouncing his name, found it there. The priest was a Basque with a tormented soul, but he was a practical man and without a word he threw the finger down the toilet. He had too many problems with his numerous parishioners to waste time digging into the origin of a single finger.

Gregory and Judy Reeves attended school for the first time in their lives. They were the only blue-eyed blonds in a population of Latin immigrants in which the rule of survival was to speak Spanish and to run like a deer. Students were forbidden to speak their native language in school; they were to learn English in order to integrate more quickly. When someone let a Spanish word slip out where the teacher could hear, he rated a couple of whacks to his backside. If English was all Jesus needed to write the Bible, the world had no need of any other languages, was the explanation for such strict measures. Out of defiance, the children spoke Spanish whenever they could, and anyone who did not was regarded as a *besa-culo*—ass-kisser being the worst epithet in the student repertory. Judy and Gregory had been quick to sense racial antagonism and were afraid that if they made the slightest misstep they would be beaten to a pulp. The first day of classes, Gregory was so frightened he could not get a word out, not even to say his name.

"We have two new students," said the teacher, smiling, enchanted to have two white children among so many dark skins. "I want you to treat them well and help them study and learn the rules of this institution. What are your names, my dears?"

Gregory was mute, clinging to his sister's dress. Finally Judy rescued him.

"I am Judy Reeves, and this dunce is my brother," she announced. All the class, including the teacher, burst out laughing. Gregory felt something warm and sticky in his trousers.

"All right, you may sit down," she told them.

Two minutes later Judy began to hold her nose and glare at her brother with a fierce expression. Gregory fixed his eyes on the floor and tried to imagine he wasn't there, that he was riding down the road in the truck in the open air, that his father had never got sick and that the damned school didn't exist, that it was all only a nightmare. Soon the smell reached the other children, who began stamping and hooting.

"Let's see now, who was it?" the teacher asked, wearing a false smile that looked as if it were pasted to her teeth. "There is nothing to be ashamed of; it was an accident, it could happen to anyone. . . . Who was it?"

"I did not dirty my pants, and my brother didn't either, I swear it!" Judy shouted defiantly. A chorus of jeers and snickers met her declaration.

The teacher leaned over and whispered in Gregory's ear that he should leave the classroom, but he held on to the desk with both hands, with his head buried between his shoulders and his eyelids clamped shut, red with shame. The teacher tried to lead him out by one arm, gently at first and then tugging and pulling, but the boy clung to his seat with the strength of desperation.

"*Váyate a la chingada!*" Judy howled at the teacher in her newly acquired Spanish. "This school is a shitpile!" she added in English.

The teacher was stunned, and the class fell silent. "*Chingada, chingada, chinnnngada!* Let's go, Greg," and the two Reeveses walked from the classroom hand in hand, she with her head high and he with his glued to his chest.

Judy took Gregory to a gas station, hid him among some oil drums, and managed to hose down his trousers without anyone's seeing them. They walked home in silence.

"Well, how did it go?" Nora Reeves asked, puzzled to see them back so soon.

"The teacher said we don't have to come back. We're much more intelligent than the other students. Those runny-nosed little kids don't even speak like real people, Mama. They don't know English!"

"What kind of talk is that?" Olga interrupted. "And why are Gregory's clothes wet?"

The result was that they returned to school the next day, herded by Olga, who marched them into the classroom and made them apologize to the teacher for the insults; for good measure, Olga warned the other children that they had better think twice before bothering the Reeveses. As she left, she faced the compact mass of brown-skinned students, flashing the curse sign: fist closed, with the index and little fingers pointed like horns. Her bizarre appearance, her Russian accent, and her gesture had the effect of calming the beasts, at least for a while.

A week later, Gregory turned seven. No one celebrated; in fact, no one remembered, because the family's attention was focused on his father. Olga, the only one who went every day to the hospital, brought the news that Charles Reeves was finally out of danger and had been transferred to a ward where they could visit him. Nora and Inmaculada Morales scrubbed the children till they glowed, dressed them in their best clothes, put ribbons in the girls' hair and slicked down the boys' with pomade. They set out for the hospital in a procession, carrying small bunches of daisies from the garden and a platter of Inmaculada's chicken tacos and refried beans with cheese. The room was as big as a hangar, with identical rows of beds on either side and an endless corridor down the center; they tiptoed along until they reached the patient's bed. The name *Charles Reeves* written on a card allowed them to identify him; otherwise they would never have recognized him. He was a stranger to them: he had aged a thousand years, his skin was waxen, his eyes had sunk in their sockets, and he smelled of almonds. The children, crushed together, elbow-to-elbow, stood holding their flowers, not knowing where to put them. Flushing, Inmaculada Morales covered the platter of tacos with her shawl, as Nora Reeves began to tremble. Gregory had a presentiment that something irreparable had happened in his life.

"He's much better, he'll be able to eat soon," Olga said, adjusting the intravenous needle in his arm.

Gregory retreated back down the corridor, raced down the stairs two at a time, and ran toward the street. At the hospital gate, he curled up in a ball, head between his knees, arms around his legs, repeating *chingada, chingada,* like a litany.

As immigrants from Mexico arrived, they descended on friends or relatives, where often several families were already crowded together. The laws of hospitality were inviolable; no one was denied a roof and food during the first days, but after a while each person was to fend for himself. They streamed in from towns south of the border, looking for work, with nothing to their names but the clothes on their backs, a bundle over their shoulders, and the will to get ahead in that Promised Land where, they had been told, money grew on trees and a clever man could become an impresario with his own Cadillac and a blonde on his arm. What they had not been told, however, was that for each success, fifty were left by the wayside and another fifty went back home defeated, nor did they realize that they themselves would not benefit but were destined to open the way to the children and grandchildren born on that hostile soil. They had no idea of the hardships of exile, how they would be abused by their employers and persecuted by authorities, how much effort it would take to reunite their family, to bring their children and old people, or how great would be the pain of telling their friends goodbye and of leaving their dead behind. Neither were they warned that they would quickly lose their traditions, or that recollections would corrode and leave them without memories. There was no way they could have foreseen that they would be the lowest of the low. But even had they known, they might still have undertaken the voyage north. Inmaculada and Pedro Morales called themselves "wire-cuttin' wetbacks" and, rocking with laughter, liked to tell how many times they had crossed the border, sometimes swimming the Rio Grande and other times cutting wire fences. They had returned to their native land several times on vacation, entering and leaving with children of all ages and even the grandmother, whom they had brought from her village after she was widowed and her mind had begun to fade. After several years they obtained legal papers, and their children were born as American citizens. There was always room at the Morales table for new arrivals, and the second generation grew up hearing stories of poor devils who crossed the border hidden like contraband in the false bottom of a truck, or who jumped from moving trains or crawled underground through old sewer pipes, always with the terror of being caught by the immigration officers, the feared

"Migra," and sent back to their country in fetters after being booked as criminals. Some were shot by the guards or died from hunger and thirst; others smothered to death in the secret compartments of vans run by the "coyotes," whose business it was to transport desperate people from Mexico to a town on the other side. At the time Pedro Morales made his first trip, Latinos still had the feeling they were reclaiming territory that had always been theirs. For them, slipping across the border was not a crime but a righteous adventure. Pedro Morales had been twenty then; he had just completed his military service, and as he did not want to retrace the footsteps of his father and grandfather, impoverished *campesinos* on a hacienda in Zacatecas, he decided to make the trip north. He went as far as Tijuana, where he hoped to get a contract as a *bracero* and work in the fields, because North American agriculturists needed cheap labor. Since he had no money, however, he could not wait for the formalities or bribe officials and police; neither did he like that town of transients, where, in his view, men lacked honor and women respect. He was tired of beating the bushes for work, and he did not want to ask for help or accept charity. Finally he decided to cross the cattle fence marking the border; he cut the wires with pliers and, following the directions of a friend with more experience, started walking straight toward the sun. That was how he had found himself in southern California. The first months were very difficult; it was not as easy to earn a living as he had been told. He went from farm to farm, picking fruit and beans and cotton, sleeping on the road, in train stations, in car graveyards, living on bread and beer, sharing adversity with thousands of men in the same situation. The bosses paid less than they had promised and at the least complaint went to the police, who were always on the lookout for illegal aliens. It was a long time before Pedro could establish himself in one place; the "Migra" was on his heels, but finally he discarded his sombrero and huaraches, adopted blue jeans and a wool cap, and learned to reel off a few phrases in English. As soon as he was situated in the new land, he went back to his village to get his childhood sweetheart. Inmaculada was waiting for him, with her wedding gown starched and ready.

"The gringos are all crazy: they put peaches on meat and jam on fried eggs; they take their dogs to the beauty parlor and don't believe in the Virgin Mary; men wash the dishes inside the house and women wash the cars outside on the street, wearing a bra and short shorts that show everything. But if we don't have anything to do with them, we can live the good life," Pedro reported to his betrothed.

They were married with the customary ceremonies and fiestas; they slept their first night as man and wife in Inmaculada's parents' bed—on loan for the occasion—and the next day caught the bus north. Pedro had a little money in his pocket and was already expert at crossing the border; he was in better shape than he had been the first time but just as scared, because he did not want to expose his wife to any danger. People were telling hair-raising stories of thefts and killings by bandits, of corrupt Mexican police and mistreatment by American police, stories to serve as warning to the most macho of men. Inmaculada, in contrast, walked happily one step behind her husband, protected against bad fortune by the scapulary of the Virgin of Guadalupe, with the bundle of her belongings balanced on her head, a prayer on her lips, and her eyes wide open to see the world that lay before her like a magnificent coffer overflowing with surprises. She had never been outside her village and did not have any idea that roads could go on forever. Nothing could dampen her spirits, not humiliation, nor fatigue, nor the snares of nostalgia, and when finally she found herself with her husband in a squalid room in a boardinghouse on the other side, she thought she had crossed the threshold of heaven. A year later their first child was born; Pedro obtained a job in a Los Angeles tire factory and took a night course in mechanics. To help her husband, Inmaculada took work in a garment factory and then worked as a domestic servant until the number of pregnancies and babies forced her to stay home. The Moraleses were orderly people, without vices; they saved their money and learned to take advan-

tage of the benefits of the country where they would always be foreigners but where their children would belong. Their door was
open at all times to offer shelter; their house became a kind of step-
ping-stone for new immigrants. Today, you; tomorrow, me,
Inmaculada always said. There's a time to give and a time to
receive, that's the natural law of life. They learned that generosity
is returned in many ways, they did not lack for good fortune or
work, their children were healthy and their friendship valued, and
with time they worked their way out of the poverty of their origins. Five years after arriving in the city, Pedro set up his own
automobile repair shop. At the time the Reeveses came to live in
their patio, they were the most respected family in the barrio.
Inmaculada had become a universal mother figure, and Pedro was
consulted as being the most levelheaded member of the community. In surroundings where no one ever dreamed of going to the
police or to court to resolve a conflict, Pedro acted as arbiter in mis-
understandings and as judge in disputes.

Olga was at least partly right. A month after the operation,
Charles Reeves walked out of the hospital on his own two feet, but
his hope of hitting the road again was out of the question; it was
obvious that he had a long convalescence ahead of him. The doctor had ordered tranquillity, a special diet, and lifelong self-
restraint; he was not even to consider a nomadic life for a very
long time, perhaps years. Everything the family had saved had
been exhausted long ago, and they owed a sizable sum to the
Moraleses. Pedro would not listen to a word about money, because
he owed his Maestro a spiritual debt impossible to repay. Charles
Reeves, however, was not a man to accept charity, not even from a
good friend and disciple, nor could they continue to camp in the
patio of someone else's house, so despite the pleas of his children,
who could see their hope of escaping the oppression of school
rapidly slipping away, the sign and the loudspeaker were removed
and the truck was sold. With the money from the sale and a bit
more from loans, the Reeveses were able to buy a run-down cottage on the edge of the Mexican barrio.

The Moraleses mobilized their relatives to help rebuild the shack. For Gregory Reeves, that weekend formed an indelible memory: Latin music and food would be forever linked with the concept of friendship. Early Saturday morning there appeared a caravan of assorted vehicles—from a pickup truck driven by Inmaculada's brother, a hefty man with a contagious smile, to a column of bicycles carrying cousins, nephews, and friends, all loaded down with tools and construction materials. The women set up temporary tables in the yard and rolled up their sleeves to cook for the crowd. Heads of chickens rolled, cuts of pork and beef rose in a pile, corn, beans, and potatoes bubbled in pots, tortillas toasted, knives danced, chopping, slicing, and peeling, trays of fruit glistened in the sunlight, and in the shade sat more trays, holding chopped tomato and onion, hot salsa, and guacamole. Enticing aromas escaped from the kettles, tequila and beer flowed from carafes and bottles, and guitars sang with the rhythms of the generous land on the far side of the border. Little boys and dogs raced among the tables; little girls, very grown-up, helped set the tables; a retarded cousin with a placid Asiatic face washed dishes; the moonstruck grandmother ensconced beneath a tree added to the chorus with a voice like a song finch. Olga served tacos to the men and kept the children in line. Through the entire weekend, far into the night, everyone worked happily under the direction of Charles Reeves and Pedro Morales, sawing, nailing, and welding. It was a binge of sweat and song, and by Monday the house had reinforced walls, windows on proper hinges, sheets of zinc on the roof, and a new plank floor. The Mexicans took down the tables of their feasting, packed up their tools, guitars, and children, climbed back into or onto their vehicles, and slipped away whence they had come, to avoid being thanked.

When the Reeveses walked into their new home, Gregory, astounded by the steadiness of the walls, wondered how the house could be taken apart. To him and his sister, those modest rooms seemed like a palace; they had never had a solid roof over their heads, only the canvas of a tent—or the sky. Nora installed her kerosene stove, set the old typewriter in her room and, in the living room, in the place of honor, her hand-cranked phonograph for listening to opera and classical music; she was immediately ready to begin a new phase of her life.

Olga, with little or no explanation, decided to live on her own. At first she stayed on in the Moraleses' patio, using the excuse that the Reeves house was too remote and her clients could not come that far; soon after, she rented a room above a garage on the other side of the barrio, where she hung out a sign advertising her services as fortune-teller, midwife, and healer. Word of her talents spread rapidly, and her reputation was assured when she rid the lady who owned the grocery store of her beard and mustache. In that society where not even men had much hair on their faces, the shopkeeper was the butt of savage jokes until Olga intervened, liberating the lady with a poultice of her own invention, the same she used to cure mange. When at last the bearded woman's cheeks were exposed to the full light of day, sharp tongues said that at least the beard had made her interesting; without it she was just another woman with a face like a pirate. Rumors spread of how, just as Olga could heal with her salves and ointments, she could do harm with her witchcraft, and she was treated with respect. Judy and Gregory often visited her, and from time to time she showed up for Sunday lunch with the Reeveses, but the visits grew further and further apart and finally were completely suspended. Gradually even her name was no longer mentioned, because to do so filled the air with tension. Judy, distracted by her new life, did not miss her, but Gregory never lost touch.

Charles Reeves went back to earning a living by painting. Working from a photograph, he could produce a quite faithful image of a man; when it came to the ladies, the representation was enhanced: he erased signs of age, modulated Indian or African features, lightened skin and hair tones, and gowned his subjects with elegance. As soon as he had the strength, he also returned to his preaching and to writing books, which he himself printed. Despite the financial strain of keeping *The Infinite Plan* afloat, he staggered on tenaciously. His audiences were composed principally of laborers and their families, many of whom barely understood English, but he learned several key words in Spanish, and when his vocabulary failed he turned to the blackboard and sketched his ideas. At first only friends and relatives of the Moraleses attended, more interested in getting a close look at the boa than they were in the philosophical aspects of the lecture, but soon they learned that the Doctor in Divine Sciences was very eloquent and that fast as lightning he could draw wonderful cartoons—Imagine, you have to come see how he does it, quick as a wink, almost without looking!—and soon Morales did not have to exert pressure on anyone in order to fill the hall. When Reeves learned of the precarious conditions in which his neighbors lived, he spent weeks in the library studying the laws, and thus in addition to spiritual aid could offer his listeners counsel on how to navigate the unknown seas of the system. Through him, immigrants learned that even though they were illegal aliens they had certain civil rights: they could go to the hospital, bury their dead in the county cemetery—although they preferred to take them back to their home village—and claim countless other privileges they had previously been ignorant of. In that barrio, *The Infinite Plan* had to compete with the pageantry of the Catholic ceremony, the drums and tambourines of the Salvation Army, the novel polygamy of the Mormons, and the rites of seven Protestant churches, including the Baptists, who submersed their fully clothed converts in the river, the Adventists, who served lemon pie on Sundays, and the Pentecostals, who went about with hands uplifted in order to receive the Holy Spirit. Since Charles Reeves's course accommodated all doctrines and it was not necessary for followers to renounce their own religion, Padre Larraguibel of the Church of Our Lady of Lourdes and the pastors of the other affiliations could not object—although for once they were in accord, and each from his own pulpit accused the preacher of being an unprincipled charlatan.

From their first meeting, when the Reeveses' truck had disgorged its contents onto the Moraleses' patio, Gregory and Carmen, the Moraleses' youngest daughter, had been fast friends. One look was enough to establish the complicity that was to last throughout their lifetimes. The girl was a year younger, but in practical matters she was much better informed; it was she who would reveal to him the tricks to surviving in the barrio. Gregory was tall, thin, and very blond, and she was small, plump, and the color of golden brown sugar. The boy's knowledge was out of the ordinary: he could recount the plots of operas, describe landscapes from the *National Geographic,* and recite Byron's verses; he knew how to bag a duck, gut a fish, and in an instant could calculate how far a truck would travel in forty-five minutes if it was moving at thirty miles per hour—none of which had much application in his new situation. He knew how to get the boa into a sack but could not go to the corner to buy bread; he had never lived among other children or been inside a classroom; he knew nothing of children's cruelty or of impassable racial barriers, because Nora had drummed into him that people are good—anything else was an abomination of nature—and all people are equal. Until he went to school, Gregory believed her. The color of his skin and his absolute lack of malice irritated the other boys, who jumped him whenever they could, usually in the bathroom, and pummeled him until he was half stupefied. Not always the innocent one, he often provoked confrontations. With Juan José and Carmen Morales, he invented gross practical jokes, such as using a syringe to remove the mint from chocolate bonbons and then to fill them with the hottest salsa from Inmaculada's kitchen; they then offered these treats to the Martínez gang: Let's smoke the peace pipe and be friends, OK? After that trick, they had to hide for a week.

Every day, as soon as the last bell rang, Gregory ran home like a streak, chased by a pack of boys ready to slaughter him. He was so fast that he often stopped in midcourse to yell insults at his enemies. As long as his family was camping in the Morales patio, he had no fear, because the house was close to the school; Juan José ran with him, and no one could catch him in such a short distance. When they moved to their new house, however, the distance was ten times greater, and the possibilities of reaching his goal in safety were diminished by alarming proportions. He changed his route, learned different shortcuts, and found hiding places where he could crouch and wait until his pursuers tired of hunting for him. Once, he slipped into the parish church, because in the Padre's religion class he had been told that since the Middle Ages the church had traditionally served as a place of asylum; the Martínez gang nonetheless followed him inside and after a horrendous chase across the pews caught him before the main altar and kicked and beat him beneath the indifferent gaze of plaster saints wearing gilt brass halos. The energetic priest had come running at Gregory's cries and lifted his enemies off him by the hair of their heads.

"God didn't save me!" the boy yelped, more humiliated than hurt, pointing to the bloodied Christ presiding over the altar.

"What do you mean, he didn't save you?" roared the priest. "Didn't I come help you, you ingrate?"

"Too late! Look what they did to me," Gregory howled, displaying his bruises.

"God has no time for such harebrained feuds. Get up and blow your nose," the Padre commanded.

"You said it was safe here. . . ."

"It is, if the enemy knows it's a holy place; those blockheads don't even realize the sacrilege they committed."

"Your lousy church isn't worth a damn!"

"You watch what you say, or you'll be missing your teeth, you young runt!" The Padre's uplifted hand underlined the threat.

"Sacrilege! Sacrilege!" Gregory remembered just in time, a ploy that had the virtue of cooling the Basque blood of the priest, who took a deep breath to compose himself and attempted to speak in tones more appropriate to his holy vestments.

"Look here, son, you need to learn to defend yourself. God helps those who help themselves, as the old saying goes."

That very day, the priest, who in his youth had been a belligerent peasant boy, shut himself in the courtyard of the sacristy with Gregory and began teaching him to box—without regard for the Marquis of Queensberry. The first lesson consisted of three inviolable principles: the only thing that matters is to win; the one who strikes first strikes twice; and go straight for the balls, son, and may God forgive us. In any case, Gregory decided that the house of God was less secure than the firm bosom of Inmaculada Morales; his confidence in his fists grew in direct proportion to his flagging faith in divine intervention. From then on, if he was in trouble he ran to his friends' home, leapt over the patio wall, and ran into the kitchen, where he waited for Judy to come to his rescue. He was safe with his sister because she was the prettiest girl in the school; all the boys were in love with her, and none would have been so stupid as to do anything to Gregory in her presence. Carmen and Juan José Morales tried to serve as liaison between their new friend and the rest of their schoolmates, but they did not always succeed; it was not only Gregory's coloring that made him stand out: he was also proud, stubborn, and crafty. His head was filled with stories of Indians, wild animals, characters in operas, theories of souls in floating oranges, Logi, and Master Functionaries, none of which either the Padre or his teachers wanted to learn more about. In addition, he lost his head at the least provocation and lashed out with eyes closed and fists flailing; he fought blindly, and he almost always lost: he was the whipping boy for the entire school. Everyone laughed at him and at his dog—a mongrel with short legs and an ugly head—and even at how his mother looked: she wore old-fashioned dresses and was always handing out brochures on the Bahai religion or *The Infinite Plan*. They saved their greatest scorn for his sentimentality. All the other boys had absorbed the macho teachings of their world: men should be merciless, brave, dominant, loners, fast with a weapon, and superior to women in every sense. The two basic rules, learned by boys in the cradle, were never to trust anyone and never to cry—whatever the reason. Gregory, however, would listen to the teacher telling how seals in Canada were clubbed by fur hunters, or to the Padre recounting the woes of lepers in Calcutta, and with tears in his eyes determine to go north immediately to defend the baby seals or to the Far East to be a missionary. On the other hand, they could beat him silly and he would never shed a tear; his pride was so fierce they could have skinned him alive before he would ask for mercy. That was the only reason the other boys did not consider him a hopeless pansy. Despite everything, he was a happy young boy, with an infallible memory for jokes and the ability to coax music from any instrument—the favorite of the girls at recess time.

In exchange for the boxing lessons, the Padre required Gregory to assist him at Sunday masses. When Gregory told that to the Moraleses, he suffered a barrage of jokes from Juan José and his brothers—until Inmaculada intervened and said that because they were making fun, Juan José must serve as altar boy himself, and be proud of the honor, praise our blessed Lord. The two friends spent grudging hours in the church, swinging incense, tinkling the altar bells, and reciting parts of the Latin mass under the attentive eye of the priest, who even in his most intense moments watched them with his famed third eye—the one people said he had in the back of his head to see his parishioners' sins. The priest liked it that one of his assistants was dark-haired and the other blond; he thought such racial integration must please the Creator. Before mass the boys prepared the altar and afterward they cleaned the sacristy; when they left they received an anise bun as a reward, but the true prize was a surreptitious swig of ceremonial wine, aged, sweet, and strong as sherry. One morning their enthusiasm got out of hand and they polished off the bottle, leaving them short of wine for the last mass. Gregory, inspired, suggested that they pilfer a few coins from the collection plate and rush out and buy some Coca-Cola. They shook the bottle to kill the fizz and then poured the liquid into the cruet. During the mass they cut up like clowns, and not even murderous looks from the priest could affect the whispering, giggling, stumbling, and bells rung in the wrong sequence. When the Padre raised the goblet to consecrate the Coca-Cola, the boys collapsed on the altar steps, laughing so hard they could not stand up. Minutes later the priest reverently touched the liquid to his lips, absorbed in the words of the liturgy, but with the first sip realized that the devil had had his hand in the chalice—unless consecration had produced a verifiable change in the molecules of the wine, a possibility his practical mind immediately rejected. The Padre had undergone a long training in life's vicissitudes, and he continued the mass serenely; nothing in his demeanor hinted that anything was amiss. Unhurried, he completed the ritual and left the altar with great dignity, followed by his two staggering altar boys, but once in the sacristy he removed one of his heavy leather sandals and gave them a thrashing they would not soon forget.

That was the first of many difficult years for Gregory Reeves; it was a time of insecurity and fears, during which many things changed, but it was also a time of mischief, friendship, surprises, and discoveries.

As soon as my family settled into the new routine and my father started feeling stronger, we began improving the cottage. Because of the efforts of the Moraleses and their friends, it was no longer falling down, but it still lacked essential comforts. My father installed basic wiring, built a privy, and between us we cleared the yard of stones and weeds so my mother could plant the vegetable and flower gardens she had always wanted. He also constructed a small shed at the very edge of the ravine that bordered our property, to store his tools and gear for traveling: he still hoped someday to get a new truck and go back on the road. Then he told me to dig a hole; he said that he agreed with a Greek philosopher who had said that before he died every man should father a child, write a book, build a house, and plant a tree, and that he had done the first three. I dug where he told me, not very enthusiastically, since I had no wish to contribute to his death, but I would not have dreamed of refusing him or of leaving the job half done. "Once when I was traveling on the astral plane, I was led to a very large room, like a room in a factory," Charles Reeves would expound to his listeners. "There I saw many interesting machines. Some were unfinished and others absurd; the mechanical principles were incorrect; it was clear they would never work. I asked a Logo whom they belonged to. 'These are your unfinished works,' he explained. I remembered that in my youth my ambition had been to be an inventor. Those grotesque machines were products of that stage of my life and ever since had been there waiting for me to dispose of them. Thoughts take form— the more defined the idea, the more concrete the form. You must not leave ideas or projects unfinished; they must be terminated. If not, energy is wasted that could be better employed in other matters. You must think in a constructive way, but be careful of what you think." I had heard that story many times and was highly irritated by the obsession to complete every act and to give each object and each thought its precise place, because to judge by what I saw around me, the world was pure chaos.

My father left early that morning and with Pedro Morales returned carrying a good-sized willow tree in the pickup truck. It took both of them to drag it out and plant it in the hole. For several days I watched the tree and my father, expecting that at any moment the former would wither and die or the latter would be struck dead, but as neither occurred I decided that the philosophers of old were not worth a nickel. I was haunted by the fear of being orphaned. In my dreams I saw my father as a creaking skeleton in a dark suit, with a huge snake coiled around his ankles, and awake I remembered him shrunken to skin and bones, as I had seen him in the hospital. The idea of death terrified me. Ever since we had come to live in the city, I had felt a presentiment of danger. The standards I had known were out of kilter; even words had lost their accustomed meaning, and I was forced to learn new codes, different behaviors, and a strange language of rolled *r*'s and rasping *h* sounds. Endless roads and vast landscapes were replaced by a warren of noisy, filthy, foul-smelling—but fascinating—alleys where a new adventure lay around every corner. It was impossible to resist the lure of the streets; life was lived there: the streets were the setting for fights, love, and commerce. I was entranced by Latin music and storytelling. People talked about their lives in tones of legend. My favorite place was Inmaculada Morales's kitchen, surrounded by family activity and the smell of cooking. I never tired of the eternal circus of that life, but I also felt a need to recapture the silence of nature I had known as a boy; I searched out trees, I walked hours to climb a small hill where for a few minutes I felt again the pleasure of being inside my own skin. The rest of the time my body was a handicap; I had to protect it constantly against external threats; my light hair, the color of my skin and eyes, my birdlike skeleton, weighed on me like rocks. Inmaculada Morales says that I was a happy child, full of vigor and energy, with a tremendous appetite for life, but I do not remember myself that way. In that Latin ghetto I experienced the unpleasantness of being different, I did not fit in; I wanted to be like everyone else, to blend into the crowd, to be invisible, so I could walk through the streets or play in the schoolyard unharmed by the gangs of dark-skinned boys who vented on me the aggression they themselves received from whites the minute they stepped outside the barrio.

When my father left the hospital, we had resumed the appearance of normality, but the equilibrium of our family life was destroyed. Olga's absence hung in the air; I missed her trunkload of treasures, her magician's trappings, her bizarre clothes, her unrestrained laugh, her stories, her indefatigable energy—without her, the house was like a table with a wobbly leg. My parents drew a curtain of silence over her absence, and I did not dare ask what had happened. My mother was becoming more silent and reserved by the day, and my father, who had always been very self-controlled, became irascible, unpredictable, and violent. It's because of the operation; the chemistry of his Physical Body has been altered, that's why his aura has grown dark, but he'll be all right soon. My mother's justification was couched in the jargon of *The Infinite Plan,* but her voice lacked conviction. I had never felt comfortable with my mother; that pale, polite woman was very different from other children's mothers. Decisions, permissions, and punishment always came from my father, consolation and laughter from Olga, and my confidences were with Judy. All that tied me to my mother were literature and school notebooks, music, and love for observing the stars. She never touched me; I had grown accustomed to her physical remoteness and reserved temperament.

THE INFINITE PLAN · 55

The day I lost Judy, I felt a panic of absolute solitude I did not recover from until decades later, when an unexpected love annulled that curse. Judy had been the candid and sympathetic young girl who protected me, ordered me around, and went everywhere with me clinging to her skirts. At night I slipped into her bed and she told me stories or invented dreams, with precise instructions as to how to dream them. The sight of my sleeping sister, her warmth, and the rhythm of her breathing filled the first years of my childhood; nestled close to her, I knew no fear. When I was beside her, nothing could hurt me. One April night, when Judy was nearly nine and I was seven, I waited for everything to grow quiet, then crawled from my sleeping bag to climb into hers as I always did; that night, however, I met fierce resistance. With the covers pulled up to her chin and clawlike hands clutching the bag to her, she raged that she didn't love me, that I could never sleep with her again, that the stories, the dreams, and all the rest were over, and that I was too big for such nonsense.

"What's the matter, Judy?" I asked, frightened not so much by her words as by the rancor in her voice.

"You go to hell, and don't you ever touch me as long as you live!" and she burst out crying and turned her face to the wall.

I sat beside her on the floor, not knowing what to say, saddened more by her weeping than by the rejection. After a while, I tiptoed to the door and let Oliver in, and from that day on I slept with my arms around my dog. In the following months I had the sensation that there was a mystery in my house from which I was excluded, a secret between my father and my sister, or maybe between them and my mother, or between all of them and Olga. I sensed it was better not to know the truth, and I did not attempt to find out. The atmosphere was so charged that I tried to stay away from home as much as possible. I visited Olga or the Moraleses, I took long hikes through the nearby fields, I walked for miles, returning only at nightfall, I hid in the small shed among the tools and bundles and wept for hours without knowing why. No one asked me anything.

The image of my father began to fade and was replaced by

that of a stranger, an unfair and irascible man who pampered Judy
and beat me at the least pretext and thrust me aside: Go play outside; boys need to toughen up in the street, he would growl. There
was no resemblance between the neat and charismatic preacher of
earlier days and that revolting old man who spent the day in an
armchair listening to the radio, half dressed and unshaven. He
had stopped painting and seemed unable to spend any energy in
disseminating *The Infinite Plan.* The situation in the house deteriorated before our eyes, and once again Inmaculada Morales
showed up with her assorted spicy dishes, her generous smile, and
her sharp eye for perceiving the needs of others. Olga handed me
money, with instructions to slip it into my mother's purse surreptitiously. That uncommon income continued for many years, without my mother's ever mentioning it, as if she had never noticed
the mysterious multiplication of the bank notes.

Olga had a gift for imposing her extravagant stamp on everything around her. She was an adventurous migratory bird, but
wherever she came to roost, even for only a few hours, she created
the illusion of a permanent nest. She had few belongings, but she
knew how to arrange them so that if the space was small she kept
them in the trunk and if it was large they expanded to fill it. In a
tent at some bend in the road, in a hut, or in jail—where she
would later spend some time—she was queen in her palace. When
she moved away from the Reeveses, she found a cheap room in a
slightly sordid dwelling that had taken on the melancholy patina
of the rest of the barrio, but she livened it up with her characteristic colors, and before long the place had become a point of reference when people were looking for an address: three blocks
straight ahead, take a right, and where you see a house painted
like a rainbow, turn to the left and you're there. She decorated the
outside stairway and two windows in her personal style. clicking
curtains of shells and beads beckoned to passersby, strings of colored lights suggested a never-ending Christmas, and her name in
cursive letters crowned that strange pagoda. Her landlords tired
of requesting her to use a little more restraint and finally resigned

themselves to the strange embellishment of their property. Soon everyone for miles around knew where Olga lived. Inside, her quarters were equally bizarre. A curtain divided the room into two sections: in one she attended her clientele; the other contained her bed and her clothes, which she hung from nails in the wall. Calling upon her artistic gifts and her oil paints from the time of her venture with Charles Reeves, she covered the walls with the signs of the zodiac and words in Cyrillic, an effect that deeply impressed her visitors. She bought a set of secondhand furniture and with a flash of imagination turned it into Oriental divans; she filled shelves with statues of saints and magicians, pots with her potions, candles, and amulets; bunches of dried herbs hung from the ceiling, and it was nearly impossible to walk among the midget tables covered with braziers that hoarded dubious incense from shops run by Pakistanis. The sweetish fragrance was at war with the scent of Olga's medicinal plants and elixirs, essences for love, and wax candles for incantatory healing. She covered lamps with fringed shawls, threw a moth-eaten zebra skin on the floor, and near the window provided an altar for a large potbellied Buddha of gilded plaster. In that cave, calling on all her ingenuity, she cooked, lived, and plied her trade, all in a minimal space fitted to her needs and whims by the twist of fantasy. Once she had decorated, she spread the word that there are women who can deflect the course of misfortune and see into the depths of the soul, and that she was one of those women. Then she sat down to wait—but not for long, because many people already knew of her success with the bearded grocerywoman, and soon clients were standing in line for her services.

Gregory visited Olga almost every day. As soon as classes were out, he escaped from school pursued by the loutish Martínez, a slightly older boy who was in second grade but had not learned to read, who could not master English but already had the physique and mentality of a bully. Oliver would wait, barking, near the newspaper stand in a valiant effort to hold Gregory's enemies at bay and give his master a head start, then would race after him like an arrow to their final destination. To throw Martínez off the track, Gregory used to stop by Olga's house. His visits to the crystal gazer were a lark. Once, unbeknownst to her, he scooted under her bed and from his hiding place witnessed one of her extraordinary consultations. The owner of Los Tres Amigos bar, a conceited womanizer with a movie star mustache and an elastic waist-trimmer to hold in his belly, came to Olga, deeply perturbed, to seek a remedy for a secret malady. She received him in her astrologer's robe in the incense-perfumed room, dimly lit by red light bulbs. He sat down at the round table where she consulted with her clients and with stammering preambles and appeals for absolute secrecy told her he was tormented by constant burning in his genitals.

"Let's see; show me," Olga commanded, and with the aid of a flashlight proceeded to examine him inch by inch with a magnifying glass, while beneath the bed Gregory bit his hands to keep from exploding with laughter.

"I've used the remedies they prescribed at the hospital, but they didn't help. It's four months now, *doña,* and I'm dying!"

"There's sickness of the body and sickness of the soul," the healer intoned, returning to her throne at the head of the table. "This is a sickness of the soul; that is why ordinary medicines won't cure it. If you're going to dance, you must pay the piper."

"Huh?"

"You have mistreated your organ. Sometimes the price is a noxious disease, and sometimes an unbearable moral itch," explained Olga, who was up on all the latest gossip in the barrio; she was aware of her client's reputation and just the week before had sold powders to ensure faithfulness to the bar owner's inconsolable wife. "I can help you, but I warn you that each consultation will cost you five dollars, and I can tell you that the treatment is not going to be very pleasant. Just offhand I calculate you will need at least five sessions."

"If it will make me better . . ."

"You must pay fifteen dollars in advance. That way we'll be sure you don't change your mind in midstream; you see, once you begin the treatment you have to finish it—if you don't, your member will dry up like a prune. You understand what I'm saying?"

"Oh, yes, *doñita,* anything you say," the cocksman agreed, docile with terror.

"Take off everything below the waist; you can leave your shirt on," she ordered before disappearing behind the screen to prepare the ingredients for the treatment.

She made the man stand in the middle of the room inside a circle of lighted candles; she sprinkled white powders on his head as she recited a litany in an unknown tongue; then she rubbed the affected area with something that Gregory could not see but that was undoubtedly very effective, because in two seconds the feckless fellow was hopping like a monkey and screaming at the top of his lungs.

"Stay inside the circle!" Olga commanded, waiting calmly for the fire to subside.

"Oh, shit, oh, Christ, *madrecita*! It's worse than raw chili pepper," he howled when he had his breath back.

"If it doesn't hurt, it isn't doing its work," she asserted, well aware of the efficaciousness of punishment for removing guilt, cleansing the conscience, and alleviating nervous ailments. "Now I'm going to put on something cooling," she said, and she painted his penis with tincture of methylene blue, then tied on a pink ribbon and ordered him to return the following week; he was to apply the tincture every morning and not remove the ribbon for any reason.

"But how am I going to ... well, you know what I mean ... tied like this?"

"You'll just have to live like a saint. All this happened because you were flitting around like a hummingbird. Why not be content with your wife? That poor woman has earned her ticket to heaven; you don't deserve her," and with that final recommendation for good behavior, she dismissed him.

Gregory bet Juan José and Carmen Morales a dollar that the owner of the bar had a blue dingdong tied up like a birthday present. The three spent the morning on the roof of Los Tres Amigos watching through a peephole into the bathroom until they saw the proof with their own eyes. It was not long until the whole barrio knew the story, and the bar owner was followed to his grave by the nickname Purple Pecker.

As Olga's door was not open if she was busy with some client, Gregory used to sit on the stairs and examine the newest decorations on the front of the house, amazed at the woman's talent for revitalizing herself with each new day. From time to time she would peer out, her robe barely covering her nakedness, hair like a tangle of red seaweed, and hand him a cookie or a dime: I can't see you today, Greg, I have work to do, come back tomorrow, she would say, and give him a quick kiss on the cheek. He would go home, frustrated, but understanding that she had inescapable obligations. Olga had clients of every station: desperate persons hoping to improve their luck, pregnant women ready to resort to any recourse that would thwart nature, patients disillusioned with traditional medicine, spiteful lovers eager for revenge, lonely souls tormented by silence, and ordinary people who wanted nothing more than a massage, a charm, a palm reading, or some jasmine tea for a headache. To each, Olga dispensed a dose of magic and hope, never giving a thought to the legality of her actions because in the barrio no one understood or cared about the law of the gringos.

Olga had no children of her own and in her heart had adopted Charles Reeves's son and daughter. She was not offended by Judy's rebuffs, because she knew the girl would come back when she needed her, but she was quietly grateful for Gregory's loyalty and rewarded him with affection and gifts. Through him, she kept up with the fortunes of the Reeves family. Gregory often asked why she never came to visit, but obtained only vague answers. One of the times the fortune-teller had not invited him in, he thought he heard his father's voice through the door, and his heart nearly burst from his chest; he felt he was standing at the edge of a bottomless abyss, on the verge of opening a Pandora's box of horrors. He ran away as fast as he could, not wanting to affirm what he feared, but his curiosity was stronger than his fear, and halfway home he turned back and hid outside to wait for Olga's client to come out. Night fell, and the door did not open; finally he had to go home. When he got there he found Charles Reeves sitting in his wicker chair, reading the newspaper.

How long was my father really alive? When did he begin to die? In the final months he was not himself; his physical appearance changed so greatly that it was difficult to recognize him, and his mind was similarly altered. A breath of evil animated that old man; he still called himself Charles Reeves, but he was not my father. That is why I have no bad memories of him. Judy, on the other hand, is filled with hatred. We have talked about this and do not agree about either events or people, as if we had been protagonists in different stories. We lived together in the same house at the same time; her memory, nevertheless, did not register what mine did. My sister cannot understand why I cling to the image of a wise father, of happy days of camping in the open air beneath the fathomless dome of a star-filled sky, of hiding in reeds at dawn to shoot ducks. She swears that things were never like that, that the violence in our family was always there, that Charles Reeves was a two-bit charlatan, a merchant of lies, a degenerate who died from pure perversion and left nothing good behind him. She accuses me of having blocked out the past; she says I prefer to ignore our father's vices, and that must be true, because I did not know him as an alcoholic and an evil man, which she maintains he was. Don't you remember how he beat you with his leather belt for the least little thing you did? Judy asks me. I do, but I don't harbor any hard feelings over that; in those days all boys got whippings, it was part of their education. He treated Judy better; I guess it wasn't the thing to whip girls that much. Besides, I was feisty and stubborn; my mother could never break me, which was why more than once she tried to get rid of me. But before she died, on one of those rare occasions when we were able to talk without hurting each other, she assured me she did not act the way she did out of lack of affection and that she always loved me very much. She could not look after two children, she said, so naturally she had preferred to keep my sister, who was docile, whereas I was beyond her power to control. Sometimes I dream of the courtyard of the orphan asylum. Judy was much nicer than I was, there is no doubt of that, a composed and appealing little girl, always obedient and with the natural flirtatiousness of pretty girls. She was like that until she was thirteen or fourteen, when she changed.

At first it was the smell of almonds. It came back subtly, almost imperceptibly, in the beginning, a breath that left no trace, so faint I could not decide whether I had actually smelled it or whether it was a memory from visiting the hospital when my father had his operation. Later it was the noise. The noise was the most notable change. Before, in the days when we were on the road, silence was a part of that life, each sound had its precise space. The only sounds came from the motor, and sometimes my mother's voice, reading; when we camped, it was the crackling of wood on the fire, the spoon scraping the pot, the recitation of our school lessons, brief conversations, my sister's laughter as she played with Olga, Oliver's barking. At night the silence was so heavy that the hooting of an owl or the howl of a coyote seemed thunderous. As my father said, each thing had its own place, each sound its moment. He was indignant when anyone interrupted a conversation; during his sermons we had to hold our breath, because even an involuntary cough provoked an icy stare. At the end, though, everything became a jumble in Charles Reeves's mind. In his astral pilgrimages he must have come across more than the hangar filled with unfinished machines and demented inventions: rooms bulging with smells, tastes, gestures, and senseless words; other rooms would have been filled to bursting with good intentions and there would have been one where lunacy rumbled like the bonging of a monstrous iron bell. I don't mean the noises of the barrio—traffic, loud voices, construction workers building the filling station—but the derangement that marked my father's last months. The radio, which once he had turned on only to listen to news of the war and classical music, now roared day and night with deafening information, ball games, and country music. In addition to this uproar, my father raved over trifles, shouted contradictory orders, summoned us every minute, read his sermons or passages from the Bible at the top of his lungs, coughed, spit constantly, and blew his nose with unimaginable snortings; he hammered nails in the walls and fiddled with his tools as if repairing major damage, but in fact those frenetic tinkerings served no purpose at all. Even asleep he made noise. This man, once so neat in his ways and his habits, would abruptly fall asleep at the table, his mouth still filled with food, shaken by deep snores, panting and mumbling, lost in the labyrinth of who knows what lecherous delirium. That's enough, Charles, my bewildered mother would say, and wake my father when he was fondling himself in his dreams. It's the fever, children, she would add to soothe us. My father was delirious, no doubt of it; fever ambushed him at any moment of the day, but it was particularly at night he found no rest, and dawn would find him soaked with perspiration. My mother changed his sheets every morning, to wash away not only the sweat of agony but bloodstains as well, and pus from his boils. Purulent abscesses opened on his legs, which he treated with arnica and compresses of warm water. From the first day of his final illness, my mother never again slept in his bed; she spent the night in an armchair, covered with a shawl.

Toward the end, when my father could not even get out of bed, Judy refused to enter his room; she did not want to see him, and no threat or reward could get her near the sick man. I was able to approach in stages, first observing him from the doorway and finally sitting on the edge of the bed. He was nothing but skin and bones, his complexion was greenish, his eyes were sunken in their sockets—only the asthmatic wheezing indicated he was still alive. When I touched his hand he would open his eyes, but he did not recognize me. Sometimes his fever receded and he seemed to return from a long death; he would drink a little tea, ask someone to turn on the radio, get out of bed and take a few faltering steps. One morning, half naked, he went out in the yard to look at the willow. He showed me the tender shoots: It's growing, he said; it will live to weep over me. That day after school, as Judy and I neared the house, we saw an ambulance in the lane. I ran on, but my sister sank to the sidewalk, clutching her book bag. A few people were already standing around in the yard. Inmaculada Morales was on the porch, trying to help two attendants roll a stretcher through the too narrow doorway. I ran into the house and caught hold of my mother's dress, but she pushed me away impatiently, as if she felt nauseated. At that moment I was struck by a strong blast of the odor of almonds, and a squalid old man appeared in the doorway of the room; he was standing very straight, clad only in an undershirt, and was barefoot; his remaining hair was ruffled, his eyes burning with the madness of fever, and a thread of saliva trickled from the corner of his mouth. With his left hand, he supported himself against the wall; with his right he was masturbating.

"That's enough, Charles, stop that!" my mother called to him. "That's enough, please, that's enough," she pleaded, hiding her face in her hands.

Inmaculada Morales put her arms around my mother as the attendants seized my father's arms and led him outside to the porch, where they laid him on the stretcher, covered with a sheet and secured by two straps. My father yelled terrible curses, using words that until that minute I had never heard from his mouth. I walked beside him to the ambulance, but my mother would not allow me to come with them; the ambulance pulled away, siren shrieking, amid billowing dust. Inmaculada Morales locked the door, took my hand, whistled for Oliver, and started off toward her house. Down the street we found Judy, still in the same spot, with a strange smile on her face.

"You come with me, children. I will buy you some cotton candy," said Inmaculada Morales, struggling to hold back her tears.

That was the last time I saw my father alive; a few hours later he died in the hospital, the victim of uncontainable internal hemorrhages. I spent that night, with Judy, in the home of our Mexican friends. Pedro Morales was absent; he was with my mother, attending to the details of the death. Before we sat down to dinner, Inmaculada took my sister and me aside and explained, as well as she could, that we should not worry now; our father's Physical

Body had ceased to suffer and his Mental Body had flown to the astral plane; there, surely, it was reunited with the Logi and the Master Functionaries, where it belonged.

"That is, he is in heaven with the angels," she added softly, much more comfortable with the terms of her Catholic faith than with those of *The Infinite Plan.*

Judy and I slept with the Morales children, two or three to a bed, all in the same room. Inmaculada let Oliver stay with us; he was not used to being outside and if left there moaned and whined. I was beginning to nod, exhausted by conflicting emotions, when in the dark I heard Carmen's voice whispering to make a place for her, and I felt her small warm body slip in beside me. Open your mouth and close your eyes, she said, and I felt her finger on my lips, a finger coated with something thick and sweet that I sucked like a caramel. It was condensed milk. I sat up a little and put my finger in the jar to offer to her, and we finished the treat, licking and sucking each other's fingers until it was gone. Then I went right to sleep, sated with sugar, my face and hands sticky, my arms around Carmen, Oliver at my feet, accompanied by the breathing and warmth of the other children and the snoring of the addlepated grandmother in the next room, tied by a long rope to Inmaculada's waist.

The father's death disrupted the family; they lost direction and within a very brief time were going their separate ways. For Nora, widowhood was a betrayal; she felt she had been abandoned in a cruel world with two children and no resources, but at the same time she felt inexpressible relief, because in the last years her companion had not been the man she once loved, and living with him had become a martyrdom. Even so, shortly after the funeral she began to forget Reeves's final decrepitude and to cherish earlier memories. She imagined they were joined by an invisible thread, like the one her husband had used to suspend the orange of *The Infinite Plan;* that image restored her earlier security drawn from the years he had ruled the family's fate with the firm hand of a Master. Nora yielded to her languorous nature; the lethargy born of the horror of the war was accentuated, a deterioration of will that once she was widowed subtly grew and manifested itself in all its magnitude. She never spoke of her late husband in the past tense; she alluded to his absence in vague terms, as if he had undertaken a long astral voyage, and later, when she began to communicate with him in her dreams, she would speak of it in the tone of someone repeating a telephone conversation. Her embarrassed children did not like to hear about her delusions, fearing they would lead to madness. She was alone. She was a stranger in that environment; she spoke only a few words of Spanish and saw herself as being very different from the other women. Her friendship with Olga had ended, she had little relationship to her children, she was not friendly with Inmaculada Morales or any other person in the barrio. She was amiable, but people avoided her because she was strange; no one wanted to listen to her ravings about opera or *The Infinite Plan.* The habit of dependence was so deeply rooted that when she lost Charles Reeves it was as if she began to live in a daze. She made a few attempts to earn a living as a typist or a seamstress, but nothing came of it; neither was she able to get a job translating Hebrew or Russian, as she claimed she could, because no one needed those services in the barrio and the prospect of venturing into the center of the city to look for work terrified her. She was not overly concerned about supporting her children, because she did not consider them exclusively hers; it was her theory that children belonged to society in general and no one in particular. She would sit on the porch of her house and stare at the willow for hours on end, with a placid, vacant expression on the beautiful Slavic face that even then had begun to pale. In the years that followed, her freckles disappeared, her features faded—her whole being seemed slowly to vanish. In old age she became so insubstantial that it was difficult to remember her, and as no one thought to take her photograph, Gregory feared after she died that perhaps his mother had never existed. Pedro Morales tried to convince Nora to busy herself with something; he clipped want ads for different jobs and accompanied her to several interviews, until he was convinced of her inability to face reality. Three months later, when the situation was becoming intolerable, he took her to the welfare office to sign up for payments as an indigent, grateful that his Maestro, Charles Reeves, was not alive to witness such humiliation. The check, barely sufficient to cover the most basic expenses, was the family's only regular source of income for many years; the rest came from the children's jobs, the bills Olga managed to slip into Nora's pocketbook, and the discreet support of the Moraleses. A buyer appeared for the boa, and the poor creature ended its days exposed to the eyes of the curious in a burlesque house, alongside scantily clad chorus girls, an obscene ventriloquist, and various acts intended to amuse the besotted spectators. It lived on for several years, feeding on live mice and squirrels and the scraps thrown into its cage for the thrill of watching the bored creature open its jaws; it continued to grow and fatten until it was truly awe-inspiring, though it was lethargic until the day it died.

The Reeves children survived on their own, in their individual ways. Judy found a job in a bakery, where she worked four hours every day after school; by night she baby-sat or cleaned offices. She was an excellent student; she learned to imitate any handwriting and for a reasonable sum would do homework for her classmates. She maintained her clandestine trade without ever being caught, all the while enjoying her reputation as a model young girl, always smiling and docile, never revealing the demons in her soul until the first symptoms of puberty transformed her personality. When two firm cherries budded on her breasts, her waistline slimmed, and her baby features became more modeled, everything changed. In that barrio of dark-skinned, rather short people, her golden color and Valkyrie-like stature made it impossible for her to pass unnoticed. She had always been pretty; once she emerged from girlhood, however, and males of all ages and conditions began to hound her, the once sweet child became a raging animal. She felt violated by men's lustful glances and often came home shouting curses and slamming doors; she sometimes wept impotently because someone had whistled at her in the street or made lewd gestures. She acquired a sailor's vocabulary to rebuff these advances, and for anyone who tried to touch her she kept a long hatpin at hand, which she would bury like a dagger, without compunction, in her admirer's most vulnerable parts. In school she got into fights with boys over the look in their eye and with girls over racial differences and the jealousy she inevitably provoked. More than once Gregory saw his sister engaged in the strange wrestling matches females indulge in, rolling, scratching, hair-pulling, insults—so different from the way boys do battle, which is generally brief, silent, and conclusive. Girls look for a way to humiliate their enemy, while boys seem prepared to kill or be killed. Judy did not need any help in defending herself; with practice she became a true champion. While other girls her age were trying out their first makeup, practicing French kisses, and counting the days until they could wear high heels, she cut her hair like a jailbird, dressed in men's clothes, and compulsively ate leftover bread and rolls in the bakery. Her face broke out in pimples, and by the time she entered high school she had gained so much weight that no trace remained of the delicate porcelain doll she had been as a child; she looked like a sea lion, a description she used when she wanted to denigrate herself.

When he was seven, Gregory turned to the streets. He was not bound to his mother by any emotion; between them there were only a few shared routines and a tradition of honor drawn from didactic stories about self-sacrificing sons who were rewarded and ungrateful ones who ended up in the witch's oven. He felt sorry for his mother; he was sure that without Judy and him, Nora would die of attrition, sitting in her wicker chair staring into empty air. Both children thought of their mother's indolence not as a vice but, rather, as a sickness of the spirit; perhaps her Mental Body had gone in search of their father and had wandered astray in the labyrinth of some cosmic plane, or had fallen behind in one of those vast spaces filled with weird machines or baffled souls. Gregory's closeness with Judy had vanished, and when he tired of trying to reestablish contact with her, he replaced his sister with Carmen Morales, with whom he shared the unceremonious affection, the spats, and the loyalty of best friends. Gregory was mischievous and restless; he was a problem in school and spent half his time serving out various punishments—whether wearing donkey's ears and standing with his face to the wall or suffering the principal's spankings. He lived like a boarder in his own home, staying out as late as possible, coming home only to sleep—he much preferred visiting the Moraleses, or Olga. Most of his time he was to be found in the jungle of the barrio, learning its most secret secrets. Everyone called him El Gringo, and despite racial animosity, many people liked him, because he was cheerful and obliging. He had several friends: the cook at the taco stand, who always had some tasty dish to offer him; the lady at the grocery store, who let him read comic books without buying them; and the usher at the movies, who from time to time let him in the side door to watch the film. Even Purple Pecker, who never suspected Gregory's role in tagging him with that name, used to treat him to soda pop in Los Tres Amigos bar. Trying to learn Spanish, he lost much of his English and ended up speaking both languages poorly. For a while he stuttered badly, and the principal called Nora Reeves to recommend that she place her son in the nuns' school for retarded children, but his teacher, Miss June, intervened, promising she would help him with his homework. He was not much interested in school; his world was the streets—where, incidentally, he learned considerably more. The barrio was a citadel within the city, a rough, impoverished ghetto born of spontaneous growth around an industrial zone where illegal immigrants could be employed without anyone's asking questions. The air was tainted with the stench of the tire factory; added to that on weekdays was smoke from exhausts and streetside grills, which formed thick clouds like a heavy mantle above the houses. On Fridays and Saturdays it was dangerous to venture out after nightfall, when the barrio was crawling with drunks and drug addicts, ready to explode into homicidal combat. At night you could hear couples arguing, women screaming, children crying, men brawling, and sometimes gunshots and police sirens. During the day, the streets boiled with activity, while unemployed men with time on their hands loafed on the street corners, drinking, hassling women, shooting craps, and wishing away the hours with the fatalism of five centuries of Indian forebears. Shops displayed the same low-priced goods seen in any Mexican town, restaurants served typical dishes, the bars tequila and beer, and in the dance hall they played Latin music; during celebrations there was never a shortage of mariachis dressed in enormous sombreros and matador suits and singing of honor and despair. Gregory, who knew them all and never missed a fiesta, became a kind of mascot to the musicians; he would sing along with them, yelling the obligatory *ay, ay, ay* of Mexican *rancheras* like a pro, stirring the enthusiasm of the crowd that had never known a gringo with such talent. He called half the barrio by name and had such an angelic expression that he won the confidence of most who knew him. More comfortable in the labyrinth of alleys and passageways, empty lots and abandoned buildings than at home, he played with the Morales brothers and a half-dozen other boys his age, always avoiding confrontation with older gangs. Just as with young blacks, Asians, or poor whites in other parts of the city, for young Hispanics the barrio was more important than family; it was their inviolable territory. Each gang was identified by its language of signs, colors, and wall graffiti. From a distance the gangs all seemed the same, formed of ragged, belligerent boys unable to articulate a thought; seen more closely, they were distinctive, each with individual rites and intricate symbolic language. For Gregory, learning the codes was a prime necessity; he could distinguish members of the different gangs by the jacket or cap they wore or the hand signs they used to flash messages or to challenge a fight; he had only to see the color of a single slogan on the wall to know who had put it there and what it meant. Graffiti marked boundaries, and anyone who ventured into alien territory, whether through ignorance or daring, paid dearly; that is why every time he went out, he had to take long detours. The Martínez boys had the only gang in grade school; they were training to become members of Los Carniceros, who lived up to their name as "Butchers" and were the most feared in the barrio. They could be identified by the color purple and the letter *C;* their drink was tequila and grape juice—because of the color—and their sign a hand hooked in a C covering mouth and nose. In constant warfare with other groups and the police, they existed solely to provide a sense of identity to the youths, most of whom had dropped out of school, had no job, and lived in the street or in communal pads. The gang members had records—numerous arrests for robbery, dealing marijuana, drunkenness, assault, and car theft. A few were armed with homemade pistols fashioned from a piece of pipe, a wood grip, and a detonator, but more generally they carried knives, chains, razors, and clubs, which did not preclude serious injury: the ambulance carried away two or three after every street battle. The gangs were the greatest threat Gregory faced; he could never join one—that, too, was a matter of race—and to confront them would be an act of madness. He did not attempt to build a reputation for bravery, all he wanted was to survive; neither, however, did he want to be thought of as a coward, because his weakness would be exploited. It took only one or two beatings to demonstrate that lone heroes triumph only in the movies, that he must learn to negotiate with his wits, not attract attention, know his enemies in order to profit from their weaknesses, and avoid fights, because as that pragmatist Padre Larraguibel had told him, God helps the good guys when they outnumber the bad guys.

The Morales house became Gregory's true home, a place where he was always welcomed as a son. In that family confusion he was merely one child more, and Inmaculada herself used to wonder absently how she could have had a blond son. In the Morales tribe no one complained of loneliness or boredom, everything was shared, from existential anguish to the only bathroom; inconsequential matters were discussed at top pitch, but important problems were held in strict familial secrecy, in accordance with an age-old code of honor. The father's authority was never questioned: I wear the pants here, Pedro Morales roared whenever anyone trod too near his toes, but in fact Inmaculada was the true head of the family. No one approached the father directly, preferring to be processed through the maternal bureaucracy. Inmaculada never contradicted her husband before witnesses but always managed somehow to get her way. The first time their eldest son came to the house dressed like a zoot-suited *pachuco,* Pedro Morales thrashed him with a leather strap and threw him out of the house. The boy was fed up with working twice as much as any American for half the pay and was hanging out in pool halls and bars most of the day with his buddies, with no money in his pockets but what he won from bets or what his mother quietly slipped him. To avoid an argument with his wife, Pedro Morales had played blind as long as he could, but when his son appeared gussied up like a pimp and with a tear tattooed on one cheek, he had beat him to a pulp. That night, when everyone else was in bed, the murmur of Inmaculada's voice could be heard for hours, wearing down her husband's resistance. The next day Pedro went out to look for his son; when he found him standing on a corner throwing verbal bouquets to every woman who passed by, he took him by the collar and marched him to their garage; he ripped off his son's outlandish *pachuco* garb, gave him greasy overalls to put on, and for several years worked him from sunup to sunset, until he became the best mechanic in the entire area, set up in his own shop at his father's expense. On Pedro Morales's fiftieth birthday, his married son, now with three children and a house in the suburbs, had the tear removed from his cheek as a birthday present for his father; the scar was all that remained of his fling with rebellion. Inmaculada spent her life slaving for the men of her family. As a girl she had been trained to serve her father and brothers, and now she did the same for her husband and sons. She rose at dawn to cook a huge breakfast for Pedro, who opened his repair shop early in the morning, and she never served leftover tortillas at her table; that would have been an affront to her dignity. The rest of the day went by in a thousand unsung chores, including preparation of three complete meals, as she was convinced that her men had to be nourished with large amounts of constantly varied dishes. It never entered her mind to ask her sons, four young giants of men, to help her sweep the floors, shake out the bedclothes, or wash the rough work clothes, stiff with motor oil—garments she scrubbed by hand. She expected her two girls, on the other hand, to serve the males, because she considered it their duty. It was God's will—and our misfortune—that we were born women; our fate is hard work and suffering, she used to say in a resigned tone, without a hint of self-pity.

In those years Carmen Morales was already a balm for Gregory Reeves's hard knocks and a light in his moments of darkness, a role she would always play in his life. The girl scurried around busily, untiring and competent, and she had a strong practical sense that allowed her to escape rigid family traditions without confrontation with her father, who had his own very clear ideas about a woman's place—silent, and in the home—and who never thought twice about physically punishing an insurgent, including his two daughters. Carmen was his favorite, but his expectations for her were no different from those for the meek young girls from his village in Zacatecas. In contrast, Morales worked unstintingly to educate his four male children, on whom he pinned disproportionate hopes; he wanted to see them rise higher than their humble grandfathers and than himself. With inexhaustible tenacity, through preaching, punishment, and good example, he held his family together, saving his children from alcohol and delinquency, forcing them to finish high school, and guiding them into various trades. With the exception of Juan José, who died in Vietnam, each attained a measure of success. At the end of his days, Pedro Morales, surrounded by grandchildren who spoke no word of Spanish, congratulated himself on his descendants, proud of being the trunk of that family tree, although he would joke that none had made millions or become famous. Carmen very nearly achieved that, but her father never publicly acknowledged her worth; that would have been a surrender of his macho principles. He sent his two daughters to school because that was the law, and although it was not his intention to keep them in ignorance, neither did he expect them to take their studies seriously; instead, they were to learn domestic skills, help their mother, and guard their virginity until the day they were married—the only ambition for a decent girl.

"I don't intend to get married," Carmen whispered secretly to Gregory. "I want to work in a circus with trained animals and a high trapeze, where I can swing upside down and show the whole world my britches."

"My girls will be good mothers and wives, or go to the convent," Pedro Morales boasted every time someone came to him with the story of a girl who found herself pregnant before she left school.

"Oh, blessed Saint Anthony, find them good husbands!" Inmaculada Morales implored, hanging her statue of the saint upside down to oblige him to hear her modest pleas. It was obvious to her that neither of her girls had the calling to be a nun, and she did not want even to think of the tragedy of watching them turn out like the easy girls who played around before they were married, the ones who left a trail of condoms in the cemetery.

But all that came much later. During the years of primary school, when Carmen and Gregory had sealed their pact of undying friendship, those questions were still to be raised, and no one preached virtue to prevent them from playing together unsupervised. Everyone was so accustomed to seeing them together that later, as they became adolescents, the Moraleses trusted Gregory to look after Carmen more than they did their own sons. When Carmen asked permission to go to a party, they first ascertained that Gregory would go too, in which case the parents felt secure. From the day he first walked into their house, they had welcomed him without reservation, and through the following years, convinced against all logic and experience of the purity of Gregory and Carmen's sentiments, they turned a deaf ear to the inevitable gossiping of the neighbor women. Thirteen years later, when Gregory left that city forever, he was homesick for only one thing: the Morales household.

Gregory's shoeshine box contained black, brown, yellow, and oxblood polish, but it lacked neutral saddle soap for the gray and blue leathers that were also in vogue, and black dye to run around the edge of the soles. He always meant to put his earnings toward completing his supplies, but that determination faltered the minute a new movie came to town. Movies were his secret addiction; in the dark he was but one of a horde of noisy kids. He never missed a show in the barrio, where they ran Mexican films, and on Saturdays he went into the city with Juan José and Carmen to see the American serials. The episode seemed always to end with the protagonist bound hand and foot in a shed filled with dynamite and the villain lighting the fuse; at the climactic moment the screen would go black and a voice would invite the audience to come back in a week for the next installment. Sometimes Gregory was so miserable he wanted to die but postponed his suicide until the following week: how could he quit this world without knowing how the devil his hero had escaped the trap? And escape he always did; it was truly amazing how he could drag himself through the flames and emerge unscathed, with his ten-gallon hat in place and his clothes clean as new. The film transported Gregory to another dimension; for an hour or two he became El Zorro or the Lone Ranger and all his dreams were fulfilled. By magic, the hero recovered from contusions and wounds, freed himself from ropes and bonds, triumphed over his enemies by virtue of his superior abilities, and won the girl. To the soft strains of strings and woodwinds, they kissed in the foreground, silhouetted against the sun or the moon. Gregory could relax; the movies were not like his barrio; the only surprises were agreeable ones, and the bad guy was always bested by the hero and paid for his crimes with prison or his life. Sometimes he repented, and following the inevitable humiliation confessed the error of his ways and was led off to music that sounded a warning, usually trumpets and kettledrums. Life was beautiful, and America was truly "the land of the free and the home of the brave," a land where someone like Gregory could become President; all you had to do was stay pure of heart, love God and your mother, be forever faithful to one girl, respect the law, defend the weak, and scorn money—because heroes never expected to be compensated. Gregory's uncertainties vanished into the air of that formidable universe of black and white. He walked out of the theater reconciled with life, brimming with admirable intentions that lasted at least a couple of minutes, until the shock of being outside restored his sense of reality. Olga took it upon herself to inform him that the films were made in Hollywood, only a short distance from her house, and that it was all a monumental lie; only the songs and dances of the musical comedies were what they seemed, everything else was a trick of the camera; Gregory, however, did not let that revelation disturb him.

He worked his trade a long way from home in a district of offices, bars, and small businesses. He covered a five-block radius of action, walking back and forth, offering his modest services, eyes to the ground, observing shoes as worn and shapeless as those of his Latin neighbors. As in the barrio, no one wore new footwear except for a few gangsters and drug dealers, who sported patent-leather moccasins, boots with silver studs, and two-tone shoes that were hell to shine. He could guess people's faces by their way of walking and by their shoes: Hispanics wore red with a stacked heel, blacks and mulattoes preferred sharp-toed yellow, the Chinese had tiny feet, and whites had turned-up toes and run-down heels. The shine was the easy part; what was difficult was finding clients ready to pay a dime and give up five minutes for the sake of their shoes. "A good shine, a good impression!" Gregory shouted at the top of his lungs, but very few listened. With luck he would make fifty cents in an afternoon, the price of one marijuana cigarette. The few times he smoked grass he concluded it was not worth working so many hours only to blow it on crap that turned his stomach and left his head throbbing like a drum, but not to seem a fool, he pretended to be high. The Mexicans who had seen marijuana growing like a weed in fields of their homeland thought it really was like grass, but gringos smoked it as a sign of manhood. To imitate them, and to impress the blondes, the boys in the barrio smoked all they could get. Given his meager success with marijuana, Gregory's affectation was to dangle a cigarette from the corner of his mouth, movie-villain style. He was so good at it that he could talk and chew gum and never lose his smoke. When he wanted to act the macho before his

friends, he would pull out a homemade pipe and fill it with a mixture of his invention: tobacco from salvaged butts, a little sawdust,
and powdered aspirin, which according to popular belief got you
as high as any drug known. On Saturdays he worked all day, usually earning a little over a dollar; he handed almost all of it to his
mother, keeping only a dime for the weekly movie and sometimes
a nickel for the collection box for missionaries in China. If he
could save five dollars, the priest would give him a certificate of
adoption for a Chinese baby girl, but the real trick was to earn ten,
which would give him the right to a boy child. May God bless you,
the priest said every time Gregory brought his nickel for the collection box, and once God more than blessed him, He rewarded
him with a billfold containing fifteen dollars that He had put in
the cemetery for Gregory to find. The cemetery was the favorite
spot for couples to go after dark; there they hid among the tombs
to make love at their ease—although spied on by the children
from the barrio, who followed every gambol and gallop of
the tempestuous spectacle. Ay, I'm so afraid! I hear a lost soul, the
girls would whimper, mistaking the choked laughter of the
voyeurs for the moaning of spirits, but at the same time letting
their skirts be slipped higher and higher for the roll among the
tombstones and crosses. "Our cemetery is the best in the city,
much prettier than the one the millionaires and Hollywood
actresses have; theirs is nothing but trees and grass and looks more
like a golf course than holy ground. Did you ever see a cemetery
where the dead hadn't a single statue to keep them company?"
Inmaculada Morales would ask, even though in truth only the
wealthy could afford mausoleums and stone angels; immigrants
could barely pay for a headstone with a simple inscription. In
November, to celebrate the Day of the Dead, Mexicans visited the
relatives they had not been able to take back to their villages,
bringing offerings of music, paper flowers, and sweets. From early
morning the air was filled with *ranchera* songs, guitars, and toasts,
and by nighttime everyone was tipsy, including the souls in purgatory, who were drunk from the tequila liberally sprinkled into the
ground. The Reeves children went to the cemetery with Olga,

who bought them candy skulls and skeletons to eat at their father's grave. Nora always stayed home; she said she disliked pagan festivals, that they were merely a pretext for drunkenness and vice, but Gregory suspected that the real reason was her wish to avoid meeting Olga. Or perhaps she was denying that her husband was dead and buried, because for her Charles Reeves was somewhere on a different plane, busily administering *The Infinite Plan*. The billfold with the fifteen dollars was half hidden beneath some bushes. Gregory was looking for trap-door spiders; at his age, he was still more attracted by the fantastic insect-catching trap the spiders wove and their egg sacs, containing a hundred tiny young, than he was by the clumsy bucking and incomprehensible moans of the couples. He also collected the scattered white rubber balloons that after they were blown up looked like long sausages. It was as he bent down to a spider hole that he saw the billfold and felt a jolt in his heart and temples; he had never found anything valuable and now was unsure whether this was a gift from heaven or the devil's temptation. He glanced quickly around him to be sure he was alone, snatched up the wallet, and ran to hide behind a mausoleum to examine his treasure. He opened it with trembling hands and extracted three brand-new five-dollar bills, more money than he had ever seen at one time. He thought of Padre Larraguibel, who would tell him God had placed the money there to test him and to observe whether he kept the windfall or deposited it in the missionary box, thereby adopting two children at one stroke. No one in the entire school was rich enough to sponsor a Chinese infant of each sex; that would make him a celebrity. Even so, he decided that a bicycle was much more practical than two babies in far-off China, beneficiaries he would never meet in any case. He had had his eye on a bicycle for months; one of Olga's neighbors had offered to sell it to him for twenty dollars, an exorbitant price, but Gregory hoped that the man could not refuse the money in hand. The vehicle was primitive and in ruinous condition but still functional. The owner was an Indian debased by a lifetime of unspeakable practices; Gregory was afraid of him because once, under a variety of pretexts, he had taken him to a garage, where he tried to put his hands inside Gregory's pants—so he asked Olga to go with him.

"Don't show your money, don't open your mouth, just let me handle everything," she told him. She bargained so well that for twelve dollars and an amulet to ward off the evil eye, the bicycle was his. "You give the three dollars you have left to your mother, you hear me?" Olga commanded as they said goodbye.

Gregory set off pedaling down the middle of the street, too happy to see the soft-drink truck coming in the opposite direction. They met head-on. Miraculously, Gregory was not crushed; there was nothing left of the bicycle, however, but a few pieces of twisted steel and the spokes of the wheels. Cursing, the driver jumped from the truck, grabbed Gregory's shirt, jerked him to his feet, shook him like a feather duster, and sent him home with a dollar as consolation.

"Look, you damned brat!" the man rumbled, more frightened than his victim. "Be glad I don't have you arrested for not looking where the hell you're going!"

"I've never seen anyone as stupid as you! You should have got two dollars, at least!" Judy scolded when she learned what had happened.

"That's what you get for being disobedient. I've told you a thousand times not to go into that cemetery. Nothing good comes of ill-gotten gains," was Nora Reeves's analysis, as she sponged whiskey onto scraped knees and elbows.

"Blessed Jesus, be thankful you're alive," said Inmaculada Morales, hugging him.

Earning money became an obsession with Gregory. He was willing to do any job, even shelling the corn for making tortillas, a tedious process that skinned his knuckles and left him nauseated for hours from the smell. Then he decided he would take up stealing, although it never occurred to him to steal money—his was an adventure, a sport, not a way to earn a living. At night he would crawl through a hole in the school fence, climb onto the roof of the ice cream stand, pry up a sheet of zinc, and slip inside to steal ice cream bars; after he ate two or three, he would take one to give to

Carmen. Those nocturnal excursions provided a blend of excitement and guilt; the rigid norms of honesty learned from his mother pounded in his head. He felt perverse, not so much for defying her as because the owner of the stand was a nice old lady who favored him among all the boys and was always treating him to ice cream. One night she returned to look for something she had forgotten, opened the door, switched on the light before he could flee, and caught him with evidence of the crime in his hand. He stood frozen in his tracks, while she moaned, How could you do this to me? I've been good to you! Gregory burst into tears, begging her to forgive him and swearing to pay back everything he had stolen. What! This isn't the first time? Gregory had to confess that he owed her more than six dollars' worth of ice cream bars. From then on, he went near her only to pay back a little of his debt. Even though she forgave him, he never again felt comfortable in her presence. He was less fortunate in the army-navy surplus store, where he shoplifted war castoffs that were of absolutely no use to him: canteens, buttons, caps, even an enormous pair of boots he carried out of the store in his schoolbag, never suspecting that the owner had his eye on him. One afternoon he picked up a flashlight, stuffed it under his shirt, and was going out the door as a police car pulled to a stop. There was no way to escape; he was taken to jail and locked in a cell where he witnessed the ferocious beating of a dark-skinned youth. In terror, he waited his turn; he was well treated, however: the police merely booked him, reprimanded him, and told him to return everything he had hidden at home. They went to talk with Nora Reeves, despite Gregory's nearly hysterical pleas not to, that it would break her heart. She came to the jail wearing her blue dress with the lace collar, looking like a ghost from an old daguerreotype; she signed for his release, listened to the charges in silence, and, no less silent, departed, followed by her son. Be grateful you're white, Greg, said Inmaculada Morales when she learned of the incident. If you were the color of my sons, you'd have been in for it. Nora was so embarrassed that for several weeks she did not speak, and when finally she did, it was to tell Gregory to bathe and put on his only suit, the one that he had worn to his father's funeral and was now too small, because they had an important errand. She took him to the orphanage run by the nuns and begged the mother superior to accept him because she felt she could no longer cope with a son who was such a troublemaker. Standing behind his mother, staring at his shoes, muttering, I won't cry, I won't cry, while tears poured down his face, Gregory swore that if she left him there he would climb the church steeple and leap off headfirst. Such dramatic measures were fortunately unnecessary because the nuns refused to take him; they already had too many orphans to house, and he had a family. He lived in his own house, and his mother received welfare payments; he could not qualify as an orphan. Four days later Nora bundled up his things and took him by bus to the house of a farming couple who had agreed to adopt him. She bade her son goodbye with a sad kiss on his forehead, promised him she would write, and left without a backward glance. That night Gregory sat down to eat with his new family, not speaking, not looking up, worried that no one would feed Oliver, that he would never see Carmen Morales again, and that he had left his pocketknife in the shed.

"Our only son died eleven years ago," the farmer said. "We are God-fearing, hardworking people. There'll be no time here for play, only school, church, and helping me in the fields. But the food is good, and if you behave we'll treat you well."

"Tomorrow I'll make you a custard," his wife said. "You must be tired; I'm sure you want to go to bed. I'll show you your room; it belonged to our son; we haven't changed a thing since he left us."

For the first time, Gregory had his own room and a bed; up till then he had used a sleeping bag. It was a small, sparsely furnished room with an open window looking out toward the horizon across cultivated fields. On the walls were pictures of veteran baseball players and old warplanes, not at all like those he had seen in the newsreels. He inspected everything without daring to touch, thinking of his father, the boa, Olga's necklaces for invisibility, Inmaculada's kitchen, and Carmen Morales and the sticky-sweet taste of condensed milk, as a painful, icy knot grew in his chest. He sat on the edge of the bed with his modest belongings on his knees; he waited until the house was asleep, then stole out, carefully closing the door. The dogs barked, but he ignored them. He began walking in the direction of the city, returning along the same route he had followed in the bus, which was etched in his mind like a map. He walked all night and early the next morning, totally drained, appeared at his own front door. Oliver welcomed him, barking happily. Nora Reeves came to the door; with one hand she took the bundle of clothes from her son and with the other reached out to pat him, but stopped before the gesture was completed.

"Try to grow up soon," was all she said.

That afternoon Gregory thought of racing against the train.

I run up the hill with Oliver behind me, looking for the trees, chest heaving; the undergrowth is scratching my legs, I fall and cut my knee, shit, I yell, shit, and let the dog lick the blood; I can scarcely see where to put my feet, but I keep running toward my green refuge, the place where I always hide. I don't have to see the blazes on the trees to find my way; I've been here so many times I could come blindfolded; I know every eucalyptus, every patch of wild blackberries, every boulder. I lift a branch, and the entrance is before me, a narrow tunnel beneath a thorny bush—it must have been a fox's den—just the width of my body. If I drag myself forward on my elbows, snaking along carefully with my face between my arms and calculating the curve correctly, I can slip through without getting scratched; Oliver is waiting outside; he knows the drill. It has rained during the week, and the ground is soft; it's cold, but my whole body has been feverish for hours, ever since this morning in the broom closet, a fire that will never die, I know. Something pricks me from behind, and I yell out; it's only thorns caught in my sweater. That was how Martínez took me, from behind; I still feel the knife blade against my throat, but I don't think I'm bleeding anymore. If you move I'll kill you, you fucking sonofabitch gringo, and I had no way to defend myself, all I could do was cry and curse while he was doing it to me. Now run tell Miss June and I'll cut your sister's face here on the spot, and you already know what I'll do to you, he said when he was through, while he was fastening his pants. He walked away laughing. If anyone finds out, I'm fucked; they'll call me a pansy for the rest of my life. No one must ever find out! But what if Martínez tells? I'd like to kill him! My hands, my clothes, my face, are covered with mud; my mother will be furious; I'd better think up some excuse: I got hit by a car, or the gang worked me over again, but then I remember I don't have to make up any lie because I'm going to die, and when they find my body the dirt won't matter. I'll wait like I am. She'll be grief-stricken, she won't think about the bad things I've done, only my good side, that I wash the dishes and give her almost everything I make shining shoes, and at last she'll realize that I've been a good son and she'll be sorry she wasn't more loving to me, sorry she wanted to give me away to the nuns and the farmers and that she never cooked eggs for my breakfast even once, it's not even hard, Doña Inmaculada does it with her eyes closed, even a retard can fry a couple of eggs. She'll be sorry, but it will be too late because I'll be dead. They'll have an assembly at school and say nice things about me the way they did for Zarate when he drowned in the ocean; they'll say I was their best classmate and that I had a great future, and all the students will have to line up and walk past my coffin to kiss me on the forehead. The first graders will be crying, and I'll bet the girls will faint: women can't stand to see blood; they'll all squeal except for Carmen, who will put her arms around my corpse and never even flinch. I hope Miss June doesn't get the idea to read the letter I wrote her at the funeral, jeez, why did I do that? I can't ever look her in the face again; she's so pretty, as pretty as a fairy princess or a movie actress. If she only knew what I'm thinking in class when she's standing up there at the blackboard going over the arithmetic problems and I'm sitting at my desk staring at her like a moron, with my head in the clouds— who can think about numbers when she's around! Like, for instance, I dream that she tells me, I'll help you with your home- work, Greg, your grades are a disaster, so I stay after class and all the others are gone and we're alone in the building, and without me saying a word she goes wild and lies down on the floor, and I peepee between her legs. Never, not in all the days of my life, will I confess to the Padre the dirty things I think up; I'm a pervert, a pig. And I had to go and write that farewell letter to Miss June! What a screwup. Well, at least I won't have to suffer the shame of seeing her again; I'll be dead and gone by the time she reads it. And Carmen, poor Carmen ... The only reason I feel sad about dying is that I won't ever see her again. If she knew what Martínez did to me she would come here and die with me, but I can't tell anyone, especially her.

This is the worst thing that ever happened in my life, it's the very worst thing that rat Martínez ever did to me, worse than the First Communion when he made me bite off a piece of bread before I took communion, so when I swallowed the host I'd be struck by lightning and go straight to hell. But nothing happened; I didn't feel anything. I guess it was because it wasn't my sin, it was his, and he's the one who'll boil in Satan's caldrons, not me, for leading me to sin—which is a greater offense than the sin itself, that's what Padre Larraguibel explained to us when he told us about Adam and Eve. That time I had to write five hundred times *I must not blaspheme,* because I said that God committed the sin when He put the apple in the Garden of Eden knowing that Adam would eat it one day, anyway, and if that wasn't leading someone to sin, what was? Oh, this is worse than when Martínez stripped me in the gym and hid my clothes; if the cleaning lady hadn't come and helped me, I would have had to spend the night in the shower and the next day the whole school would have seen me stark naked. It's worse than when he shouted to everyone in the schoolyard that he had spied me in the bathroom playing doctor with Ernestina Pereda. I hate him! I hate him from the bottom of my heart! I wish he would die, not just get sick but be killed— but not before someone cuts off his dick. I want that lousy Martínez to pay. I hate him, I hate him!

I'm inside my den now, I whistle to Oliver and listen to him crawling through the tunnel. I put my arms around him, and he lies very still, panting, with his tongue hanging out; he looks at me with his honey-colored eyes, he understands, he's the only one who knows all my secrets. Oliver is a pretty ugly dog; Judy despises him; he's a real mutt and has a long fat tail like a baseball bat. He's bad besides; he eats clothes and rolls in dog shit and then jumps on the beds; he loves fights and sometimes comes home all chewed up, but he's warm and when he hasn't been rolling in anything he smells great. I bury my nose in his neck; his outside hair is short and stiff, but next to his skin it's soft as cotton, and I like to sniff him there—nothing smells better than dog. The sun's gone down, and shadows are everywhere; it's cold, one of those rare winter afternoons, and in spite of the fact that I'm afire, my hands and ears are freezing cold—it feels clean. I've decided not to slit my throat with my pocketknife as I planned to; I'll just die of the cold: I'll slowly freeze through the night, and tomorrow morning I'll be stiff as a board, a slow death but more peaceful than being hit by a train. That was my first idea, but every time I run in front of the train I'm too big a coward and at the last second jump and save myself by a hair. I don't know how many times I tried it, but I've decided not to die that way, it must hurt a lot, and besides, the idea of all the guts makes me sick; I don't want to be scraped up with a shovel or have some smartass keep my fingers for souvenirs. I'm going to push Oliver away, because he keeps me warm and I'll never freeze this way. I'll scratch this hollow in the dirt to get comfortable and turn over on my back and lie perfectly still— oh, that pain there . . . that damn, miserable Martínez *queer*! My head is filled with thoughts and visions and words, but then after a very long time I stop crying and begin to breathe normally and then smell the soft, fresh earth gathering me into her arms the way Doña Inmaculada hugs me; I sink, I let go and think about the planet, round, floating free of gravity in the black abyss of the cosmos, spinning and spinning, and I think of the stars in the Milky Way and how it will be at the end of the world, when everything explodes and particles spray out like fireworks on the Fourth of July, and I feel like I'm a part of the earth, made of the same stuff, and when I die I will disintegrate, crumble like a cake, and be part of the soil, and trees will grow from my body. I start thinking how the world doesn't turn around me, how I'm not anything special—I must be about as important as a hunk of clay—and maybe I don't have a soul of my own; suddenly I wonder if there isn't just one big soul for all living creatures, including Oliver, and no heaven or hell or purgatory, maybe they're just something cooked up by the Padre, who's so old his mind's gone soft, and my father's Logi and Masters don't exist either, and the only one who's anywhere close to the truth is my mother with her Bahai religion, although she gets all wound up with shit that may be fine for Persia but doesn't make much sense here. I like the idea of being a particle, of being a grain of cosmic sand. Miss June says that comets' tails are formed of stellar dust, thousands of tiny little rocks that reflect the light. I'm feeling really calm now, I've forgotten about Martínez, about being afraid, about the pain and the broom closet, I am at peace, I rise up and am flying with my eyes wide open toward the starry void. I'm flying . . . flying with Oliver. . . .

From the time she was a little girl, Carmen Morales had the manual skills that characterized her for the rest of her life; in her hands any object was transformed from its original form. She made necklaces from soup beans, soldiers from toilet paper rolls, toys from spools and matchboxes. One day, playing with three apples, she discovered that she had no trouble at all keeping them in the air at the same time; soon she was juggling five eggs, and from that moved naturally to more exotic objects.

"Shining shoes is a lot of sweat and not much cash, Greg. Learn some trick, and we'll work together," Carmen suggested to her friend. "I need a partner."

Dozens of eggs later, Gregory's definitive clumsiness was established. He had no interesting talent to offer other than wiggling his ears and eating live flies, although he did have a good ear for the harmonica. Oliver was more gifted; they taught him to walk on his hind legs with a hat clamped in his jaws and how to select small slips of paper from a box. At first he swallowed them, but he eventually learned to deliver them delicately to the client. Carmen and Gregory assiduously perfected a routine for their show and to escape the scrutiny of friends and neighbors planned to perform as far from home as possible, since they knew that if Pedro or Inmaculada Morales knew what they were doing, nothing could save them; they had already earned one spanking for their idea of posing as beggars in their own barrio. Carmen made a skirt from brightly colored scarves and a bonnet trimmed with chicken feathers, and asked to borrow Olga's yellow boots. Gregory sneaked out the top hat and bow tie his father had worn while preaching, items Nora had preserved as relics. They asked Olga to help them in drafting the slips with fortunes, telling her it was a game for the end-of-school party; she pierced them with one of her looks but without further questions sat down and wrote out a handful of prophecies in the style of Chinese fortune cookies. They rounded out their supplies with eggs, candles, and five kitchen knives, which they hid in a sack because they could not leave their houses carrying such things without raising suspicion. They washed Oliver down with a hose and tied a ribbon around his neck, hoping to make him look a little less like a cur. They chose a street corner far from the barrio, donned their minstrel outfits, and tried out their act. A small crowd soon gathered around the two children and the dog. Carmen, with her petite figure, her eye-catching clothes, and her extraordinary skill in tossing burning candles and sharp knives in the air, was an instant attraction; Gregory devoted himself to playing the harmonica. In pauses between the juggling, he put aside his mouth organ and invited the spectators to buy a fortune. For a small sum, the dog would select a folded slip and carry it to the client—slightly damp with slobber, it is true, but perfectly legible. In an hour or two the children earned as much as a laborer received for a full day's work in any of the area factories. As it began to grow dark, they removed their costumes, packed up their equipment, divided their earnings, and returned home, after swearing that torture could not make them reveal what they had done. Carmen buried her money in a box in her patio, and Gregory doled his out at home, to avoid prying questions, keeping a small share to go to the movies.

"If we earned that much here, imagine what we could do in Pershing Square. We'd be millionaires! Hundreds of people go there to listen to the hotheads, and there are all those rich people going in and out of hotels," Carmen proposed.

Such a bold move would never have entered Gregory's mind. He believed there was an invisible frontier that people of his status never crossed; the world was different on the other side: men strode along purposefully with work to do and urgent errands, gloved women strolled at a more leisurely pace, the stores were luxurious and the automobiles shiny. He had been there once or twice with his mother, when she had legal matters to attend to, but he would never in the world have thought of going there alone. In one instant, Carmen revealed the possibilities of the market: for three years he had been shining shoes for a dime among the poorest of the poor, without a glimmer of how only a few blocks away he could find customers more easily and charge triple the amount. The idea intimidated him, however, and he immediately rejected it.

"You're crazy."

"Why are you so chicken, Gregory? I bet you don't even know the hotel."

"The hotel? You've been in the hotel?"

"Of course. It's like a palace: it has paintings on the ceilings and the doors; there are pom-poms on the curtains, and I can't even describe the lamps: they look like ships strung with lights. Your feet sink into the rugs like sand at the beach, and everyone looks elegant—and they serve tea and cakes."

"You had tea in the hotel?"

"Well, not exactly, but I've seen the trays. You have to walk in without looking at anyone, as if your mama was waiting for you at a table, you understand?"

"And what if they catch you?"

"The first rule is, you never admit anything. If someone says

THE INFINITE PLAN · 89

something to you, you act like a rich kid, you turn up your nose and say something rude. I'll take you one day. At any rate, that's the best place to work."

"We can't take Oliver on the streetcar," Gregory argued weakly.

"We'll walk," she replied.

From then on they went to Pershing Square every time Carmen Morales could escape her mother's vigilant eye. They attracted more people than the soapbox speakers expounding with futile passion on subjects no one cared to hear about. Without the juggling their act was too flat, so if Carmen was unable to go, Gregory resumed his shoeshine routine—although now he worked the streets of the business district. The two children were united by mutual want and their shared secret, in addition to many other complicities.

At sixteen, Gregory was attending high school with Juan José Morales. Carmen was one year behind them, and Martínez had dropped out of school and joined the Carniceros gang. Reeves tried never to go anywhere near him and as long as he could avoid him felt safe. By that time the rebelliousness that formerly kept him on the move had diminished, but he was tortured by other, silent agonies. In high school most of the students were white; he no longer felt people were pointing a finger at him or that he had to run home the minute the bell rang in order to elude his enemies. Mandatory education was not always a fact among the poor, and even less among Latins, who often had to take a job as soon as they were out of grade school. Gregory's father had implanted in him an ambition to obtain an education, a desire that he himself had never satisfied because by the time he was thirteen he was traveling across Australia shearing sheep. Gregory's mother, too, encouraged him to learn a profession, so he would not have to break his back doing hard labor: Figure it out, son—a third of your life is spent sleeping, a third in daily routines, and the most interesting third will be spent working; that's why it's best to do something you like. The one time Gregory had mentioned leaving school to look for a job, Olga read his fortune in the tarot cards and he turned up the card for Law.

"Not a chance. You'll be a thief or a policeman, and in either case, your studies will stand you in good stead," she pronounced.

"I don't want to be either one of those things."

"This card says very clearly that you'll have something to do with the law."

"Doesn't it say I'll be rich?"

"Sometimes rich and sometimes poor."

"But I'll get to be someone important, won't I?"

"You don't *get to* anywhere in life, Gregory! You just live it."

Carmen Morales taught Gregory to dance to North American rhythms, and they became so expert that people would form a circle around them and applaud their exhibitions of jitterbug and rock 'n' roll. Gregory would fling Carmen above his head in a kind of headstand and before she tumbled to the floor toss her over his shoulder in a breathtaking maneuver, sweep her back between his legs, just grazing the floor, and pull her to her feet safe and sound—all without losing the beat or her teeth. Gregory saved for months to buy a black leather jacket and tried to train a curl to flip over his forehead, but as no amount of hair ointment could conquer the limp bangs that resulted, he opted for short hair combed straight back, more comfortable but less suitable for the rebel image that made girls tremble with apprehension and pleasure. Carmen herself was very different from the teenage movie star image—blonde, virtuous, and slightly silly—that boys sighed over and plump brunette Mexican girls tried vainly to imitate by peroxiding their hair. Carmen was pure dynamite. On weekends the two friends dressed in the latest version of what was "in"—he in his black leather jacket, even if it was hellishly hot, she in tight pants she hid in her purse and changed into in the ladies' room, because if her father had seen her he would have ripped them off her—and went off to dance halls where they were known and not charged an entrance fee because they were the main attraction for the night. They danced without pause, not stopping even to drink a Coke, because they had no money to pay for it. Carmen had developed into an intrepid young girl with a black mane of hair and an attractive face with thick eyebrows and lips; she had an easy laugh and impressive curves, with breasts too large for her height and age, protuberances she detested as grotesque but that Gregory swore grew larger by the day. When they danced, he swung her about only to enjoy the sight of those calendar girl's breasts defying the laws of gravity and decency, but when he saw anyone who was equally admiring, he felt a blind rage. He was not consciously attracted to his friend; the mere idea would have horrified him as a sin of incest. Carmen was as much his sister as Judy, yet at times all his good intentions faltered before the treachery of his hormones, which were at constant fever pitch. Padre Larraguibel tried to fill his young charges' heads with apocalyptic predictions about the consequences of sinful thoughts about women and about touching themselves. He threatened lightning bolts as punishment for lechery, vowed that hair would grow in the palms of their hands, that they would break out with running sores, that gangrene would rot their penises, and that finally the sinner would die after atrocious suffering, plus, should he die without confession, he would plummet headfirst into hell. Gregory doubted the divine lightning bolt and the hair on the palms of his hands, but he was sure the other inflictions were true because he had seen his father, he remembered how he had been covered with pustules and that he died for abusing himself. Gregory never dreamed of finding solace with any of the girls in his school or the barrio—they seemed off limits—nor did he want to visit the prostitutes, who seemed almost as terrifying as Martínez. He was desperate for love, inflamed by a brutal and incomprehensible ardor, frightened by the drumming of his heart, by the sticky honey in his sleeping bag, by turbulent dreams, and by the surprises dealt him by his body; his bones lengthened, he developed muscles, hair grew on new parts of his body, and his blood boiled with inextinguishable fire. At the most insignificant stimulus he exploded into a sudden gratification that left him dismayed and half faint. A woman brushing by him in the street, the glimpse of a shapely leg, a scene in the movies, a phrase in a book, even the vibration of the streetcar—everything excited him. In addition to studying, he had to work; even exhaustion, however, did not neutralize his unfathomable desire to sink into the swamp, to lose himself in sin, to suffer that wild delight, that always-too-brief death, yet once more. Sports and dancing helped burn his energy, but only a more drastic remedy could cool his raging instincts. Just as in his childhood he had fallen madly in love with Miss June, in adolescence he suffered sudden passionate crushes on inaccessible girls, usually older than he, whom he never approached but resigned himself to adoring from afar. A year later, after a sudden spurt, he would reach his full height and weight, but at sixteen he was still a slim adolescent with too large knees and ears, slightly pathetic, although there were indications of the good temperament to come. "If you can escape being a thief or a policeman, you'll be a movie star, and women will fall all over you," Olga promised, trying to console him when she saw him suffering inside the hair shirt of his own skin.

It was Olga, finally, who rescued him from the incandescent torment of chastity. Ever since Martínez had cornered him in the grade school broom closet, Gregory had been besieged by unconfessable doubts concerning his virility. He had not explored Ernestina Pereda again—or any other girl—under the guise of playing doctor, and his knowledge about that mysterious side of existence was vague and inconsistent. The crumbs of information garnered on the sly in the library merely confused him further, because they contradicted the experience of the street, the jokes the Morales brothers and other friends told, the preachments of the Padre, the revelations of the movies, and the alarms of his fantasies. He wrapped himself in solitude, denying with stubborn determination the perturbation of his heart and the restlessness of his body, attempting to imitate the chaste knights of the Round Table or the heroes of the Far West, but at any moment he could be betrayed by an upsurge of nature. That dull pain and nameless confusion weighed on him for an eternity, until it was more than he could live with, and had Olga not come to his aid he would

have been half mad. Olga had seen him born, she had been present at every important moment of his childhood, she knew him
like a son; nothing about him escaped her eye, and what she could
not deduce through simple common sense she divined through
her gifts as a seer, which at best consisted of knowledge of
another's heart, an observant eye, and boldness in improvising
counsel and visions of the future. She had no need to call on her
gift of clairvoyance to recognize Gregory's helpless state. Olga was
in the fourth decade of her life; the curves of her youth had turned
to fat, and the reversals of her gypsy vocation had aged her skin,
but she had not lost her grace and style, the lush foliage of her red
hair, the swish of her skirts, or her boisterous laugh. She lived in
the same house but no longer in one room; she had bought the
property and made it into her private temple. In one room she dispensed medicines, magnetized water, and all manner of herbs; in
another, therapeutic massages and abortions; and in the large living room she held spiritualist, magic, and divination sessions. She
always received Gregory in the room above the garage. One day
he seemed especially pale, and she was moved by the primitive
compassion that recently had been her essential feeling for him.

"Who are you in love with now?" she said, laughing.

"I've got to get out of this fucking place," he muttered, his
head in his hands, defeated by the enemy below his waist.

"Where do you plan to go?"

"Anywhere, straight to hell, I don't care. Nothing happens
here, I can't breathe, I'm suffocating."

"It isn't the barrio; it's you. You're drowning inside your own
hide."

The soothsayer took a bottle of whiskey from the cupboard,
splashed a stout drink into one glass and another for herself,
waited for Gregory to drink it, then poured another. He was not
accustomed to strong liquor, and it went to his head; the windows
were closed, and the aroma of incense, medicinal herbs, and
patchouli was heavy in the air. With a shudder, he caught Olga's
scent. In a flash of loving inspiration, the heavyset woman walked
up behind him and wrapped her arms around him; her drooping

breasts pressed against his back, her beringed fingers blindly unbuttoned his shirt while he turned to stone, paralyzed by surprise and fear, but then she began to nuzzle his neck, trace his ear with her tongue, whisper words in Russian, explore his body with her expert hands, touch him there where no one had touched him, ever, until with a sob, plunging down a steep precipice, shaken with terror and anticipated joy, and without knowing what he was doing, or why, he turned to her, desperate, tearing at her clothes in his urgency, throwing himself on her like an animal in rut, rolling with her across the floor, kicking his pants down, groping his way into her skirts, penetrating her in a burst of desolation, and immediately collapsing with a scream, as his being gushed from him as if an artery had exploded in his groin. Olga allowed him to rest a moment on her bosom, scratching his back as she had so often when he was a boy, but as soon as she calculated that he was feeling remorse, she got up and went to close the curtains. Calmly, she removed her torn blouse and wrinkled skirt.

"Now I am going to teach you what we women like," she said with a new smile. "The first thing, my son, is never to hurry. . . ."

"I have to know something, Olga; swear that you'll tell me the truth."

"What is it you want to know?"

"My father and you . . . I mean, the two of you. . . . "

"That's none of your business; it has nothing to do with you."

"I have to know . . . you were lovers, weren't you?"

"No, Gregory. I will say this only once: no, we were not lovers. Don't bring up the subject again, because if you do, that will be the last time I ever see you. Is that clear?"

Gregory wanted so badly to believe her that he asked no more questions.

Beginning with that afternoon, the world changed color for Gregory. He visited Olga almost every day and like an inspired student learned what she had to reveal; he pried into her every hiding place, boldly whispered every known obscenity to her, and discovered, amazed, that he was not totally alone in the universe and that he wanted to live. As his soul soaked everything in like a

sponge, his body developed and within a few weeks he grew out
of boyhood and his expression became that of a contented man.
When Olga realized that he was falling in love from pure gratitude, she berated him furiously and forced him to look at her
naked body and make a meticulous inventory of her pounds, her
gray hair, and her wrinkles, of the fatigue that came from being
cudgeled so many years by destiny, and then she solemnly threatened to send him away if he persisted in such twisted ideas. She
described in very clear terms the limits of their relationship and
added that he should be beating his breast because he had a brutal
fate in store: he would not find another woman who would provide him with free sex at his whim, iron his shirts, put money in
his pockets, and ask nothing in return; furthermore, he was still a
runny-nosed kid, and by the time he grew up she would be an old
woman, and it was up to him to concentrate on his studies and see
whether he could climb out of the hole he'd been born in and
make something of himself; after all, he lived in the land of opportunity, and if he failed to take advantage of that good fortune, he
was a hopeless idiot.

Gregory's grades improved, he made new friends, he began
working on the school newspaper and soon found himself writing
inflammatory articles and chairing student meetings for various
causes—some bureaucratic, like the schedules for the sports program, others having to do with principle, such as discrimination
against blacks and Latins. You got that from your father, Nora
sighed, worried, because she did not want to see him become a
preacher. Appeased by Olga, he could enjoy reading and spent
every spare minute in the public library, where he struck up a
friendship with Cyrus, the elderly bibliophile in charge of the elevator. Cyrus manned the controls with one hand and held a book
in the other, so absorbed that the elevator operated itself, like a
machine on the loose. He looked up only when Gregory appeared;
then for a few seconds his anemic, prophet's face lighted up and a
faint smile flickered across the rictus of his lips, but he would
immediately regain control and greet Gregory with a growl—to

make it very clear that the only bond between them was a certain intellectual affinity. The boy usually showed up about midafternoon, after school, and stayed only half an hour, because he had to work. The old man waited for him from early morning, and as the hour approached caught himself glancing at his watch, always on guard to rein in any untoward emotion, but if Gregory failed to come it was as if the sun had not risen. They were soon good friends. Reeves liked to spend his Saturdays with the old man; he visited him in his shabby room in the boardinghouse where he lived, and at other times they went to the movies or out for a walk, although as it started to get dark Gregory always left to take Carmen dancing. After they knew each other better, Cyrus made an appointment to meet Gregory in the park, using the pretext of discussing philosophy and sharing a picnic lunch. He waited for Gregory, holding a basket from which French bread and the neck of a wine bottle protruded, and when he arrived led him to an isolated spot where no one could hear and whispered that he wanted to reveal a life-and-death secret. After making Gregory swear he would never betray him, he solemnly confessed that he was a member of the Communist Party. The boy did not entirely understand the significance of such a confidence, even though the country was at the height of a witch hunt unleashed against liberalism, but he imagined Cyrus's proclivity as something as contagious and disreputable as a venereal disease. He made inquiries that only further muddied the waters. His mother gave him a vague response about Russia and the massacre of a royal family in a Winter Palace, all so remote that it was impossible to relate it to his time and place. When he mentioned communism to the Moraleses, Inmaculada crossed herself in fright; Pedro forbade him to utter obscenities in his house and warned him of the danger of getting involved in affairs that were none of his business. Politics is a vice; honest, hardworking people have no need for it, declared Padre Larraguibel, whose inclination toward the horrific had increased with the years. He accused Communists of being the Antichrist incarnate and the natural enemies of the United States. He assured Gregory that to speak to one of them constituted an automatic betrayal of a Christian culture and nation, since everything that was said was immediately transmitted to Moscow for diabolical ends. Be careful, you'll find yourself in trouble with the law and end up in the gas chamber—which you'd deserve for being a damn fool. The Reds are atheists, Bolsheviks: plain bad people who have no business in this country; let them go back to Russia if that's what they want, he concluded, with a thump of his fist that made his coffee-and-brandy leap from the table. Gregory realized that Cyrus had offered him the ultimate proof of friendship in telling his secret, and in return he vowed not to disappoint his friend as he followed the intellectual path he had recently undertaken. Cyrus stirred Gregory's passion for certain authors and, every time he posed a question, sent him to look up the information for himself—which was how he learned to use encyclopedias, dictionaries, and other library resources. If everything else fails, he counseled, go through old newspapers. A vast horizon opened before Gregory's eyes; for the first time it seemed possible that he might leave the barrio, that he was not condemned to stay buried there for the rest of his days. The world was enormous, his curiosity was awakened, along with the desire to live adventures that previously he had seen only in the movies. When he was free from school and work, he spent hours with his teacher, riding up and down the elevator until he was dizzy and had to stagger outside for a breath of fresh air.

He had dinner every night with the Moraleses, and in passing helped Carmen, who was a terrible student, with her homework; then he went to visit Olga, arriving home after his mother and Judy were asleep. Occasionally on the weekend he would seek Nora's company to talk about what he was reading, but their relationship cooled day by day, and they were never again to enjoy conversations like those from their bohemian life, times when she had told him the plots of operas and deciphered the mysteries of the firmament in the starry skies. He had very little in common with his sister and must have been very distracted not to perceive her unyielding hostility. Their cottage had begun to deteriorate— the wood creaked, and there were leaks in the roof—but the land had risen in value as the city advanced in that direction. Pedro Morales suggested they sell the property and move into a small apartment where their expenses would be lower and maintenance more simple, but Nora feared that if they moved she would lose contact with the ghost of her husband.

"The dead need a permanent hearth; they can't be moving from one place to another. And houses need a death and a birth. One day my grandchildren will be born here," she said.

Besides Olga, with whom he shared the wondrous intimacy of uninhibited lovers, Carmen Morales was the person Gregory was closest to. Once Olga had mollified his instincts, he could contemplate his friend's improbable bosom without discomfort. He wished for her a less sordid fate than that of women from the barrio, who were mistreated by their husbands, worn down by their children, and inconsolably poor; he felt that with a little help Carmen could finish school and learn some skill. He tried to initiate her into reading, but the library bored her; she detested school-work and demonstrated no interest whatever in newspapers.

"If I read more than half a page my head hurts. Why don't you read it and tell me about it," she would apologize when he cornered her between a book and a wall.

"It's because she has those large breasts. The more bosom, the less brain, that's a law of nature; that's why the poor miserable females are the way they are," Cyrus explained to Gregory.

"That old poop is a moron!" Carmen erupted when she learned what he had said, and started wearing falsies in her bra out of pure defiance, with such spectacular results that everyone in the neighborhood had some comment on how extremely well developed the younger Morales girl was.

Her breasts were not all that attracted comment. Her busy-as-a-mouse days were far behind; she had become a fiery girl surrounded by a whirlwind of suitors who dared not cross the delicate line of honor, since on the other side, resolute and suspicious, stood Pedro Morales and his four strapping sons. In many ways, Carmen was no different from other girls her age; she loved parties, she wrote her romantic musings and copied verses in her diary, she fell in love with movie stars and batted her eyes at any boy within flirting distance—that is, if she had eluded her family's vigilance, or Gregory's, for he had assumed the role of guardian knight. Nevertheless, unlike other girls, she had a seething imagination that later would save her from a banal existence.

One Thursday as they left school, Gregory and Carmen found themselves facing Martínez and three of his gang. The flow of youngsters leaving the building slowed for an instant and then branched off to avoid them, not wanting to provoke trouble. Martínez had seen Carmen the previous Saturday at a dance and was waiting for her with the arrogance of one who knows he is the stronger. She stopped short, like the students around her who could sense the menace in the air but were incapable of reacting. Martínez had grown very large for his age; he was an insolent giant with a Latin lover's mustache and assorted tattoos; he affected extreme *pachuco* style: pomaded hair combed into two high pompadours, pleated pants, shoes with metal tips, a leather jacket, a purple shirt.

"Come 'ere, baby, give us a kiss." He stepped forward and gripped Carmen's chin.

She slapped his hand away, and his eyes narrowed to two slits. Gregory seized Carmen by the arm and tried to walk away from that unheroic ambush, but the gang blocked their way. There was no one to turn to: the street had emptied, leaving a terrible void; the remaining students had backed away to a prudent distance, forming a large semicircle around Carmen, Greg, and the aggressors.

"Hey, I know you, you little shitass," Martínez jeered, giving Gregory a slight push, then added for the benefit of his cronies, "This is the fuckin' gringo pansy I told you about."

Still holding Carmen's arm, Gregory tried once more to make an escape, but Martínez stepped forward menacingly, and Gregory realized that the moment he had feared had come, that there was no way to avoid the threat that had stalked him for years. He breathed deeply, trying to control his terror, forcing himself to think, realizing he was on his own and that none of his schoolmates would come to his defense. There were four gang members, and it was a sure bet they carried knives or brass knuckles. Hatred washed over him like a hot tide, rising from the pit of his belly to his throat; memories flooded back, and for a moment his mind went blank and he sank deep into a murky quagmire. Carmen's voice pulled him back to the street.

"Keep your hands off me, you bastard," and she fended off Martínez's aggression as the sidekicks snickered.

Gregory pushed Carmen to one side and confronted his enemy, their faces inches apart, fists balled, eyes filled with animosity, chests heaving.

"Which do you want, you gringo homo? You want me to ream your ass again, or would you rather mix it up with me?" Martínez murmured, his voice soft and slow, as if he were speaking of love.

"Motherfucker! Four of you punks against one unarmed person—you call that a fight?" Gregory spat out.

"Say what! OK, then, this will be between the two of us," and Martínez signaled the other three to back off.

"I'm not talking about some stupid fistfight. What I want is a duel to the death," Gregory growled, teeth clenched.

"What the fuck is that?"

"Just what you heard, you stinking greaser," and Gregory raised his voice so everyone around them could hear. "In three days, behind the tire factory, at seven o'clock at night."

Martínez glanced uneasily around him, not fully comprehending what this was about, and the other gang members shrugged their shoulders, still mockingly, as the circle of onlookers closed in a little: no one wanted to miss a word of what was happening.

"Knives, clubs, chains, or pistols?" Martínez asked, unbelieving.

"The train," Gregory replied.

"The fuckin' train *what*?"

"We're going to find out who has the balls," and Gregory took Carmen's hand and walked off down the street, turning his back with the feigned contempt of the bullfighter for the beast he has yet to defeat, walking rapidly so no one could hear the pounding of his heart.

It had been several years since I raced the train, first with the intention of killing myself and later just for the sheer joy of living. It passed four times a day, huffing like a stampeding dragon, convulsing the wind and silence. I always waited at the same spot, a flat, empty lot where for a while junk and garbage would collect but then be cleaned up so kids could play ball. First I would hear the distant whistle and the sound of the engine, and then I would see the train, an awesome, enormous snake of iron and thunder. My challenge was to judge the exact moment I could dart across the track ahead of the locomotive: to wait till the very last instant, until it was almost upon me, then run like crazy and leap to the other side. My life hung on the slightest miscalculation—hesitating too long, tripping over a rail, the spring in my legs, keeping a cool head. I could tell the different trains from the sound of their engines; I knew the first train of the morning was the slowest and the seven-fifteen the fastest. Now I felt confident, but as I had not actually taunted the bull for some time, I practiced with each train that passed during the next few days. Carmen and Juan José went with me to check the results. The first time they watched, Carmen dropped the stopwatch and screamed hysterically; fortunately, I didn't hear her until the locomotive had passed, because I would probably have wavered and not be here to tell the story. We discovered the best site for the contest, a place where the rails were clearly visible; we removed the loose stones and marked the distance with a line in the dirt, moving it closer to actual impact each time, until we could not cut it any shorter because the last train grazed my back. Evenings were the most dangerous; at that time of day, when it was nearly dark, the light on the locomotive was blinding. I suppose that Martínez was practicing in a different place, so no one could see him and his excessive pride would remain undamaged. He could not evidence the slightest concern about the challenge before any Carnicero; he must show total indifference to danger, be the absolute macho. I was counting on that to give me the edge, because during my years in the jungle of the barrio I had learned to accept fear with humility, a burning in the stomach that sometimes tormented me for days on end.

By the appointed Sunday, the word had spread throughout the school, and by six-thirty there was a string of cars, motorcycles, and bicycles parked at the empty lot and about fifty of my schoolmates sitting on the ground near the track, waiting for the show to begin. The tire factory was closed, but the sickening smell of hot raw latex lingered on the air. There was a party atmosphere; some people had brought snacks, some were downing whiskey or gin disguised in soft-drink bottles, some had even brought cameras. Carmen avoided the general hubbub; she stood apart from the rest, praying. She had begged me not to do it: It's better to have people think you're a coward than to lose your life in the blink of an eye; after all, Martínez didn't do anything to me, this duel of yours is crazy, it's a sin, God will punish us all. I explained that this had nothing to do with what happened at school, that she wasn't the cause but only the pretext—this confrontation sprang from old debts too numerous to tell, something about manhood. She hung a small rectangle of embroidered cloth around my neck:

"It's the scapulary of the Virgin of Guadalupe my mother wore when she came here from Zacatecas. It can work miracles. . . ."

At seven o'clock exactly, four beat-up cars painted the bright purple of Los Carniceros appeared, carrying the gang members who had come to back up Martínez. They drove through the crowd, making the sign of the hooked hand before their faces and grabbing their crotches as an act of provocation. I had a vision of how there would be a battle royal if things did not turn out well and how even though there were more of my friends, they were no match for the Carniceros, who were armed and were experienced in turf wars. I had to look twice to tell which was Martínez; they all looked alike: the same Vaselined hair, leather jackets, studs and chains, and cocky walk. Martínez had not changed one iota of his gang uniform, not even the stacked heels; I, on the other hand, was comfortably dressed—I could only afford clothes I bought in rummage sales at church bazaars—and was wearing gym shoes. I reviewed my advantages: I was lighter, and faster; in fact, in any head-to-head contest he could never defeat me, but this was a duel to the death, and at the moment of truth, daring would count for more than agility. In grade school Martínez had been a good athlete, whereas I was only mediocre in sports—but I tried not to think about that.

"At exactly seven-fifteen the express will go by. We will start at the same time, separated by the width of three paces, so you don't have a chance to push me, you shit." I was shouting loud enough for everyone to hear me. "I'll take the position closest to the train; I'll give you that on a platter."

"Don't do me any favors, you little gringo flit!"

"Choose, then: the position nearer the train or starting farther away."

"I'll start farther away."

With a stick I drew two lines in the dirt, while three gang members and some of my buddies, headed by Juan José Morales, went to the other side of the track to monitor the duel from that vantage.

"So close? You 'fraid, queer?" Martínez sneered.

I had anticipated his reaction; I scuffed out the lines with my foot and drew them farther away. Juan José Morales and one Carnicero measured the distance between us, and at that moment we heard the whistle of the train. The spectators surged forward, the gang to the left in a tight bunch, my friends to the right. Carmen gave me a last encouraging look, but I could tell she was near collapse. We took our places on the marks; surreptitiously I touched the scapular, and then I blocked out everything around me, concentrating on myself and that mass of iron racing toward me, counting the seconds, muscles tensed, attuned to the increasing clamor, alone against the train as I had been so many times before. Three, two, one—now! and with no conscious thought of what I was doing I felt a savage roar rise from my belly, as my legs rocketed forward of their own volition, an electrifying charge shot through my body, my muscles strained, and terror blinded my eyes with a veil of blood. The racketing of the train and my howl sank into my pores, filled my body until I became a single terrible bellow. I saw the gargantuan light bearing down on me, my skin burned from the heat of the engine and the air was riven by that gigantic arrow, sparks from steel wheels against rail showered upon my face. There was an instant that lasted a millennium, a fraction of time congealed for an eternity, and I was suspended above a bottomless abyss, floating in front of the locomotive, a bird petrified in mid-flight, every particle of my body straining in the last leap forward, my mind focused on the certainty of death.

I have no idea what happened next. All I remember is coming to on the far side of the track, nauseated, drained, gasping in the smell of hot metal, dazed by the furious snortings of the enormous beast clacking by, clacking, clacking interminably, and when finally it was gone I heard an abnormal silence, a soundless void, and I was in total darkness. A century later, Carmen and Juan José took my arms to help me to my feet.

"Get up, Gregory. Let's get out of here before the police come...."

Only then did I have a flash of lucidity; through the darkness I could see people running for the road. The purple cars of the Carniceros were streaking away, and there was no one there but Carmen, Juan José, and myself, splashed with blood. Pieces of Martínez were scattered across the landscape.

PART TWO

PART TWO

The story of the duel of the train was repeated so many times, and embroidered to such fantastic proportions, that Gregory Reeves became a hero among his classmates. Something fundamental changed at that point: he shot up overnight and lost his naiveté, the source of so many misadventures and fistfights; he was more assured and for the first time in years felt good about himself and finally stopped wishing he were dark-skinned like everyone else in the barrio—in fact, he began to evaluate the advantages of not being like them. There were nearly four thousand students, from different sectors of the city, in his high school—almost all middle-class whites. Girls wore their hair in a ponytail, never said bad words or painted their fingernails, went to church, and some already had the immutable matronly air of their mothers. They lost no opportunity to neck with the latest boyfriend in the last row of the movie theater or back seat of a car, but they preferred not to talk about it. They dreamed of a diamond on their ring finger, and in the meantime their boyfriends took as much liberty as they were allowed before being domesticated by the blinding flash of love. They were living their last chance for fun, for games and contact sports, for drinking themselves blind, for drag racing—a time of boyish mischief, some of it innocent, such as stealing the bust of Lincoln from the principal's office, some not so innocent, such as trapping a black or a Mexican or a homosexual and smearing him with excrement. They made fun of romance but used it when they wanted to get a girl. Among themselves they spoke of little but sex, but very few had the opportunity to practice it. Gregory Reeves was too discreet to mention Olga among his friends. He felt entirely at ease in school; he was not segregated by color anymore, and no one knew anything about his home or his family, especially that his mother was on relief. He was one of the poorest students, but he always had money in his pocket because he worked; he could invite a girl to the movies, he had enough to buy a round of beers or make a bet, and during his senior year his earnings stretched far enough to buy a car that looked like a rattletrap but had a good motor. That he was poor was noticeable only in his shiny pants, threadbare shirts, and lack of free time. He looked older than he was, and was slim, agile, and as strong as his father before him; he thought he was handsome and acted as if he was. For the next few years he took advantage of the Martínez legend and of his knowledge of the two cultures in which he had grown up. The intellectual oddities of his family and his friendship with the library elevator operator had stimulated his curiosity; in an atmosphere where men barely read the sports page and women preferred gossip magazines about Hollywood stars, he had read, in alphabetical order, the world's major thinkers from Aristotle to Zoroaster. He had a skewed vision of the world, but in any case it was broader than that of the other students, even of some teachers. He was dazzled by each new idea, believing he had discovered something unique, and felt duty bound to reveal it to the rest of humanity; he quickly learned, however, that a display of knowledge was about as welcome among his friends as a kick in the ass. As a result, he was cautious before them, but with the girls he could not avoid the temptation to show off his act: walking the high wire of words. Endless discussions with Cyrus had taught him to defend his ideas with passion, although his teacher had frustrated any attempt to dizzy him with his eloquence. More foundation and less rhetoric, son, he would say, but Gregory found that his oratorical bombast impressed other people. He knew how to work his way to the head of any group, and his classmates grew accustomed to deferring to him. As modesty was not one of his virtues, he naturally imagined himself on his way to a political career.

"That's not a bad idea. In a few years, socialism will have triumphed in the world, and you can be the first Communist senator in the nation." This was but one of Cyrus's enthusiastic ideas, expressed during their whispered conferences in the basement of the library, where for years he had tried, without great success, to sow in his disciple's mind the seeds of his burning passion for Marx and Lenin. Gregory found his theories inarguable from the point of view of justice and logic, but intuitively he knew they had no chance of succeeding, at least in his half of the planet. Besides, he found the idea of making a fortune more seductive than owning an equal share of poverty, though he never dared confess such mean thoughts.

"I'm not sure I want to be a Communist," was always his prudent rejoinder.

"Well, what will you be, then?"

"Maybe a Democrat. . . ."

"There's no difference between Democrats and Republicans—how many times do I have to tell you? At any rate, if you're going to make it to the Senate, you need to start right now. The early bird catches the worm. You need to be elected student body president."

"You're crazy, Cyrus. I'm the poorest boy in the class, and I speak English like a Chicano. Who'd vote for me? I'm not a gringo and not a Latino; I don't represent anyone."

"That's the very reason you can represent everyone," and his aged friend lent him a copy of *The Prince,* along with other works by Niccolò Machiavelli, so he could learn about human nature. After three weeks of superficial reading, Gregory Reeves returned, confused.

"This isn't any help, Cyrus. What do fifteenth-century Italians have to do with the loafers in my school?"

"Is that all you have to say about Machiavelli? You've missed the whole point; you're a dunce. You don't deserve to be secretary at a preschool, much less president of the student body."

So Gregory put his nose in the books again, this time with greater dedication, and gradually the illumination of the Florentine statesman shone through five centuries of history, the distance of half the globe, cultural barriers, and the fog of a youthful brain, to reveal the art of power. Gregory took notes in a notebook he modestly titled "President Reeves," which turned out to be prophetic because, using the strategies of Machiavelli, the advice of his mentor, and manipulations of his own inspiration, he was elected president by a crushing majority. It was the first year the school was free of racial problems, because students and teachers worked together, convinced by Reeves that they were all in the same boat and nothing was to be gained by rowing in opposite directions. He also organized the first sock hop—to the scandalized dismay of the school board, which considered the dance a definitive step toward a Roman orgy. Nothing sinful occurred, however; it was an innocent party at which shoes were all the celebrants removed. The new president was determined to leave a spotless record behind him and thus start himself down the road to the White House, but the task was more arduous than he had calculated. Not only was he saddled by the responsibilities of his office; he worked in the kitchen of a taco stand until late at night, on weekends he repaired tires in Pedro Morales's garage, and summers he worked as a *bracero,* picking fruit. He kept himself so busy that he was spared the vices of the alcohol, drugs, betting, and drag races in which several of his friends lost a large part of their innocence, when not their health or even their lives.

Girls became Gregory's obsession, manifested sometimes as a euphoric bemusement capable of making him forget his own name but usually as a martyrdom of molten metal in his veins and well-worn obscenities in his mind. Delicately, because she was very fond of him, but with unyielding determination, Olga exiled

THE INFINITE PLAN · 111

him from her bed, using the pretext that it was time for him to find consolation from a different source. I'm too old for this, she told him, but the truth was that she had fallen in love with a truckdriver ten years her junior, who liked to visit her between runs. So for several years that once independent woman darned the socks and put up with the chicanery of a low-down lover— until on one of his long hauls he turned down a new road, to follow another love, and never returned. It was true, anyway, that Olga and Gregory's encounters had lost the allure of novelty and the thrill of secrecy and had degenerated into discreet gymnastics between a grandmother and grandson. Olga was replaced by Ernestina Pereda, Gregory's grade school classmate, who now worked in a restaurant. For a moment he imagined himself smitten with her, an illusion that dissipated almost immediately, leaving the bad taste of guilt. Of all Ernestina's lovers, he may have been the only one with such scruples, and to banish them he had to betray his romantic nature and the chivalry he had absorbed from his mother and his reading; he did not want to take advantage of Ernestina, as so many others had done, but neither could he lie about his feelings for her. The social climate that would view sex as a healthful exercise without risk of pregnancy or obstacle of guilt had not yet appeared on the horizon. Ernestina Pereda was one of those beings destined to explore the abyss of the senses, and it was her fate to have been born fifteen years too soon, at a time when women had to choose between decency and pleasure—and Ernestina lacked the courage to renounce either. As long as she could remember, she had lived in wonder of the potential of her body; at seven she had converted the school bathroom into her first laboratory and her schoolmates into guinea pigs with whom she conducted research, performed experiments, and reached astounding conclusions. Gregory had not escaped her scientific zeal; they sneaked off with high enthusiasm to the sordid intimacy of the bathroom for mutual exploration, a game that would have continued indefinitely had the brutish Martínez and his band not cut it short. At recess, the boys had climbed onto a large box to spy on the pair, had discovered them playing doctor, and had stirred up such a storm that Gregory was sick with shame for a week and never again attempted such diversions until the day Olga rescued him from his adolescent befuddlement. By the time Gregory returned to her, Ernestina Pereda was a veteran; there was scarcely a boy in the barrio who hadn't bragged about having her—some justifiably, many merely to boast. Gregory tried not to think about her promiscuity; their times together were free of any pretense of sentiment, and if love was never mentioned, kindness was never absent. Gregory's infatuations usually took the form of ephemeral passions for girls from better parts of town, with whom he could not practice the forbidden pirouettes from Olga's repertoire or Ernestina Pereda's frenetic caracoles. He had no difficulty finding sweethearts, but he never felt sufficiently loved: the affection he received was but a pale reflection of his consuming desire. He liked tall, slim girls but yielded to any temptress of the opposite sex, even the plumpest girls from the barrio. Only Carmen was exempt from his erotic delirium; he considered her his best friend, and their pure friendship was impervious to her feminine charms. They were, nonetheless, very different in temperament, and gradually an intellectual gap opened between them. Gregory shared confidences with Carmen, took her dancing and to the movies, but there was no point in discussing anything he had read with her, or any of the social and metaphysical questions Cyrus had sowed in his consciousness. When he journeyed down those paths, his friend did not even attempt to flatter him by feigning interest; she froze him with an icy stare and told him to cut the shit. He had no better intellectual communication with other girls; they were initially attracted because of his reputation for being wild and a good dancer, but they had little tolerance for his insistent urging and soon went their way, complaining that he was a conceited bookworm who could not keep his hands to himself. Watch out if he asks you to take a ride alone in that junk heap of his; first he'll bore you to death with some political jazz and then try to get you out of your bra. Even so, Reeves did not lack for amorous adventures. Juan José Morales thought it was not worth the effort to try to under-

stand women; as the old Spanish song said—and Padre Larraguibel when he was inflamed with Catholic ardor—they were
creatures of lust and damnation. For the machos of the barrio
there were only two kinds of girls: those like Ernestina Pereda
and the others, the ones who were untouchable, destined for
motherhood and hearth. But a man should not fall in love with
either of them; love made a man a slave or, worse, a poor deceived
fool. Gregory never accepted those standards and for the next
thirty years relentlessly pursued the chimera of perfect love, stumbling more times than he could count, falling and picking himself
up, running an interminable obstacle course, until he gave up the
search and learned to live in solitude. Then, in one of life's ironic
surprises, he found love when he least expected it. But that is
another story.

Gregory Reeves's senatorial aspirations ended abruptly the day
after his high school graduation, when Judy asked him what he
meant to do with his life and told him it was time for him to move
out of his mother's house because it was too crowded for the three
of them.

"It's long past time for you to live somewhere else. There's no
room here; it's terribly uncomfortable."

"All right, I'll look for a place," Gregory replied, with a blend
of sadness for this brusque manner of being expelled from the
family and relief for leaving a home where he had never felt
loved.

"We need to have Mama's teeth fixed; we can't put it off any
longer."

"Do you have anything saved?"

"Not enough. We need three hundred dollars. And besides,
there's the television we promised her for Christmas."

Judy had suffered an unhappy adolescence, to become a
woman soured by unspoken indignation. Her face was still sur-
prisingly beautiful, and her hair, even slashed by scissors, was the
gold of her childhood. Pernicious layers of fat had settled over her
bones, but because she was still very young she was not totally

misshapen; despite her obesity, the original contours of her figure were discernible, and on the rare occasions that she forgot her self-loathing and laughed, she regained her earlier charm. She had had several love affairs with the Anglo men she met at work or in other neighborhoods; her Hispanic neighbors had long ago abandoned the chase, convinced that she was unattainable. She made it her business to frighten off her most diligent pretenders with fits of arrogance or cool silences.

"That poor girl will never marry; you can see she hates men," Olga predicted.

"Unless she loses some weight, she's had it," Gregory added.

"Weight has nothing to do with it, Gregory. She won't end up an old maid because she's fat but because she's so mad at the world that she *wants* to be fat."

For once, Olga's clairvoyance failed her. Regardless of appearance, Judy married three times and had countless lovers, some of whom lost their peace of mind pursuing a love she could not or would not give. She had several children by different husbands and adopted others, all of whom she raised with great affection. The natural tenderness that had left its mark on the first years of Gregory's life, something he tried many times to recapture throughout his stormy relationship with his sister, had lain dormant in Judy's soul until it could be channeled toward the responsibilities of motherhood. Her own and her adopted children helped her overcome the emotional paralysis of her youth and to bear with fortitude the tragic secret hidden in her past. She eventually dropped out of school and went to work in a garment factory; the family situation was precarious and the money that she and Gregory brought home insufficient for their needs. After a year of cleaning houses after school, with work-reddened hands and the conviction that she was going nowhere down that road, she decided on a full-time job at the factory. Sitting beside other badly paid and badly treated women, she stitched away in a dark, airless room where cockroaches paraded unmolested. In that industry, laws were violated with impunity and workers exploited by unscrupulous bosses. She brought home bundles of cloth and sat at her mother's sewing machine far into the night. She was not paid overtime for her piecework, but she needed the money: at the first complaint, her employers would turn her out into the street—there were many desperate people waiting in line.

As for Gregory, he, too, was used to hard work; he had contributed to the household income since he was seven. Several improvements were made from his earnings: the old icebox was exchanged for a modern refrigerator, the kerosene camp stove for a gas range, and the wind-up gramophone for an electric record player on which his mother could listen to her beloved music. Gregory was not daunted by the idea of living alone. Both his friend Cyrus and Olga tried to convince him that instead of toiling for subsistence wages he should try to work his way through college; that alternative, however, was not one often considered among young people from his surroundings, who were forced by an invisible ceiling to keep their eyes on the ground. Once he finished high school, Gregory found himself again limited by the low horizons of the barrio. For eleven years he had done everything possible to be accepted and, despite his color, had nearly succeeded. Although he could not have put it into words, the real reason he became a laborer may have been his desire to remain part of the world in which he had grown up: the idea of using education to rise above the others seemed a betrayal. During the happy years of high school he had deceived himself briefly, believing he could escape his fate; deep down, however, he had accepted his social marginality and at the moment of confronting his future had been crushed by reality. He rented a room, furnishing it with crates containing his few belongings and books lent to him by Cyrus, with Oliver as his only company. The dog was old and half blind, had lost several teeth and large patches of his coat, could barely drag his heavy mongrel bones around, but he was still a discreet and faithful friend. A few weeks of working at a wetback's wages were enough to teach Reeves that the American dream was not within everyone's reach. He would return to his room at night, exhausted, throw himself on his bed, stare at the ceiling, and review the extent of his despair; he felt trapped in a bottomless pit. He worked all summer in a freight warehouse, lifting and carrying heavy loads; he developed muscles where he hadn't known he had them and was beginning to look like a gladiator, when an accident forced a change in his life. He and another man were carrying a refrigerator, strapped between them, up a narrow stairwell; it was suffocatingly hot, and on each step Gregory bore all the weight on one side of his body. Suddenly he felt a burning electric charge in his right leg; he had to call on all his strength not to drop the load, which would have crushed his mate. A terrible bellow escaped him, followed by a string of curses, and when he could set down the refrigerator and examine his leg, he saw a purple tree with thick trunk and branching limbs; he had ruptured the veins, and in a matter of minutes his leg was grossly deformed. He was taken to a hospital, where he was told that absolute rest was required and that only surgery would repair the varicose veins. His employer gave him a week's pay, and Reeves spent his convalescence in his room, sweating beneath the ceiling fan, sustained by the faithful companionship of Oliver, therapeutic massages by Olga, and Mexican dishes prepared by Inmaculada Morales. Cyrus's books, classical music, and visits from friends were his entertainment. Carmen came often to tell in detail the plots of the latest movies; she had a gift for narrating, and listening to her, he felt he was watching the screen. Juan José Morales, who like Gregory had reached his eighteenth birthday, came to say goodbye before enlisting in the armed forces. As a remembrance he left a photograph album of naked women, which Gregory put aside to spare himself additional torture; he had enough with the scorching heat, his immobility, and boredom. Cyrus came to see him every day and reported the latest news in a sepulchral tone: humanity was on the verge of catastrophe, the cold war was endangering the planet, there were far too many atomic bombs ready to be activated and far too many arrogant generals willing to use them—at any moment someone would press the fatal button, the world would go up in a final blaze of light, and that would be the fucking end of everything.

"We've lost our sense of ethics; we live in a world of small-mindedness, of gratification without happiness and actions without meaning."

"Come on, Cyrus. How many times have you warned me about the dangers of bourgeois pessimism?" his disciple replied mockingly.

From time to time Nora would materialize, discreet and tenuous. She would bring cookies for Gregory and a bone for Oliver, sit near the door on the edge of her chair, and discuss with greatest formality her perennial topics: history, recollections of his father, and music. With each visit, she seemed more ethereal, less substantial. On Saturdays they listened to the opera on the radio, and Nora, with teary eyes, would comment that those were surely the voices of supernatural beings, for humans could not achieve such perfection. With habitual good manners, she looked at the stack of books from her chair and courteously inquired what he was reading.

"Philosophy, Mama."

"I don't care for philosophers, Greg; they are against God. They try to rationalize Creation, which is an act of love and magic. To understand life, faith is more useful than philosophy."

"You would like these books, Mama."

"Yes, perhaps I would. We have to read a lot, Greg. With knowledge and wisdom, evil could be vanquished on this earth."

"These books say with different words what you taught me: that all men and women are one in the eyes of God, that no one should possess the earth, because it belongs to everyone, and that one day there will be justice and equality for all."

"And those are not religious books?"

"Just the opposite; they're about men, not gods. They're about economics, politics, history—"

"I pray, son, that those are not Communist books."

As she left, she would hand him a pamphlet on Bahaism or some new spiritual guide among the many to be found everywhere and leave with a quiet wave of her hand, without having touched her son. Her presence in the room would have been so faint that Gregory wondered whether she had really been there or whether that lady with the mist-colored hair and old-fashioned dress was only a trick of his imagination. He felt a painful affection for her; she seemed seraphic, untouched by evil, as fine and delicate as a ghost in a tale. At times he was devoured by his anger toward her; he wanted to shake her out of her persistent haze, shout at her to open her eyes, just once, and look at him—Look at me, Mother, here I am, can't you see me?—but usually he wanted only to be near her, to touch her, laugh with her, tell her his secrets.

One evening Pedro Morales closed the garage early to come see him. Following the death of Charles Reeves, he had tacitly assumed the task of watching over his Maestro's family.

"You were injured on the job. They should pay you compensation," he explained to Gregory.

"They told me they don't owe me anything, Don Pedro."

"Your boss has insurance, doesn't he?"

"The boss said that he's not the boss and that we're not his employees, that we're independent contractors. They pay us in cash, fire us at will, and there's no insurance. You know how that goes."

"But that's illegal. You need a lawyer, son."

Reeves had no money for lawyers, however, and he was discouraged by the idea of slogging through years of tangled negotiations. The minute he was back on his feet he found a less demanding but no more agreeable job in a furniture factory, where the workers were always half dazed from the fine sawdust in the air and fumes from glue, varnish, and solvent. For several months he made chair legs, all exactly alike. The accident to his own leg had put him on his guard, and he confronted the foreman so many times, demanding rights written in the contract but ignored in practice, that he was branded an incorrigible troublemaker and fired. After that he bounced from job to job, dismissed from each after only a few weeks.

"Why do you raise such a ruckus, Greg? You're not in high school now, you're not the president of anything. As long as they pay you, keep your mouth shut and don't complain," Olga counseled, with little hope of being heard.

"That's the way, son; we have to have class solidarity. In union there is strength," Cyrus exclaimed, pointing a trembling forefinger at an invisible red banner. "Work is elevating; all labor is equally worthy and should receive equal pay. All men do not have the same abilities, however. This isn't for you, Greg, this is wasted effort; you're not getting anywhere; it's like shoveling sand into the sea."

"Why don't you be a painter?" Carmen asked. "Your father was an artist, wasn't he?"

"And he died a pauper, leaving us on public welfare. No, thanks. I'm up to here with being poor. Poverty is a piss-poor way to live."

"No one gets rich working in a factory. Besides, you don't know how to take orders, and you get bored too fast. The only thing you're good for is to be your own boss," insisted his friend, who had applied the same principles to herself.

Carmen was too old now to go out in bright clothes and juggle on some street corner, but she had no desire to earn a conventional living; the idea of spending the day locked up in an office or sitting at a sewing machine appalled her. She earned a little money from crafts she sold in gift shops and traveling fairs. Like Judy and many other girls in the barrio, she had never finished high school and had no skills, but she had imagination to spare, and secretly she counted on her father to help her escape the torture of a routine job. Pedro Morales's resolve weakened before the blandishments of his untraditional daughter, and he allowed her liberties he would not tolerate in his other children.

The work was simple in the plant for manufacturing tin cans, but a moment's inattention could cost a worker a couple of fingers. The machine Gregory was in charge of sealed cans on the endless rows passing before him on a conveyor belt. The noise was earsplitting: the ring of levers and sheet metal, grinding presses and gears, squeals from badly oiled machinery, hammering screeching blades. Gregory, even with wax earplugs, was ne~ crazed by the din in his head; he felt as if he were inside a cl~ bell tower. The noise left him drained; once outside, h~

dazed he was not even aware of the roar of traffic but felt as if he were at the bottom of a silent sea. All that mattered was productivity; each worker was forced to the limit of his strength, and often past that limit if he wanted to keep his job. On Monday the men reported for work limp from weekend hangovers and could barely stay awake. When the five o'clock whistle blew and the racket abruptly ceased, Gregory was always disoriented for a few minutes, suspended above a void. The workers washed up at faucets in the factory yard, changed clothes, and poured out toward the bars. At first Gregory hung around with the other men, swimming in smoke, saturated with cheap tequila and dark beer; he laughed at their dirty jokes and sang their raucous *rancheras,* more bored than enjoying himself. For a few minutes he could pretend he had friends, but as soon as he was outside and the vapors of the bar cleared from his head, he realized he had been fooling himself. He had nothing in common with the men he worked with; they distrusted him as much as any other gringo. He soon renounced that false camaraderie and went straight from the factory to his room, where he locked the door and read and listened to music. To gain the men's confidence, he organized protests; he was the first to declare war when someone was injured or had an accident, but in practical terms it was difficult to disseminate Cyrus's ideas on social justice when he could not count on the support of the intended beneficiaries.

"They want security, Cyrus. They're afraid. Everyone's looking after himself; no one cares about anyone else."

"Fear can be overcome, Gregory. You must teach them to sacrifice self-interest for the common good."

"In real life it seems that every person defends his stake. We live in a very selfish society."

"You must talk to them, Greg." The tireless socialist's lectures never slowed. "Man is the only animal governed by ethics, that ︎︎ progress beyond his instincts. If that were not so, we would es ︎ in the Stone Age. This is a crucial moment in history; if we birth ︎m an atomic cataclysm, all the elements are ripe for the New Man."

"I hope you're right, but I'm afraid that the New Man will be born somewhere else, Cyrus, not here. In this barrio no one thinks about leaps in evolution, only survival."

And that was how it was; no one wanted to attract attention. The Hispanics, most of them illegal aliens, had overcome countless obstacles to come north and had no intention of provoking new misfortunes through political agitation that could attract the feared agents of the "Migra." The factory foreman, a huge man with a red beard, had observed Reeves for months, but because he was one of Judy's patient admirers had not fired him. This man dreamed of the day he would remove Judy's clothes and sink into her generous flesh, and hoped to worm his way into Judy's heart through her brother. He missed no opportunity to have a few drinks with Gregory, always hoping for an invitation to the Reeves house in return. I don't want him around here, Judy groaned when her brother suggested inviting him, and Gregory never dreamed that the redhead would win the round through sheer tenacity and in time become his sister's first husband.

Once he had caught Gregory distributing fliers in badly written Spanish and wanted to know what the hell they were about.

"These are articles of the Work Law," he replied defiantly.

"What the fuck is that?"

"Conditions in this workplace are unhealthy, and we're owed a lot of money in overtime."

"Come to the office, Reeves."

Once they were alone, the foreman offered him a seat and a drink from the bottle of gin he kept in the first-aid cabinet. For a long moment, he observed Gregory in silence, looking for a way to express what was on his mind. He was a man of few words and would never have gone to such trouble had Judy not been involved.

"You can go a long way here, man. The way I see it, in less than five years' time you could be foreman. You're educated, and you're a natural leader."

"And I'm also white, right?" Reeves returned.

"That too. Even in that you're lucky."

"Apparently, none of my comrades will ever get any farther than the conveyor belt. . . ."

"Those lousy *indios* are no good, Reeves. They fight and steal; you can't trust them. They're stupid, besides; they can't understand anything, and they're too lazy even to learn English."

"You don't know what you're talking about. They have more ability and sense of honor than either of us. You've lived in this barrio all your life and you don't know a single word of Spanish, but any one of them learns English in a few weeks. And they're not lazy either; they work harder than any white, for half the pay."

"What do you care about a few stupid Mexicans? They're nothing to you; you're different. Believe me, you'll be foreman; who knows, one day you could own your own factory. You got the stuff, and you should be thinking of your future. I'll help you, but I don't want any hassle; it's not in your best interests. Besides, these Mexicans never complain; they're perfectly happy."

"Ask them and see what they say. . . ."

"If they don't like it, let them go back home; no one asked them to come here."

Reeves had heard that line too many times, and he angrily stalked out of the office. In the yard where the workers were washing up, he saw the trash barrel overflowing with his pamphlets; he kicked it over and walked away cursing. To work off his bad mood, he went to see two horror movies; then he stood at a counter and ate a hamburger and at midnight returned to his room. His rage, meanwhile, had turned to an agonizing sense of impotence. When he got home, he found a message on his door: Cyrus was in the hospital.

For two days his aged friend lay dying, his only companion Gregory Reeves. Cyrus had no family, and he had not wanted to ~~a~~dvise any other of his friends because he considered death to be a ~~priva~~te matter. He detested sentimentality and warned Gregory ~~that at~~ the first tear he would have to go, because Cyrus was not ~~going to s~~pend his last moments on earth consoling a blubberer. ~~He had aske~~d him to come, he explained, because there were still a few things he wanted to teach him, and he did not want to leave with remorse for a job unfinished. During those two days his heart was rapidly failing; he passed hour after hour concentrating on the exhausting process of withdrawing from life and drawing away from his body. At certain moments he found strength to speak and was sufficiently lucid to warn his disciple one last time about the dangers of individualism and to dictate a list of books, with instructions to read them in the order indicated. Then he gave Gregory the key to a locker in the train station and, pausing frequently to catch his breath, outlined his last instructions.

"You will find eight hundred dollars there, in bills. No one knows I have them, so the hospital won't be able to claim them to pay my bill. Public charity or the library will take care of my funeral—they won't throw me onto the dump, I'm sure of that. That money's for you, son, for you to go to the university. A man can begin at the bottom, but it's much easier to begin at the top, and without a diploma you'll have a hard time getting out of this hole. The higher you are, the more you'll be able to change things in this damned capitalistic society, you understand?"

"Cyrus—"

"Don't interrupt; I'm getting weaker. Why do you think I filled your head with reading all these years? So you'll use it! When a man's earning his living doing things he doesn't like, he feels like a slave; when he's doing what he loves, he feels like a prince. Take the money and go somewhere far away from this town, you hear? You had good grades in school, you won't have any trouble being admitted into a university. Swear you'll do it."

"But—"

"Swear it!"

"I swear I'll try. . . ."

"That's not enough. *Swear* you'll do it."

"All right, I'll do it," and Gregory Reeves had to step out in the corridor so his friend would not see the tears. He had suddenly been gripped in the claws of an ancient fear. After he had seen Martínez's body strewn across the track, he thought he had overcome his phobia about death and in fact had not thought about it for years, but with the faint scent of almonds in Cyrus's room the terror had returned with all the intensity of his childhood years. He wondered why that particular odor nauseated him, but could not remember. That night Cyrus died, quietly and with dignity, as he had lived, in the company of the man he had thought of as his son. Shortly before the end, the dying man had been removed from the ward and taken to a private room. Notified by Carmen Morales, Padre Larraguibel arrived to offer the consolation of his faith; Cyrus was already unconscious, and Gregory thought it disrespectful to disturb his friend, an unreconstructed agnostic, with holy water and a spate of Latin.

"It can't do him any harm, and who knows, it might help," the priest argued.

"I'm sorry, Padre; Cyrus wouldn't like it, begging your pardon."

"It isn't up to you to decide, boy," the priest replied emphatically, and with no further discussion pushed Gregory aside, extracted his stole and the oils for extreme unction from his kit, and performed his moral obligation, capitalizing on the dying man's inability to defend himself.

Death came calmly, and it was several minutes before Gregory realized what had happened. He sat a long while beside the body of his friend, speaking with him for the last time, thanking him for all the things he owed him, asking him never to leave him and to watch over him from the heaven of nonbelievers.... Look what a fool I am, Cyrus, to ask that of you of all people, because if you don't believe in God, you sure as hell aren't going to believe in guardian angels. The next morning Reeves collected the modest treasure from the locker and to it added savings of his own to pay for a solemn funeral with organ music and a profusion of gardenias; he invited all the library personnel and others who had never known Cyrus existed but attended only because they were invited, like his mother, Judy, and the Morales tribe—including the grandmother, who was close to a hundred but still capable of enjoying a funeral, happy it was not she in the coffin. A brilliant sun shone the day of the burial; it was hot, and Gregory sweated profusely in his dark rented suit. Walking behind the casket down the cemetery path, he silently said goodbye to his teacher, the first stage of his life, the city, and his friends. One week later he caught a train to Berkeley. He had ninety dollars in his pocket and very few good memories.

I leapt from the train with the anticipation of a person opening a blank notebook; I was beginning a new life. I had heard so much about that profane, subversive, and visionary city where lunatics lived elbow-to-elbow with Nobel laureates that it seemed I could feel the energy in the air, the buffeting of an infectious wind that stripped me of twenty years of routine, fatigue, and asphyxia. Enough was enough; Cyrus was right: my soul was rotting within me. I saw a string of yellow lights in the moonlit mist, a scarred platform, shadows of silent travelers with their suitcases and bundles, and I heard a dog barking. There was an impalpable, cold dankness in the air and a strange odor, a blend of the metal of the locomotive and of coffee vapors. It was a drab station, no different from many others, but nothing could dampen my enthusiasm; I slung my canvas bag over my shoulder and set off, skipping like a kid and shouting at the top of my lungs that this was the first night of all the remaining stupendous days of my fantastic life! No one turned to stare at me, as if that fit of sudden madness were absolutely normal; in fact it was, as I confirmed the next morning almost as soon as I left the hostel and stepped into the street to undertake the adventure of enrolling in the university, looking for a job, and finding a place to live. It was another planet. To someone like me who had grown up in a kind of ghetto, the cosmopolitan and libertarian atmosphere of Berkeley made me feel drunk. On a wall, in bold green letters, I saw ANYTHING IS TOLERATED EXCEPT INTOLERANCE. The years I spent in Berkeley were intense and splendid years; still today when I visit, something I often do, I feel I belong to that city. When I went there at the beginning of the decade of the sixties, it was not a shadow of the indescribable circus it would become after I moved to the other side of the bay, but it was already an unconventional place, the cradle of radical movements and audacious forms of rebellion. It was my luck to be present at the transformation of the caterpillar into the large-winged, brilliantly colored butterfly that animated an entire generation. Young people came from the four corners of the nation in search of new ideas that still had no name but could be felt in the air, throbbing like muted drums. Berkeley was the Mecca of godless pilgrims, the far extreme of the continent, where people came to escape old delusions or to find a utopia, the very essence of California, the soul of these vast reaches, enlightened and without memory, a Tower of Babel of whites, Asians, blacks, a few Latinos, children, old people, and the young—especially the young: *Never trust anyone over thirty.* It was in vogue to be poor, or at least to appear to be so, and would continue to be fashionable in future decades, even after the entire nation had abandoned itself to the intoxication of greed and success. The residents all gave the impression of being ragged, and often the beggar on the corner looked as prosperous as the generous passerby who dropped a few coins into his cup. I observed all this with provincial curiosity. In my barrio in Los Angeles there was not a single hippie—the Mexican machos would have destroyed him—and even though I had seen a few on the beach and in the city center and on television, nothing compared to this spectacle. Around the university, heirs to the Beatniks had taken over the streets with their wild hair, beards, and sideburns, their flowers, necklaces, Indian tunics, patched jeans, and monks' sandals. The fragrance of marijuana blended with traffic fumes, incense, coffee, and waves of spices from Eastern restaurants. In the university itself, people still wore their hair short and dressed conventionally, but you could already see signs of the changes that a couple of years later would put an end to all such prudent monotony. In the gardens, students took off their shoes and shirts and soaked up the sun in a foreshadowing of the time soon to come when men and women would remove all their clothes and celebrate the revolution of communal love. YOUNG FOREVER, said the graffiti on a wall, while every hour the merciless carillon of the campanile reminded us of the inexorable passage of time.

I had seen close at hand the several faces of racism; I am one of few whites who has lived it. When the older daughter of the Moraleses was lamenting her Indian cheekbones and cinnamon skin, her father seized her by the arm, dragged her to a mirror, and commanded her to take a good look and thank the blessed Virgin of Guadalupe that she was not a "filthy black." On that occasion, I could only think how little good had resulted from the diploma of *The Infinite Plan* hanging on the wall as evidence of the superiority of Morales's soul; at heart, he shared the prejudices of other Latins who despised blacks and Asians. No Hispanic attended the university in those days, everyone was white, with the exception of a few descendants of Chinese immigrants. And you never saw a black in the classroom, only on the sports teams. There were almost no people of color to be found in offices, stores, or restaurants; in contrast, the hospitals and jails were filled. While blacks were segregated, they were not treated like foreigners, the humiliation suffered by my Latin friends; at least they were walking on their own soil—and many were beginning to take great, noisy strides.

I made the circuit of the offices, trying to find my way through the labyrinth of the campus, calculating how much money I would need to survive and how I was going to find a job. I was sent from window to window in a round of form-filling, like the proverbial serpent biting its own tail. The bureaucracy was crushing; no one knew anything, we newcomers were considered an inevitable nuisance, to be got rid of as quickly as possible. I didn't know whether they treated us like garbage to toughen us up or whether I was the only one who was so lost; I came to believe they were discriminating against me because of my Chicano accent. Occasionally some good-natured student, a survivor of earlier obstacles, passed on information that set me on the right track; without such help I would have spent a month circling around like a slug. No rooms were available in the dormitories and I wasn't interested in fraternities—they were strongholds of conservatism and class consciousness, with no room for a person like myself. One fellow I ran into several times during madhouse of those first days told me he had found a room to and would share it with me. His name was Timothy Duane, and as I would later find out, girls thought he was the handsomest man in the university. When Carmen met him many years later, she said he looked like a Greek statue. There is nothing Greek about him; he's a typical blue-eyed, dark-haired Irishman. His grandfather, he told me, escaped from Dublin at the beginning of the century, just ahead of the arm of English justice; he arrived in New York with one hand out and another behind him, and after a few years in some questionable business dealings, had made a fortune. In his old age he became a benefactor of the arts, and everyone forgot his somewhat murky past; when he died, he left his heirs a pile of money and a good name. Timothy had grown up in Catholic boarding schools for sons of the wealthy, where he learned various sports and cultivated an overwhelming sense of guilt that must have been with him from the cradle. In his heart of hearts, he wanted to be an actor, but his father believed there were only two respectable professions, medicine and law, everything else was a great stew of crooks and incompetents—especially the theater, which in his eyes was a hotbed of homosexuals and perverts. Half his income was diverted into the arts foundation his grandfather Duane had established, a beneficence that had not made the father any more sympathetic to artists. He remained a healthy autocrat for nearly a century, depriving humanity of the pleasure of viewing the fine figure of his son on stage or screen. Tim became a doctor who hated his profession and told me that he chose pathology as a specialty because at least when your patients were dead you didn't have to listen to their complaints or pat their hands. When he renounced his dream of being an actor and exchanged the boards of the theater for the icy slabs of dissecting theaters, he became a recluse, tormented by unrelenting demons. Many women pursued him, but all those affairs had foundered by the way, leaving behind misgivings, regret, and insecurity—until late in his life, after he had lost laughter, hope, and a large part of his cha when someone came along to save him from himself. But I'm ing ahead of my story; that happened much later. At the time t him, he was deceiving his father, promising to

after coming to Berkeley, I was living in the attic with my friend Duane; I was regularly attending classes and had found two jobs to keep my head above water. Studying presented no difficulty: the university was not yet the terrible brain factory it would later become; it was like high school, only less orderly. I was required to attend ROTC courses for two years. I liked the exercises and the summer camp so much, and was so taken with the uniform, that I signed for all four years and reached officer's rank. When I enlisted, I had to sign a sworn declaration that I was not a Communist. As I was writing my signature at the bottom of the page, I felt Cyrus's ironic gaze on the back of my neck, so strong that I turned around to speak to him.

The foreman of the plant for manufacturing tin cans dreamed every night of Judy Reeves, and in his waking hours relentlessly pursued a vision of her. He was not obsessed with corpulent women; he had simply never noticed that she was fat. In his eyes Judy was perfect, neither too little nor too much, and if anyone had told him she was carrying nearly double her normal weight, he would have been truly amazed. He did not focus on the extent of her defects but on the worth of her virtues; he loved the spheres of her breasts and her voluminous buttocks and was thrilled her flesh was so plentiful—all the more to hold. He was dazzled by her baby-fine skin, by her hands, roughened by sewing and house-work but nobly formed, by the radiant smile he had glimpsed only twice, and by her hair, fine and pale as strands of silver. The girl's determination to reject him merely fed his desire. He looked for opportunities to be near her, despite the arrogant indifference that met every overture. Fresh from the shower, wearing a clean shirt and splashed with cologne to dissipate the acrid odor of the plant, he stationed himself every evening at the bus stop to await his beloved's return from work; he would reach for her hand to help her from the bus, knowing that she would choose to lurch down the steps rather than accept his help. Then he walked her home, speaking in a conversational tone as if they were the closest of friends; undiscouraged by Judy's stubborn silence, he would tell her details of his day, the baseball scores, news about people she had never met. He would walk her as far as her door, invite her out to dinner—sure of her silent refusal—and say goodbye with the promise to meet her the next day at the same place. This patient siege was maintained for two months, without variation.

"Who is that man who comes here every day?" Nora Reeves finally asked.

"No one, Mama."

"What is his name?"

"I've never asked him. I'm not interested."

The next day Nora was waiting at the window, and before Judy could close the door in the gigantic redhead's nose she stepped out to greet him and invite him in for a beer, ignoring her daughter's murderous gaze. Sitting in the tiny living room, on a chair too fragile for his enormous body, the suitor sat tongue-tied, cracking his knuckles while Nora observed him with interest from her wicker chair. Judy had disappeared into the bedroom, where her furious snorting could be heard through the paper-thin walls.

"Allow me to express my appreciation for your courteous attentions to my daughter," said Nora Reeves.

"Unh-huh," the man replied, unaccustomed to such formal language and unable to offer a more articulate response.

"You appear to be a decent person."

"Unh-huh. . . ."

"Are you?"

"Am I what?"

"I asked whether you are a decent person."

"I don't know, ma'am."

"What is your name?"

"Jim Morgan."

"My name is Nora, and my husband is Charles Reeves, Master Functionary in Divine Sciences: Surely you have heard of him; he is very well known. . . ."

Judy, listening in the next room, had heard all she could bear;

she swept into the room like a typhoon, facing her timid admirer with arms akimbo.

"What the hell do you want of me? Why don't you stop bugging me?"

"I can't. . . . I think I'm in love; I'm really sorry . . . ," her miserable caller stammered, his face flushing red as his hair.

"All right, if the only way I can get rid of this nightmare is to go to bed with you, let's get it over with!"

Nora Reeves uttered a horrified exclamation and jumped up so quickly she overturned her chair; her daughter had never spoken such words in her presence. Morgan also stood up, made a slight bow to Nora, and clamped his cap on his head; at the door, he turned.

"I see I was mistaken about you. What I have in mind is marriage," he said succinctly.

As she descended from the bus the next day, Judy found no one waiting to take her hand to help her. She heaved a sigh of relief and started majestically homeward, swaying like a slow freighter, observing the activity in the street: people going about their errands, cats pawing through garbage pails, dark-skinned children playing cowboys and Indians. It was a long walk, and by the time she reached home her happiness had faded, replaced by acute dejection. That night, desolate, she could not sleep but tossed and turned like a beached whale. At dawn she arose, drank a cup of chocolate, and ate two bananas, three fried eggs with bacon, and eight pieces of toast slathered with butter and marmalade. Her mother found her on the porch, chocolate mustache and egg yolk still on her upper lip, with two rivulets of tears running down her cheeks.

"Your father came again last night. He told me to have you bury chicken livers at the foot of the willow tree."

"Don't talk to me about him, Mama."

"It's for the ants. He says that will get them out of the house."

Judy did not go to work that day; instead, she visited Olga. The divine looked her over from top to bottom, evaluating the rolls of fat, the swollen legs, the labored breathing, the unbecoming dress hurriedly stitched from cheap cloth, the terrible desolation in the girl's definitively blue eyes, and she did not have to gaze into her crystal ball to suggest advice.

"What do you want more than anything else, Judy?"

"Children," she replied unhesitatingly.

"For that you need a man. And while you're at it, it's best if the man's a husband."

Judy went straight to the pastry shop on the corner and devoured three millefeuille pastries and two glasses of apple cider; from there she went to the beauty shop, a place she had never visited before, and in the next three hours a short, sympathetic Mexican woman gave her a permanent, painted her fingernails and toenails a bright pink, and used a wax depilatory on her legs, while Judy patiently and methodically ate her way through two pounds of chocolates. Then she took the bus into the city to buy a new dress at the only store for fat women in the entire state of California. She found a blue skirt and a flowered blouse that slightly minimized her bulk and brought out the childlike freshness of her skin and eyes. Thus arrayed, at five o'clock she was standing with crossed arms and a fierce expression at the door of the factory where her lovesick admirer worked. The whistle blew, and she watched the herd of Latino workers troop by; twenty minutes later the foreman appeared, unshaven, sweaty, and wearing a grease-stained shirt. When he saw her, he stopped dead, dumbfounded.

"What did you say your name was?" To hide her embarrassment, Judy spoke in a loud, rather unfriendly voice.

"Jim. Jim Morgan. . . . You look really pretty."

"Do you still want to marry me?"

"Do I!"

Padre Larraguibel celebrated the mass in Our Lady of Lourdes parish church, even though Judy was Bahai like her mother and Jim belonged to the Church of the Holy Apostles; all her friends were Catholics, and in the barrio the only valid marriage was one that followed the ritual of the Vatican. Gregory made a special trip in order to escort his sister to the altar. Pedro Morales shouldered expenses for the party, while Inmaculada and her daughters and friends spent two days cooking Mexican dishes and baking wedding cookies. The bridegroom provided the liquor and the music. The result was an uproarious affair held in the middle of the street with the best mariachis in the barrio and more than a hundred guests dancing the night through to Latin rhythms. Nora Reeves made her daughter an exquisite wedding gown, with so many organdy ruffles that from a distance Judy looked like a pirate ship and at closer range the cradle of the heir to a throne. Jim Morgan had saved a little money and so was able to install his wife in a small but comfortable house and to buy a new bedroom suite with a special-sized bed big enough for the two of them and strong enough to withstand the rhinoceros charges with which, in all good faith, they made love that first week. The following Friday, the husband did not come home. His wife waited for him until Sunday, when he finally appeared, so drunk he could not remember where or with whom he had been. Judy picked up a milk bottle and broke it over his head. The blow would have killed a weaker man, but it barely split Jim Morgan's brow and, far from deterring him, stirred him to a frenetic state of arousal. He swiped the blood from his eyes with his shirt sleeve, threw himself on his wife, and despite her furious kicking, that night they conceived their first son, a beautiful boy who weighed ten pounds at birth. Judy Reeves, illuminated by a happiness she had never believed possible, offered the baby her breast, determined to give this infant the love she had never received. She had discovered her calling as a mother.

For Carmen Morales, Gregory's departure was a personal affront. In the depths of her heart, she had always known that he would not stay in the barrio and that sooner or later he would search for new horizons; she had thought, however, that when that moment came they would leave together, perhaps live a life of adventure with a traveling circus, as they had so often planned. She could not imagine an existence without him. For as long as she could remember she had seen him nearly every day; nothing great or small had happened to her that she had not shared with him. It was he who had unveiled the childhood myths: that there is no Santa Claus and that babies don't grow under cabbages to be delivered from Paris by the stork, and he was the first to know when at eleven she discovered a red stain on her underpants. He was closer to her than her own mother or her brothers and sister; they had grown up together, they told each other even those things forbidden by the norms of propriety their parents had taught them. Like Gregory, Carmen had fallen in love at the drop of a hat, always with breathtaking passion, but unlike him she was bound by the patriarchal traditions of her family and her society. Her fiery nature was at odds with the double standard that made prisoners of women but granted a hunting license to men. She knew she had to protect her reputation because the least shadow could unleash a tragedy: her father and her brothers watched her like hawks, ready to defend the honor of the house while they themselves tried to do to other girls what they never allowed women of their own blood. Carmen was ungovernable by nature, but at that stage in her life she was still enmeshed in the cobwebs of "what will people say." She feared her father most of all, then the explosive Padre Larraguibel, and then God, in that order— and, last, the evil tongues that could destroy her future. Like so many girls of her generation, she had been raised by the axiom that marriage and motherhood were the perfect destiny—"They got married and had a lot of children and lived happily ever after"—but she could not find a single example of wedded bliss around her, not even her parents; they stayed together because they could not imagine any alternative, but they were light-years from the image of romantic couples in the movies. She had never seen them embrace, and it was rumored that Pedro Morales had a son by another woman. No, that was not what she wanted for herself. She continued to dream, as she had in her childhood, of a different life, a life filled with adventure, but she lacked the courage to make the break and leave home. She knew that people were gossiping behind her back: What is that youngest Morales girl up to? She doesn't have a steady job, she goes out alone at night, she wears too much eye makeup, and isn't that a bracelet she wears on her ankle? And she runs around with Gregory Reeves too much—after all, they're not related. The Moraleses should keep a closer eye on that girl; she's old enough to get married, but it won't be easy to find her a husband when she acts like one of those easy gringas. Carmen had not, nevertheless, lacked for enthusiastic candidates for her hand in marriage. She was barely fifteen when she received her first proposal, and by the time she was nineteen, five young men had desperately wanted to marry her; she loved all of them with a chimerical passion, and after a few weeks, at the first hint of predictable routine, she became bored. About the time Reeves went away she was involved with her first American boyfriend, Tom Clayton—all the others had been Latinos from the neighborhood. Clayton was an ironic, intense newspaperman who dazzled her with his knowledge of the world and his exciting theories about free love and the equality of the sexes, subjects she had never dared broach at home but had discussed extensively with Gregory.

"Empty words! All he wants is to get you to bed and then cut out," her friend reproved her.

"Screw you, Greg, you're nuts! You're farther behind the times than Papa!"

"Has he mentioned marriage?"

"Marriage kills love."

"What doesn't kill it, Carmen, for God's sake!"

"I'm not interested in a church wedding, all in white, Greg. I'm different."

"Just say it: you've already gone to bed with him. . . ."

"No, not yet." Then, after a pause filled with sighs, "How does it feel? Tell me what it feels like."

"Oh, like an electric shock, I guess. The truth is that sex is overrated; all that dreaming about it, and when it's over, you're only half satisfied."

"Liar! If that was how it is, you wouldn't keep panting after every girl you see."

"But, Carmen, that's the trap. You always think it will be better with the next one."

Gregory left in September; the following January, Tom Clayton went to Washington to join the press corps of the most charismatic President of the century, drawn by fascination for his ringing political pronouncements. He wanted to feel the aura of power and play a part in historic events; as he explained it to Carmen, there was no future for an ambitious newsman in the West; it was too far from the heart of empire. He left behind a tearful Carmen, because by then she was in love for the first time; compared to the emotion she was feeling, all her other affairs had been insignificant flirtations. By telephone and in notes spotted with grammatical blunders, she related the day-by-day details of her romantic martyrdom to Gregory, reproaching him not only for having gone away at such a crucial moment but also for having lied about the electric current; had she known, she said, what it was really like, she would not have waited so long.

"It's sad you're so far away, Greg. I don't have anyone to talk to."

"People are more up-to-date here; everyone goes to bed with everyone, and then they discuss it."

"If my parents find out, they'll kill me."

The Moraleses did find out, three months later, when police came to their house to question them.

Tom Clayton had not answered Carmen's letters, and she had no sign he was even alive until some weeks later, when she finally reached him by telephone at an ungodly hour and announced, in a voice choked with panic, that she was pregnant. Clayton was pleasant but unmoved. It wasn't his problem; he was devoting his life to political journalism, and he had to think about his career; there was no way he could come back just then—and besides, he had never uttered the word "matrimony." He believed in spontaneous relationships, and he had supposed that she shared his beliefs. Hadn't they discussed that very subject many times? In any case, he didn't want to see her hurt, he would accept his responsibility; the very next day he would put a check in the mail, and she could resolve that minor inconvenience in the usual manner. Carmen stumbled from the telephone booth and walked in a daze to the nearest café, where she slumped into a chair, at a loss to know what to do. She sat there with her eyes on her cup until they announced closing time. Later, lying on her bed with a mute throbbing in her temples, she decided that her first priority was to keep her condition secret, or her life would be ruined forever. Several times she was at the point of dialing Gregory's number, but she did not want to confess her disgrace even to him. This was her hour of truth, and she must face it alone; it was one thing to talk a big game, making vaguely feminist statements, but something quite different to be an unmarried mother in her corner of the world. She knew that her family would never speak to her again; they would throw her out of the house, out of her clan, even out of the barrio. Her father and her brothers would die of shame; she would have to bring up the baby all by herself, support it and look after it alone, and find some kind of work to survive. Women would repudiate her, and men would treat her like a prostitute. She knew that the child, too, would bear a terrible stigma. She did not have the courage to fight such a long battle—or the courage to make a decision. She argued back and forth for what seemed forever, unable to make up her mind, masking the incapacitating nausea every morning and the drowsiness that paralyzed her every evening, avoiding her family and barely communicating with Gregory, until the day came when she could not button her skirt and she realized the need for urgent action. She called Tom Clayton once again but was told that he was away on a trip and no one knew when he would return. She immediately went to Our Lady of Lourdes, praying the Basque priest would not see her; she knelt at the altar, as she had so many times in her life, but for the first time spoke to the Virgin as woman to woman. For years she had had silent doubts about religion; Sunday mass had become a mere social ritual, but being so frightened, she longed for a renewal of the solace of faith. The statue of the Madonna, robed in silk and crowned with a halo of pearls, did not meet her halfway; the colored-glass eyes in the plaster face stared into empty space.

Carmen explained her reasons for the sin she planned to commit, asked the Virgin's mercy and blessing, and from there went directly to Olga.

"You shouldn't have waited so long," said Olga, palpating Carmen with expert hands. "It's no problem during the first weeks, but now. . . ."

"And it's not a problem now. You have to do it."

"It's very risky."

"I don't care. Please help me," and she burst out weeping hopelessly in Olga's arms.

Olga had known Carmen since she was a child, and the Moraleses were like her own family; she had also lived in the barrio long enough to know what awaited the girl from the minute someone noticed her burgeoning belly. She set an appointment for the next night, prepared her instruments and medicinal herbs, and vigorously rubbed her Buddha, because both she and Carmen were going to need a great deal of luck. Carmen told her parents that she was going to the beach with a friend and would be gone a couple of days, and she moved in with Olga. Nothing remained of the girl's cheerful self-assurance; fear of imminent pain overshadowed any other fears, and she could not consider the possible risks or consequences; all she wanted was to sink into a deep sleep and wake liberated from her nightmare. Despite Olga's potions, however, and the half bottle of whiskey she drank straight down, she did not lose consciousness, and no merciful dream floated her through this crisis. Bound by wrists and ankles to the kitchen table, a rag stuffed in her mouth to prevent her screams from being heard outside, she bore the pain until she could stand no more and made signs that she would prefer anything to this torture. Olga's response was that it was too late for second thoughts; they must follow the brutal procedure to the end. After it was over, Carmen, with an ice pack on her belly, lay weeping uncontrollably, curled in a ball like a baby until she was overcome by exhaustion, the calming herbs, and the alcohol, and fell asleep. Thirty hours later, when she still had not awakened but seemed to be wandering in the delirium of a different world, while a thread of blood, thin but constant, was staining the sheets red, Olga knew that for once her lucky star had failed her. She struggled to lower Carmen's fever and stop the hemorrhaging, but the girl was growing steadily weaker; it was clear her life was draining away. Olga realized she was trapped. Carmen could die beneath her roof, which would mean her ruin; on the other hand, she could not put her out in the street, nor could she advise the family. As she held Carmen's head to force some water down her throat, she thought Carmen murmured Gregory's name, and immediately she realized that he was the only person she could turn to for help. Her call waked him from his sleep. Come this minute, was all she said, but from the tone of her voice Gregory grasped her urgency and asked no questions; he took the first morning plane and within hours was holding Carmen in his arms. He took her by taxi to the nearest hospital, cursing because through all those horrible weeks she had not confided in him. Why did you shut me out? I should have been with you. I told you, Carmen, Tom Clayton is a selfish sonofabitch, but all men aren't like that; not every man wants to bed you and then dump you, the way your father always warned you they would. I swear there are better men than Clayton. Why didn't you let me help you earlier? Maybe the baby would have lived. You shouldn't have gone through this alone. What are friends for? Why are we brother and sister if it isn't to help each other? Life can get so fucked up, Carmen; don't die, please don't die.

While the surgeons were operating, the police, notified by the hospital of the condition in which the patient had arrived, were trying to extract information from Gregory Reeves.

"Let's make a deal," the exasperated officer proposed after three hours of fruitless interrogation. "You tell me who performed the abortion, and I'll let you walk out of here a free man; you won't even be booked. No more questions. Nothing. You'll be free and clear."

"I don't know who did it, I've told you a hundred times. I don't even live here; I came on the morning plane—here's my ticket. My friend called me, and I brought her to the hospital. That's all I know."

"Are you the father?"

"No. I haven't seen Carmen Morales in more than eight months."

"Where did you pick her up?"

"She was waiting at the airport."

"No way! She can't even walk! Tell me where you picked her up, and I'll let you go. Otherwise I'll book you as an accomplice and accessory after the fact."

"That's something you'll have to prove."

And once again the same cycle of questions, answers, threats, and evasions. Finally the police released Gregory and went to the Morales home to question the family. That was how Pedro and Inmaculada found out what had happened, and though they suspected Olga they did not say so, partly because they knew her intentions were good and partly because in the Mexican barrio informing was an unthinkable crime.

"God has punished her, so I won't have to," said Pedro Morales, his voice thickening when he learned of the gravity of his daughter's condition.

Gregory Reeves stayed with his friend until she was out of danger. For three nights he slept upright in a chair at her bedside, waking frequently to be sure she was still breathing. On the fourth morning, Carmen awakened without fever.

"I'm hungry," she announced.

"Thank God!" Gregory smiled and pulled a tin of condensed milk from a bag. Together they slowly drank the thickly sweet liquid, holding hands, as they had so often done as children.

Olga, meantime, had packed her suitcase and flown to Puerto Rico, the farthest place she could think of, telling everyone in the barrio that she was going to try her luck at the Las Vegas casinos because the ghost of an Indian had come and whispered in her ear a system for beating the house at faro. Pedro Morales put on a black armband. Publicly he said a relative had died, at home he made it known that his daughter had never been born and that it was forbidden to mention her name. Inmaculada promised the Virgin she would say a rosary every day for the rest of her life if

She would forgive Carmen's sin; she collected the money she kept hidden beneath a floorboard and, behind her husband's back, went to visit her daughter. She found her in a coarse green hospital gown, sitting in a chair and staring out the window toward the brick wall of the building across the street. She looked so miserable that Inmaculada swallowed her reproaches and her tears and simply put her arms around her daughter. Carmen hid her face in her mother's bosom and, as she was hugged and rocked, breathed in the scent of clean clothes and cooking that always recalled her childhood.

"Take these savings, daughter. It would be best for you to go away for a while, until your father misses you so much that his heart softens. Write me—not at the house but through Nora Reeves. She is the most discreet person I know. Take good care of yourself, and may God be with you. . . ."

"God has forgotten I exist, Mama."

Inmaculada cut her off. "Don't say that, even as a joke! Whatever happens, God loves you . . . and so do I. We will always be beside you, do you understand?"

"Yes, Mama."

When Gregory Reeves first saw Samantha Ernst she was on the tennis court; she was playing, and he was trimming the shrubbery. One of his jobs was supervising the dining room in a women's dormitory across from where he lived. Two cooks prepared the food, and Gregory oversaw a crew of five students who served the meals and washed dishes, a position much to be envied since it gave him free access to the building and to the girls. In his off-hours, he worked as a gardener. Except for cutting grass and pulling weeds, he knew nothing at all about plants when he began, but he had a good teacher, a ferocious-looking but tender-hearted Romanian named Balcescu, who shaved his head and then rubbed his scalp to a rosy glow with a scrap of felt. He spoke a dizzying mélange of languages and loved flowers as he loved himself. In his country he had been a border guard, but the moment the opportunity presented itself, he capitalized on his knowledge of the terrain and escaped; after wandering a long while he had entered the United States from Canada, on foot, with no money, no papers, and two words in English: "money" and "freedom." Convinced that that was what America was all about, he made little effort to enlarge his vocabulary and got along principally through mime. He taught Gregory how to battle worms, whiteflies, slugs, ants, and other enemies of vegetation, and to fertilize, graft, and transplant. More than work, those hours in the open air were a pleasant pastime, and Gregory learned to decipher his boss's instructions by constant exercise of intuition. The day he was trimming the hedge, one of the tennis players caught his eye; he stood watching a few minutes, not so much because of the girl's looks, which off the court might not have warranted a second glance, as for her precision as an athlete. She had firm muscles, quick legs, a long face with aristocratic bones, short hair, and the slightly earth-colored tan of people who are always in the sun. Gregory was attracted by her animal health and agility; he waited until she finished the match and then stationed himself at the gate to the court to wait for her. He could not think what to say, however, and when she walked by with her racket over her shoulder and her skin glistening with sweat, he still could think of nothing clever to say. He followed her far enough to see her get into an expensive sports car. That night, in a tone of studied indifference, he told Timothy Duane about her.

"You wouldn't be so stupid as to fall in love, Greg."

"Of course not. I like her, that's all."

"She doesn't live in the dormitory?"

"I don't think so. I've never seen her there."

"Too bad. For once, the key would have been of some use."

"She doesn't look like a student; she has a red convertible."

"She may be the wife of some executive."

"I don't think she's married."

"Then she's a whore."

"When have you seen whores playing tennis, Tim? They work at night and sleep during the daytime. I don't know how to talk to a girl like that—she's very different from the girls I've known."

"Well, don't talk. Invite her to play tennis."

"I've never had a racket in my hand."

"I can't believe that! What have you been doing all your life?"

"Working."

"What the hell *do* you know how to do, Greg?"

"Dance."

"Then take her out dancing."

"I wouldn't dare."

"Do you want me to talk to her?"

"You stay away from her!" Gregory exclaimed, not wishing to compete with his friend for anyone's favor, especially this woman's.

The next day he spied on her while pretending to work on the shrubs and when she walked by made a move to stop her but again was overcome by shyness. That scene was repeated until finally Balcescu noticed that the shrubs had been trimmed to the nub and decided to intervene before the rest of the landscaping suffered the same fate. His solution was to walk onto the court, interrupt the game with a torrent of words in his Transylvanian tongue, and, when the terrified girl did not obey his urgent gesticulating in the direction of her admirer, who was watching with stupefaction from the other side of the fencing, take her by the arm and, muttering something about money and freedom, lead the greatly confused woman to his assistant. That was how Gregory Reeves found himself face-to-face with Samantha Ernst, who, to escape Balcescu, turned to Gregory with relief; with the approval of the colorful master gardener, they went off together to have a cup of coffee. They took a wobbly table in the most popular café in the city, an overcrowded hole-in-the-wall in a state of constant disrepair where several generations of students had written volumes of poetry and argued every theory known and where many couples, like themselves, had cautiously begun the process of getting to know one another. Gregory had thought he would impress Samantha with his knowledge of literature, but when she seemed distracted he quickly abandoned that tactic and began casting about for common ground. She exhibited no enthusiasm for civil rights or the Cuban revolution; in fact, she seemed to have no opinions about anything, but Gregory confused her passivity with depth of spirit and tightened his clutch on his prey.

Outside of tennis, Samantha Ernst had few interests— although more than the girls in Gregory's high school or the barrio had evidenced. She had thought of becoming an archaeologist; she liked the idea of working in the fresh air in her shorts and exploring exotic places in search of ancient civilizations, but when exposed to the discipline that was required, she had renounced that career. She was not cut out for meticulous classification of crumbling bones and shards of unserviceable pitchers. Then came a few unsettled years that affected many aspects of her life. The daughter of a Hollywood producer, she had grown up in a beautiful house with two swimming pools; her father married four times and lived surrounded by nymphs just out of the cocoon, to whom he promised instant stardom in exchange for small personal favors. Her mother, a Virginia aristocrat with the hauteur of a queen and the prim manners of a governess, stoically endured her husband's philandering with the help of an arsenal of drugs and a variety of credit cards—until the day she looked into the mirror and could not see her own face; it had been eroded by loneliness. They found her floating in the rosy foam of the marble bathtub where she had slit her wrists. Samantha, who by then was sixteen, managed to pass unnoticed in the paternal mansion among the tumult of stepbrothers and stepsisters, ex-wives, current girlfriends, servants, friends, and pedigreed dogs. She continued to swim and play tennis with her usual tenacity, without indulging in useless nostalgia and without ever judging her mother. She did not miss her; they had never been close, and she might have forgotten her completely had it not been for recurrent nightmares of rosy foam. Like so many others, Samantha had come to Berkeley because of its reputation for liberalism; she had had her fill of both the bourgeois etiquette imposed by her mother and her father's revels with ephebes and maidens. Her car stood out among the wrecks driven by other students, and her house—provided by her father—was a bohemian refuge hidden among trees and gigantic ferns and commanding a superb view of the bay. Gregory Reeves was intimidated by Samantha's refinement; he had never known anyone who could master the intricacies of a six-course dinner or determine the authenticity of a cashmere jacket or Persian rug at a glance—except Timothy Duane. Duane, however, made fun of everything, especially cashmere jackets and Persian rugs. The first time Gregory invited Samantha to go dancing, she looked radiant in a low-cut yellow dress and pearl necklace. Feeling ridiculous in the suit Duane had lent him, he knew he would have to take her to a much more expensive place than his budget could afford. Samantha danced badly, listening carefully to the music and counting steps, two, one, two, one, stiff as a broom in her partner's arms. She drank fruit juice, had very little to say, and had a cold and distant air that to Gregory seemed laden with mystery. He clung to his love obstinately and convinced himself that shared tastes and passion were not indispensable requisites for forming a family. For that was exactly his intention, even though he had not yet admitted it in his heart of hearts—much less put it in words. All his life he had wanted to be part of a real family, like the Moraleses, and he was so in love with that dream of domesticity that he was determined to carry it out with the first available woman, without bothering to ask whether she shared the same plans.

Reeves graduated with an honorable mention in literature—his mentor, Cyrus, must have been celebrating in the other world—and then entered law school in San Francisco. The idea of becoming a lawyer had occurred to him first as a form of rebuttal to Timothy Duane's opinion that the nearest thing to a lawyer is a privateer; gradually he was seduced by the idea. As soon as he made up his mind, he called Olga to tell her that she had been wrong in her prediction and, if he had anything to do with it, he was not going to be either a criminal or a policeman. Olga, who had returned from Puerto Rico some time earlier with a new store of divining and medicinal lore, told him that as always she was at least half right, because he would be working with the law—and besides, lawyers were nothing but thieves with a license. Gregory had another reason for continuing his studies: to avoid military service as long as possible. The Vietnam war, which at first seemed an insignificant conflict in a far-off corner of the globe, had taken an alarming turn, and now he took no pleasure in wearing his officer's reserve uniform or participating in war games on weekends. A delay of three or four years, as he worked for his degree, would save him from shipping overseas.

"How do you explain the fierce resistance of those little Oriental runts?" Timothy Duane's tone was bantering. "They can't seem to understand that we are the most crushing military power in history. A blind man could see we're winning. According to our official counts, their losses are so high there can't be any enemies left; any fire from the other side has to be coming from ghosts."

What for Duane was sarcasm, many others held as truth; they were convinced that all that was needed was one final push, and the deceitful enemy would be vanquished once and for all, if not wiped off the face of the planet. That was what the generals kept assuring the public on television while, behind them, cameras panned the rows of body bags containing American soldiers lined up on the landing fields. Hymns, flags, and parades in every city in America. Noise, ash, and confusion in Southeast Asia. A silent list of the names of the dead; no list of those mutilated in body or mind. In street protests, young pacifists burned flags and draft cards. Traitors, Commie fairies, their opponents yelled. Love it or leave it—we don't want you. Police broke up demonstrations with nightsticks and occasional gunfire. Peace and love, man, the hippies crooned, meanwhile handing flowers to uniformed men who aimed rifles at them and dancing in circles, their eyes blurred in a paradise of marijuana, forever smiling with that shocking happiness no one could forgive. Gregory vacillated. He was drawn by the adventure of the war, but he felt an instinctive mistrust of such fervent war fever. Crazy, they're all crazy, Timothy Duane sighed, exempted from military service by a dozen questionable medical certificates detailing a multitude of childhood infirmities.

After a long period of friendship, Gregory's initial passion for Samantha grew into love; her suspicion dissipated, and their relationship settled into the age-old routines and rituals of courtship. They went to the movies and on long rides in the evening air, to concerts and theater; they sat together beneath the trees to study; sometimes they met after Gregory's classes in San Francisco and strolled through Chinatown like two tourists. Reeves's plans were so bourgeois that he dared not reveal them even to Samantha: they would build a house with a rose garden, and while he earned a living as a lawyer she would bake pies and raise the children—all proper and decent. The memory of his family's home-on-wheels during the days his father was still healthy had lingered in his mind as the only happy time of his life. He was convinced that if he was able to reproduce that little tribe he would feel safe and tranquil once again; he dreamed of sitting at the head of a long table with his children and friends, a scene he had witnessed so many times at the Moraleses' home. He thought about them often, because despite poverty and the limitations of the barrio where they lived, they were the best example of family in his experience. In those days of hippie communities and fast food, his secret hope for a patriarchal existence was suspect and better not mentioned aloud. Reality was changing with frightening speed; every day there was less time for the family table; the world was whirling, traditions were being turned upside down, life had become one long hassle, and even the movies—once Gregory's only secure terrain—offered less and less consolation. Cowboys, Indians, chaste lovers, and brave soldiers in spotless uniforms were to be found only in old TV movies interrupted every ten minutes by commercials for deodorant and beer; in the sanctuary of the movie theaters themselves, once a refuge, an oasis of fleeting tranquillity, the greater likelihood now was a blow to the solar plexus. John Wayne, the hardfisted, brave, and solitary hero he had tried unsuccessfully to emulate, had retreated before an onslaught of avant-garde films. Captive in his seat in the audience, he endured

150 · Isabel Allende

Japanese warriors committing hara-kiri on a giant screen, Swedish lesbians in full flower, and extraterrestrial sadists taking over the planet. He could not even enjoy melodramas, because instead of kisses and violins, they ended in depression or suicide.

During the summer vacation, the couple was separated. Samantha went to visit her father, and Gregory divided his time between obligatory military summer camp and politics, working with other students for the advancement of civil rights. Two more diverse realities could not be imagined: rough military training in which blacks and whites were equally subject to the sergeant's orders, and the dangerous assignments in southern states where he worked in black communities, practically going underground to elude groups of white thugs prepared to prevent any thought of racial justice. Those were the days when Black Panthers, with berets, inflammatory rhetoric, and militant marches, were eliciting both fear and fascination. Blacks arrogant about their blackness, blacks dressed in black, with black sunglasses and I-dare-you expressions, occupied the width of the sidewalk; walking elbow-to-elbow with their women—black women with bold, jutting breasts—they no longer stepped aside for white pedestrians, no longer cast their eyes to the ground, no longer lowered their voices. Defiance had replaced timidity and humility. At the end of the summer, the sweethearts came together again, without urgency but with sincere joy, like two good friends. They rarely argued or discussed controversial topics, but neither were they bored; they were comfortable with their silence. Gregory never asked Samantha's opinion or told her about his activities because she seemed not to hear; the effort of communicating his ideas was too great a strain. She was not excited by anything except sports or an occasional innovation introduced from the Orient, such as whirling dervishes or the techniques of Transcendental Meditation. In that area there was much to choose from, because the city offered an infinity of marathon courses for people who wanted to acquire in the space of an easy weekend the hard-won wisdom of the great mystics of India. Reeves had been raised among the Logi and Master Functionaries, he had seen his mother divorce herself from reality and disappear down spiritual paths, and he knew Olga's sorcery: it was not strange that he should mock such disciplines. Samantha lamented his lack of sensitivity but was not offended, nor did she attempt to change him—the task would have been too exhausting. Her energy was very limited, perhaps she was simply lazy, like her cats; in that place and that time it was easy to confuse her abulic temperament with the vogue for Buddhist serenity. She lacked vigor even in lovemaking, but Gregory persisted in calling her coldness timidity and invested all his imagination in their lukewarm courtship, inventing virtues where few existed. He learned to play tennis in order to join his sweetheart in her one passion, even though he detested the game; he never won, and as the match was between only two players, there was no way to dilute defeat by sharing it equally among members of a team. She, on the other hand, made no attempt to pursue any of his interests. On the one occasion when they went to the opera, she fell asleep in the second act, and every time they went dancing they ended up in a bad mood, because she was unable to relax and feel the beat of the music. The same thing happened when they made love; they moved in different tempos and were left with a sensation of emptiness. Neither of the two, however, saw any warnings for the future in those miscounters; instead, they placed the blame on their fear of a pregnancy. Samantha objected to any form of contraception, some for being unaesthetic or uncomfortable and others because she was not inclined to interfere with the delicate balance of her hormones. She cared for her body obsessively; she worked out for hours, drank two liters of water a day, and took nude sunbaths. While Gregory was learning to cook with his friends Joan and Susan, and reading the *Kamasutra* and any erotic manual he could get his hands on, she was nibbling raw vegetables and defending chastity as therapeutic hygiene for the body and discipline for the soul.

Reeves's initial enchantment with the university diminished at the same rate as his Chicano accent. By the time he graduated, he had concluded, like many others, that he had learned more in the street than in the classroom. A university education attempted to prepare students for a productive and docile existence, a project at odds with their increasing rebelliousness. Professors considered themselves more or less exempt from that earthquake; blinded by their petty rivalries and their bureaucracy, they did not perceive the gravity of what was taking place. In four years of study, Gregory had no memorable teachers, despite the fact that many were celebrated scientists and humanists; no one but Cyrus had ever forced him to examine his ideas and to spread his wings in intellectual exploration. He had spent his time looking up pointless information, memorizing facts, and writing papers that no one analyzed. His romantic ideas about student life had been buried under meaningless routine. Even so, he did not want to leave that incredible city, although for practical reasons it would have been easier to live in San Francisco. The People's Republic of Berkeley was by now under his skin; he liked losing himself in streets swarming with swamis in cotton tunics, women with the air of Renaissance ghosts, sages with no ties to this earth, revolutionaries without a revolution, street musicians, preachers, lunatics, peddlers, craftsmen, police, and criminals. A vogue for Indian fashion predominated among the young, who wanted to distance themselves as much as possible from their bourgeois parents. Everything was for sale in the streets and squares: drugs, shirts, records, used books, cheap jewelry. The traffic was a pandemonium of graffiti-covered buses, bicycles, ancient lime-green and watermelon-pink Cadillacs, and the decrepit conveyances of a fleet of taxis that were cheap for ordinary people and free for special people like bums and protesters.

To earn more money, Gregory began baby-sitting; he collected the children after school and entertained them until their parents returned home. He started with five children, but soon the number grew and he was able to resign his jobs as waiter in the girls' dormitory and gardener with Balcescu; he bought a small bus and hired a couple of assistants. He earned more money than any of his classmates, but although the work looked easy from a distance, it was extremely demanding. The children were like sand—from a distance they were identical, when he tried to collect them they escaped through his fingers, and when he wanted to be free of them he could not brush them off—but he was fond of them and actually missed them on weekends. One of the smallest boys had a talent for disappearing; he made such an effort to go unnoticed that he became the one Gregory would never forget. One afternoon he did in fact vanish. Before starting home, Gregory always counted the children, but that day he was late and failed to do so. He followed his usual route, and as he reached the shy child's house he realized in horror that the boy was not on the bus. He turned around and rushed back to the playground, arriving just as it was growing dark. He ran through the park, calling the child at the top of his lungs, while the remaining children, tired and out of sorts, sat sobbing in the bus. Finally Gregory ran to a telephone to ask for help. Fifteen minutes later there was a gathering of several policemen with flashlights and dogs, volunteer searchers, a waiting ambulance—should it be needed—two reporters and a photographer, and fifty or so neighbors and bystanders, watching from beyond ropes.

"You better notify the parents," the officer decided.

"My God! How am I going to tell them?"

"Come on, I'll go with you. These things happen; I've seen everything in my time. The bodies turn up later—I wouldn't describe that—some raped . . . tortured. . . . Too many perverts on the loose. If I had my way, I'd send them all to the gas chamber."

Reeves's knees were like water, and he was on the verge of throwing up. When he reached the house the second time, the door opened and the little cherub stood in the doorway, his face smeared with peanut butter. He said he had been bored and decided to go home and watch television. His mother was not back from work yet and never suspected that her son had been reported missing. From that day on, Gregory's slippery charge was restrained by a rope tied around his waist, just like the cord that bound Inmaculada Morales's daft mother-in-law, to both prevent a repetition of the problem and quash any flowering of independence among the other children. Great idea! So what does it matter if they have to pay a psychiatrist later to treat them for a puppy-dog complex, Carmen commented when Gregory called to report his solution.

Joan and Susan moved to an old, run-down, but still structurally sound mansion, where they opened a vegetarian and macrobiotic restaurant that came to be considered the best in the city. A colony of hippies moved into their former house. First there were two couples and their children, but that number rapidly multiplied; the doors were open to welcome anyone who wanted to find refuge in their oasis of drugs, crafts, yoga, Eastern music, free love, and communal kitchen. Timothy Duane could not tolerate the disruption, confusion, and filth, and he rented an apartment in San Francisco, where he was studying medicine. He offered to share it, but Reeves was still reluctant to leave the attic, even though he, too, was attending classes in the city across the bay and was fed up with the hippies. It annoyed him to come home and find strangers in his room, he detested the monotonous music of drums, whistles, and flutes, and his hackles rose every time his personal belongings disappeared. The flower children would smile benignly when he came raging downstairs to reclaim his shirts: Peace and love, man. He almost always retreated with his tail between his legs to the last private corner of his room, without his possession and with a feeling of being a rotten capitalist. Berkeley had become a center for drugs and rebellion; every day new nomads poured in, searching for paradise. They came riding roaring motorcycles, driving broken-down cars, and in buses fitted out as temporary homes; they camped in the public parks, gently made love in the streets, and lived on air, music, and grass. The odor of marijuana predominated over any other. There were two revolutions in progress: one of hippies, who wanted to change the laws of the universe with Sanskrit prayers, flowers, and kisses, and a second of iconoclasts who meant to change the laws of the nation with protests, yelling, and rocks. The second was more in line with Gregory's nature, but he did not have time to participate and he lost his enthusiasm for street skirmishes when he realized they had become a way of life, a common pastime. He stopped feeling guilty to be studying instead of bedeviling the police, he believed that his unsung efforts during the summer, going house to house to register southern blacks to vote, were more valuable. When there were no civil rights protests, there were marches against the war in Vietnam; it was a rare day without some public altercation. The police used military tactics and combat units to maintain an illusion of order. Among those horrified by the promiscuity, chaos, and contempt for private property, a counteroffensive was organized to preserve the values of the Founding Fathers. A chorus of voices rose in defense of the sacred American Way of Life: They are tearing down the pillars of Western Christian civilization! This nation will end up a Communist and psychedelic Sodom and Gomorrah, that's all these misfits want! Blacks and hippies are ripping the guts out of our system! Timothy Duane parodied perfectly his father and other gentlemen at the club. They were not the only ones to place all the dissidents in one package: the press tended to fall into the same trap of oversimplification, even though the most superficial examination revealed significant differences. The cause of civil rights was growing stronger in direct ratio to the disintegration of the hippie movement. The revolution against racism advanced powerfully and inexorably, while the flower revolution was a pipe dream. The hippies, tripped out on hallucinogenic mushrooms, grass, sex, and rock, gave little heed to their own weaknesses and to the strength of their detractors; they believed that humanity had moved onto a higher plane and that nothing would ever be the same again. We should never underestimate human stupidity, Duane said with conviction. A few loonies may run around kissing each other and tattooing doves on their chests, but I can assure you no trace will remain of them; they will be swallowed up by history. In the friends' late-night conversations, he always sounded the skeptical note, convinced that mediocrity would in the end defeat the great ideals and that therefore no one should consume any energy getting excited about the Age of Aquarius, or any other age. He maintained that it was a waste of Gregory's time to spend his summer registering blacks, because they would not bother to vote or else would vote Republican. Every time, however, there was an effort to raise funds for civil rights campaigns, Duane managed to wheedle a four-figure check from his mother. He defended feminism as a magnificent concept that released him from paying the woman's share on a date—and incidentally might lead to a cost-free evening in bed—but in fact he never took advantage of such opportunities. He had a cynicism that both shocked and amused Gregory.

Freedom and money, money and freedom, was Balcescu's continuing enigmatic preachment. By then he had acquired a slightly more extensive vocabulary in English, had added a mandarin's pigtail to his shaved skull, dressed like a feudal Russian peasant, and among his plants taught his brand of philosophy to a small clique of followers. Duane attributed Balcescu's success to the fact that no one understood anything he was saying and to his extraordinary skill in cultivating bathtubs of marijuana and flowerpots of magic mushrooms. The Romanian had a small LSD laboratory in his garage, a flourishing business that in a relatively short time made him a rich man. Although Gregory had not worked with him for years, they had remained good friends, a relationship based on love of roses and the pleasures of the table. Balcescu had a natural instinct for inventing garlic-based dishes to which he gave unpronounceable names, presenting them as the typical cuisine of his country. He taught Gregory to cultivate roses in wine barrels so he could take them with him in case he moved or left the country.

"I'm not thinking of leaving." Gregory laughed.

"You never know. Without freedom, without money, what's to do? Emigrate." Balcescu sighed with a pathetic expression of nostalgia.

Samantha Ernst studied literature in her spare time, after her workouts and her sports. She had never held a job and never would. Her father had recently been ruined financially by producing a high-budget film on the Byzantine Empire that was such a monumental fiasco it destroyed his own empire in less time than it takes to tell. Like all her stepbrothers, stepsisters, and stepmothers, who until then had profited from the producer's generosity,

Samantha was forced for the first time to provide for herself; she never suffered any real want, however, because Gregory Reeves was there. They had planned to be married after he completed law school and found a good job, but the magnate's ruin precipitated events and they had to set the wedding forward a couple of years. They were married in a ceremony so private it seemed secret, with Timothy Duane and Samantha's tennis instructor as the only witnesses; after the wedding they called relatives and friends with the news. Gregory visited Nora and Judy Reeves once a year, at Thanksgiving time; they were semiestranged, and the mother and sister were not surprised not to be invited to the wedding, but the Moraleses were deeply offended and for a while stopped speaking to their "gringo son," as they called him—until Margaret's birth softened their hearts and they forgave him. Gregory moved his belongings into Samantha's house, including the wine barrels of roses, prepared to begin his dream of the perfect family. Married life was not as idyllic as he had imagined; marriage resolved none of the problems of courtship, it merely added new ones, but he did not lose hope and looked forward to better times once he received his law degree, found a normal job, and had fewer pressures. His baby-sitting enterprise provided enough money for his wife's comfort, although he could not share any of the benefits. His schedule had deteriorated into a veritable marathon. He rose at dawn to do his chores, then traveled one hour to class. In the afternoon he took his charges to museums, parks, and entertainments, keeping one eye on them and another on his books. Once a week he went to the laundromat and the market; many nights he earned a few dollars helping Joan and Susan in their restaurant. By the end of the day he arrived home exhausted; he usually put some meat on the grill and ate while he continued to study. Samantha was revolted by the sight of raw meat and nauseated by the smell of it cooking, so she preferred not to be around at dinnertime. Their schedules never meshed anyway; she slept till noon, began her activities in the afternoon, and always had some class at night: African drums, yoga, Cambodian dance. While her husband outdid himself to meet all his obligations, she seemed perpetually confused, as if mere existence were a major challenge to her elusive nature. Conjugal life did nothing to increase her interest in games of love, and she continued to be as indifferent as ever in bed—with the added aggravation that now they had more opportunities to be together and fewer excuses for her coldness. Gregory tried to follow the advice in his manuals, even though he felt ridiculous performing the erotic gymnastics Samantha seemed not to appreciate anyway. Mulling over the meager results of his efforts, Gregory came to the conclusion that with the happy exception of Ernestina Pereda, women had no great enthusiasm for lovemaking. He was ignoring countless publications that proved the contrary, and as the Western world acknowledged an outburst of female libidos, he substituted patience for passion, although he never completely abandoned the hope that gradually he could lead Samantha into the sinful gardens of lust, which was how Duane, with his tormented Catholic conscience, referred to pure and simple sexual diligence.

When Samantha discovered she was pregnant, she was totally demoralized. She felt that her tanned body, which had never known a gram of excess fat, had become a loathsome receptacle housing a rapidly growing, gluttonous tadpole that she could not imagine had any connection with her. During those first weeks she wore herself out doing the most violent exercises in her repertory, subsconsciously hoping to be liberated from pernicious servitude, but then she was felled by exhaustion and did nothing but lie in bed staring at the ceiling, devoid of hope and furious with Gregory, who seemed enchanted by the idea of a child and responded to her complaints with sentimental platitudes—absolutely inappropriate behavior, as Samantha never failed to tell him, given the circumstances. It's your fault, all your fault, she reproached him. I don't want children, at least not yet. You're the one who's always talking about having a family—God knows where you got such a stupid idea—and from talking so much about it, now it's happened. Damn you! She could not believe her bad luck; she had assumed she was barren, because in years of not taking precautions she had never been caught. She kept repeating to herself, like a spoiled child who always got her own way, If I don't want it, it won't happen. She suffered attacks of nausea brought on more by her revulsion toward herself and rejection of the baby than by her pregnancy. Gregory bought a natural foods cookbook and asked Joan and Susan to advise him how to prepare healthful meals, an empty exercise since Samantha seemed barely able to tolerate a stalk of celery or a slice of apple. Three months later, when she could see the changes in her waistline and breasts, she abandoned herself to her fate with a kind of rabid dedication. Her lack of appetite turned to voraciousness, and contrary to all her vegetarian principles, she methodically devoured greasy pork chops and sausages that Gregory cooked at night and she nibbled cold all day long. One night while eating with a group of friends at a Spanish restaurant, she discovered the special of the day, *callos a la madrileña,* a concoction of tripe with the consistency of a wet towel soaked in tomato sauce. She went so often at odd hours to order the same dish that the chef took a liking to her and gifted her with plastic containers running over with his insalubrious stew. She gained weight and broke out in welts, she suffered severe depression, she felt ill and guilty, poisoned by putrid food and animal cadavers, but as if accepting some form of punishment, she could not stop eating. She slept too much and the rest of the time watched television from her bed, surrounded by her cats. Reeves, who was allergic to cat hair, moved to a different room, without ever losing his good humor or his patience. He would smile to himself and say, She'll get over it; she gets these whims because she's pregnant. Even though Samantha despised housework, her house had once been presentable; now relative order had turned to chaos. Gregory tried to do some cleaning, but however much he tried, the odor of cat urine and Spanish tripe permeated the house.

That was the year the aquatic childbirth technique came into vogue, an original combination of breathing exercises, balms, Eastern meditation, and common, everyday water. Some training was necessary if one was to accomplish a delivery in a bathtub, supported by the baby's father and accompanied by friends and anyone else who wanted to participate; the baby was ushered into the world without the trauma of being ejected from the warm, silent, liquid ambience of the maternal womb into the horror of a delivery room blazing with lights and bristling with surgical instruments. It was not a bad concept but in practice was rather complicated. Samantha had refused even to discuss the subject of the birth, faithful to her theory that if she did not want something it would not happen, but toward the seventh month she had no choice but to face reality because within a finite period of time the baby would be born and she, inevitably, would play a role in the event. To give birth in a warm tub under soft light, assisted by a pair of beatific midwives, seemed less threatening than the same process carried out on a hospital table, given into the hands of an aproned and masked man no one could recognize; she was not agreeable, however, to turning the moment into a social event— despite the midwives' promises that she needn't worry about anything and the price included drinks, marijuana, music, and photographs. We were married in private, so why would I have the baby in public? And I certainly don't want anyone taking my picture with my legs spread apart. Samantha's mind was made up, putting an end to the dilemma of her nonparticipation. She got up from her bed and began attending the classes with Gregory; there she saw other women in the same condition and discovered that pregnancy is not necessarily a disgrace. She noticed with surprise that other women seemed content and even exhibited their bellies with pride. That had a healthy effect; she partially regained respect for her body and determined to take care of herself; she did not forgo the tripe *a la madrileña,* but she did add vegetables and fruit to her diet, take long walks, and rub almond oil and sage-and-mint lotion into her skin. She bought clothes for the baby and for a few weeks seemed her old self. The extensive preparations for the delivery included installation of an enormous wood tub in the living room; in principle it could be rented, but they were persuaded to buy it. After the baby was born it could be used in other ways, they were told; this was also the time when friends were beginning to sit naked in large tubs to enjoy a communal soak in steaming hot water. The purchase turned out to have been for naught, however, because five weeks before the baby was due, Samantha gave birth to a girl; they named her Margaret, after the maternal grandmother who died in the rosy foam. Gregory had come home one evening to find his wife sitting in a puddle of amniotic fluid, so befuddled it had not occurred to her to call for help, to say nothing of practicing the seal breathing she had learned in the childbirth courses. Gregory helped her into the bus he used for his work and sped to the hospital, where a caesarean was performed to save the baby. Margaret did not enter the world in a wood tub, lulled by soporific chants and clouds of incense, but prematurely began life in an incubator, a pitiable, solitary fish in an aquarium. It was two days later, as Samantha was taking her first tentative steps down the hospital corridor, that Gregory remembered to call the spiritual midwives, relatives, and friends to tell them the news. He regretted that Carmen had not been by his side, the only person with whom he would have wanted to share the trials of those moments.

For Samantha Ernst, the wind of disaster had begun to blow on the very day of her birth, when her aristocratic mother had placed her in the hands of a nurse and forever renounced responsibility for her, and the moment her own daughter was born, that wind had turned into a hurricane that swept Samantha beyond the bounds of reality. Much later she would confess to her analyst, with absolute sincerity, that the only feeling she had for the tiny creature gasping for breath in the glass cage was denial. Secretly she was grateful she did not have milk to nurse the infant and was not obliged to hold her in her arms. Nothing she had learned during the courses was of any use to her; she was never able to accept her daughter, dismissing her as one more baby girl among the thousands born on the planet at that hour of that day. Nor could she absorb the idea that she had the basic care of that tiny wormlike creature. She looked at herself in the mirror and saw a long incision across her belly, once smooth and tanned and now flabby and covered with stretch marks, and she wept inconsolably for her lost beauty. Her husband tried to comfort her, but every time he came near she repulsed him with undisguised venom. She'll get used to it, it's all very new, she's upset, Gregory thought, but after three weeks, when they were ready to release the infant from the hospital and the mother had not stopped examining herself in the mirror and sobbing, he had to ask his sister for help. Perhaps his mother would have been the logical person in a crisis of that nature, but Samantha could not bear her mother-in-law; she had never perceived any of her virtues and thought of her as a weird old woman who would drive a turtle out of its mind. Gregory also thought of Olga, who truly enjoyed babies and bringing them into the world, but he knew that if his wife could not tolerate Nora, she would have even less patience with Olga.

Gregory called Judy and pleaded with her. "I need your help. Samantha is depressed and ill, and I don't know anything about babies. Please come."

"I'll ask for the day off Friday and spend the weekend with you, but that's all I can do," she replied.

Weary of the drunken sprees of the gigantic redhead Jim Morgan, by whom she had two children, Judy had divorced him and gone back to live with her mother in the old cottage. Nora looked after the two grandchildren, one of whom was still a babe in arms, while Judy supported the family. Jim Morgan loved his wife and would love her till the day he died, regardless of the fact that she had become a harpy who chased him screaming through the house, stood at the door of the factory to insult him before his workers, and prowled the bars looking for him in order to create a scene. When she threw him out of the house once and for all and filed for divorce, he felt as if his life were over; he had gone on a monumental bender from which he awakened behind bars. He could not explain how the tragedy had occurred; he did not even remember the person he had killed. Some witnesses said it was an accident, that Morgan had not meant to kill the man—he had polished off his hapless victim with one punch—but the circumstances did not favor the accused. The victim was, by all lights, a sober, mild-mannered featherweight who when the altercation began was standing on a corner ringing a bell for the Salvation Army. Once in prison, Jim Morgan could not contribute to the children's support, but Judy was happy with that, convinced that the less contact her children had with a criminal father, the better it would be for them. Since she did not make enough money to live in her own house, she went back to live with her mother.

When Gregory met his sister at the airport, he was shocked to see how much weight she had gained. He could not hide his feelings, and she noticed immediately.

"Don't say anything. I know what you're thinking."

"You need to go on a diet, Judy!"

"That's easy to say; and the proof of that is how often I've done it. I must have lost two thousand pounds in all."

With difficulty she climbed into Gregory's bus, and they drove to the hospital to pick up Margaret. They were handed a small bundle wrapped in a shawl, so light they looked inside to be sure she was there. Among the folds of wool they found a tiny infant, calmly sleeping. Judy bent down to her niece and began to kiss and nuzzle her like a bitch with her whelp, transfigured by a tenderness Gregory had not seen in decades but had not forgotten. All the way home, she talked to Margaret and petted her, while Gregory observed from the corner of his eye, amazed at Judy's transfiguration: the unsightly layers of fat disappeared, revealing the radiant hidden beauty below. At home they found the cats sleeping in the cradle and Samantha in her room standing on her head, seeking relief from her emotional anxiety in a fakir's acrobatics. Gregory shook the cat hair from the baby's bedding while Judy, short-tempered from the trip and from hours on her feet, jolted her sister-in-law from nirvana with one shove, turning her right side up and returning her to the hard facts of reality.

"Come let me show you how to sterilize the bottles and change the baby's diapers," she commanded.

"You'll have to explain it to Greg. I'm not any good at those things," Samantha stammered, retreating.

"It's better if he doesn't spend too much time with the baby;

you don't want the same shit from him I got from my father," Judy grumbled testily.

"What are you talking about?" asked Gregory, who was holding the child.

"You know damn well what I'm talking about. I'm not a cretin; do you think I haven't noticed that you always have kids around?"

"Kids are my job!"

"Your job, sure. Of all possible jobs, you had to choose that one. I wonder why. I bet you look after little girls too, don't you? All men are perverts!"

Gregory deposited Margaret on the bed, took his sister roughly by one arm, and dragged her into the kitchen, closing the door behind them.

"Now you're going to explain what the fuck you mean!"

"You have an amazing ability to play dumb, Gregory. I can't believe you don't know. . . ."

"I *don't* know!"

And then the venom spilled from Judy, all that she had borne in silence from that night over twenty years before when she had not let Gregory crawl into her sleeping bag, the secret zealously guarded with the fear it was not a mystery and that everyone knew, the hidden theme of all her bad dreams and rancor, the unspeakable shame that she was exposing now only to protect her niece—an innocent baby, she said—to prevent the sin of incest from happening again in the family, because those things are in the blood, they're genetic curses, what a black day it was when that piece of garbage brought us into the world, he was a filthy, sinful lecher, and if you need more details I can give them to you, because I remember everything, it's burned into my memory, if you want me to I'll tell you how he got me into the shed with a hundred excuses and made me open his fly and he put it in my hands and told me it was my doll baby, my sugar candy, to do it like that, like that, more, until—".

"That's enough!" screamed Gregory, clapping his hands over his ears.

· · ·

Every Monday morning Gregory Reeves called Carmen Morales, something they do to this day. After the abortion that nearly cost her her life, Carmen had told her mother goodbye and disappeared without a trace. Her name was never spoken in the Morales house, but no one forgot her, least of all her father, who quietly dreamed about her but was too proud to admit he was dying of pain for his absent daughter. She did not communicate again with her family, but two months later Gregory received a postcard from Mexico with a telephone number and the drawing of a small flower, Carmen's unmistakable signature. He was the only one to have news of her during that period, and through him Inmaculada Morales learned what her daughter was doing. In their brief Monday conversations, the two friends kept up-to-date about their lives and plans. Their voices were distorted by static and by the strain of talking long-distance; it was difficult to communicate in interrupted sentences, and their memories of each other began to dim: they were as if blind, with their hands outstretched in the darkness. Carmen had rented a sordid room on the outskirts of Mexico City and was working in a silver workshop. She spent so many hours traveling by bus across that huge accursed city that she had no time for anything else. She had no friends or lovers. The disillusion she had experienced at the hands of Tom Clayton had destroyed her ingenuous tendency to fall in love at first sight, and besides, being where she was, it was nearly impossible to find someone who would understand and accept her natural independence. Her father's and her brothers' machismo was pale compared to what she was encountering, and, prudently, she settled for solitude as the lesser evil. Because of Olga's unfortunate procedure and the subsequent operation, she would never be able to have children; she was freer than before, but also sadder. She lived on the implicit boundary where the official city ended and the inadmissible world of the marginal began. The building she occupied consisted of a narrow passageway with a row of rooms on either side, a couple of water taps, a trough for laundry in the center, and communal bathrooms in the rear—always so filthy she tried to avoid using them. It was a more violent place than the ghetto where she had grown up: people had to fight for their minuscule space, and there were many quarrels and few hopes; she was in a nightmare world, unknown to tourists, a terrible labyrinth ringing the beautiful city founded by the Aztecs, an enormous conglomerate of wretched shacks and unpaved and unlighted streets suffocating in garbage that stretched toward an endless horizon. She walked among downtrodden Indians and indigent mestizos, naked children and starving dogs, women bowed by the weight of pregnancies and drudgery, idle men resigned to their fate but with a hand on the grip of a dagger, ready to defend their eternally threatened dignity and manhood. Now she could not count on the protection of her family and soon realized that as a young woman living alone she was a rabbit surrounded by a pack of hounds. She never went out at night; she slept with a bar across her door, another over the window, and a butcher knife beneath her pillow. When she went out to wash her clothes, the other women stared at her with distrust because she was different. They called her "gringa," in spite of her having explained a thousand times that her family was from Zacatecas. Men she never spoke to at all. Sometimes she bought candy and sat in the alley, waiting for children to gather around her; those were her few happy moments. In the workshop she sat beside silent Indians with magic hands, who rarely spoke to her but taught her the secret of their art. The hours raced by unnoticed; she was absorbed in the laborious process of modeling the wax, pouring the metals, engraving, polishing, mounting the stones, and assembling each minute piece. At night she designed earrings, rings, and bracelets in her room; first she practiced with tin and pieces of glass; later, when she had saved a little money, she used silver and semiprecious stones. In her free hours she sold the pieces door-to-door, taking care that her employers never learned of their modest competition.

The birth of her daughter had launched Samantha Ernst into a quiet but fierce depression; there were no scandalous rages or dramatic changes in behavior, but she was not the same. She continued to get up at noon, watch television, and lie in the sun like a lizard, without resisting reality but also without participating in it. She ate very little, was always sleepy, and came to life only on the tennis court, while Margaret vegetated in a carriage in the shade, so forsaken that at eight months she still could not sit up and hardly ever smiled. The only time her mother touched her was to change her diapers and put the bottle in her mouth. At night Gregory bathed her and sometimes rocked her, trying always to do it in Samantha's presence. He loved the baby very much and when he held her in his arms felt a painful tenderness, an overpowering desire to protect her, but he did not feel free to cuddle her as he would have liked. His sister's confession had raised a Wall of China between his daughter and himself. He felt equally uncomfortable with the children in his charge and found that he was examining everything he did in the light of a possible licentiousness inherited from his father. When he compared Margaret to other babies her age, he saw she was slow in developing; something was obviously wrong, but he did not want to share his doubts with his wife for fear of frightening her and distancing her even more from her daughter. He performed little tests to see whether Margaret could hear; he thought she might be deaf, which would explain why she seemed so quiet, but when he clapped his hands near the cradle, she jumped. He thought Samantha had not noticed anything, but one day she asked him how you know when an infant is retarded; for the first time, he could speak of his fears. After a thorough examination, Margaret was diagnosed as being healthy but in definite need of stimulation; she was like an animal in a cage, suffering from sensory deprivation. The parents took a course in which they learned how to express affection toward their daughter, how to gurgle at her, how little by little to focus her attention on the world around her, and other elemental skills any orangutan is born knowing but they had to learn from an instruction manual. The results were evident within a few weeks, when the child began to crawl, and a year later she spoke her first two words—not "papa" and "mama" but "cat" and "tennis."

Gregory was studying for final examinations, hours, days, months spent buried in his books and thanking his lucky stars for his good memory, the only thing left functioning while around him everything else seemed rapidly to be falling apart. Far from being over, as he had calculated it would be, the war in Vietnam was reaching the proportions of catastrophe. Along with relief at finally passing the bar came the inevitable nightmare of going overseas, for he could not continue to postpone his obligatory service with the army. His family was his principal worry; his relationship with Samantha was stumbling along, and a separation would undoubtedly mean the end to it; in addition, he was afraid to leave Margaret, who was developing into a very strange child. She was so quiet and secretive that sometimes Samantha forgot about her and when Gregory came home at night he found she had not eaten since breakfast. She did not play with other children but entertained herself for hours watching soap operas on television; she was never hungry, and she washed herself obsessively, pulling a footstool up to the basin to soap her hands over and over, saying, Dirty, dirty. She wet her bed and wept disconsolately when she waked to the clammy sheets. She was very pretty and would stay pretty even after the offenses she later committed against her body: she had the grace of her Virginia grandmother and the exotic Slavic face of Nora Reeves, as she looked in a photograph taken on the refugee ship that brought her from Odessa. While Margaret hovered in the shadow of the furniture and in dark corners, her parents, busy with their own affairs and deceived by the good-little-girl facade, failed to see the demons gestating in her soul.

It was a time of great changes and continuing surprises. The novelty of free love, for so many years kept under lock and key, spread rapidly, and what had begun as another hippie fantasy became the favorite parlor game of the bourgeoisie. Astonished, Gregory observed people who only shortly before had defended the most puritanical ideas now practicing libertinism in homey, private orgies. In his bachelor days, it had been almost impossible to find a girl who wanted to make love without a promise of marriage: pleasure without sin or fear was unthinkable before the pill. He seemed to remember devoting the first ten years of his youth to finding women; all his determination and inventiveness had gone into that exhausting chase—and often in vain. Suddenly things had turned around, and in a matter of a year or two chastity ceased to be a virtue and became a defect demanding treatment before the neighbors found out. It was such an abrupt reversal that Gregory, enveloped in his problems, did not have time to adapt and was not touched by the revolution until much later. Despite his failure with Samantha, it never occurred to him to capitalize on the hints boldly thrown his way by some of the girls he studied with and by mothers of his charges.

One Saturday in spring the Reeveses were invited to dinner at the home of some friends. Sit-down dinners were no longer in style; the meal was waiting in the kitchen, and the guests served themselves on paper plates and tried to find a place to sit while balancing a full glass, a dripping plate, bread, napkin, and sometimes a cigarette. Everyone was drinking too much, and some were smoking marijuana. Gregory had had a hard day; he was tired and wondered whether he would not have been better off at home than trying to cut a piece of chicken on his knees without throwing it all over himself. After dessert there was a general move to shed clothes and step into a large hot tub in the moonlit garden. The vogue for the Laboyer birth method had passed without much flurry, and many families had been left with an outsize tub as a remembrance. The Reeveses still had theirs in the living room and used it as a playpen for Margaret and as a place to throw the odds and ends that collected on the floor. More daring tub owners had converted these artifacts into a conversation piece inspired by communal baths in Japan, until an industry sprang up in manufacturing large tubs specifically for that purpose. Gregory was not tempted to go outside to freeze on the patio just after eating, but it seemed bad manners to remain dressed when everyone else was in the buff, and furthermore he did not want to give the impression he had something to be ashamed of. So he took off his clothes, all the while watching Samantha from the corner of his eye, amazed at his wife's naturalness in exposing herself. She was not a prudish woman, she was proud of her body and often went about naked at home, but this public exhibition made him a little nervous; on the other hand, everyone else seemed as comfortable as any aborigine from the Amazon basin. The women generally tried to stay submerged, but the men seized every opportunity to show off; the most arrogant offered the spectacle of their nakedness while they served drinks, lighted cigarettes, or changed records; some even knelt at tubside inches from the face of someone else's wife. Gregory realized this was not the first time his friends had practiced the sport, and he felt betrayed, as if everyone were sharing a secret he had purposely been excluded from. He also suspected that Samantha had attended such parties previously and not felt it necessary to tell him. He tried not to stare at the women, but his eyes kept drifting to the perfect breasts of the host's mother, a sixtyish matron he had not noticed before the watery revelation of attributes unexpected in a woman her age. In a restless lifetime, Reeves would travel the maps of so many female geographies that it would be impossible to remember them all, but he never forgot that grandmother's breasts. Meanwhile, Samantha, with her eyes closed and her head thrown back, more relaxed and content than her husband had ever seen her, was humming happily, a glass of white wine in one hand and the other beneath the water, suspiciously close to Timothy Duane's leg. On the way home, Gregory wanted to talk about the evening, but she fell asleep in the car. The next morning, as they sat before a cup of steaming coffee in the sunlit kitchen, the nudist party seemed like a distant dream, and neither of them mentioned it. After that night, Samantha took advantage of any opportunity to enjoy new group experiences; in contrast, in the privacy of the marriage bed she was as cold as ever. Why deprive ourselves? the evangelists of open marriage were preaching. We should add experiences to life, not subtract them; we emerge the richer from every encounter and therefore have more to offer to our spouse; love is big enough to go around; pleasure is a bottomless well from which we may drink our fill. Gregory suspected there was a flaw in this reasoning but did not dare to manifest his doubts for fear of sounding like a cave dweller. He felt as if he were in a foreign country; he was not convinced of the benefits of promiscuity, and as he watched his friends' enthusiastic acceptance he told himself that he was held back by his background in the barrio, and that was why he could not adapt. He did not like to admit how much it bothered him to see other men touching Samantha's body under a variety of excuses: detoxifying massages, activation of holistic points, and stimulation of spiritual growth through bodily communication. Samantha mystified him; she must be concealing certain aspects of her personality from him and living a secret life. She never showed him her true face but, rather, assumed a succession of masks. He thought it was perverse to fondle another woman in the presence of one's wife, but, again, he did not want to be left behind. Every week trendy sexologists discovered new erogenous zones, and apparently they must all be explored if one was not to be thought ignorant; manuals piled up on Gregory's night table, awaiting their turn to be studied. Once, he dared object to a method for exploring the Self and awakening Consciousness through collective masturbation, and Samantha accused him of being a barbarian, an unawakened and primitive soul.

"I don't know what the quality of my soul has to do with the perfectly natural fact that I don't like to see other men's hands between your legs!"

"A typical remark of an underdeveloped foreign culture," Samantha retorted, impassively sipping her celery juice.

"How is that?" he asked, nonplussed.

"You're like those Latinos you grew up with. You should have stayed in the barrio."

Gregory thought of Pedro and Inmaculada Morales and tried to imagine them naked in a hot tub with their neighbors, mutually groping for Self and Consciousness. The mere idea vented his rage, and he burst out laughing. The next Monday he told Carmen, and across two thousand miles heard his friend's uncontrollable laughter; no, no such modern innovations had reached the ghetto in Los Angeles, much less Mexico, where she was living.

172 · Isabel Allende

"Crazy, they're all crazy," was Carmen's assessment. "There's no way you would catch me parading naked in front of someone else's husband. I wouldn't know where to look, Greg. Besides, if men try things when I have my clothes on, imagine what would happen without them!"

"Don't be too optimistic, Carmen. No one would give you a second glance."

"Then why do they do it?"

I did not feel at home anywhere; the barrio where I had grown up belonged to the past, and I had never put down roots anywhere else. There was very little left of my family; my wife and daughter were as cool to me as my mother and sister had been. And I missed my friends. Carmen was on another planet; I couldn't really count on Timothy, because Samantha bored him, and I think he tried to avoid us; even Balcescu—always so close to being a caricature that he was nearly impervious to change—had done a turnabout and evolved into a kind of holy man. He lived in the midst of acolytes who worshiped the air he breathed, and from seeing himself reflected in the mirror of those adoring eyes, my bizarre Romanian had come to take himself seriously. Along with his sense of humor, he seemed to have lost interest in inventing exotic dishes and cultivating roses; we had very little in common anymore. Joan and Susan were as delightful as ever, with the delicious scent of herbs and spices still clinging to their skin, but all their time was devoted to their causes: the feminist struggle and the culinary chemistry of their vegetarian recipes—they were expert in disguising tofu so that it tasted like kidney pie. I hadn't made any friends in law school. We were fiercely competitive, all of us absorbed in our own plans and ambitions, our eyes glued to our books. I had lost my taste for meetings and had even shoved my political and intellectual interests into the background. It would have been difficult to explain to Cyrus that where I was, the only problem that confronted the left was that no one wanted to occupy the right. When I went home at night I was bone tired; on the way I would toy with the possibility of taking a detour and

wandering off toward the horizon, like my father when we were
traveling the country without a fixed itinerary or destination. The
chaos of the house got on my nerves—and I'm not a fanatic for
order, to say the least. I suppose I was drained by studying and
work; I have little doubt I was not acting like a good husband and
that was why Samantha put forth so little effort. At times we
seemed more like adversaries than allies. In such circumstances
you become blind, you don't see any way to get out of the dead-
end street you're on, you think you're stuck forever in the same
meat grinder and that there's no escape. When you get your
degree, it'll be different, Carmen would console me long-distance,
but I knew the degree alone would not cure my problems. I faithfully watched a television serial about a clever lawyer who regularly gambled his reputation, and sometimes his life, to save an
innocent man from jail or to punish a guilty one. I never missed a
program, hoping that the protagonist would restore my enthusiasm for the law and rescue me from the terrible boredom it
inspired. I had not begun to practice, and I was already disillusioned. The future looked very different from the adventure I had
imagined in my youth; the last push to finish the race was so
tedious that I began to talk about giving up law school and devoting myself to something different. Boredom, Timothy Duane
assured me, is nothing more than anger without passion. According to him, I was angry with the world and with myself, and not
without reason: my life had not been a bed of roses. He advised
me to get rid of complications—beginning with my marriage to
Samantha, which he considered an obvious mistake. I refused to
admit it, but nonetheless a moment came when at least in that
regard I had to admit he was right. It was at a party like so many
we went to during those days, in a house like any other house—
broken-down furniture, Indian rugs covering the stains on the
sofa, posters of Ho Chi Minh and Che Guevara alongside embroidered mandalas from India, the same couples, the men not wearing socks and the women not wearing bras, cold food and pieces
of cheese growing more rancid as the hours went by, too much to
drink, cigarettes and such poor-grade marijuana that the smoke

drove away mosquitoes. The same interminable conversations as well: the latest seminars on the primal scream, in which people yelled to rid themselves of aggression; or the return to the womb, in which the naked participants assumed the fetal position and sucked their thumb. I never understood those therapies and never tried them; I was sick of the subject, sick of hearing about the multiple transcendental changes in the life of everyone I knew. I walked out to the terrace to drink alone. I admit I was drinking more every day. I had given up liquor because it triggered my allergies and, between swollen mucous membranes and a terrible tightness in my chest, I could scarcely breathe. I soon discovered that wine produced the same symptoms but that I could consume more of it before I felt really sick. Some hours before, I had had a shouting match with Samantha, and I was beginning to admit to myself that our marriage was rolling toward the edge of a precipice. I had been driving into the garage when I saw a neighbor walking toward me, leading Margaret by the hand—my daughter was barely two. I think this is your child, he said, not bothering to veil his censure or his contempt. I found her wandering a couple of miles from here; to have got that far she must have been walking since morning. I picked her up in my arms, trembling. My temples were throbbing and I could scarcely speak when I confronted my wife to ask her where she had been when Margaret got out of the house and why she hadn't realized the child had been gone so long. She planted herself with her hands on her hips, as furious as I, alleging that the neighbor was a bastard who hated her because her cats had eaten his canary, that she didn't owe me any explanations, that after all she didn't ask me where I had been all day, that Margaret was very independent for her age and that she didn't choose to watch her like a jailer or tie her up with a rope the way I did with the children I looked after, and she kept yelling until I couldn't stand any more and left the room, slamming the door. I took a long cold shower to try to stop imagining the many accidents that could have befallen Margaret in those terrible two miles, but it hadn't done the trick, because at the party I was still extremely angry with Samantha. I carried my wine out on the terrace and fell into a chair, in a foul humor, a little drunk, and sick of the deadly dull music from Katmandu I could still hear from the living room. I was thinking how much time I was wasting at that boring party; my bar exams were coming up in a week, and every minute was precious. About then Timothy Duane came outside and when he saw me pulled up a chair beside me. We didn't have many opportunities to be alone. I noticed he had lost weight in recent years and his features had become deeply chiseled; he had lost that air of innocence that despite his posturing had been a large part of his charm when we first met. He took a glass vial from his pocket, sprinkled cocaine on the back of his hand, and noisily inhaled. He offered me some, but I can't use it: it kills me; the only time I tried it, I felt as if an icy dagger were buried between my eyes—the headache lasted three days, and the promised paradise was nowhere in my memory. Tim told me we'd better go inside because they were organizing a game; I told him I wasn't interested in seeing everyone bareassed again.

"This is different. We're going to trade spouses," and he insisted we go inside.

"You don't have a spouse, as far as I know."

"I brought a friend."

"She looks like a whore to me, your friend."

"She is." He laughed and dragged me back into the living room.

The men were gathered around the dining room table; I asked where the women were and was told they were waiting outside in the cars. Everyone was a little tense, slapping each other on the back and making double entendre remarks that were rewarded with great guffaws. Someone explained the operating principles: no turning back, no regrets, and no switches. They turned out the lights, dumped all our car keys on a tray, someone stirred them around, and each player chose a set at random. I was foggy from all the wine and too stunned to rush toward the tray like everyone else but not, after the lights came on, too blurry-eyed to see my key chain in the hand of a rather portly and pedantic dentist who was something of a minor celebrity because he pulled teeth with Chinese acupuncture needles in the feet as the only anesthesia. I picked up the last set of keys, wanting instead to grab the dentist by the shirt and flatten his nose with one of the never-fail punches Padre Larraguibel had taught me in the patio of Our Lady of Lourdes Church, but I was deterred by the fear of looking a fool. Everyone headed toward the cars, laughing and joking, but I went into the kitchen to clear my head under the cold-water faucet. I poured the dregs of some coffee from a thermos and sat on a kitchen stool to think back on times when life was simple and everyone understood the rules. After a while I became aware that my partner from the draw was standing before me, a pleasant freckle-faced blonde, the mother of three children and an elementary school arithmetic teacher, the last person with whom I would ever have thought of committing adultery. I've been waiting a long time, she said with a timid smile. I tried to explain that I didn't feel very well, but she thought I was avoiding her because I didn't find her attractive; she seemed to shrink against the doorjamb like a little girl caught doing something she shouldn't. I smiled the best smile I could, and she came to me, took my hand, helped me stand up, and led me to the car with a blend of delicacy, modesty, and determination that disarmed me. She drove us to her house. We found her children asleep in front of the television and carried them to their beds. She put on their pajamas, kissed their foreheads, pulled up the covers, and stayed with them till they fell back asleep. Then we went to her bedroom, where the photograph of her husband, dressed in his graduation gown, presided over the chest of drawers. She said she was going to slip into something more comfortable and disappeared into the bathroom while I turned back the bed, feeling like an imbecile because I couldn't stop thinking of Samantha and the dentist or wondering why the hell I couldn't relax and play these games like everyone else and why they made me so angry. The blonde returned without her makeup and brushing her hair; she was wearing a strawberry-colored quilted robe that was perfect for a mother who gets up early to prepare breakfast for her family but less than appropriate for the circumstances. There was nothing seductive in her behavior; it was as if we were an old married couple getting ready for bed after a hard day at work. She sat on my knees and began to unbutton my shirt. She had a friendly smile, a turned-up nose, and a fresh aroma of soap and toothpaste; I was not even slightly aroused. I told her she would have to forgive me, but I had drunk too much and felt ill from my allergies.

Finally I said, "The truth is that I don't know why I came. I don't like these games—I don't like them at all, and I don't think Samantha likes them either."

"What do you mean?" and she burst out laughing, obviously amused. "Your wife goes to bed with several of your friends, so why don't you have a little fun too?"

Those were bad days for me. My life has been a series of stumbling blocks, but now, at fifty, when I look back and weigh various struggles and mishaps, I believe that period was the worst; something fundamental in my soul was forever twisted, and I was never again the same. I suppose sooner or later we all lose our naïveté. That may be for the best; I know we can't go through the world as complete innocents, defenseless, with our nerves exposed. I grew up as a street fighter. I should have been tough from the beginning, but it wasn't that way. Now that I have circled around sorrow, time and again, and can read my life as a map drawn with wrong turnings, now when I haven't a trace of self-pity and can review my life without emotion because I have found a certain peace, all I regret is the loss of innocence. I miss the idealism of youth, the time when there was still a clear dividing line between good and evil and I believed it was possible to act in accord with immutable principles. It wasn't a practical or realistic posture, I know that, but there was a pure passion in that intransigence that still moves me when I find it in others. I can't say at what moment I began to change and become the hard man I am today. It would be easy to attribute everything to the war, but in fact the deterioration began earlier than that. Or I could say that it takes a stout dose of cynicism to be a lawyer; I don't know a lawyer who isn't cynical to some degree, but that, too, is only half an answer. Carmen says I shouldn't worry, that no matter how skeptical I am, it will never be enough to get along in this world, and that I am just trying to be difficult, that despite appearances I am still the same rough and bellicose, if softhearted, animal she adopted for her brother many years ago. I know myself, however, and know what I am like inside.

Colleagues, women, friends, and clients have betrayed me, but no betrayal ever hurt as much as Samantha's, because I had not expected it. I have been suspicious ever since and am never surprised when someone disappoints me. I did not go home that night. I removed the arithmetic teacher's strawberry-colored robe, and we grappled awhile in her marital bed. She must not hold a very fond memory of me; I'm sure she expected an imaginative and expert lover, but she found herself with someone eager to get the thing over with as quickly as possible. Afterward I put on my clothes and walked to Joan and Susan's house, where I arrived at three in the morning, on my last legs and with obvious signs of being drunk. I kept my finger on the buzzer for several minutes, until they both answered, barefoot and in their nightgowns. They took me in without a question, as if they were used to receiving visitors at such an hour. While one fixed me a cup of herb tea, the other improvised a bed on the living room sofa. They must have put something in the tea, because I awoke twelve hours later with the sun on my face and my friends' dog on my feet. I think my youth ended during the hours I was asleep.

When I awoke I had in my mind and my heart the resolutions that would determine my life in future years, although I didn't know it at the time. Now that I can look at the past from a certain perspective, I realize that in that instant I began to be the person I was for a long time, an arrogant, frivolous, and greedy man I always detested—a person it has cost me a lot to leave behind.

I stayed with my friends five days, without communicating with Samantha. They took turns sitting with me and patiently listening to me retell a thousand times the story of my nostalgia, despair, and grievances. On Friday I went to take my bar examination; I was free of anxiety because I had no illusions. I didn't care about the test and was, in fact, totally indifferent in regard to my future. Several months later, when I was on the opposite side of the globe, I was notified I had passed the bar on my first try, something that rarely happens in my tortuous profession. From the exam I had reported directly to the army. I should have trained for sixteen weeks, but the war was at its peak and the course had been reduced to twelve. In some ways, those three months were worse than the war itself, but I came out of it with a hundred and ninety-eight pounds of muscle and the endurance of a camel, a brute willing to destroy my own shadow had I been ordered to do so. Two days before I shipped out, the computer selected me for the Language Institute in Monterey. I suppose that having grown up in the Mexican barrio and having heard my mother's Russian and listened to her Italian operas had trained my ear. I was almost two months in a paradise of Victorian houses, picture-postcard sunsets, and sheer cliffs overlooking rocky shores where seals lazed in the sun; I studied Vietnamese round the clock with professors who rotated on the hour and threatened that if I didn't learn quickly I would be branded a traitor to my country. At the end of the course I spoke the language better than most of the other students. I left for Vietnam harboring the secret fantasy of dying so I would not have to face the drudgery and pain of living. But dying is much more difficult than staying alive.

PART THREE

People.

War is people. The first word that comes to mind when I think about the war *is* people: us, my friends, my brothers, all united in the same desperate fraternity. My comrades. And the others, those tiny men and women with indecipherable faces whom I should hate but can't, because in these last weeks I have begun to know them. Here everything is black and white; there are no halftones or ambiguities; the manipulation is behind us, the hypocrisy, the deceit. Life or death. Kill or be killed. We're the good guys and they're the bad guys; without that conviction you're fucked for sure, and in a certain way such insane simplification is refreshing, it's one of the virtues of war. All kinds end up in this hole: blacks escaping poverty, poor farmers who still believe in the American Way of Life, a few Latins fired by the rage of centuries and aspiring to be heroes, psychopaths, and some like myself, running away from failure or guilt; in combat we're all equal, the past is irrelevant, a bullet is the great democratic experience. We must prove each day that we're not men, we're soldiers: endure, bear the pain and discomfort, never complain, kill, grit your teeth and don't think, don't ask questions, obey—that's why they broke us like horses, trained us with kicks, insults, and humiliation. We're not individuals, in this tragic theater of violence we're machines at the service of the motherfucking nation. You do anything to survive. I feel good when I've killed, because at least for now I'm still alive. I accept the lunacy and don't try to explain it; I simply hold on to my weapon and fire. Don't think, or you'll get confused and hesitate. If you think, you're dead—that is the one unequivocal law of war. The enemy has no face, he's not human, he's an animal, a monster, a demon: if I could believe that in the bottom of my heart, things would be easier, but Cyrus taught me to question everything, he forced me to call things by their names—kill, murder. I came here to shake off my indifference and to throw myself into something exhilarating, I came with a cynical attitude, ready to live recklessly, to give meaning to my life. I came because of Hemingway, in search of my manhood, the myth of the macho, the definition of masculinity, pride in the muscles and endurance I acquired during training, wanting to prove my valor because at heart I have always suspected I am a coward and to prove my fortitude because I was sick of being betrayed by my feelings. A late rite of passage. Who comes to such hell at twenty-eight? The first four months were like a life-and-death game, like placing bets against myself. I observed myself from a distance and with heavy irony sat in judgment of myself; I was haunted by the past, and pushed myself to the limits of risk and pain and exhaustion and brutality, and, when I reached those limits, found I couldn't take it. Drugs help. And then one day I woke up feeling alive, quintessentially alive, more alive than I had ever been, in love with this conflagration we call life. At that moment I faced my own mortality: I am an eggshell, a nothing that in an instant can turn to dust, leaving not so much as a memory. When the new contingents arrive I look the men over, I inspect them carefully; I have developed a sixth sense about reading the signs, I know which ones will die and which ones won't. The most courageous and daring will die first, because they believe they are invincible; these men are killed by pride. The most terrified will also die, because they are paralyzed or crazed by fear, they shoot blindly and sometimes hit a comrade; these you don't want near you, they're bad luck, you don't want them in your platoon. The best men keep their cool, they don't take unnecessary risks, they try not to attract or deserve attention, they have a strong will to live. I like the Latinos, they are surly and uncommunicative outside but dynamite inside: explosive, lethal, cool in the face of death. Not only are they brave; they're good buddies.

I carry amphetamines by the fistful, all mixed together, a kick in the stomach, a bitter taste in the mouth; I talk so fast I don't know what I'm saying, after a minute or two I can't talk at all, I chew gum to keep from biting my tongue, then I stupefy myself with alcohol and sleeping pills in order to get a little rest. I dream of rivers of blood, seas of flaming gasoline, gaping wounds— women's lips, vulvas—the dead stacked in piles, severed heads, children aflame in napalm, all those repugnant snapshots soldiers collect: red, nothing but red. I have learned to sleep in catnaps, five or ten minutes whenever I can, wherever I am, wrapped in my plastic poncho, always with my senses on alert. My hearing has grown sharper: I can hear an insect moving across the ground; my sense of smell is keener: I can smell the guerrillas from several yards away—they eat marinated fish, and when they're afraid and sweating, you can smell them. What do we smell of? Shaving lotion, probably, because we drink it like whiskey, it's forty percent alcohol. When I can sleep a couple of hours without nightmares I'm like new, but I can't always do that. If I'm not sending out the guard or on patrol, I spend the night in camp, shivering beneath a rain-soaked tarp in a tent stinking of urine, boots, mold, rotting rations, and sweat, and listening to the gnawing of busy rats and men on routine shitwork, with mosquitoes so thick they're even in my mouth. Sometimes I wake up crying like an idiot; how Juan José would laugh at me. I wonder how many times he led me to a corner of the schoolyard so the others wouldn't see me cry: Shut up, you gringo fairy, men don't cry. He would shake me, mad as hell, and as his threats didn't solve the problem but only made things worse, he finally would beg me please to shut up—For all you hold holy, *mano,* before they take us both for sissies and kick the shit out of us. To get going in the morning I take aspirins with coffee—cold, of course—smoke the first joint of the day, and before I go out gulp down the amphetamines. What I miss is a warm meal, a shower, a cold beer; I'm up to here with the rations they drop from the air in blue-and-yellow packets—ham and beans, and fruit salad. It's like being a kid again, being here; it's a strange sensation: there are no personal responsibilities, no questions, only obeying, although in fact that's hard for me; I'm better at giving orders, not blindly obeying them. I will never make a good soldier. It's easy to get by unnoticed, to fade into the shadows. Unless you do something really stupid, the days tick by one after the other, your only goal to survive; the terrible, invincible machine takes over everything, your superiors make the decisions, and you have to hope they know what they're doing; I have no worries, I can be invisible in the ranks, I'm like everyone else, a number without a face, a past, or a future. It's like going crazy: you float in the limbo of eternal time and warped space, and no one can hold you accountable for anything; all I have to do is my job, and as for the rest, I do whatever I damn well please. Nothing is more dangerous, though, than to feel you're superior; you're on your own, as lonely as your belly button, Juan José warned me that day on the beach, peering through the smoke of a reefer moistened in opium. The only thing that saves us is the obstinate brotherhood of the grunts. I feel overwhelming compassion, I want to weep for all the accumulated pain, mine and everyone else's, I want to grab a machine gun and go out and kill, howl until the whole universe shatters, I will have a wail stuck in my throat as long as I live. You're crazy, *mano;* you can't feel sorry about things during a war. Juan José and I ran into each other on the beach during a couple of days' leave, a miracle that among half a million servicemen we were in the same place at the same time. We hugged each other, unable to believe in such a coincidence: what fantastic luck to run into you, *mano,* and we clapped each other on the back and laughed, happy, for a minute forgetting where we were, and why. We tried to catch up on what had happened, an impossible task because we hadn't seen each other for ten years, ever since Juan José joined the army and was strutting around in his uniform while I was working for a buck and a half an hour. We had gone our own ways, he toward his destiny as a soldier and I to work for wetback's wages for a year, until Cyrus convinced me to leave the barrio. I don't intend to work forever in my papa's craphole of a garage, *mano,* Juan José had told me, my old man's a slave driver, the army's the best I can do; I'll serve in that fucker until I'm thirty-eight or forty and then retire with a good pension—and the world's mine, *mano.* What else am I gonna do with this Mexican skin and face? Besides, women love uniforms. We laughed like idiots on that beach. You remember the time we stole old Purple Pecker's cigarettes and Padre Larraguibel's wine? And the fights with horse dung? And when we shaved Oliver and painted him with Mercurochrome and took him to school and told everyone he had the bubonic plague?—Hey, *mano,* what the shit *is* the bubonic plague?—all with the old joking, offhanded affection, the rough language and good feelings we shared since we were boys. He told me he'd fallen in love with a Vietnamese girl, and when he showed me the photograph he kept in a plastic case in his wallet, he became serious, and his voice changed. It was an overexposed Polaroid snapshot, in which the woman's face looked like a pale moon framed by the shadows of her hair. I particularly noticed the eyes, but everything else looked like all the Asiatic faces I'd been seeing in recent months.

"Her name's Thui," he told me.

"That's the name of a fairy princess."

"It means water."

I had heard rumors about my friend; soldiers talk, whispers fly through the ranks. He confirmed what I'd heard through the grapevine: he was on a difficult mission, the officer in charge of the platoon was new, they saw they were surrounded, the firing began, five were hit, and the officer ordered them to retreat without taking their wounded. The guy was a fuckup, *mano,* how could we leave them there? Imagine if it was you: I wouldn't leave you to the enemy; that's what I tried to explain to him, but the dickhead sonofabitch was crazy, *mano,* he drew his pistol and threatened us, and he was yelling and waving his arms, I mean, out of control. I couldn't wait for him to calm down, there wasn't time, so I shot him, point-blank. He went down without knowing what hit him. We got the hell out of there—with our wounded, like you should, *mano.* We saved all of them but one who was too far gone; they'd shot out his guts. Poor bastard, he was holding his intestines in his hands and looking at me, wild. Don't leave me alive, Lucky Star, don't leave me; he was beggin'. I had to shoot him in the head, may God forgive me. What a fucking mess this is, *mano.*

Bodies were supposed to be placed in bags, with the names neatly on tags, but there wasn't always time for formalities—not enough time or not enough bags. You pick them up by the wrists and ankles and throw them into the helicopters, or tie them up like packages in their own ponchos, swarming with flies. In a few hours the corpses are swollen, bloated, infested with maggots, a bubbling broth of putrefaction. The helicopters are windbirds; they land in a tornado, swirling dust, garbage, and befouled clay for thirty yards around. When the dead have been lying for hours in the heat or rain, bits of flesh tear loose in the whirlwind and, if you're standing too close, hit you in the face. On the mountain I refused to load bodies. I helped the wounded, but afterward I turned to stone and no one dared give me orders; I was beyond life and death, operating on a different plane. A crisis of nerves, a psychotic breakdown—I forget what name they gave it. They wash down the choppers with a hose, but they can't get rid of the stench. Or the echoes of the screams; the dead aren't really gone. I'm not crying, it's the damned allergies or the smoke, who knows; it's no wonder my eyes are irritated: you live breathing in filth. Every time, I give thanks I'm not one of the ones leaving in a body bag, or even worse, one of the others, the ones loaded on with their chest slit open like a piece of fruit, red stumps where legs or arms should be, but still alive, maybe for years, dogged forever by intolerable memories. Thank you, God, I'm still alive, I shouted in

English there on the mountain, O Guardian Angel, *dulce com-pañía,* watch over me by night and by day, I added in Spanish, but no one heard me; between the fire of the battle and screams of the wounded, I couldn't even hear myself. Fucking-Holy-Mother-of-God, get me out of this alive, I cried out; I had the scapulary of the Virgin of Guadalupe around my neck, a scrap of cloth stiff and black from the dried blood of Juan José. A chaplain had given it to me several weeks after my brother was killed. He was the one who had closed his eyes; he told me that Juan José was already as gray as a ghost when he took off the scapulary and asked the chaplain to give it to me for luck, to see if it would help me get out alive. What were his last words? was all I could think to ask the chaplain. Hold me, *Padre,* I'm falling. Hold me, it's so dark down there, was the last thing you said, *mano,* and I wasn't there to hear you or hold you tight and yank you back from death. Oh, shit. Oh, bloody shit! What good was the damn scapulary, *mano*! You lose your faith here, but you get superstitious and begin to see fatal omens everywhere: Tuesdays are bad luck, it's been exactly a week since something happened, it's the calm before the storm, the planes always go down in threes, and two were shot down today.... You'll live to be an old man, Greg, Olga swore to me, you'll have time to make a lot of mistakes, to be sorry for some and suffer like hell; it won't be an easy life, but I guarantee it'll be a long one, it's written here on your palm and in the tarot cards. But she could have made it up, she doesn't know anything, she's a worse fake than my father, worse than all the people who tell fortunes and sell amulets in this whole godforsaken country. She told Juan José Morales the same thing, and he believed it; what a stupid bastard you were, *mano.* You were sure of your good luck, that's why you weren't more careful; your confidence was so contagious that two guys from your squad did everything they could to stick close to you: they were sure they'd be safe there. Now none of you can go to Olga and get your money back.

The jungle is filled with sounds, animal cries, padding paws, swishing noises, murmurs, but not the forest; the forest is silent, an opaque silence. I imagine that from the air it looks purified by the fire, and clean, but on the ground it's hell. You get used to it after a while; the worst perversion, the most obscene part of war, is that it can seem normal. At first I was confused, then euphoric; in both cases my conscience was dormant. Now, in the village, I'm beginning to think again. There's no reason to think in a firefight; you become a noise- and death-dealing machine. No one wants a thinking man, a critic with a conscience, only machos bursting with testosterone—illiterate blacks, Latin bandits, criminals released from prisons to serve: guys like me are dead weight. After each patrol, my muscles twitch, I can't control my hands, my teeth are clenched, and a tic pulses in my face. It's like a demented smile; many of the men have it. It goes away, they say. In the months I've been here I've become accustomed to being wet to the bone, to feet rubbed raw inside my boots, to fingers frozen around my weapon, to being ringed by shadows, waiting for the shot that will come at any instant from anywhere, to counting the steps between me and that bush, the minutes to reach the river, the hours to end this patrol, the days to complete my hitch and go home. Counting the seconds of life and computing the odds that the next burst of machine gun fire will kill my buddy, not me. And asking myself what the shit I'm doing here, not wanting to admit, not even in the depths of my soul, the strange fascination of violence, the vertigo of war. That dawn on the mountain when it began to grow light, I saw that only nine of us were still alive; the dead and wounded were too many to count. We had fought through the night. With daylight the bombers came and strafed the mountainside, forcing the guerrillas to retreat, and then the helicopters landed. The sound of the engines was music to my ears, the sound of my mother's heartbeat before I was born, tic-tac tic-tac ... life. Let us pray, says the Methodist chaplain, and the others sing *A mighty fortress is our God* while I sing *O, Susanna*. Confess, my son, says the Catholic chaplain, and I tell him to go confess to his whorish mother, but then I repent: I'd just as soon not be struck by a bolt of lightning, as Padre Larraguibel used to say, and be taken out in mortal sin. Do not fear, for God is with you. In the Sunday sermon they read the story of Job. Worn down by the trials the Lord has visited upon him, Job says, "For the thing which I greatly fear is come upon me, and that which I was afraid of is come unto me. I was not in safety, neither had I rest, neither was I quiet; yet trouble came." Don't think bad things, *mano,* because they'll happen. Don't call up devil death by thinking about him, Juan José Morales used to warn me, laughing. Lucky Star they called Juan José. Lucky Star Morales.

There's the smoke too. My mind is in a fog. Smoke from tobacco, pot, hashish, whatever crud I'm smoking, the mist of cold mornings in the mountains and steaming heat of valleys at noon, dust and diesel fumes, fetid clouds from napalm, phosphorus, and more bombs than I can count, and the burning that knows no beginning or end and is turning this country into a desert crisscrossed by black scars. All kinds of smoke, smoke of all colors. From above they must look like clouds, and sometimes they are: down here the smoke is part of the terror. We can't stop, even for an instant, no one can; if we keep moving we have the illusion we're outwitting death, we scurry like poisoned rats. In contrast, the enemy stays quiet, no wasted anxiety; they wait silently, they have generations of training for pain behind them—who can decipher the immutable expression on those faces? Those bastards don't feel anything, a marine told me who specialized in getting information from prisoners; they're like laboratory frogs. We keep on the move in our frenzy to stay alive—and then on the way to where we're going meet death face-to-face. The enemy crawl silently through their tunnels, blend into the foliage, melt away in a breath, and they can see in the dark. We are never safe. Figure it out, Juan José Morales said, count how many men have come to this stinkhole, and then count the casualties. The percentage is really low, *mano,* we're going to get out in one piece, don't you worry. I suppose that he was right and that most of us will live to tell about it, but here all we think about is the dead and the atrocities told by survivors. Yes, many come out looking normal, but no one is ever the same, we're marked forever; but who cares? We're garbage anyway. This is a war fought by blacks and poor whites, country boys, boys from small towns, from the worst barrios; the sons of the wealthy don't end up as common grunts: their fathers find ways to keep them at home or their colonel uncles assign them safe duty. My mother argues that racism is the worst perversion; Cyrus always said it is class injustice. They're both right, I guess; we're not even equal when we go to war. *No Dogs or Mexicans Allowed* you'd see on some restaurants not long ago. And *Whites Only* painted on public rest rooms. Here, on the other hand, men of color are welcome, very welcome, but racial tension burns beneath the superficial camaraderie: whites hang out with whites, blacks with blacks, Latinos with Latinos, Asians with Asians, all with their own language, music, rites, superstitions. In the camps the barrios have inviolable boundaries; I wouldn't dare walk into black territory without being invited. It's no different from where I grew up; nothing's changed. Every man has his story, but I don't want to hear it; I don't want friends either, I can't give myself the luxury of becoming fond of someone and then seeing him die, like Juan José, or that poor kid from Kansas up on the mountain; all I want is to do my job, do my tour, and get out alive. I pray for a wound serious enough to send me home but not serious enough to cripple me. One helicopter pilot I know, a cheerful mulatto from Alabama, used to say, if only they don't get me in the balls; he went home covered with medals but in a wheelchair. That will never happen to me, that business of the medals, I told myself, and then they gave me one because I went crazy. I'm a war hero, I have a fucking Silver Star. I never meant to do anything more than my duty; I've always said that it's better to live like a coward than die like a fool, but by one of life's ridiculous ironies now I'm Mr. Shitass Hero. First lesson of the barrio: There's no virtue in heroism, only in survival. Oh, Juan José, why didn't you pay attention to what you taught me yourself when we were a couple of snotty-nosed kids? And now how am I going to explain to your parents and your brothers and sisters? how the hell can I look Carmen and your mother in the face? how can I tell them the truth? I'll have to lie to them, *hermano,* and keep on lying, because I don't have the courage to tell them they blew away half your body and that those decorations you won for bravery—I'm sure they sent them to your mother to hang on the living room wall—are nothing but painted tin stars that don't mean much at the time you're dying.

I know violence: it's a crazed beast. You can't reason with it; you have to try to outwit it. I envy the pilots; up there you cash it in with more elegance; you drop like a stone or explode in a million pieces, with no time even to pray, like Martínez when the train hit him—*pachuco* bastard, I don't even hate him anymore. But down here on the ground in the infantry they can get you a thousand ways: spitted on the sharpened stakes of a leaf-covered pit, decapitated by machete, blown up by a grenade or a mine, cut in half by machine gun fire, torched to a crisp—and that's not even counting the ingenious deaths that come with being taken prisoner. Dig a hole in the ground and hide until this is all over; crawl into some animal's den, as Oliver and I used to when I was a boy. Why wasn't it my luck to pull an office job? Lots of guys are sitting out the war under a ceiling fan; if I'd been more clever I wouldn't be here, I would have done my service when I got out of high school, for example, instead of slaving like a peon at a time when no one was even talking about the war. And now I'm here, stupid fool that I am, too old to be in a hell like this; I feel like a grandfather to these baby-faced kids in camouflage uniforms. I don't want my bones to end up under a cross in a military cemetery, one among thousands; I want to die an old man in Carmen's arms. Jesus, I hadn't thought about Carmen in a long time. Why did I say Carmen and not Samantha? Where did that flash come from? In her last letter she told me about a new boyfriend; Chinese or Japanese, I think she said, but she didn't give his name. I wonder who it is this time? She has a real talent for choosing the worst possible men for herself; this one's probably some ragged, long-haired lotus-eater; they have them in Europe too, by the gross. The last snapshot she sent showed her standing in front of the cathedral in Barcelona, dressed like a flamenco dancer or some such thing. I'm no puritan, but I thought of Pedro Morales and I wrote her and told her she was too old to act like a teenager, that she should take off that junk and put on a bra: Oh, well, what do I care, it's your business, go ahead and screw things up. Carmen . . . how I wish I could hear your voice, Carmen.

I'm afraid I've completely crossed over the line, lost any sense of good and bad, of what's decent. I'm so used to atrocity that I can't imagine life without it. I try to remember what friends do to have a good time, how you share breakfast with your family, what you say to a woman on your first date, but all that has evaporated, and I doubt if it will ever come back. The past is a swirl of hazy fragments: the dance contests with Carmen, my mother listening to the opera in her wicker chair, the duel with Martínez that made me the asshole hero of the school—my God, the crazy things you do at that age; no girl could refuse me, and when I bought the Buick they begged me. I was as poor as a church mouse, but I bought that wreck of a car; when I was at the wheel I felt like a sheik, and in the back seat I sinned more than I care to remember. We didn't, as the girls said, go all the way, of course; the boy attacked and the girl defended herself—not very enthusiastically, but she couldn't cooperate in her own seduction even if she was dying to; hot necking was what we did, more like a cat fight than lovemaking, a wrestling match that left us both limp—come outside her, God, don't get her pregnant, if you go to bed with her you'll have to marry her, you're a gentleman, aren't you? Only Ernestina Pereda did it with everyone, God bless Ernestina Pereda, I hope you're well and happy, Saint Ernestina, you were wild for it, but afterward you'd cry, and you'd make us swear we'd keep the secret, a secret trumpeted from the housetops, everyone knew about you and took advantage of your passion and your generosity, if it hadn't been for Olga and you, my blood would have turned to poison from all my obsessions. Here women are like tiny, preadolescent girls, nothing but a handful of bones; they don't have breasts or hair anywhere on their bodies, and they're always sad; you feel more pity for them than desire. Only one thing about them is lavish, their hair, their long smooth black hair sparked with blue lights. I took one young girl to bed in a room filled with people; her family was eating in one corner, and a baby was crying in a quartermaster's supply box. We were in the bed, separated from the others by a threadbare curtain; she was reciting a string of obscenities in English that she'd learned by heart. I'm sure there's a manual for dirty phrases; the War Office thinks of everything; if there are manuals for how to use the latrines, why wouldn't there be one for training prostitutes? We want the best for our boys, no matter what, the cream of the nation, right? Shut up, I begged her, but she didn't understand or didn't want to be quiet, and her family was talking on the other side of the curtain and the baby kept crying. Suddenly I remembered something I'd seen in a dusty southern town when I was five years old: two men raping a young Negro girl, two giants crushing a terrified little girl between them, a girl as small and fragile as the one I was with, and I felt like one of them, huge and satanic, and my desire flowed from me, and my erection with it. I don't know why at just that moment I remembered something that happened more than twenty years before on the other side of the world. Leo Galupi, that engaging scoundrel, took me to see the Granny, a local curiosity, a wrinkled old woman who crawls around beneath the tables in the bar, peddling her services; she's a wizard, they say, and once she's had you in the clutches of those monkey mandibles, you get real choosy. She asks ten dollars, and you don't have to worry about anything; she takes charge, she even cleans you up afterward and zips your fly for you. She makes the rounds, busily entertaining her clients under the table, while everyone else keeps drinking and playing cards and telling dirty jokes. I couldn't do it; I don't know whether it was repugnance or pity. The Granny's hair is almost white; she's a not at all venerable old lady, with the biceps of Charles Atlas and a few razor-sharp teeth; one time she'll do what we all fear: rip off someone's prick with one fierce, tearing motion. That risk is part of the game; each client fears that she will decide to do it just when his turn comes, and . . . zap!

Here in the village I've begun to feel human again. They invite me by turns, one day in each home; they cook for me, and the family gathers around to watch me eat, all smiling, proud of feeding me even though there's not enough for them. I've learned to accept what they offer me and to thank them without offending them by being too effusive. The most difficult thing in the world is to accept a gift without a fuss. I had forgotten that; since the time the Moraleses took us in, no one had ever given me anything without expecting something in return. This has been a lesson in affection and humility: we can't go through life without owing something to somebody. Sometimes one of the men takes my hand, like a sweetheart, and I've also learned not to pull my hand away. At first I was embarrassed: men don't hold hands, men don't cry, men don't feel pity, men ... men.... How long has it been since someone touched me out of pure sympathy or friendship? I shouldn't get soft, let anyone get to me, trust anyone—if you get careless, you're a dead man. And don't think; the most important thing is not to stop and reflect; if you imagine death, it happens, it's like a premonition, but I can't stop thinking about it, my head is filled with visions of death, words of death. I want to think about life. ...

Toward the end of February the company found itself on the crest of a mountain, with orders to defend the position at any cost. In a later investigation, the reason why the men should have resisted as they did was not clear; bureaucracy and time contrived to blanket events in obscurity. We're all going to die here, a trembling young man from Kansas told Gregory Reeves. It was not the boy's baptism of fire, he had been in the forward units for months, but he had an unshakable premonition that he would die and felt he hadn't really had time to taste life—he had turned twenty less than a week before. You're not going to die—Reeves shook him—don't talk like that. They waited, digging trenches and stacking dirt- and rock-filled sandbags to form a barricade, not so much with any thought of protection as to keep busy and take their minds off their fear. Even so, the wait was endless; they were tense, anxious, weapons primed, tormented by cold after sunset and heat during the day. The attack came at night, and from the first moment they knew they were facing an enemy that outnumbered them ten to one and they would not escape. A few hours later the perimeter was reduced to a desperate handful of men, still firing but without hope, encircled by the corpses of more than a hundred comrades scattered on the slopes. In the orange light of an explosion, Gregory Reeves saw the body of the soldier from Kansas lifted in the air and tossed to the far side of the barricade; without knowing what he was doing, or why, he leapt over the stacked bags and crawled toward the boy through an inferno of crossfire, grenades, and choking smoke. He propped him up in his arms, calling him by name: Don't worry, I'm here, it's all right. He felt the youth's hands clutching his jacket and heard the rattle of his dying breath; Reeves's nose was filled with the stench of fear and blood and raw flesh, and in another burst of light he saw death in the boy's eyes and in the color of his skin; he also saw that his legs were missing: where legs should have been there was only a blackish puddle. It's all right; I'll carry you back. The choppers are on the way, and soon we'll be drinking beer and celebrating we're safe. Hang on. Don't leave me alone, please, don't leave me alone, and Reeves felt the darkness closing in around them and wanted to shield the wounded man from terror, but his life was slipping through Reeves's fingers like sand, crumbling, turning to smoke, and when he felt the weight of the boy's head fall against his chest and his hands release their grip, and when a last spasm of warm blood bathed his neck, he knew that inside him something had broken into a million fragments, like an exploded mirror. Carefully, he laid the body on the ground, then he stood up and threw his own weapon as far as he could. He heard the awesome sound of an enormous bell ringing inside him, and a metallic scream rose from his gut to convulse the night and for an instant quell the roar of the explosions; it congealed time and stopped the forward movement of the world. And he kept yelling and yelling until there was no breath and no yell left inside him. The echo of the bell receded, but time did not resume its march, and from that moment until the dawn, everything happened in a single fixed image: a photograph in black and red in which the events of the night were forever captured. Reeves is not in that bloody mural. He looks for himself among the corpses and the wounded, among the sandbags and in the furrows of the trenches, but he cannot find himself. He has disappeared from his own memory. One of the men he rescued told later how he watched him throw away his gun and stand up, arms raised above his head, as if challenging the next round of fire, and when he had emptied his lungs in that long howl, Reeves turned to where the man was lying, two yards away, bleeding painlessly, and picked him up and tossed him over his shoulder and, unmindful of the rounds of fire whizzing around him, carried him in a straight line toward the crest of the hill, where four hands reached out to receive the wounded man. Then Gregory Reeves went back to look for another casualty, and then another, and all through the remainder of that fateful night he transported injured men through dense enemy fire, certain that as long as he continued what he was doing nothing could happen to him: he was invulnerable. In his lifetime, he had never before had and would never have again that sensation of absolute power.

Help arrived at dawn. The helicopters carried off first the wounded, then the nine survivors, and finally they unloaded the plastic bags to bundle up the dead. Of the men who emerged without a mark, eight were weak from the strain and terror, trembling so hard in their soaked clothes that they could not hold the flask in their hand to take a swig of whiskey, but when hours later they were set down at the beach for three days of R and R, they recovered and were able to talk in some detail about what had happened. Filthy, adrenaline flowing, as one man, a family of desperadoes, they threw themselves like animals on the ice-cold beer and sizzling hamburgers, which they hadn't seen in months, and when someone tried to remind them of canteen regulations, they raised a storm that nearly degenerated into another slaughter. When the military police arrived and saw their faces and heard what they'd been through, they relieved the men of their weapons and released them, to see whether a little salt water and sand could bring them back to the land of the living. The ninth survivor, Gregory Reeves, was the last into a helicopter after helping all the others aboard. He sat mute and rigid in his seat, eyes straight ahead, deep furrows of fatigue creasing his face, without a scratch but completely bathed in the blood of his comrades. His nerves were gone. They could not send him to the beach; they gave him a shot, and he awakened two days later in the camp hospital, in restraints, to prevent him from harming himself in the torment of his nightmares. They told him he had saved the lives of eleven infantrymen and for acts of extreme valor he would receive one of the nation's highest decorations. In line with the superstitious codes of war, the nine who had not been wounded knew they had cheated death and that they were marked men. If they stayed together they would not have a second chance to escape, but separately they might be able to hoodwink fate a little longer. They were sent to different companies, with the tacit agreement that they would not get in touch with one another for a while. They had no desire to meet, anyway, because the euphoria of having been rescued was followed by the terror of not being able to explain why they were the lucky ones among more than a hundred men. Of the wounded, two recuperated within a couple of weeks, and once or twice Gregory Reeves crossed paths with them. They did not speak to him but pretended not to recognize him; their debt was too great, they could not repay him, and they were shamed by that knowledge.

After Reeves had been several months in Vietnam, his superiors remembered that he spoke the language, and he was sent by the intelligence service to a village in the mountains as liaison with friendly guerrillas. His official mission was to teach English, but no villager had the least doubt about the true nature of his assignment, and not even Reeves bothered to pretend. The first day of classes, he reported to the school with a machine gun in one hand and a satchel of books in the other; he walked through the room without glancing to the right or left, set his briefcase on the table, and turned toward his students. Twenty men of various ages, bent double in a deep bow, greeted him. From ancestral respect for knowledge, they were bowing not to him but to the figure of the teacher. He felt the blood rush to his face; at no time in the war had he felt a responsibility as grave as at that moment. Slowly he removed his weapon from his shoulder and walked to the wall and hung it on a peg, then he returned to the blackboard and in turn bowed to salute his students, silently thanking his stars for twelve years in public school and seven at the university. From that day, the English course, which in principle was a screen for gathering information, became an urgent obligation, the only way to repay the villagers in some small measure for all he received from them.

He lived in a modest but cool and comfortable house that had belonged to a French official, one of the few for several miles around that had its own privy at the back. The cats and mice scurrying around in the roof became so familiar that when occasionally they were still during the night he awakened with a start. He spent much of his time preparing his classes. In truth he had very little to do; the military mission was a joke: the friendly guerrillas were unpredictable shadows. His sporadic contacts were surreal, and his reports were exercises in divination. He communicated daily by radio with his battalion but only rarely could offer any information. He was in the middle of the combat zone, but at times the war seemed to be a story he had heard about another place and another time. He strolled among the thatched houses, walking through clay and pigshit, greeting everyone by name, helping farmers ready the rice paddies with heavy, buffalo-drawn wooden plows, helping women with their packs of children fetch water in large pitchers, helping small children fly kites and make rag dolls. In the evenings he heard mothers singing as they rocked their babies and men conversing in their language of trills and whispers. Those sounds marked the rhythm of the hours, they were the people's music. He also listened to his own music for the first time in an eternity; playing his tapes of concerts for hours, he could imagine the war was a bad dream. It seemed he had been born among these tolerant, gentle people who were nonetheless capable of picking up a weapon and giving their life to defend their land. He soon was speaking the language fluently, although with a harsh accent that provoked happy giggles—but never in the classroom. Men who treated him as a friend when he was invited to eat greeted him with salaams in the school. At night he played cards with a group whose custom it was to trade quips in true verbal duels of sarcastic humor, most of which he lost, because while he paused to translate the joke the others had gone on to something new. He had to tread a difficult line because there was a tenuous boundary between the traditional jokes and a strict protocol imposed by respect and good manners. Superficially the Vietnamese behaved as equals, but they were ruled by a complex and subtle system of hierarchies within which each man was zealous in guarding his honor. They were a hospitable and friendly people, and the doors of their houses were always open to Reeves; in turn, visitors arrived at his house without notice and stayed for hours and hours in amiable chatter. What they most esteemed was the ability to tell a story. There was among them an aged storyteller who could transport his listeners to heaven or hell; he could soften the heart of the bravest men with his love stories, his complex tales of maidens in danger and sons in disgrace. When the story ended, everyone would sit suspended in silence, and then the old man himself would laugh, mocking his audience, who had listened like children spellbound by his words. Reeves would sit among his friends like one member more of a huge family. Soon he stopped seeing himself as a white giant, he forgot differences in size, culture, race, language, and goals, and allowed himself the pleasure of being like everybody else. One night he stood staring at the black dome of the sky and had to smile at the realization that in almost thirty years of life, this remote village in Asia was the only place where he had felt accepted as a part of a community.

Reeves wrote to Timothy Duane with a list of materials for his classes—the texts he was using were infantile and antiquated—and he also contacted a high school in San Francisco to arrange an exchange of letters with his students. In their painstaking English his pupils wrote a page or two about their lives and some weeks later received a return packet from the United States, an event that was celebrated the same evening. Among other trifles, as an illustration of the Halloween tradition, Timothy Duane sent a rubber mask with gorilla features, green hair, shark teeth, and

pointed ears that wiggled like gelatin. Reeves draped himself in a
sheet, put on the mask, and went leaping through the streets with
a lighted torch in each hand, never imagining the terror his prank
would evoke. An air raid would not have produced greater panic:
women and children ran toward the jungle, screaming at the top
of their lungs, and those men who were able to overcome their
fright organized to beat back the monster with sticks. The gorilla
had to run for its life, tangled in the sheet, while trying to tear off
the mask. Reeves identified himself just in time, although not
before being struck by several stones. The mask became a prized
trophy; the curious paraded by to admire it and poke at it with a
hesitant finger. Reeves intended to offer it as a prize to the best
student in his course, but so many were inspired to earn top marks
that he decided to contribute the treasure to the community. The
face of King Kong took its place in the council hall beside a bloody
flag, a first-aid kit, a radio transmitter, and other war relics. In
return, the villagers gave their English teacher a small wooden
dragon, a symbol of prosperity and good luck, whose visage was
angelic in comparison to the rubber mask.

The illusory tranquillity of those months in the village ended
sooner than Reeves had anticipated. First he began to suffer a kind
of dysentery; he blamed his symptoms on contaminated water and
unfamiliar food and by radio requested medication. He was sent a
box containing various vials and a sheet of instructions. He began
to boil his water, tried to refuse invitations without causing offense,
and religiously took the prescribed medicines. For a few days he
felt better, but then the symptoms returned and he felt worse than
before. He thought he was experiencing a recurrence of his earlier
problem and was not overly concerned. He planned to kill the
virus with indifference; he wasn't going to cry about it like an old
woman—men don't complain, *mano*—but he grew perceptibly
worse: he lost weight, he could scarcely drag himself around, and it
took an extraordinary effort to get out of bed and focus on preparing his classes or correcting his students' work. He would stand,
chalk in hand, without the energy to move his arm, staring at the
blackboard with a dazed expression, not knowing what the

chicken tracks he himself had written meant or what the white-hot coals burning a hole in his gut might be. *Is this pencil red? No, this pencil is blue,* and he could not remember which pencil was which or what the hell difference it made what color it was. In less than two months he lost forty pounds, and when someone mentioned that he was getting thin and turning the color of a squash, he replied with a weak smile that a good spy was supposed to blend into the landscape. By then no one in the village made any mystery about his coded messages, and he allowed himself the liberty of joking about it. Everyone took his presence as an inevitable consequence of the war; it was nothing personal: if it weren't Reeves it would be someone else, no two ways about it. Of the numberless foreigners who had passed through the village, enemies or friends, this was the one they felt comfortable with—they had real affection for him. At times some little boy would come and whisper in his ear that it was going to be a stormy night and it would be a good idea to turn out his lights, lock the door tight, and not go outside for any reason. Nothing seemed very different; Reeves would glimpse the pale crescent of the moon through a slit in his window, listen to the cries of night birds, and turn a deaf ear to movement through the alleyways of the village. He made no report about those episodes; his superiors would not understand that if the people were to survive, they had no choice but to yield to those who were stronger—from either side. One word from him about those strange nights of silent activities, and a search-and-destroy party would wipe out his friends and reduce the village to a pile of burned-out huts, a tragedy that would not change the plans of the guerrillas in any way. Because of the dearth of information, suspicions were raised at battalion headquarters, and someone was sent to bring Reeves back to base to make a personal report. On the way there, Reeves fainted, and when they reached the base two men had to lift him from the jeep and carry him to a chair in the shade. They handed him a bottle of water, which he drank without taking a breath and then immediately vomited up. Blood tests eliminated the usual maladies, and the doctor, fearing a contagious disease, sent him by plane directly to a hospital in Hawaii.

* * *

The hospital experience was decisive for Gregory Reeves, because it gave him time to think about his future, a luxury he had never known until then. Only rarely had he had so much free time. He was in a bubble floating in a void; each hour was eternal. The months of fighting had sharpened his senses, so that now in the relative silence of his sickbed he jumped when a thermometer was dropped on a metal tray or when a door blew shut. The smell of a meal made him ill, a whiff of a medicinal odor nauseated him, and the stench of a wound triggered uncontrollable vomiting. The friction of the sheets against his skin was torture, and food tasted like sand. For several days he was fed intravenously, then thanks to a nurse who spooned baby food into his mouth, he slowly recovered his appetite. During the first days he thought of nothing but his body; all his senses were focused on getting well, on monitoring how his organism was reacting to his various ills, but when he felt better he was able to take a look around. Once his system was free of the drugs on which he had operated during the days of combat, a mist lifted from his mind, and a merciless light permitted him to examine his life. Lying flat on his back, his eyes fixed on the ceiling fan, he mulled over his fate, his bad fortune in being born among the poorest of the poor and of having worked hard all his life without reward. He had succeeded in escaping the slums of his youth to become a lawyer, which was more than any of his childhood friends had accomplished, but he had not rid himself of the stigma of being poor. His marriage had done nothing to change that feeling; his wife's whims and her general lassitude, which once had been a source of puzzlement, were now a matter for concern. Timothy Duane had said that the world is divided into queen bees, destined for pleasure, and drones, whose mission was to provide for the queens. People like Samantha and Timothy had been born with a silver spoon in their mouth; they hadn't a worry in the world, and there was always someone to pay their bills if their own inheritance was not sufficient. Damn them, he muttered, when he compared his life to theirs. He kept repeating, I swear by all that's holy, I'll beat old Lady Luck—trying not to think that his "luck" might be the grave. No, that won't happen; I have less than two months to go, he would comfort himself; they'll never send me back into that hell. He felt sorry for the other patients, losers like himself, but he was upset by their moaning, the sound of their slippers shuffling across the linoleum, their wretchedness and misery. He listened to the few words they had to say and their complaints, thinking how they were throwaways, all of them, numbers on a roll—trash. They could disappear tomorrow, and there would be no trace of their passage through the world.

And what about me? Would anyone remember me? No one. My wife and daughter wouldn't cry over me, or my mother. Carmen? She would be mourning for her brother; she adored Juan José, the only one of the family who kept in touch when all the others turned away from her. Careful, there I go again, getting sentimental. The truth is I don't give a fuck whether anyone remembers me or not; all I want is to be rich and powerful. My father had power in the proletarian world he lived in; he could hypnotize a hall filled with people and leave them convinced that he was the representative of the Supreme Intelligence; he made us all believe he knew the plans and rules for the universe, but look how he died: tied to a bed coughing up blood and oozing pus through sores over all his body, crazy as a loon. I know what you're muttering, Cyrus, that the only power that counts is the power of morality. You were a good example of that, but you spent your whole life shut up in an elevator without air or light, reading on the sly, and I'll bet your soul is still scrabbling around in heavenly tomes. What did you gain from being such a good man? You gave me a lot, I can't deny that, but you had nothing yourself, you lived a miserable, lonely life. Pedro Morales is another just man. When I was a kid I thought he was powerful; I was afraid of his patriarchal rumble and that stony Indian face sparked with gold teeth. Poor Pedro Morales, he couldn't hurt a fly, another victim of this shithole society; they say that since Carmen went away he's failed, grown old, and now there's Juan José's death on top of that. I'm going to have true power—money and prestige—something I never saw in the barrio; then no one can look down on me or raise his voice to me. You must be whirling in your grave to hear such cynicism, Cyrus. Try to understand: the world belongs to the strong, and I'm fed up with standing in line with the weak. Well, enough of that. The first thing is to get well. As it is, I can't lift my arm to comb my hair, I can scarcely breathe, and my brain is at the boiling point, and none of it has anything to do with whatever made me sick, it's from the past, I'm being eaten alive by my allergies. I'm not going to take any more drugs, I'm killing myself, well, at the most a little marijuana to get through the day, but no more pills or shooting up that shit, I want to get back to the world of the healthy. I *won't* be another veteran in a wheelchair, an alcoholic-drug-addict-dregs-of-the-world veteran, there's enough of them already. Damn it to hell, I'm going to be rich!

Thoughts were hurtling through his mind. When he closed his eyes he saw spiraling images, whirling and whirling; when he opened them he saw his memories projected on the gray ceiling. It was nearly impossible to sleep; he lay awake in the darkness, struggling to suck air into his lungs.

The doctors identified his infection, administered antibiotics, and in three weeks he was back on his feet. He had gained weight, but he would never regain his former strength, and he came to understand that muscles have little to do with manhood. His allergies improved, the headache went away, he no longer bubbled when he breathed or looked at the world through bloodshot eyes, but he still felt weak, and the least expenditure of effort clouded his vision. One day, unbelieving, he heard the doctor say he was releasing him, and his orders were to return to his unit. He could not imagine how he would carry a weapon again; he had expected he would complete his remaining weeks of service in some office assignment or be sent back to the village. Instead, he was flown to Saigon with two days' leave and incontrovertible orders to use that forty-eight hours to get back in shape. He used the time to look up Thui, Juan José Morales's sweetheart. Through inquiries made by his friend Leo Galupi, a man from whom the world held no secrets, he located Thui by telephone and made an appointment to meet her at a small restaurant. Gregory awaited her arrival with terrible anxiety; he could not think how to soften the blow of what he had to tell her. Thui had said she would be wearing a blue dress and white bead necklace, so he could recognize her. Reeves watched Thui enter the restaurant and before making a move took a second or two to study her from a distance and to quiet the wild thumping of his heart. She was not beautiful; her skin was dull, as if she had been ill, and she had a flat nose and short legs. Her best feature was her eyes, oblique and set wide apart: two perfect black almonds. She held out a small hand, which was engulfed by his own, and murmured a greeting without meeting his eyes. They sat down at a plastic-covered table; she waited quietly with her hands in her lap and her eyes lowered while he studied the menu with absurd dedication, asking himself why the hell he had ever called her: now he was in this mess, when all he wanted was to get away. The waiter brought them beer and a dish that was difficult to identify but doubtlessly lethal for someone recovering from an intestinal infection. The silence became uncomfortable; Gregory stroked the scapulary of the Virgin of Guadalupe beneath his shirt. Finally Thui looked up at him, her face expressionless.

"I already know," she said in her halting English.

"Know what?" Reeves immediately regretted having asked.

"About Juan José. I already know."

"I'm so sorry. I don't know what to say; I'm not very good at this kind of thing. . . . I know you loved each other very much. I was fond of him too," Gregory blurted, and his grief cut off his words and filled his heart with tears he could not shed, as he pounded the table with his fist.

"Can I do anything for you?" she asked.

"That's what I should be asking you. That's why I called. Forgive me, I don't want to butt in. Did Juan José speak of me?"

"He told me about his family and his country. You're his brother, aren't you?"

"You might say. He told me about you too, Thui. He said he

was in love for the first time in his life, and that you were a very sweet person, and that when the war was over you two would be married and he would take you back to America."

"Yes."

"Do you need anything? Juan José would want me to . . ."

"Nothing, thank you."

"Money?"

"No."

There was nothing more to say. They sat for a while and finally she announced that she must go back to work and stood up. Even though Gregory was still seated, her head was only slightly higher than his. She placed her childlike hand on his shoulder and smiled, a faint, slightly mischievous smile that added to her elfin air.

"Don't worry. Juan José left me everything I need."

Fear. Terror. I'm suffocating with fear. It's not like anything I've felt before; this is new. Before, I was programmed for this shit, I knew what to do, my body obeyed me; I was always alert, on edge, a dyed-in-the-wool grunt. Now I'm a weakling, twitching with ineffectiveness, a bag of rags. Lots of men die in their last few days of service because they relax or get scared. I'm afraid of dying in an instant, without time to say goodbye to the light, and even more afraid of dying slowly. I'm afraid of blood, of my own blood pouring from me, of pain, of living as a paraplegic, of going crazy, of the syphilis and other horrors we pick up here, of being taken prisoner and tortured in a cage for monkeys, of being swallowed up by the jungle, of falling asleep and dreaming, of getting used to killing, to violence, drugs, filth, whores, to the mindless obedience, the screams, and afraid that afterward—if there is an afterward—I won't be able to walk through the streets like a normal person but will rape old ladies in the park and fire a carbine at kids playing in a schoolyard. I'm afraid of everything that lies ahead. Brave is he who is calm in the face of danger. Cyrus underlined that in a book for me; he told me not to be cowardly, that the honorable man does not lose heart or yield to fear, but this is different, these are not fanciful dangers, not the shadows and monsters of my imagination: this is the fire of the end of the world, Cyrus.

And rage. I should feel hatred, but despite the training, the propaganda, and what I see and am told, I can't feel the hatred I should. That must be my mother's fault—she filled my head with her Bahai teachings—or maybe the fault of my friends in the village, who taught me to see our similarities and to forget our differences. No hatred but more than enough rage, a simmering anger against everyone, against the enemy, those motherfuckers tunneling through the ground like moles and multiplying as fast as we exterminate them and looking just like the men and women in the village, who invited me to their homes to eat. Rage against every single one of the corrupt bastards getting rich on this war, against the politicians and generals with their maps and their computers, their hot coffee, their deadly mistakes and infinite arrogance, against the bureaucrats and their casualty lists, their long columns of numbers, their body bags in endless rows, against all those who stayed home and burned their draft cards and also against those who wave flags and applaud when we appear on the television screen but don't know why we're getting killed. Cannon fodder or heroic defenders of liberty, those sonsofbitches call us both; they can't pronounce the names of the places where we fall, but they have opinions, they all have their ideas on the subject. Ideas! What we don't need here is their goddam ideas. And rage against the skies that open to pour buckets of water on us, soaking us through and rotting everything we touch, against this climate from outer space where when we're not freezing we're boiling, against this scarred country and its defiant jungle. We're winning, of course, we're winning; that's what Leo Galupi always tells me, the king of the black market, who served his two years and then came back to stay and never intends to leave because he loves the frigging place and because he's making a mint selling us contraband ivory and selling the Vietnamese our socks and deodorants. We come out on top after every skirmish, at least according to Galupi; I don't know why, then, we have this sense of defeat. But good always triumphs, the way it does in the movies, and we're the good guys, aren't we? We control the sky and sea; we could blast this country to a heap of ashes and leave nothing on the map but a crater, an enormous crematorium where nothing will grow for a million years, all we have to do is press the famous button, it would be easier than Hiroshima—you remember that, Mama, or have you forgotten? You haven't mentioned Hiroshima in years; what do you talk about these days with my father's ghost? Those bombs are obsolete, we have others now that kill more people more efficiently. What do you think of that, eh? But wars aren't won in the air or at sea, they're won on land, inch by inch, man to man. The extreme in brutality. Why don't we just launch a nuclear attack and get this over with and get back home? marines say with their second beer. I don't want to be anywhere around when we do it. I don't want to think of vanished friends, blown to bits, their homes in flames, the masses of refugees, monks ablaze in gasoline, nor do I want to think of Juan José Morales or the poor kid from Kansas, or think of my daughter every time I see one of these little girls blind or covered with scars and burns. I need to concentrate on getting out of here alive, I can't spare any room for emotion; get out alive, and that's it. I can't look anyone in the eye; we're marked for death, and I'm frightened by the empty eyes of these eighteen-year-old kids, all with the dark void in their gaze.

The enemy are all around us, they know our every thought, they hear our whispers, they smell us, follow us, watch us ... wait. They have no choice: win or die. They're not the ones asking themselves what the shit they're doing here; they've been born on this soil for thousands of years and have been fighting for at least a hundred. The little kid who sells us fruit, the woman without ears who leads us to the whorehouses, the old man who burns the garbage, they're all enemies. Or maybe none of them is. During the three months in the village I was a human being, not a grunt, a man, but now I'm a hunted animal again. What if all this was just a nightmare? A nightmare ... Soon I'll wake up in a clean desert, holding my father's hand and watching the sunset. The skies here are magnificent; it's the only thing the war hasn't devastated. The dawns are long, and the sun rises so slowly: orange, purple, yellow, an enormous disk of pure gold.

I never thought they'd send me back to this hell; I only have a month—less than a month, exactly twenty-five days. I don't want to die now; that would be a stupid way to go. It's not possible to have survived the beatings of the barrio gangs, a race against a moving train, the massacre on the mountain, and three months of firefights, only to end up with no fame and no pain in a body bag, wiped out at the last minute like some damn moron. That can't happen. Maybe Olga's right, maybe I am different from the rest and that's why I'll come down safe and sound from the mountain: I'm invincible, I'm immortal. That's what everyone believes; if we didn't, we couldn't keep fighting. Juan José thought he was immortal. Fate, karma, destiny. . . . Careful with those words; I've been using them too often. There's no such thing; that's just bull-shit my father and Olga used to cheat the ignorant. You shape your own destiny, you take your hard knocks. I will make what I want of my life—that is, as long as I get out alive and make it home. And *that's* not fate? Going home's not up to me; nothing I do or don't do can guarantee I won't lose my arms or my legs or my life during the next twenty-five days.

Inmaculada Morales realized that her husband was sick before he had his first attack; she knew him so well she noticed changes he had not perceived. Pedro had always enjoyed splendid health; the only medicine he trusted was the eucalyptus oil he rubbed on his back after overworking, and the only time he had ever been anesthetized was when his sound teeth were replaced with gold ones. He did not know his exact age; he had obtained his birth certificate from a forger in Tijuana when he had to provide one for his immigration papers and had chosen a date at random. His wife calculated that he was about fifty-five at the time Carmen left home. After that, Pedro Morales had never been the same. He became a taciturn man with a solemn expression, a man not easy to live with. His family never questioned his authority; they would not have dreamed of defying him or asking for explanations. Some time later, when the older children married and had children of their own, he mellowed a little; when he watched his grandbabies babbling and crawling around his feet like cockroaches, he would smile as he had in the good times. Inmaculada could not mention Carmen's name. She had tried once, and he had nearly struck her. Look what you're making me do, woman! he roared when he found himself with his arm raised against her. Unlike many men in the barrio, Morales thought it cowardly to strike a wife; it's different with daughters, he said: they have to learn. Despite his old-fashioned severity, Inmaculada could guess how much he missed Carmen and devised a way to keep him informed. She began a sporadic correspondence with Gregory Reeves, in which the main topic was the absent girl. She sent Reeves postcards with pictures of flowers and doves, recounting the news of the family, and her "gringo son" wrote back about his most recent telephone conversation with Carmen. This was how Inmaculada followed the details of her daughter's life: her stay in Mexico, her trip to Europe, her love affairs, her work. Inmaculada left the cards lying around, where her husband could read them without damaging his injured pride. Customs were changing drastically during those years, and mistakes like Carmen's became a daily occurrence; it seemed senseless to continue to punish her as if she were the spawn of Satan. Pregnancies outside marriage were a common theme in films, television serials, and novels, and in real life famous actresses were having children without identifying the father, feminists were advocating women's right to an abortion, and hippies were coupling in public parks in full view of anyone who wanted to watch, so that not even the hard-shelled Padre Larraguibel could understand Pedro Morales's intransigence.

Then came the bitter Wednesday when two young officers called at the Morales home, a pair of frightened young men who attempted to hide their discomfort behind absurd military rigor and the formality of a too often repeated speech. They brought the news of Juan José's death. There would be a religious service if the family agreed, and the body would be buried within the week in a military cemetery, they said, and then they presented the parents with the decorations their son had won for heroic actions beyond the call of duty. That night Pedro Morales suffered his third attack. He felt a sudden weakness in his bones, as if his body had turned to wax, and collapsed at the feet of his wife, who could not lift him into bed and was afraid to leave him alone to seek help. When Inmaculada saw he was not breathing, she threw cold water in his face, but without effect. Then she remembered a television program she had seen and began to administer mouth-to-mouth resuscitation and to shock his heart by pounding his chest. A minute later, her husband, streaming water like a duck, regained consciousness, and as soon as the dizziness had passed drank two glasses of tequila and devoured half an apple pie. He refused to go to the hospital, convinced that his attack was nothing but nerves and that he would feel fine after a little sleep—which in fact he did. The next morning he got up early, as usual, opened the garage, and after giving orders to the mechanics, left to buy a black suit for his son's funeral. There was no aftermath from his attack other than aching ribs where his wife had beaten on his chest. Faced with the impossibility of getting her husband to the doctor, Inmaculada decided to consult Olga, with whom she had reconciled following Carmen's tragic incident because she realized she had only wanted to help. She knew Olga was experienced and would never have risked performing such a late abortion if it had been someone other than Carmen, whom she loved as if she were her own niece. That things had worked out badly was not Olga's fault but the will of God. Olga had heard about Juan José's death and, like everyone in the barrio, was getting ready to attend Padre Larraguibel's mass. The two women hugged and patted each other and then sat down to drink a cup of coffee and discuss Pedro Morales's fainting spells.

"He just isn't the same. He's getting thin. He drinks quarts of lemonade; he must have holes in his belly from all the lemonade he's swallowed. He doesn't even have the energy to grumble at me when I tell him some days he shouldn't go to the shop."

"Anything else?"

"He cries in his sleep."

"Don Pedro is so macho he can't cry when he's awake. His heart is filled with tears over his son's death; it's normal he should shed them when he's asleep."

"But the tears began before Juan José died—may God shelter him in His Loving Bosom."

"One of two things: either his blood is bad or he is sick with grief."

"I think he's really sick. That's how my mother was—you remember her?"

Olga remembered very well; she had made history when she appeared on television to celebrate her hundred and fifth birthday. She was normally a happy person, if more than a little unbalanced, but she awoke one morning bathed in tears and no one could console her; she knew she was going to die, and it made her sad to be going alone—she liked her family's company. She thought she was still in her village in Zacatecas; she had never realized she had lived thirty years in the United States, that her grandchildren were called Chicanos, and that beyond the boundaries of the barrio everyone spoke English. She ironed her best dress, because she meant to be buried decently, and asked to be taken to the cemetery to locate the grave of her ancestors. The Morales boys had hastily ordered a stone with the names of their great-grandparents and placed it in a strategic spot where their grandmother would be able to see it with her own eyes. My, how the dead multiply! was her only comment when she saw the size of the county cemetery. In the next weeks she continued to weep for herself, in anticipation, until she was consumed like a candle and her flame was snuffed out.

"I'm going to send him some La Magdalena syrup; it's very effective in these cases. And if Don Pedro doesn't get better, you must take him to a doctor," Olga recommended. "And forgive me, *doñita,* but making love is good for the body and good for the soul. I'd recommend you be affectionate with him."

Inmaculada blushed. That was a subject she had never been able to discuss with anyone.

"If I were in your shoes, I'd also call Carmen to come home. It's been a long time, and her father needs her. It's time they made their peace."

"My husband would never forgive me, Doña Olga."

"Don Pedro has just lost a son. Don't you think it would be a consolation for him to have the girl he thought of as dead brought back to life? Carmen was always his favorite."

Inmaculada took the syrup with her, not to seem ungrateful. She did not have much confidence in the healer's potions, but she trusted her blindly when it came to advice. When she got home she threw the bottle into the trash and searched through the tin box where she kept Gregory Reeves's postcards until she found her daughter's most recent address.

Carmen Morales lived in Mexico City for four years. The first two had been so lonely and filled with poverty that she had begun to enjoy reading, something she'd never imagined possible. At first Gregory sent her novels in English, but eventually she registered at a public library and began reading in Spanish. That was where she met an anthropologist, twenty years her senior, who initiated her into the study of other cultures and of her own heritage. He was as fascinated with the girl's cleavage as she was with his erudition. At the beginning, Carmen was horrified by the violent and bloody past of the continent—she could find nothing to admire in priests caked with dried blood who engaged in ripping hearts from their sacrificial victims—but when the anthropologist explained the significance of those rituals, told her the ancient legends, taught her to decipher hieroglyphics, took her to museums, and introduced her to a myriad of books on art, feather mantles, weavings, bas-reliefs, and sculptures, she came to appreciate that ferocious aesthetic. Her greatest interest lay in the designs and colors of cloth, paintings, ceramics, and ornaments; she entertained herself for hours making sketches to use in her jewelry. The anthropologist and his pupil spent so much time together observing mummies and blood-curdling Aztec statuary that they became lovers. He suggested they live together and share ecstasy and expenses; she left the pestilent hovel where she had been existing marginally and moved into his apartment in the very center of the city. The air pollution was so bad that sometimes birds dropped from the sky, but at least she had a bathroom with hot water and a sunny room where she could set up her workshop. She believed she had found happiness and imagined she would acquire wisdom through osmosis. She was eager to learn and lived in a constant state of amazed admiration for her lover; every crumb of knowledge he scattered fell onto fertile soil. In exchange for the first-rate education she was acquiring from the anthropologist, she was willing to serve him, to wash his clothes, clean the house, prepare the meals, and even cut his fingernails and his mane of hair—besides turning over to him everything she earned selling her silver pieces to tourists. He not only knew about phantasmagoric Indians and cemeteries of friable pots, he was also informed about film, books, and restaurants; he decided how she should dress, speak, make love, even think. Carmen's submissiveness lasted much longer than could have been expected in a person of her temperament; for almost two years she reverently obeyed him. She even put up with his having other women and telling her about it in salacious detail, "because there should be no secrets between us," and quietly endured being slapped around when he had had too much to drink. After every violent incident her erudite companion brought home flowers and put his head in her lap, weeping, begging her to understand—the devil in him had got the upper hand—and swearing he would never do it again. Carmen forgave him, but she did not forget, and in the meanwhile she was absorbing information like a sponge. She was embarrassed about being roughed up; she felt humiliated and sometimes thought she must deserve it. Maybe that was normal treatment; hadn't her father often beat her? Finally one day she dared mention it to Gregory Reeves in one of their secret Monday telephone conversations; her friend screamed to high heaven, called her stupid, terrified her with statistics of his own invention, and convinced her that the anthropologist would never change—just the opposite, his abuse would increase until it reached extremes she could not even imagine. Ten days later Carmen received a bank draft for a plane ticket and a letter offering to help and begging her to return to the United States. Gregory's gift arrived the day after a skirmish in which with one sweep of his hand the anthropologist had emptied a soup pot over Carmen. It was an accident, they both knew that, but even so she spent two days dousing her chest with milk and olive oil. As soon as she could bear to wear a blouse she went to a travel agency, meaning to buy a ticket home, but as she was leafing through some brochures she remembered her father's fury and decided she lacked the strength to confront him. In a fit of inspiration, she spun the needle and bought a ticket for Amsterdam. She traveled light and did not even say goodbye to her lover; she had meant to leave a letter but in the haste of packing forgot. She carried her jeweler's tools and supplies in a tote bag, along with two tins of condensed milk to ease the distress of the journey.

She was dazzled by Europe, which she toured from end to end with a pack on her back, earning her living with no great difficulty, teaching English, selling her jewelry when she had time to make some, and knowing that if she was threatened by hunger she could call on Gregory for help. No cathedral, castle, or museum escaped her, until she reached the saturation point and swore never again to set foot in a temple of tourism; she would stroll through the streets and enjoy life. One summer she got off the train in Barcelona and was immediately surrounded by a group of noisy gypsies, who insisted on telling her fortune and selling her amulets. She thought they were stunning and decided on the spot that this style was made for her, not only for her jewelry design but for her personal life. Later she discovered the Moorish influence in the south of Spain and the color of North Africa, all of which she adopted in a happy mélange. She moved into a *pension* in the Gothic barrio, notable for its uninterrupted clanking and moaning of pipes and absence of natural light, but her room was large, with coffered ceilings, and contained an enormous worktable. Within a few days she had stitched up a number of ruffled skirts that reminded her of Olga in her younger years and of the costumes she herself had worn for her juggling act in Pershing Square. That look would be her style for the rest of her life; in years to come she refined it to perfection for her personal pleasure, never knowing that in a future time it would make her wealthy and famous.

After wandering from Oslo to Athens with her belongings on her back, and nearly penniless, she decided she had had enough of the vagabond life and that the time had come to settle down. She was convinced that the only occupation she was suited for was jewelry making, but there was merciless competition in that field. To excel, it was not enough to have original designs; before she went any further she must discover the secrets of her craft. Barcelona was an ideal place for that. She enrolled in several courses, where she learned centuries-old techniques and gradually developed her unique style, a blend of solid traditional craft with a bold gypsy flavor, touches of Africa, Latin America, and even a hint of India, so popular during that decade. She was always the most original student in the class, and her creations sold so quickly she could not keep up with the orders. Everything was going better than she could have hoped, until her path crossed that of a fellow student, a Japanese craftsman slightly younger than herself. Carmen had succeeded in placing her work in exclusive shops; he, on the other hand, was peddling his with little success along the Ramblas, a contrast he found humiliating. As consolation, Carmen went back to selling in the street, using the excuse that the soul of the city was to be found there. The young Japanese moved into Carmen's crepuscular *pension*. Very quickly, their cultural differences outweighed their mutual attraction, but Carmen's need for companionship was so great that she ignored the symptoms. Her lover would not renounce his ancestral customs: he came first, and he expected to be served. He lay for hours in a steaming tub and then yielded it to her when the water was cold. It was the same with food, bed, supplies, and work tools; in the street he walked ahead of her, and she had to follow two paces behind. If there was sun, he went out to sell and Carmen stayed behind in the dark, sunless room, working, but if they awoke to rain, it became her turn to peddle their wares, because her lover would be suffering an opportune rheumatic pain related to the damp weather. At first she found his behavior amusing—strange Oriental customs, she told herself good-naturedly—but after a while she grew impatient, and the arguments began. He never lost his composure and met her recriminations with long, glacial silences; she felt his withdrawal pressing in around her but did not complain because at least this man refrained from striking her or scalding her with boiling soup. Finally she would give in, tired of being lonely, and also yielding to her fascination for him; she was attracted by his long black hair, his small, extremely muscular body, his strange accent, and the precision of his movements. She would circle around him timidly, purr in his ear like a cat, and usually succeed in breaching his shell; their reconciliation was accomplished in bed, where he was expert. They would have stayed together out of inertia had a telegram from Inmaculada not intervened. It announced Pedro Morales's illness and asked Carmen for the love of God to come home because she was the only one who could save her father from being consumed by sadness. Carmen realized then how much she loved the headstrong old man, how much she wanted to bury her head in her mother's welcoming bosom and again be, if only for an instant, the indulged girl she had been as a child. Thinking that the trip would be for only a couple of weeks, she took nothing with her but the minimum of clothing she hurriedly stuffed into a bag. Her lover accompanied her to the airport, wished her luck, and, because they never touched in public, bade her farewell with a slight bow.

From looking death in the face so often, I learned the value of living. Life is all we have, and no life is more valuable than another. Juan José Morales's life was worth no more than the lives of the men I killed, yet their deaths don't weigh on me: those men are always with me; they are my comrades. Kill or be killed, it's that simple. For me, it isn't a moral question; my doubts and confusions are of a different nature. I'm one of the lucky ones who came out of the war unharmed.

When I arrived home, I went directly from the airport to a motel; I didn't call anyone. San Francisco was cloudy, and a wintry wind was blowing, the way it does in summer, and I decided to wait for the sun to come out before I called Samantha. I don't know why I thought the weather might make our meeting more amicable. The truth is that when I went away we were prepared to get a divorce; we never wrote to each other, and the day I called her from Hawaii it was obvious we had nothing to say to each other. I was tired, with no appetite for arguments or reproaches, much less for telling her or anyone else my war experiences. I wanted to see Margaret, of course, but my daughter might not recognize me; at that age children forget in a few days, and she hadn't seen me for months. I left my things in the room and went out to look for a café. I was longing for a cup of San Francisco coffee; it's the best in the world. I walked through that urban delirium where the ocean can rarely be seen, straight lines rising and falling, laid out in accord with a geometric design indifferent to the topography of the city's hills. I looked for familiar landmarks, but everything was deformed by the fog. It was a place I didn't know; I couldn't identify the buildings and began to wander disoriented in that city of contradictions and smells, depraved like all ports, and as full of tricks as a frivolous girl. I can't explain San Francisco's air of elegance, seeing that it was founded by prostitutes and outlaws and bands of adventurers flushed with easy gold. A Chinese man brushed my arm, and I jumped as if I had been stung by a scorpion, fists clenched, reaching for the sidearm I no longer carried. The man smiled. Have a good day, he said, as he walked on. I stood there paralyzed, feeling strange eyes on me, although actually no one was paying attention to me, while the cable cars clanged by, students, secretaries, the ubiquitous tourists, Hispanic laborers, Asian businessmen, hippies, black prostitutes with platinum-blond wigs, homosexuals hand in hand, all like actors in a movie set illuminated by klieg lights, while I stood watching on this side of the screen, uncomprehending, totally outside everything, thousands of years away. I walked through the Italian district, through Chinatown, through streets frequented by sailors, where liquor, drugs, and pornography were the major commerce—inflatable sheep were the latest novelty—along with Saint Christopher medals as protection against the perils of the sea. I returned to the motel, took several sleeping pills, and was out for twenty hours; I was awakened by sun streaming through the window. I picked up the telephone to call Samantha but couldn't remember my own number and decided to wait a while longer, to give myself a couple of days alone to compose body and soul; I needed to cleanse myself, inside and out, of scores of sins and terrible memories. I felt contaminated, dirty, dead tired. I also waited to call the Moraleses; I would have had to leave immediately for Los Angeles, and I didn't have the courage to do it. I wasn't ready yet to talk about Juan José, to look Inmaculada and Pedro in the eye and assure them their son had died for his country, a hero, fully confessed and without pain, almost without realizing, when in fact he died in agony, and only half of his body was left to bury. I couldn't tell them his last words were not a message for them; he had clung to the chaplain's hand and said, Hold me, Padre, I'm falling ... it's so deep down there. Nothing happens the way it does in the movies, not even death; we don't die cleanly, we die stricken with terror in a pool of blood and shit. In the movies no one really dies; in war no one really lives. In Vietnam I used to imagine that soon someone would turn on the lights and I would walk out of the theater and get a cup of coffee and before long forget everything. Now that I've learned to live with the canker of a good memory, I no longer make believe that life is like fiction; I accept it with all the pain it carries with it.

My sister and I had grown apart; we hadn't seen each other since Margaret was born. I didn't want to call her, or my mother. What would we have said? My mother was opposed to the war; she thought it was more honorable to desert than to kill. Any form of violence is shameful and perverse; remember Gandhi, she always told me; we cannot support a culture based on armaments; we are in this world to celebrate life and to promote compassion and justice. Poor woman; innocent of reality, she wandered through the planes of *The Infinite Plan* after my father, half out of her head but with an unquestionable lucidity in her digressions. I left for Vietnam without saying goodbye because I didn't want to hurt her; for her, the war was a matter of principle, it had nothing to do with my personal safety. I suppose she loved me in her way, but there was always a chasm between us. What would my father have advised me? He would never have told me to go to jail or leave the country; he would have invited me to go hunting, and in the frozen silence of dawn, waiting for the ducks, would have clapped me on the back, and we would have understood each other without need for words, as men sometimes understand each other.

I spent my first three days home shut up in the motel, sitting before the television with cartons of beer and bottles of whiskey; then I took my sleeping bag down to the beach and spent two weeks staring at the sea, smoking pot, and conversing with the ghost of Juan José. The water was cold, but I swam just the same, until I felt my blood congealing in my veins and my brain growing numb and free of memories—blank. The ocean over there is warm; soldiers swarmed over the sand like ants: three days of play, beer, and rock to compensate for months of fighting. For two weeks I did not exchange a complete sentence with anyone, merely mumbling a word or two to ask for pizza or a hamburger. I think deep down I wanted to go back to Vietnam. At least there I had comrades and something to do; here I had no friends, I was alone, I didn't belong anywhere. In civilian life no one spoke the language of war; there was no vocabulary to describe the experience of the firefights, and even had there been one, nobody would have wanted to hear my story; nobody likes bad news. Only among veterans could I feel at ease and talk about the things I would never discuss with a civilian. Only grunts would understand why you harden yourself to affection and are afraid to get close to anyone; they know that physical courage comes much easier than emotional courage, because they, too, lost friends they loved like brothers and made up their minds that in the future they would spare themselves that unbearable pain: it's best not to love anyone too much. Without realizing it, I had begun to slip down into that abyss where so many are lost; I began to see the glamorous side of violence, to think that nothing so exhilarating would ever happen to me again, that the rest of my life would be a gray desert by comparison.

I believed I had discovered the secret that explains why we keep on fighting wars. Joan and Susan maintain that war is a way for old machos to eliminate young men; they hate them and fear them and don't want to share anything with them, not women or power or money, because they know that sooner or later the younger men will depose them. That's the reason they send the young to their deaths, even if it's their own sons. That may be a logical rationale for the old men, but why do the young men go? Why throughout so many millennia have they not rebelled against these ritual massacres? I have an answer. It's something more than the primordial instinct to do battle, more than blood lust: pleasure. I discovered that on the mountain. I don't dare say the word aloud, it would bring bad luck, but I repeat it over and over to myself: *pleasure, pleasure.* The most intense pleasure you can experience, much more intense than sex: thirst satiated, first love requited, divine revelation, say those who know what it is.

That night on the mountain I was within a fraction of a second of death. A bullet grazed my cheek and struck the forehead of the soldier behind me. Panic paralyzed me for an instant; I was suspended in the fascination of my own fear, but then consciousness was blacked out and I began to fire in a frenzy, screaming and cursing, unable to stop or to reason, while bullets sped past me and the world exploded in a cataclysmic roaring. I was blanketed in heat and smoke, trapped in the airless void that followed each flash of fire. I have no idea how long all that lasted or what I did or why I did it; I remember only the miracle of finding myself alive, the rush of adrenaline and the pain over every inch of my body, sensual pain, an atrocious pleasure unlike anything I had known, deeper than the most prolonged orgasm, a pleasure that invaded every pore, turning my blood to caramel and my bones to sand, submerging me finally in nothingness.

After nearly two weeks in the motel on the beach, I woke up one night screaming. In my nightmare I was alone on the mountain at dawn; bodies were strewn below me, and the shadows of guerrillas were climbing toward me in the mist. They were coming closer. Everything was very slow and very quiet, a silent movie. I fired my weapon, felt the recoil, my hands ached, I saw the sparks, but there was no sound. The bullets passed through the enemy without stopping them; the guerrillas were transparent, as if sketched on glass; they moved forward inexorably, encircling me. I opened my mouth to scream but was so filled with horror that no voice came out, only shards of ice. After waking, the pounding of my heart kept me from falling asleep again. I got out of bed, took my jacket, and went to walk on the beach. All right, enough moaning, I announced to the gulls at dawn.

Carmen Morales did not dare go straight home to her family, because she did not know what welcome she might expect from her father, whom she had not seen for seven years. From the airport she took a taxi to the Reeveses' house. As they drove through the streets of the barrio she was surprised by the transformations; it looked more prosperous, cleaner, more orderly, and much smaller than she remembered. Besides the actual changes, she was influenced by comparisons to the enormous squatters' cities that ring the Mexican capital. She smiled when she thought how this complex of streets had been her universe for so many years and how she had fled from it as an exile, weeping for her lost family and home. Now she felt like a foreigner. The taxi driver observed her with curiosity in the rearview mirror and could not resist the temptation to ask where she was from. He had never seen anyone like that woman in the brightly colored skirts and clinking bracelets; she was different from those sleepwalking hippies, who wore similar garb: this one had the determined air of a woman of business.

"I'm a gypsy," Carmen told him, with absolute aplomb.

"Where is that?"

"We gypsies don't have a country; we're from everywhere."

"You speak very good English," was his comment.

Carmen had difficulty locating the Reeves cottage; over the years, weeds had swallowed up the garden, and the willow tree blocked the house from view. She walked down the path toward the front yard. She recognized the place where she had buried Oliver, following the instructions of Gregory, who wanted his childhood companion's remains to rest near the family home and not on the garbage dump like some stray. She found Nora Reeves sitting on the porch in the same rickety wicker chair, a worn old woman with a meringue-white bun and an apron as faded as the rest of her. She was much smaller and wore a sweet and slightly addled expression, as if her soul had already left her body. She stood up unsteadily and greeted Carmen politely, without recognizing her.

"It's me, Doña Nora, I'm Carmen, Pedro and Inmaculada Morales's daughter."

It took Nora Reeves a minute to situate the visitor in the confused map of her memory; she stood looking at Carmen with her mouth agape, unable to relate the image of the dark-haired girl who used to play with her son to this apparition escaped from a sheik's harem. Finally she held out her arms and embraced Carmen, trembling. Nora Reeves made hot tea, served in glasses, and they sat down to catch up on news of the past. They were interrupted by Judy's noisy brood, back from school, four children of indeterminate age, two flaming redheads and two with Latin features. Nora explained that the first two were Judy's own and that the other two also lived with her although they were her second husband's children by a previous marriage. Their grandmother served them milk and bread and jam.

"Do they all live here?" Carmen asked, surprised.

"No. I watch them after school until their mother comes to pick them up in the evening."

Judy appeared about seven, and she, too, failed to recognize her friend. Carmen remembered her as being large, but she could not have imagined that Judy could continue to add so much weight; she was too huge for any of the chairs, so she lowered herself gingerly to the porch steps, giving the impression that it would take a crane to get her up again. She looked radiant, nevertheless.

"Not all of this is fat," she announced with pride. "I'm pregnant again."

Both her own and her foster children ran to clamber over the amiable mountain of their mother, who hugged them, laughing, and accommodated them among her rolls of flesh with a skill born of practice and affection, at the same time handing each a sugar bun and in passing eating several herself. When Carmen saw Judy playing with the children, she understood that motherhood was her friend's natural state and could not avoid the prick of envy.

"After dinner I'll take you home, but first let's call Doña Inmaculada, so she can prepare your father. Don't you have anything a little less colorful to wear? That old man disapproves of any wild stuff in women. Is that the style in Europe?" Judy asked without a hint of irony.

Pedro Morales was waiting for his daughter dressed in his funeral suit enlivened with a red necktie and a carnation in his buttonhole. Inmaculada had announced the news with extreme caution, expecting a violent reaction, and was amazed when her husband's face lighted up as if he had shed twenty years. "Brush off my suit, woman," was all he could manage as he blew his nose to hide his emotion.

"I expect she's changed a lot—with God's blessing," Inmaculada warned him.

"Don't worry, woman. Even if she shows up with blue hair, I'll recognize her."

Still, like Nora and Judy, he was not fully prepared for the woman who walked into his house a half hour later, and his jaw hung slack for several seconds before he closed his mouth. Carmen seemed taller to him, but then he noticed the high-heeled sandals and measured the cloud of curly, tangled hair that added inches to her height. She was festooned with necklaces like an idol, her eyes were painted with black lines, and she resembled something he had seen in a Moroccan tourism poster hanging in Los Tres Amigos bar. Even so, his daughter looked beautiful to him. They hugged each other for a long time and wept together for Juan José and for the seven years she'd been away. Then she curled up beside him to tell him some of her adventures, omitting certain portions to avoid scandalizing him. In the meantime, Inmaculada busied herself in the kitchen, repeating, *gracias, bendito Dios, gracias, bendito Dios,* and Judy, glued to the telephone, called all the Morales children and friends to announce that Carmen had come home turned into an outlandish, wild-haired gypsy, but that she was still the same girl: bring beer and your guitars, because Inmaculada is making tacos to celebrate.

His daughter's presence restored Pedro Morales's good humor. At the insistence of Carmen and the other members of his family, he agreed to see a doctor, who told him he had advanced diabetes. None of my ancestors ever had any such thing, this is some newfangled American disease; I have no intention of sticking myself every time I turn around, like some stinking addict, the offended patient grumbled; that doctor doesn't know what he's talking about, they mixed up the tests in the laboratory, they're always making stupid errors. Once again, however, Inmaculada gained the upper hand and forced Pedro to stay on a diet and herself took charge of administering his medication at the proper times. I'd rather argue with you every day of the week than end up a widow, she said; it would be hard work to break in another husband. It had never entered Pedro's mind that he could be replaced in what he had thought was his wife's unconditional love, and the knowledge made a considerable dent in his stubbornness. He refused to admit he was ill but resigned himself to the treatment, "just to please that crazy woman," as he liked to say.

The barrio quickly seemed too small for Carmen Morales; after a few weeks with her parents, she felt she was suffocating. In the years she was away, she had idealized the past; in moments of greatest loneliness she longed for her mother's tenderness, for her father's protection, and for the companionship of family, but she had forgotten the narrow-mindedness of the barrio. She had changed during those years; the dust of much of the world was on her shoes. She paced through the house like a caged leopard, filling the house and disturbing its peace with her whirling skirts, her tinkling bracelets, and her impatience. In the street, people turned to stare at her, and children came up to touch her. It was impossible to ignore the criticism and whispering going on behind her back: Just look how the younger Morales girl has got herself up; that hair hasn't seen a comb for centuries; she's got to be either a hippie or a whore, they said. Nor could she find a job; she was not willing to work in a factory like Judy Reeves, and there was no market for her jewelry in the barrio—women wore false gold and rhinestones; no one would be caught dead in her aboriginal earrings. She imagined it would be reasonably easy to place her pieces in shops in the city, where actresses and sophisticated shoppers and tourists would buy them, but in the claustrophobia of her parents' house she had no stimulus for creativity; her ideas dried up along with her desire to work. She wandered around the rooms, depressed by the porcelain figurines, the silk flowers, the family portraits, the red plush furniture encased in plastic covers, all the symbols of the Moraleses' new opulence. The bric-a-brac that was her mother's pride and joy gave her nightmares; she preferred a thousand times over the more modest house of her childhood. She could not bear the radio and television programs blaring night and day with stories of romance and tragedy, or the earsplitting commercials touting various brands of soap and automobiles and lotteries. Worst of all was the widespread pursuit of gossip: everyone lived on what everyone else did; not a hair stirred in the neighborhood that escaped comment. Carmen felt like a visiting Martian and consoled herself with her mother's cooking. Inmaculada had adapted her recipes to her husband's strict diet without losing any of their flavor and spent hours among her pots and pans, bathed in delicious odors of salsas and spices. Carmen was bored. Apart from playing checkers with her father, helping do household chores, and seeing relatives when the family got together for Sunday dinner, she had nothing to do. She had

plump bitch's lover, an idea that must have been in the back of their minds for years. Let them make the most of it, she muttered, unsure why the prospect should make her so angry.

Carmen could not pay much longer for the motel room where she was staying, so she started looking for work and a place to live. She bought a newspaper and took a table in a café near the university, and among countless notices for holistic massages, aroma therapies, miraculous crystals, copper triangles to improve the color of your aura, and other novelties that would have enchanted Olga, discovered the help-wanted ads. She called several places before one restaurant gave her an appointment for the next day: she was to bring her social security card and a letter of recommendation, two things she did not possess. The first was not difficult—she simply found out where to sign up, filled out a form, and was assigned a number—but she had no idea how to obtain the second. She knew Gregory Reeves would have given her a letter in a minute; what bad luck he wasn't there, but she couldn't let a small setback become a major blow. She located a hole-in-the-wall shop where she could rent a typewriter and wrote a letter praising her expertise in child care, her reliability, and her pleasant manner in dealing with the public. The style was somewhat flowery, but out of sight, out of mind, as her mother would say: Gregory did not need to know the details. She knew her friend's signature by heart; it was not for nothing they had corresponded all those years. The next day she presented herself at the restaurant, which turned out to be an old house decorated with plants and strings of garlic. She was met by a gray-haired, pleasant-faced woman wearing baggy pants and the sandals of a Franciscan monk.

"Interesting," she said after reading the letter of recommendation. "Very interesting. . . . So you know Gregory Reeves?"

"Yes; I worked for him." Carmen blushed.

"As far as I'm aware, Gregory has been in Vietnam for more than a year. So how do you explain a letter dated only yesterday?"

The person Carmen was speaking to was Joan, Gregory's friend, and she was in the macrobiotic restaurant where he had gone so often to eat vegetarian hamburgers and seek comfort. Knees trembling, voice quivering, Carmen admitted her deception, explaining in a few sentences her relationship to Reeves.

"Well, I can see you're resourceful." Joan laughed. "Gregory is like a son, though I'm not old enough to be his mother—don't let my gray hair fool you. He slept on the sofa in my living room the night before he left for the war. It was so stupid to go! Susan and I wore ourselves out telling him not to, but what could we do? I hope he comes back the same man; it would be a terrible waste if something happened to him; he always seemed like a super guy to me. If you're his friend, then you're our friend too. You can start today. Put on an apron and tie a kerchief around your head so your hair doesn't end up in our customers' food, then go on in the kitchen and let Susan explain the work."

Soon Carmen Morales was not only waiting tables; she was also helping in the kitchen. She had a flair for stuffings and sauces and ideas for new combinations to vary the menu. She became such a good friend of Joan's and Susan's that they rented her the attic of their house, a large room that became an ideal refuge once the junk was cleared out. It had two windows overlooking the bay from the superb prospect of the hills and a skylight in the roof that let in the starlight. In the daytime Carmen enjoyed the natural light, and at night the room was illuminated by two huge Victorian lamps rescued from a flea market.

She worked afternoons and part of the evenings in the restaurant but had her mornings free. She bought tools and materials and in her leisure time started designing jewelry again, finding, to her relief, that she had lost neither her inspiration nor her will to work. The first earrings she made were for her patronesses, who had to have their ears pierced to wear them; they both had slightly sore ears but took off the earrings only to sleep, persuaded that the jewelry enhanced their personality: feminists but still feminine, they would say, laughing. They considered Carmen the best coworker they had ever had but told her she should not be wasting her talent waiting tables and stirring pots; she should devote herself entirely to her jewelry making.

"It's the only thing you're suited for. Every person is born with a talent, and happiness depends on discovering that talent in time," they would say when they were all sitting around drinking mango tea and telling their life stories.

"Don't worry. I'm happy," Carmen replied truthfully. She had a premonition that the hard times were behind her and the best part of her life lay ahead.

Back in the world of the living, Gregory made a pile of his war souvenirs—snapshots, letters, music tapes, clothes, and his medal for bravery—sprinkled them with gasoline, and set them afire. He kept only the painted wood dragon, a memory of his friends in the village, and Juan José's scapulary. He meant to return that to Inmaculada once he discovered how to remove the dried blood. He had sworn not to behave like so many other veterans, hooked forever on the nostalgia of the only momentous event in their lives, crippled in spirit, unable to adapt to everyday routine or to rid themselves of the multiple addictions acquired in the war. He avoided news reported in the press, protests in the street, friends from that time who met to renew the adventures and camaraderie of Vietnam. Nor did he want to hear about the others, comrades in wheelchairs or emotional cripples—or about suicides. For the first few days he was grateful for every small detail: a hamburger with french fries, hot water in the shower, a bed with sheets, the comfort of civilian clothes, conversations with people in the street, the silence and privacy of his room; but soon he realized that this appreciation held its own dangers. No, why should he celebrate anything, even the fact of having a whole body? The past was the past—if only he could erase it from his memory. During the day he nearly succeeded, but at night he had nightmares and woke, bathed in sweat, to the sound of rattling weaponry and the onslaught of visions of red. He dreamed of a small boy lost in a park, and he was that boy, but most of all he dreamed of the mountain, where he was firing against transparent shadows. He would reach out and grope on the table for pills or a joint, turn on the light, half awake, not knowing where he was. He kept the whiskey in the kitchen; that gave him time to think before taking a drink. He thought up small obstacles to help: no booze before I get dressed or eat something; I won't take a drink on odd-numbered days or if the sun isn't shining; first I'll do twenty push-ups and listen to a concerto all the way through. Using these tricks, he postponed the time for opening the cabinet where he kept the bottle and usually was able to control his impulse, although he decided not to forgo liquor altogether; he wanted always to have something on hand for an emergency. When at last he called Samantha he did not tell her that for two weeks he had been only twenty miles from their house; he acted as if he had just arrived and asked her to pick him up at the airport, where he waited for her, fresh from the shower, shaved, sober, and wearing civilian clothes. He was amazed to see how much Margaret had grown and how pretty she had become; she looked like a princess in a nineteenth-century illustration, with her navy-blue eyes, blond curls, and fine-featured, strangely triangular face. He also noticed how little his wife had changed; she was even wearing the same white pants she had worn the last time he saw her. Unsmil-ingly, Margaret held out a limp hand but refused to give him a kiss. She moved with the coquettish gestures she had copied from adult actresses in soap operas and, like them, swayed her little hips as she walked. Gregory felt uncomfortable with her; he could not see her as the young girl she truly was but as an indecent parody of the femme fatale; he felt ashamed of himself—maybe Judy was right, after all, and the perversity of his father was latent in his blood, a hereditary curse. Samantha gave him a lukewarm wel-come. She was happy to see him looking so well, he was thinner but stronger, and the tan was becoming, she said. Apparently, the war had not been that traumatic for him; for her, on the other hand, things were not going at all well, she hated to say it but her finances were in terrible shape, she had run through his savings and was finding it impossible to live on a soldier's salary; she wasn't complaining, of course, she understood the circumstances, but she wasn't used to hardship and neither was Margaret. No, she hadn't been able to keep his baby-sitting business going; it was hard work, and boring, and besides, she had to look after their daughter, didn't she? As they got into the car she told him very smoothly that she had reserved a hotel room for him, but she had no objection to his keeping his things in her garage until he had a better place. If Gregory had had any illusions about a possible reconciliation, those few sentences were more than enough to remind him of the chasm between them. Samantha was as courteous as ever; she had remarkable control over her emotions and was able to maintain a conversation for an indefinite time without saying anything. She did not ask any questions, because she did not want unpleasant answers; with remarkable effort she had managed to live in a fantasy world in which there was no room for sorrow or ugliness. Faithful only to herself, she had tried to ignore the war, their divorce, the breakup of her family—anything that might affect her tennis schedule. Gregory realized with a kind of relief that his wife was a blank page and that he had no remorse about beginning a new life without her. For the remainder of the drive he tried to talk with Margaret, but his daughter was not disposed to cooperate. Sitting in the back seat, she chewed on her red fingernails, played with a lock of her hair, and watched herself in the rearview mirror, replying with monosyllables if her mother spoke to her but stubbornly silent when it was her father.

Gregory found a house to rent across the bay; its principal attraction was that it had a dock—in questionable repair. He planned to buy a boat sometime in the future, more for show than from any desire to sail. Every time he had gone out in Timothy Duane's boat he had been convinced that so much work could be justified only to save the life of someone drowning, never as a pastime. Following the same criterion—appearances—he bought a Porsche, hoping to elicit admiration from males and attention from females. Cars are phallic symbols, Carmen teased when she learned of his purchase, so I don't know why you would want one that's so short and stubby and trembly. At least he had the good sense not to buy furniture before he had a steady job; he made do with a bed the size of a boxing ring, one multipurpose table, and two chairs. Thus installed, he traveled to Los Angeles, his first trip since taking Margaret to meet the Morales family several years before.

Nora Reeves welcomed him casually, as if she had seen him only yesterday, offered him a cup of tea, and told him the news of the barrio and of his father, who continued to communicate with her every week to keep her informed about the progress of *The Infinite Plan*. She did not refer to the war, and for the first time Gregory noted the striking similarities between his mother and Samantha: the same coolness, apathy, and courtesy, the identical determination to ignore reality—although the latter had not been as easy for his mother because she had lived a much more difficult life. For Nora Reeves, indifference had not been enough; it had taken a strong will to remain untouched by life's problems. Gregory found Judy in bed, with a newborn baby in her arms and her other children playing about her. Her obesity was disguised beneath the sheet; she looked like an opulent Renaissance Madonna. Busy raising her brood, she made no attempt to ask Gregory how he was, assuming that if he was standing before her, apparently in one piece, there was no news to tell. His sister's second husband turned out to be a taxi driver; he was a widower, the father of the two older children and the baby. He was a Latino born in the United States, one of the many Chicanos who speak Spanish badly but who bear the unmistakable stamp of their ancestors: small and slim, with the long drooping mustache of a Mongol warrior. Compared to his predecessor, the gigantic Jim Morgan, this man looked like an undernourished wimp. Gregory wondered whether he loved Judy as much as he feared her. He imagined a quarrel between them and could not help smiling; his sister could crack her husband's skull with one hand, as easily as breaking an egg for breakfast. Gregory, fascinated, tried to imagine how they made love.

The Moraleses gave Gregory the reception he had not had until that moment, hugging him, with tears flowing. Fleetingly, Gregory was tempted to believe that they were grieving because it was he and not their son Juan José who was returning unharmed, but the expression of unqualified happiness on the faces of his friends cleansed his heart of that unworthy doubt. They removed the plastic from one of the armchairs and sat him down to question him in detail about the war. Gregory had promised himself not to talk about it but to his surprise told them everything they wanted to know. He realized this was part of the mourning process; among them, they were burying Juan José for the last time. Inmaculada forgot to turn on the lights and offer Gregory something to eat; no one moved until well after dark, when Pedro went to the kitchen to get some beer. Alone with Inmaculada, Gregory took off the scapulary and handed it to her. He had given up the idea of washing it, fearing it would disintegrate, but he did not need to explain the origin of the dark stains. She took it without examining it and immediately put it on, hiding it beneath her blouse.

"It would be a sin to throw it out, because it was blessed by a bishop, but if it couldn't protect my son, I don't know what good it is." She sighed.

Then Gregory was able to tell about Juan José's last moments. The Moraleses, sitting side by side on the ugly ruby-red sofa, hand in hand for the first time in anyone's presence, listened, shivering, to what Gregory Reeves had sworn not to tell them but now could not keep secret. He told them about Juan José's reputation for being lucky and brave, how, miraculously, they had run into each other on the beach, and how very much he wished he had been the one to be at Juan José's side and hold him in his arms when he was falling: Padre, hold me, I'm falling, and it's so deep.

"Did he have time to think of God?" his mother wanted to know.

"He was with the chaplain."

"Did he suffer much?" Pedro Morales asked.

"I don't know; it was over so fast. . . ."

"Was he afraid? Did everything seem black? Was he crying out?"

"No; they told me he was calm."

"At least you're back, thanks be to God," said Inmaculada, and for a wonderful moment Gregory felt absolved of all guilt, redeemed from anguish, saved from his worst memories, as a wave of gratitude swept over him. That night the Moraleses would not allow him to go to a hotel; they insisted he stay with them and made up Juan José's bachelor bed for him. In the night table Gregory found poems his friend had written in pencil in a lined notebook. They were love poems.

Before he flew back, Gregory visited Olga. She was showing her years; little remained of her former brilliant plumage, she had become a tangle-haired old witch, although her vigor for healing and fortune-telling had not diminished. By this time in her life she was thoroughly convinced of human stupidity; she had more faith in her sorcery than in her medicinal herbs, because sorcery appealed more directly to her clients' boundless credulity. It's all in the mind, she maintained; the imagination works miracles. Her home, too, showed the wear and tear of time; it looked like a medicine man's bazaar, crammed with the dusty items of her magic, with more disorder and less color than he remembered. Dried twigs, barks, and roots still hung from the ceiling, the shelves holding flasks and small boxes had multiplied; the old aroma of incense from the Pakistani shops had disappeared, swallowed by more powerful odors. Many pots still bore labels suggesting their contents: Forget-Me-Not, Business Blossoms, Invincible Conquerer, Secret Vengeance, Savage Pleasure, Removes All Cares. With an eye trained to discover the invisible, Olga immediately noted the changes in Gregory, the impenetrable wall around him, the hard eyes, the harsh, joyless laugh, the dry voice, and the new twist to the mouth that on thinner lips would have been scornful but on his was mocking. He radiated the power of a rabid animal, but beneath the armor she perceived pieces of a shattered soul. She knew instinctively it was not the moment to offer her broad experience as a counselor, because his mind was closed, and so she spoke of herself.

"I have many enemies, Gregory," she confessed. "You try to do good, but you're repaid with envy and resentment. Now there are people saying I'm in league with the devil."

"Fatal for business, I should think. . . ."

THE INFINITE PLAN · 239

"Don't you believe it; as long as there are frightened people, people in pain, my skill never drops in value," Olga replied with a crafty wink. "And incidentally, is there anything I can do for you?"

"I don't think so, Olga. What's wrong with me can't be cured with incantations."

The Moraleses gave Gregory Carmen's address. He had thought she was still in Europe and could scarcely believe they were living only the length of a bridge apart. Their Monday telephone calls had been deferred, and mail was erratic in Vietnam, so his last contact had been a postcard from Barcelona telling him of the Japanese lover. It seemed an extraordinary coincidence that Carmen had moved into Joan and Susan's house; reality sometimes is as improbable as the absurd soap operas Inmaculada followed so faithfully.

All through his eventful life, especially when he was particularly lonely after becoming involved with a new woman and finding that she still was not the one he sought, Gregory Reeves often asked himself why it had not worked out for Carmen and him. By the time he dared ask her that question, she replied that in those days he was closed to the only kind of love worthy of sharing, protected by a mantle of cynicism that benefited him very little in the long run, since with the least breeze he was once again exposed to the elements—but that cynicism had been enough to fence off his heart.

"At that time you were obsessive about money and sex. We can blame the war, if you like, although I think there were other reasons: you were still carrying a lot from your childhood," Carmen told him many years later, when both had traveled their separate labyrinths and met as they emerged. "The strange thing is that you barely had to scratch the surface to see that beneath those defenses you were crying out for help. But I wasn't ready for a meaningful relationship either; I hadn't matured and couldn't give you the unbounded love you needed."

After his visit to the Moraleses, Gregory postponed his reunion with Carmen, finding a spate of new excuses. He was intimidated by the idea of seeing her; he was afraid they would have changed and not know each other or, worse still, not like each other. Finally it became impossible to invent new excuses, and two weeks later he looked her up. He wanted to surprise her, so he appeared at the restaurant without warning, only to find that she had left her job a few days before. Joan and Susan welcomed him enthusiastically, checked him over from head to toe to confirm that he was in one piece, stuffed him with vegetarian lasagne and pistachio and honey pastries, and finally told him where he could find Carmen. He noticed the transformation in the way his friends looked: they were wearing earrings visible at ten paces, they had cut their hair, and judging by the unwarranted flush on her cheeks, Joan was wearing rouge. They explained, laughing, that they had abandoned Indian braids and grandmotherly buns because their Tamar earrings demanded something more dashing; there was nothing wrong with that, as they had discovered, rather tardily, it was true, and so they were going to make up for lost time. We can be feminists with these doodads in our ears and a little makeup; don't worry, man, we've not renounced any of our principles, we promise you. Gregory wanted to know who Tamar was, and was told that Carmen had changed her name with a view to devoting herself full time to making jewelry, adopting both a new style and a new name because she didn't think her own was very exotic. She went every morning to the street where hippies could be found selling their merchandise on trays set on folding legs. Positions were drawn in a daily lottery, a system that avoided the squabbles of previous years when street merchants fought over their favorite spots. To get a good location you have to get up early, but Carmen is very disciplined, Joan and Susan said, and so you're sure to find her on the first corner; that's the most popular location because it's near the university, where you can use the bathrooms.

Both sidewalks were lined with vendors and artisans who earned their daily bread from the day's sales and survived on metaphysical dreams, political ingenuousness, and drugs. A few lunatics rambled among them, attracted by who knows what mys-

terious forces. The government had slashed funds for medical services, leaving already economically troubled psychiatric hospitals
without resources and forcing them to release their patients.
These outcasts got by on charity during the summer months and
then were collected in the winter to avoid the embarrassment of
numb bodies littering the public streets. The police ignored these
poor maniacs unless they became troublesome; their neighbors
knew them, had lost their fear of them, and had no objection to
feeding them when they began to grow faint with hunger. Often
they could not be distinguished from drugged-out hippies, but
some were unmistakable, even famous, like a dancer who wore
transparent tights and the flaming cape of a fallen archangel and
floated silently about on point, startling inattentive pedestrians.
Among the most familiar was a hapless visionary who read fortunes with cards of his own invention and wandered around
moaning about the horrors of the world. One day, despairing at
such evil and greed, he reached the breaking point and gouged
out his eyes with a tablespoon. He was taken away in an ambulance and shortly afterward was back again, silent, and smiling
because now he did not have to view cruelty. Someone pricked
holes in his cards so he could tell them apart, and he continued to
read fortunes for passersby, with greater success now that he had
become a legend. This was the scene of Gregory's search for Carmen. He fought his way through the confusion and noise of the
street, looking for her but not finding her; it was the Christmas
season, and the sidewalks were filled with a welter of shoppers
intent upon completing their purchases. When he did see Carmen,
it took him several seconds to adapt this image to the one in his
memory. She was sitting on a small bench behind a portable table
on which her work was displayed in glittering rows; her hair tumbled over her shoulders, she was wearing an odalisque's embroidered jacket, her arms were deep in bracelets, and her strange
dark cotton dress was bound like a tunic at the waist by a chain of
silver and copper coins. She was attending a tourist couple who
undoubtedly had made the trip from their farm in the Midwest to
see at first hand the horrors of Berkeley they had glimpsed on

television. Carmen did not notice Gregory, and he stood apart, watching her, screened by the streams of people. During those minutes, he remembered how much he had shared with her, the tender dreams of adolescence, the hopes she had inspired, and he knew he must have loved her since the long-ago night they slept together in the same bed on the day his father died. She had changed; her movements were assured and graceful, her Latin heritage was more pronounced: her eyes were blacker and her gestures broader, her laugh was bolder. Travel had sharpened his friend's intuition and made her more astute; thence the change of name and style. By then the word "ethnic" had been coined to designate styles from places no one could locate on the map, and Carmen had capitalized on it because she knew that in her part of the world no one would value jewelry made by a humble Chicana. On her table was a placard announcing TAMAR, ETHNIC JEWELRY. From where he stood, Gregory listened to her chatting with her customers; she told them she was a gypsy, and they recoiled slightly, fearing they would be cheated. She spoke with a slight accent she had acquired since he last saw her. Gregory knew she was not capable of affectation, but she well might have adopted the accent for the sport of it, just as she had invented a mysterious past, more for the pleasure of the game than from any conscious lie. If anyone had reminded Carmen that she was the daughter of illegal immigrants from Zacatecas, she herself would have been surprised. In her letters she had written the extravagant autobiography she was creating by chapters like a television serial, and he had warned her more than once to be careful, because if she kept repeating her fantasies she would end up believing them. Now, seeing her only a few yards away, he understood that Carmen had become the protagonist of her own novel, and that the name Tamar better suited this colorful merchant of beautiful baubles. At that moment, she looked up and saw him.

They hugged each other like a couple of lost children and then sought each other's lips and kissed with all the passion nurtured through years of secret fantasies. Carmen quickly put away her wares and folded her table, and they left pushing a small shopping

THE INFINITE PLAN · 243

cart containing the small boxes with her jewelry, staring at one another hungrily, looking for a place where they could make love. Their urgency was so great that they could not take time to talk; they needed to touch each other, explore, verify that each was as the other had imagined. Carmen did not want to share Gregory with Joan and Susan; she was afraid that if they went to her room they would inevitably run into their friends, and however discreet the two women might be, it would be difficult to avoid their company. Gregory had the same thought and, without consulting Carmen, drove to a run-down motel whose only virtue was being near at hand. There they stripped off their clothes and fell onto the bed, giddy in their eagerness, their hunger. Their first breathless embrace was intense and violent; they attacked without preamble, in a tumult of sheets; they took their pleasure of one another and then fell briefly into a stupefied slumber. Carmen waked first and sat up to observe the man she had grown up with, now a stranger. She had dreamed about him more times than she could count, and now he was lying naked before her, as close as her kisses. He had been honed by the war; he was thinner, more muscular, his tendons stood out like rope beneath his skin, and one leg had prominent blue veins, the legacy of his accident while delivering the refrigerator. Even asleep he was tense. She kissed him, sadly; she had imagined a very different coming together, not this kind of mutual violation, this all-out warfare; they had not made love but done something that left the taste of sin in her mouth. She felt as if Gregory had not been altogether present, that his mind was somewhere else, that he had embraced not her but someone else, some unidentified ghost from his past or his nightmares; he had not been tender or sharing or good-humored, he had not whispered her name or looked into her eyes. She herself had not been her most giving, but she did not know at what point she had failed; Gregory had set the tempo, and everything happened with such desperation that she had lost her way in a dark jungle from which she emerged hot, moist, a little sore, and sad. Her failed love affairs had not diminished her capacity for tenderness. Opening herself, however, she had encountered unexpected resistance from this friend she had been waiting for since girl-hood; she attributed it to the privations of war and still hoped to find a chink in his armor through which she could slip into his heart. She leaned over to kiss him again, and he was instantly awake, on the defensive, but when he recognized her he smiled and for the first time seemed to relax. He took her shoulders and pulled her to him.

"You're a loner, Greg, ready for a fight, like a movie cowboy."

"I've never ridden a horse in my life, Carmen."

He did not realize how much on target Carmen's analysis was, or how prophetic. Loneliness and strife had determined his destiny. Memories he had tried to hold at bay came flooding back, bringing with them a deep bitterness impossible to share with anyone, not even Carmen in that moment of intimacy. Like the weeds in the front yard of his house, he had grown without water or care, surrounded by the metaphysical madness of his father, the stony silences of his mother, the tenacious animosity of his sister, and the violence of the barrio, suffering because of the color of his skin and his bizarre family, divided always between the call of a sentimental heart and that combative fever, that savage energy, that made his blood boil and his judgment evaporate. One part of him inclined toward compassion and the other toward reckless-ness. He lived trapped in continual indecision between opposing forces that split him into two irreconcilable halves, a raw wound that tore him up inside and isolated him from others. He felt con-demned to being alone. Just accept it, Gregory, and then forget it; we're born, we live, and we die alone, Cyrus had lectured him. Life is confusion and suffering and, more than anything, solitude. There are philosophical explanations, but if you prefer the story of the Garden of Eden, consider it a punishment upon the human race for having bitten into the fruit of knowledge. That idea merely exacerbated Reeves's rebelliousness; he had not given up his childhood dream that the anguish of living would disappear by magic. During the years he used to hide in the shed behind his house, overcome by irrational fear, he had imagined that one day he would awake liberated forever from that dull ache in the center of his being—it was only a question of adjusting to the principles and rules of decency. But it had not worked out that way. He had fulfilled the rites of passage and the successive steps along the road to manhood; he had made himself a man, silently enduring repeated bumps and knocks along the way, faithful to the national myth of the independent, proud, and free individual. He considered himself a good citizen willing to pay his taxes and defend his country, but somewhere he had fallen into an insidious trap, and instead of living the expected reward he was still slogging through a swamp. It was not enough to do your share and do it again; life was like an insatiable sweetheart, always demanding more strength, more courage. In Vietnam he had learned that to survive you had to break many rules. The world belonged to the bold, not the meek; in real life the villain fared better than the hero. There was no moral resolution to the war, nor were there victors; they were all part of the same unholy debacle, and now in civilian life it seemed it was the same, but he was determined to escape the curse. I'm going to get to the top, even if it means climbing over my own mother, he said every day to the image in the bathroom mirror, hoping the repeated exhortation would overcome the depression that weighed him down each morning. He was not ready to talk about these things with anyone, not even Carmen. He felt the whisper of her hair on his mouth, breathed in her musky scent, and again abandoned himself to the clamor of desire. He saw her body swaying against the shadows of the curtains, heard her laughter and her moans, felt the trembling of her breasts on the palms of his hands, and for one too brief instant believed himself redeemed from the anathema of loneliness, but immediately the throbbing in his groin and the chaotic drumming of his heart blotted out that chimera and he sank deeper and deeper into the absolute abyss of pleasure, that ultimate and most profound of isolations.

Much later they dressed, when their need for fresh air and something more to eat than the cold pizza and warm beer the motel had to offer brought them back to the real world. They had had time to make love more calmly and to catch up on the past, to finish conversations begun on the telephone over the years, to remember Juan José, to tell each other of their broken dreams, failed loves, unfinished projects, adventures, and accumulated pain. In those long hours Carmen perceived that Gregory had changed not just in body but in his soul, although she supposed that with time the bad memories would fade and he would be the old sentimental, fun-to-be-with Gregory with whom she had won rock 'n' roll contests—her confidant, her brother. No, not my brother ever again, she thought sadly. When their curiosity in exploring one another had been satisfied, they put on their clothes and went outside, leaving Carmen's cart and jewelry in the room. Sitting before steaming mugs of coffee and crisp toast, they looked at each other in the red afternoon light and felt uncomfortable. They did not know why a shadow had fallen between them, but neither could ignore its injurious effect. They had satisfied the compulsions of desire but had not truly come together; their spirits had not fused, nor, as expected, had they found a love capable of transforming their lives. Once they were dressed and appeased, they understood how widely divergent their paths had grown, how little they had in common, how different their interests were, how they no longer shared either plans or values. When Gregory revealed his ambition to become a successful and wealthy lawyer, Carmen thought he was joking; such greed did not suit the man she remembered. What had happened to his ideals, the effect of the inspirational books and Cyrus's lectures? He had bored her with his idealism when they were teenagers, and she had made fun of it to tease him, but in the long run had adopted those norms as her own. For years she had considered herself the more frivolous of the two and had thought of him as her guide; now she felt betrayed. As for Gregory, he lacked the patience to listen to Carmen's opinions about important subjects, from the war to the hippies, dismissing them as the nonsense of a spoiled bohemian who had never known true want. The fact that she was completely content to sell her work on the street and planned to spend the rest of her life like a vagrant, pushing her little cart and living on air, elbow-to-elbow with loonies and misfits, was sufficient proof of her immaturity.

"I think you've become a capitalist!" Carmen accused him with horror.

"Well, why not? And you don't have the faintest idea what a capitalist *is*!" Gregory replied. Carmen could not express what was in her heart but mumbled some disjointed thoughts that came out sounding like adolescent drivel.

They had paid for the motel room for another night, but after they had finished their third cup of coffee in silence, isolated in their separate thoughts, and strolled for a while observing the spectacle of the street as it grew dark, Carmen announced she must get her things from the motel and go back home; she had a lot of work to do. Her declaration saved Gregory the unpleasant-ness of having to invent a similar excuse. They parted with a quick kiss and a vague promise to see each other very soon. They did not communicate for almost two years, when Carmen Morales called Gregory to ask for his help in rescuing a child on the other side of the world.

Timothy Duane invited Gregory Reeves to a dinner at his parents' home, unknowingly giving him the push he needed to get ahead in the world. Duane had welcomed his friend with the customary handshake, as if he had just returned from a brief vacation; only the shine of his eyes betrayed the emotion he felt, but like everyone else he did not want to hear anything about the war. Gregory had the impression he had done something shameful; returning from Vietnam was like getting out of jail after a long sentence: people pretended that nothing had happened and treated him with exaggerated courtesy or ignored him completely—there was no place for soldiers outside of Vietnam. The dinner at the Duanes' was boring and formal. The door had been opened by an elderly and beautiful black woman in an impeccable uniform, who showed Gregory to the drawing room. Dumb-founded, he saw there was not an unadorned square inch of wall or floor; a profusion of paintings, tapestries, sculptures, furniture, rugs, and plants left no serene space on which to rest the eyes. There were tables with inlaid mother-of-pearl and gold filigree, ebony chairs with silk cushions, silver cages for stuffed birds, and a collection of porcelain and crystal worthy of a museum. Timothy came forward to meet him.

"How luxurious!" escaped from Reeves as greeting.

"Bel is the only luxurious thing in this house. Let me introduce you to Bel Benedict," his friend replied, motioning to the servant, who resembled an African sculpture.

Gregory at last met his friend's father, about whom he had heard so little good, a pompous, wizened patriarch who could not utter two sentences without parading his authority. That night would have been detestable for Gregory had it not been for the orchids that both saved the evening and opened doors for his career. His friend Balcescu had initiated him into the vice with no return—flowers—which began with a passion for roses and with the years extended to other species. In that palace replete with precious objets d'art, what most attracted Gregory were Timothy's mother's orchids. They flourished in a thousand forms and colors, planted in jardinieres, clinging to tree bark suspended from the ceilings, and growing like a jungle in a garden room in which the grande dame had reproduced the climate of the Amazon. While others were having coffee, Gregory slipped away to admire them and there found an old man with diabolical eyebrows and impressive bearing who was similarly taken with the orchids. They chatted about the plants, each surprised at the other's knowledge. The gentleman turned out to be one of the nation's foremost lawyers, an octopus whose tentacles embraced the entire West, who when he learned Gregory was looking for a position handed him his card and invited him to come have a talk. A week later Reeves was working in his firm.

Gregory Reeves was one among some sixty attorneys—all equally ambitious but not all equally determined—under the direction of the three founding partners, who had become millionaires from the misfortunes of others. Their offices occupied three floors of a tower in the center of the city, from which the bay was framed in squares of steel and glass. The windows could not be opened; the air was circulated mechanically, and a system of lights hidden in the ceilings created the illusion of an eternal day at the Pole. The number of windows in each office determined the occupant's importance: at first Gregory had none, but when he left the firm seven years later he could boast of two corner windows offering a glimpse of the building across the street and an insignificant scrap of sky; that glimpse, however, represented his ascent in the firm and on the social ladder. He had, in addition, several potted plants and a handsome English leather sofa that suffered heavy use without losing its stoic dignity as various female fellow lawyers and an undetermined number of secretaries, clients, and friends lightened the burden of the boring cases involving inheritances, insurance, and taxes it was his duty to resolve. Gregory's boss soon visited him under the pretext of exchanging information about a rare variety of fern, and then once or twice invited him to lunch. Observing Gregory from a distance, he had detected his new employee's aggressiveness and energy, and he began to send him more interesting cases to sharpen his claws on. Excellent, Reeves; you keep it up and before you know it you could be my partner, he would congratulate him from time to time. Gregory suspected that he told his other junior members the same thing, but after twenty-five years very few had achieved senior rank in the firm. He had no vain hopes of significant advancement and was aware he was being exploited; he worked twelve to fifteen hours every day, but he considered it part of his training to fly solo one day and did not complain. The law was a web of bureaucratic intricacies, and the trick consisted in being the spider and not the fly; the judicial system had become an aggregate of regulations so entangled they no longer served the purpose for which they had been created, and far from expediting justice had made it extremely difficult to achieve. The aim had shifted from the pursuit of truth, from punishing the guilty and compensating the victim—as he had been taught in his law classes—to winning by any means; to be successful you had to know the most recherché legal loopholes and use them to advantage. Hiding documents, confusing witnesses, and falsifying information were common practices; the challenge was the degree of efficiency and discretion you could achieve. The force of the law should never fall upon clients able to pay the firm's clever lawyers. Gregory's life took a turn that would have alarmed his mother and Cyrus; he lost most of his illusions about his profession and began to see it only as a vehicle for getting ahead. He had similar disillusions in regard to other aspects of his life, especially love and family. Samantha's divorce had ended without undue hostility; they had arranged the settlement in an Italian restaurant, over two glasses of Chianti. Since he had nothing valuable to share, Gregory agreed to pay Samantha alimony and child support for Margaret. As they said goodbye, Gregory asked Samantha whether he might have the wine barrels with the roses; after long neglect they were nothing more than dried sticks, but he felt duty-bound to revive them. Samantha had no objection and even offered to throw in the wood tub of the unsuccessful aquatic birth, which one day might serve as a container for an indoor jungle. At first Gregory made weekly trips to see his daughter, but soon the visits grew farther apart; he always found the child waiting with a list of things to buy, and once her whims were satisfied she ignored him and seemed annoyed by his presence. He did not communicate with Judy or with his mother, and for a long time did not call Carmen, justifying his neglect with the excuse that he was too busy with his practice.

Social connections play a fundamental role in a successful career, and your friends can smooth the way, Greg's colleagues told him. You have to be at the right place at the opportune time and with the right people. Judges belonged to the same clubs as the lawyers they later heard in court; friends understand each other. Sports might not be your forte, but golf is obligatory because of the opportunity for making contacts. As Gregory had planned, he bought a boat, dreaming of yachting whites and sailing with envious colleagues and enviable women, but he never seemed to grasp the caprices of the wind or secrets of the sails; every outing on the bay was a disaster, and the boat died a sorry

THE INFINITE PLAN · 251

death, abandoned at the dock with nests of gulls in her masts and a coat of hairy algae on her hull. Gregory had known an impoverished childhood and indigent youth, but he had also been nurtured on movies that instilled a taste for the grand life. In the barrio movie theater he had seen men in dinner jackets, women dressed in lamé, and four-candelabra tables attended by liveried servants. Although all that belonged to a Hollywood that was hypothetical to begin with and had no practical application in reality, he was fascinated by it. That may have been one reason he fell in love with Samantha: it was easy to imagine her in the role of an aloof, famous blonde movie star. Gregory had his suits made by a Chinese tailor, the most expensive in the city, the same one who dressed the elderly man of the orchids and other VIPs, and he affected silk shirts and initialed gold cuff links. His tailor was an excellent arbiter of taste and forbade two-toned shoes, polka-dotted ties, checked trousers, and other temptations, and little by little Reeves refined his sartorial tastes. He also was fortunate to have a proficient teacher in interior decoration. At first he used his credit to buy every gewgaw that caught his eye—the larger and more elaborate, the better—attempting to reproduce on a small scale the house of Timothy Duane's parents, thinking that was how the wealthy lived, but even exploring every avenue for credit, he could barely finance his extravagances. He collected antique furniture, teardrop lamps, urns, even a pair of life-size bronze Abyssinians, complete with turbans and slippers. Gregory's home was on the way to becoming a Turkish bazaar when he met a young woman decorator who saved him from the consequences of bad taste. They met at a party and that same night began an impassioned, if transitory, relationship that was very crucial for Gregory because he never forgot the lessons learned from his designer. She taught him that ostentation is the enemy of elegance, an idea totally contrary to precepts learned in the Latino barrio and one that would never have occurred to him, and she peremptorily discarded almost everything in his house, including the Abyssinians, which she sold for an exorbitant price to the Saint Francis Hotel, where they may be found today at the entrance to the bar. She left only the imperial bed, the wine barrels of roses, and the wood tub, now converted into a planter. In their five-week romance she transformed Gregory's house, giving it a simple, functional look; she had the walls painted white and the floors covered in sand-colored carpeting, and she personally accompanied Gregory to buy a few modern pieces. She was emphatic in her instructions: few but good, neutrals only, minimal adornment, and in case of doubt, abstain. Thanks to her counsel the house took on the austerity of a convent, and it remained austere until its owner was married some years later.

One reason Reeves never talked about his experience in Vietnam was that no one wanted to listen, but he also believed that eventually silence would cure him of his memories. He had gone to defend the interests of his country with the image of heroes in his mind, and he had returned defeated, not understanding why his people should die by the thousands and kill without compunction on soil outside their native land. By then the war, which in the beginning had received euphoric support from the public, had become a national nightmare; the protests of pacifists had swelled to shrill defiance of the government. No one could explain how it was possible to send men into space and yet not find a way to stop this open-ended conflict. Upon their return, instead of the respect and admiration promised when they were recruited, soldiers met hostility more ferocious than enemy fire; no one cared what they had been through. Many who had endured, and survived, the rigors of the war cracked on their return to the States when they realized there was no place for them.

"This is a country of winners, Greg; the one thing no one can forgive is failure," Timothy Duane told him. "It isn't the morality or justice of this war we question, and no one wants to know about our own dead, much less that of the enemy; what royally ticks us off is that we're not winning and are going to have to slink out of there with our tail between our legs."

"Not many people here know what war is really like, Tim," Reeves replied on the one opportunity he discussed the subject with his friend. "We're never been invaded or bombed; we've been engaged in hostilities for a century, but since the Civil War not one round of mortar has fallen on United States soil. People can't imagine what it's like to live in a city under fire. They would change their ideas fast if their children were being blown apart and their houses bombed to the ground and there was no food to be had."

Reeves did not, however, waste any energy in complaints, and with the same determination that got him out of Vietnam alive, he vowed to overcome any obstacle in his path. He did not swerve a hair's breadth from the decision he had made in the hospital bed in Hawaii, and he succeeded so well that by the time the war was over, several years later, he had become the paradigm of the successful man and was managing his life with the same juggling skill Carmen had shown in keeping five knives in the air at once. He had achieved almost everything he had aspired to: he had more money, more women, and more prestige than he had dreamed of . . . but he had no peace. Because he had the arrogant and self-confident air of a master con man, no one suspected the anguish he carried on his shoulders—no one, that is, except Carmen, from whom he could never hide anything. But she could not help him either.

"The trouble with you is that you're in the bull ring but you don't have the matador's instinct for the kill," she had told him.

What was I looking for in a woman? I'm still not sure. I wasn't trying to find the other half of my soul in order to feel complete, not by a long shot. In those days I wasn't mature enough for anything spiritual, I was after something entirely earthly. I demanded something of the women I dated that I myself couldn't name, and when I didn't find it was utterly depressed. Divorce, war, and age would have cured a more clever man of romantic notions, but not me. On the one hand, I tried to lure almost every woman to bed out of pure sexual appetite; on the other, I fumed when these women did not respond to my secret sentimental demands. Confusion, pure confusion. For decades I was frustrated; after every coupling I was ravaged by melancholy and wanted only to escape as quickly as I could. That was true even with Carmen. She had good reason not to want to see me for a couple of years; she must have hated me. Women are black widow spiders; if you don't stay free of them you can never be yourself and will exist only to please them: so Timothy Duane warned me. He met every week with a group of men to talk about how masculinity was being threatened by all the feminist shit going around. I never paid much attention to Timothy, because my friend is not a very good example of abstinence. When I was young, I didn't have the poise or the knowledge to have a system for chasing girls; I chased them with all the finesse of a bear cub and with unhappy results. I was faithful to Samantha until that night I drew the arithmetic teacher whose strawberry-colored bathrobe I had no desire to remove, but I take no pride from the loyalty Samantha did not return; just the opposite: I was stupid, besides being screwed. When I was a bachelor again, I set out to profit from the revolution in mores; all the old strategies for conquest had been dissolved: no one feared the devil, sharp tongues, or an untimely pregnancy, so I put to the test the bed in my home and in countless hotels, even the Britannic springs of the sofa in my office. My boss curtly warned me that I would lose my job on the spot if he received a complaint from any female employee of the firm. I ignored him, too, and was lucky that no one came forward with a grievance, or at least that the gossip didn't reach his ears. Timothy Duane and I had specific nights during the week programmed for partying; we used to exchange information and draw up lists of candidates. For Timothy it was a sport; for me, a kind of madness. My friend was a handsome fellow, polite and wealthy, but I was a better dancer, could play a number of instruments by ear, and knew how to cook—tricks that captured certain women's attention. We thought we were irresistible, but I suppose that was true only because we settled for quantity, not quality; I can't say we were selective, we went out with anyone who accepted us. We fell in love the same day with a covetous, self-assured Philippine girl whom we besieged with our attentions in a race to see who would win her heart, but she was way ahead of us

and openly announced that she planned to sleep with both of us.
That Solomon-like solution failed at the first try: we couldn't take
the competition. After that we shared girls in such prosaic fashion
that had they suspected, they would never have gone out with us. I
had several names in my little black book that I called regularly; I
wasn't serious about any of them and made them no promises. It
was a comfortable arrangement for me, but it was not enough; as
soon as I met someone new and slightly interesting, I ran after her
with the same urgency with which I later dropped her. I suppose I
was propelled by the dream that one day my search would be justified and I would meet the ideal companion, just as I drank wine,
in spite of my allergies, hoping to find the perfect bottle, or traveled through the world in the summer, running from city to city
in the exhausting pursuit of the one marvelous place where I
would be idyllically happy. Searching, always searching, but
searching outside myself.

During that stage of my life, sex was like the violence of the
war; it was a malignant form of contact that in the end left me with
a terrible emptiness. I didn't realize at the time that in each
encounter I learned something, that I was not wandering in circles
like a blind man but in a slowly ascending spiral. I was maturing,
although at great cost, as Olga had prophesied. You're a strong,
stubborn animal, you won't have an easy life, she warned me;
you'll take your share of lickings. She was my first teacher in what
was to determine a large part of my character. When I was sixteen
she taught me more than erotic antics; her most important lesson
was about what makes a true couple. She taught me that in love,
two people open to one another, accept one another, yield to one
another. I was fortunate; few men have the opportunity to learn
that when they're young, but I didn't know enough to understand
it and soon forgot. Love is music, and sex is only the instrument,
Olga told me, but it took me more than half my life to find my
center, and that's why I had such a hard time learning to play the
music. Relentlessly, I pursued love where I could never find it, and
on the few occasions when it was right before my eyes, I was incapable of seeing it. My relationships were ferocious and fleeting; I

could not give myself to a woman, nor could I accept her. That was what Carmen knew intuitively the one time we were together in bed, but she herself had still to know a complete relationship; she was as ignorant as I; neither of us was ready to lead the other along the paths of love. She had never experienced total intimacy; she had been mistreated or abandoned by all her lovers; she trusted no one, and when she wanted to trust me, I, too, disappointed her. I am convinced that she tried with good faith to take me into her heart as well as her body. Carmen is pure affection, instinct, and compassion; tenderness comes easy to her, but I wasn't ready, and later, when I wanted to try again, it was too late. Useless to cry over spilled milk, as Doña Inmaculada says; life deals us many surprises, and in the light of things that have happened to me recently, probably it was for the best. In that earlier stage, women, like clothes or cars, were symbols of power; they succeeded one another without leaving a trace, like fireflies in a long and pointless delirium. If any of my women friends secretly wept over the impossibility of drawing me into a lasting relationship, I don't remember her, just as I have forgotten the roster of my casual companions. I have no wish to evoke the faces of the women who were my lovers in those years of libertinism, but if I tried, I think I would find only blank pages.

The letter that would change Carmen's life was delivered to the Moraleses, and they read it to her over the telephone: *Miss Carmen Tamar, I am placing my son in your care because your brother Juan José wanted him to grow up in the United States. His name is Dai Morales; he is twenty-one months old and is very healthy. He will be a good son to you and a good grandson to his honorable grandparents. Please come get him soon. I am ill and haven't long to live. Respectfully yours, Thui Nguyen.*

"Did you know Juan José had a wife over there?" Pedro Morales asked, in a voice broken by the strain of keeping calm, while in the kitchen Inmaculada stood worrying a handkerchief, vacillating between happiness over knowing she had another grandson and the doubt sown by her husband, who thought the letter smelled of fraud.

"Yes; I also knew he had a son," lied Carmen, who in fifteen seconds adopted the child in her heart.

"We don't have any proof that Juan José is the father."

"My brother told me when he called."

"Maybe the woman deceived him. It wouldn't be the first time a woman trapped a soldier with that tale. You always know who the mother is, but you can't be sure about the father."

"Then you can't be sure I'm your daughter, Papa."

"Don't be smart with me! And if you knew, why didn't you tell us?"

"I didn't want to worry you. I didn't think we'd ever see him. Papa, I'll go get our little Dai."

"It won't be easy, Carmen. We can't sneak him across the border in a crate of lettuce, the way some of our Mexican friends have with their children."

"I'll get him, Papa. You can count on it."

She picked up the telephone and called Gregory Reeves, with whom she had not communicated in a very long time, and launched straight into the story, so excited about the idea of being a mother that she completely forgot to show any sign of compassion for the dying woman or ask her friend how he had been in all the time since they had talked. Six hours later Gregory called to say he was coming to see her to bring her up-to-date about the details; meanwhile, he had made a few inquiries, and Pedro Morales was right: they could hit some difficult snags trying to bring the child into the country. They met at Joan and Susan's restaurant, now so famous it was listed in tourist guides. The food was the same, but instead of strings of garlic on the walls there were feminist posters and cartoons, portraits signed by the ideologists of the movement, and, in a corner of honor, spiked on a broomstick, the celebrated bra the owners had made an icon years earlier. The two women were glowing with their financial success, and had lost none of their warmth. Joan was enjoying an ongoing affair with the most popular guru in the city, the Romanian Balcescu, who had left the park behind and was now teaching in his own academy; Susan had inherited a piece of property from her father, where she was growing organic vegetables and contented chickens that instead of living four to a cage and eating feed with chemical additives strutted freely about, pecking real grain, until the moment they were plucked for the roasting pans of the restaurant. Balcescu grew hydroponic marijuana on the same property, and it sold like hotcakes, especially at Christmas. Sitting at the best table in the restaurant, beside a window opened to an overgrown garden, Carmen reiterated to Gregory that she would adopt her nephew even if it meant spending the rest of her life planting rice in Southeast Asia. I'll never have a child of my own, but this boy will be like mine because we have the same blood; besides, she said, I have the spiritual duty to care for Juan José's son, and no immigration service in the world can keep me from doing just that. Gregory patiently explained that the visa was not the only problem; the arrangements would be processed through an adoption agency that would examine her life to determine whether she would make a proper mother and whether she could give the baby a stable home.

"They'll ask you all kinds of uncomfortable questions. They won't like it that you spend the day on the street among hippies and drug addicts and nuts and beggars, or that you don't have a steady income, medical insurance, social security, or normal hours. Where are you living now?"

"Well, for the moment I'm sleeping in my car in a friend's yard. I bought a yellow 1949 Cadillac, a real relic; you have to see it."

"Perfect! That will delight the adoption agency!"

"It's only temporary, Greg. I'm looking for an apartment."

"Do you need money?"

"No. My sales are good; I earn more than anyone on the street, and I don't spend much. I have some money saved in the bank."

"Then why do you live like a beggar? Frankly, Carmen, I doubt they'll give you the boy."

"Can you please call me Tamar? That's my name now."

"I'll try, but it's not easy; you'll always be Carmen to me. They will also want to know if you have a husband; they prefer couples."

"Do you know that over there they treat the children of American fathers and Vietnamese mothers like dogs? They don't like our blood. Dai will be much better off with me than in an orphanage."

"Right, but I'm not the one you have to convince. You'll have to fill out forms, answer questions, and prove that he's really your nephew. I warn you, it's going to take months, maybe years."

"We can't wait that long, Gregory; that's why I called you. You know the law."

"But I can't work miracles."

"I'm not asking for miracles, only a few simple tricks in a good cause."

They worked out a plan. Carmen would take part of her savings and move into an apartment in a decent neighborhood; she would try to sell her jewelry somewhere other than the street and would designate a few friends and acquaintances to respond to the probing questions of the authorities. Carmen asked Gregory whether he would marry her in the event a husband was indispensable; amused, he assured her that the laws were not that cruel, and with a little luck she wouldn't have to go that far. Instead, he offered to help her financially, because her adventure was going to be expensive.

"I told you I have money saved. Thank you, though."

"You keep your money for looking after the boy—if you're able to bring him here. I'll pay for the tickets and give you something for the trip."

"Are you that rich?"

"What I have most of are debts, but I can always get another loan, don't worry."

Three months later, after tedious formalities in government offices and consulates, Gregory accompanied Carmen to the airport. To throw suspicious bureaucrats off the trail, Carmen, with her hair pulled back in a bun, had left her usual costume behind and was dressed in a frumpy suit; the only sign of a fire not totally extinguished was the heavy kohl rimming her eyes, something she could not give up. She looked shorter, older, and almost ugly. The exuberant breasts that were so appealing beneath her gypsy

blouses jutted like a balcony under the dark jacket. Gregory had
to admit that the exotic personality she had created was greatly
superior to the original version and promised himself not to suggest again that she change her style. Have no fear, Carmen said,
blushing; as soon as I have my boy with me I'll go back to being
my old self. When she looked in the mirror she could see no sign
of that self. In her suitcase was the small wooden dragon Gregory
had given her at the last minute—for luck, he told her; you're
going to need it. She was also carrying a bundle of documents, the
fruit of inspiration and audacity, photographs and letters from her
brother Juan José that she meant to use without any consideration
for honesty. Reeves had contacted Leo Galupi, confident that his
good friend knew everyone and that the obstacle did not exist that
could hold him back. Gregory assured Carmen that she could put
her trust in the likable Italian from Chicago, despite rumors of his
being something of a scoundrel. It was reputed that he had made a
fortune in the black market, and that was why he could not return
to the United States. The truth was different; after serving his
hitch in the army he had stayed in Vietnam, not for the easy
money, but because of his liking for disorder and uncertainty; he
had been born for a life with a surprise at every turn and was in
his element in Vietnam. He was not rich; he was a bandit betrayed
by his own generosity. In years of business dealings on the edge of
the law he had earned large sums of money, but he had spent
them supporting distant relatives, helping friends in trouble, and
loosening his purse strings whenever he saw someone in need.
The war offered him the opportunity to make money in shady
deals and at the same time forced him to spend it in countless acts
of compassion. He lived in the same warehouse where he stored
crates containing his merchandise: American products to sell to
Vietnamese and Oriental curios to interest his compatriots, from
shark fins to cure impotence to long hanks of hair to fashion wigs,
from Chinese powders for happy dreams to gold and ivory stat-
uettes of ancient gods. In one corner he had installed a gas stove,
where he liked to prepare tasty Sicilian dishes to assuage his nostalgia and to feed a half-dozen street children who were alive only

because of him. Faithful to his promise to Gregory Reeves, he was waiting for Carmen at the airport, holding a limp bouquet of flowers. He was slow to place her because he was expecting a whirlwind of skirts, necklaces, and bracelets; instead, he found an innocuous woman exhausted from the long flight and dripping with sweat. Carmen, in turn, failed to recognize Galupi because Gregory had described him as an unmistakable mafioso type, while she saw a troubadour escaped from a painting; fortunately, he was carrying a cardboard sign with the name TAMAR, which allowed them to identify each other in the crowd. Don't worry about a thing, dear; from now on I'll take charge of you and all your problems, he told Carmen, kissing her on both cheeks. He lived up to his word. He would have to perjure himself before a notary that Thui Nguyen had no family, imitate Juan José's handwriting in forged letters in which he referred to his sweetheart's pregnancy, doctor photographs to show the pair arm in arm in various locations, falsify certificates and seals, plead before incorruptible officials and bribe bribable ones, all dealings that Galupi carried out with the ease of someone who had paddled in those waters before. He was an impressive man, cheerful and good-looking, with strong Mediterranean features and a healthy head of black hair he combed back in a short pigtail. Carmen asked him to go with her on her first visit to Thui Nguyen, because after having looked forward to the moment for so long and having steeled herself for the meeting, she found her customary self-possession had deserted her; her knees buckled at the mere idea of finally seeing the boy. Thui lived in a room in a large house that prior to the war must have belonged to a family of wealthy merchants but now was divided into rooms for twenty renters. There was so much confusion from people going about their chores, children racing around, radios and televisions blaring, that they had difficulty locating the room. A wisp of a woman opened the door, an ashen shadow wearing a kerchief around her head and a dress of indeterminate color. One look was sufficient to know that Thui Nguyen had not lied; she was very ill. Obviously she had always been short, but she looked as if she suddenly had shrunk, as if her skeleton had been compressed without allowing time for her skin to adjust to the new size; it was impossible to calculate her age, because her face was as old as time but her body that of an adolescent. She welcomed them with great reserve, apologized for the room, and invited them to take a seat on the bed; then she offered them tea and without waiting for an answer put water to boil over a gas ring that occupied the only chair. In one corner they could see a household altar with a photograph of Juan José Morales and offerings of flowers, fruit, and incense. I'll bring Dai, she announced, and left the room with slow steps. Carmen Morales felt a pounding in her chest and began trembling in spite of the humid heat seeping through the walls and fostering greenish flora in the corners. Leo Galupi sensed that this was the most intense moment in Carmen's life and had the impulse to put his arms around her, but did not dare touch her.

Dai Morales, a slender, dark-skinned child, rather tall for his two years, with hair stiff as a brush and a very serious face in which almond-shaped black eyes and an absence of visible eyelids were the only Oriental features, came into the room, holding his mother's hand. He looked like a photograph Inmaculada and Pedro Morales had of their son Juan José at the same age, except that Dai was not smiling. Carmen tried to stand up, but her spirit failed her, and she fell back down on the bed. She concluded with mad certainty that this was the child that had been washed down Olga's kitchen drain ten years before, the boy who had been destined for her since the beginning of time. For a moment she lost all notion of present time and wondered with distress what her son was doing in this miserable room. Thui spoke something that sounded like trilling, and the little boy stepped forward timidly and shook Leo Galupi's hand. Thui corrected him with a second reedy bird song, and he turned toward Carmen, starting to repeat the same gesture, but their eyes met and locked for a few eternal seconds, as if they were recognizing each other after a long separation. Finally Carmen held out her arms, picked up the child, and sat him astraddle her knees. He was light as a kitten. Dai sat quietly, in silence, staring at her with a solemn expression.

"From now on, she is your mother," Thui Nguyen said in English, and then repeated it in her tongue so her son would understand.

Carmen Morales spent eleven weeks completing the formalities for adopting her nephew and waiting for the visa to take him to her country. She could have done it in less time, but she never discovered that. Leo Galupi, who at first went out of his way to help her resolve apparently unresolvable problems, at the last moment worked to complicate the proceedings and delay the final arrangements, entangling her in a web of excuses and postponements that not even he could explain. The city was much more expensive than she had imagined, and by the end of a month Carmen was running out of funds. Gregory Reeves sent her a bank draft, which vanished into bribes and hotel expenses, and just when she was ready to dip into her savings, Galupi hastened to her rescue. He had begun a new trade in elephant tusks, he said, and his pockets were stuffed with money; she had no right to reject his aid, since he was doing it for Juan José Morales, his bosom buddy, whom he had loved dearly and who had died before he could say goodbye. Carmen suspected that in fact Galupi had never heard of her brother before Gregory asked for his help, but it was just as well not to find out. She did not want Galupi to pay her hotel bill but agreed to come live at his place to cut down on expenses. She moved in with her suitcase and a bag of the beads and stones she had been buying in spare moments, including some small fossils of neolithic insects that she intended to turn into brooches. She had never imagined that this person she had seen driving a wealthy man's car and spending money with both fists would be living in a kind of furniture warehouse, a labyrinth of crates and metal shelves filled with everything imaginable. At a quick glance she saw a campaign cot, piles of books, boxes holding records and tapes, a formidable music system, and a portable television with a clothes hanger serving as antenna. Galupi showed Carmen the kitchen and other comforts of his home and introduced her to the children who came at that hour to eat, warning her not to give them money and not to leave her wallet within the reach of greedy hands. Given the camp-out casualness, the bathroom was a real surprise, an impeccable wood-paneled room with a tub, large mirrors, and red plush towels. These are the most valuable things that have passed through my hands; you don't know how difficult it is to get good towels, her host said, stroking them with pride. Last, he led Carmen to the far end of his warehouse, where he had isolated a large space with boxes piled like building blocks and an impressive Coromandel screen for a door. Inside the space Carmen found a large bed covered with white mosquito netting, delicate black lacquer furniture hand-painted with motifs of cranes and cherry blossoms, silk rugs, embroidered cloth covering the walls, and small rice-paper lamps spreading a diffuse light. Leo Galupi had created the chamber of a Chinese empress for Carmen. That would be her refuge for several weeks; there the noise of the street or the clamor of war would not reach her. Sometimes she asked herself what might be in the mysterious boxes around her; she imagined precious treasures, each with its story, and felt the air was filled with the spirit of the objects. She lived in that place with comfort and good company but gnawed by the anxiety of waiting.

"Patience, patience," Leo Galupi would counsel when he saw she was getting frantic. "If Dai were yours, you would have to wait nine months for him. Nine weeks is nothing."

During the long hours of leisure when she was not visiting Thui and her child, Carmen wandered through the markets, buying materials for her jewelry and sketching new designs inspired by that strange journey. It seemed absurd that in the midst of a conflict of such proportions she should be strolling through bazaars like a tourist. Even though by then a major part of the American troops had been withdrawn, the war continued to rage at its apogee. Carmen had imagined that the city would be one great military encampment and that she would have to look for her nephew by crawling past soldiers and through trenches, but in fact she was wending through narrow alleyways, shopping and bargaining in the midst of a motley crowd apparently indifferent

to the war. If you could talk with people you would have a different impression, said Galupi, but as she could communicate only in
English, she was isolated from their real feelings. Without meaning to, she gradually ignored reality and submersed herself in the
two subjects that mattered to her: little Dai and her work. Her
mind seemed to have expanded toward new dimensions; Asia had
worked its way into her consciousness, had invaded and seduced
her. She thought about how much of the world she had yet to
know; if she wanted true success in her craft and security for the
future, a commitment she had made as soon as she agreed to be
responsible for Dai, she would have to travel every year to distant
and exotic places, looking for rare materials and fresh ideas.

"I'll send you beads; I have contacts everywhere and can get
anything you want," said Galupi, who did not understand the
essence of Carmen's art but could sense its commercial possibilities.

"I have to choose them myself. Each stone, each shell, each bit
of wood or metal, suggests something different."

"No one here would wear what you've been drawing. I've
never seen an elegant woman with bits of bone and feathers in her
ears."

"Back home they fight over them. Women would go hungry
to buy a pair of earrings like these. The higher the price I put on
them, the better they like it."

"At least what you do is legal." Galupi laughed.

The days seemed very long to Carmen, and she was drained
by the heat and humidity. She suffered her respectable, matronly
clothes only when absolutely necessary and the rest of the time
wore the simple cotton tunics and peasant sandals she had bought
in the market. She spent hours alone, reading or sketching,
accompanied by the sounds of the large warehouse fans. At night
Galupi would arrive with his shopping bags, shower, change into
shorts, turn on the record player, and begin cooking dinner. Soon
a variety of hungry people would assemble, almost all children, to
swarm around Galupi, fill the kitchen with their chatter and
laughter, then leave as soon as they ate, without a word of good-

bye. Sometimes Galupi invited American friends, soldiers or war correspondents, who stayed very late drinking and smoking marijuana. They all accepted Carmen's presence without a question, as if she had always been part of Galupi's life. From time to time Galupi asked Carmen out for dinner, and when he had spare time he drove her around the city; he wanted to show her its many faces, from the crazy quilt of the real city to the European and American residential zones, with their air-conditioning and bottled water. We're going to buy you an outfit for a queen, Galupi announced one day; we're having dinner at the embassy. He drove Carmen to the most elegant shop in town and left her there with a wad of bills in her hand. She felt lost; for years she had sewn her own clothes, and she had no idea that a dress could cost so much. When her new friend came to look for her three hours later, he found her sitting on the steps of the shop with her shoes in her hand, muttering with frustration.

"What happened?"

"Everything was horrible and very expensive. Women are flat now. I can't fit these cantaloupes of mine in any of the dresses," she groaned, pointing to her breasts.

"That's good news." Galupi laughed, and he drove her to the Hindu district, where they bought a magnificent watermelon-colored sari embroidered in gold, in which Carmen wrapped herself with supreme assurance, feeling much more at peace with herself than in the close-fitting French dresses for emaciated women.

That night when she walked into the reception room of the embassy, she saw among the many guests the man she often thought of but had never expected to see again. There in a handsome dinner jacket, deep in conversation, a glass of whiskey in one hand, his hair gray but his face unchanged, stood Tom Clayton. He had taken a leave from his political column and come to Vietnam to write a book about the war. He spent more time at parties and in clubs than in the thick of combat, faithful to his theory that wars actually are waged in salons. He had access to places where no correspondent was welcome and knew the right people in the high command, the diplomatic corps, the government, and the small social world of the city; he was, therefore, well aware he had not seen this bewitching woman before. Judging by the olive tones of her skin, the heavy eye makeup, and the dazzling sari, he supposed she came from India. He noticed that she was observing him as well and watched for an opportunity to drift toward her. Shaking his hand, Carmen introduced herself as Tamar, the name she always used. A thousand times she had planned what she would do if she ever saw her lover again, the man who had been so decisive in her life, and the only thing she never imagined was that she would have nothing to say. The years had dissipated her rancor; she discovered, to her surprise, that all she felt for that arrogant man whose naked image she could no longer conjure up was indifference. She listened to him chatting with Galupi as he examined her from the corner of his eye, obviously interested in her, and was amazed that she could ever have loved him so deeply. She did not ask herself, as she had so often in lonely moments, what their child would have been like, because now she could not imagine any child of hers that wasn't Dai. She sighed with a blend of relief that he hadn't recognized her and profound regret for time wasted in the pangs of love.

"I haven't seen you around. Where are you from?" Clayton asked.

"From the past," Carmen replied, and turned and walked to the balcony to look out over a city glittering at her feet as if the war were in another part of the world.

Once they were back home in the warehouse, Carmen and Leo Galupi sat for a while beneath the ceiling fan to comment on the gala; they did not turn on the lights but sat in shadows filtering in from the streetlamps. He offered her a drink, but she asked whether by any chance he had a tin of condensed milk. With the tip of a knife, she punched two holes in the top of the can and settled on some cushions on the floor to sip the sweet milk, her consolation during so many moments of crisis. Galupi felt finally that he could ask Carmen about Clayton; he had noticed something odd in her behavior when they were introduced, he said. In reply,

Carmen told Galupi everything, not omitting a single detail; it was the first time she had told anyone what happened in Olga's kitchen, about her pain and fear, about her near escape in the hospital, and about the long purgatory expiating a sin that was not hers alone but that Clayton had refused to share. One thing led to another, and Carmen found herself telling Galupi her life story. Dawn came, and she was still talking, in a kind of catharsis; the dam holding back her secrets and lonely tears had burst as she discovered the pleasure of baring her soul to a sympathetic confidant. With the last sip of the condensed milk she stretched, yawning with fatigue, then leaned over to Galupi and brushed his forehead with a light kiss. Galupi caught her by the wrist and drew her toward him, but Carmen pulled away, and his kiss was lost on the air.

"I can't," she said.

"Why not?"

"Because it's not just me now; I have a son."

The next morning Carmen Morales waked just before dawn and thought she saw Leo Galupi standing beside the Coromandel screen, watching her, but in the pale light he might have been part of her dream. She had been dreaming the same nightmare that had tormented her for years, but this time Tom Clayton was not in it and the head of the child who held its arms out to her was not covered by a paper bag; this time she could see clearly, and the face was Dai's face.

Carmen and Galupi adjusted comfortably to sharing their living space, like an old married couple. Carmen was easing into motherhood; every day she took Dai out for a slightly longer time. She learned a few words in Vietnamese and taught Dai others in English, she learned what he liked, what he feared, the stories of his family. Thui took Carmen with her on a two-day visit in the country to give her relatives an opportunity to say goodbye to Dai. They wanted to keep the boy, horrified at the idea of sending one of their family across the ocean, but Thui was aware that in Vietnam her son would always be a bastard half-breed, a second-class citizen, poor, and with no hopes for making his way out of that poverty. The challenge of adapting in America would not be easy, but at least there Dai would have opportunities for something better than working the family's small plot of land. Leo Galupi insisted on going with them, because those were not times for two women and a baby to be traveling without protection. For Carmen this was yet one more instance of something she had known since childhood and that Joan and Susan had hammered home so often: that men and women live in the same time and space but in different dimensions. She lived looking back over her shoulder, watching for real and imagined dangers, always on the defensive, working twice as hard as any man, for half the reward. What for men was a trivial matter that did not warrant a second thought was for her a risk requiring careful calculations and strategies. Something as simple as a trip to the country could be considered a provocation on a woman's part, an invitation to disaster. She mentioned this to Galupi, who was amazed that he had never considered such differences before. Dai's relatives were poor, suspicious farmers who received the strangers with hatred in their eyes, even after Thui Nguyen's long explanations. The sick woman was failing very rapidly; it was as if she had held the cancer at bay until she met Carmen and when she felt comfortable that her child was in good hands had yielded to its ravages. She was leaving life without the slightest commotion. She was gently fading into the background so Dai would begin to forget her before she died, forget she had ever existed, making the separation more bearable. Thui explained this to Carmen with great delicacy, and Carmen could not go against her wishes. Thui often asked Carmen to keep Dai for the night: I'm not feeling well and am better alone, she said, but as Carmen and Dai left she would turn her head to hide her tears, and her eyes came alive when they returned. She could scarcely walk and was in constant pain, but she did not complain. She stopped taking the prescribed medications, which left her exhausted and nauseated without offering relief, and consulted an elderly acupuncturist. Carmen went with her several times to those strange sessions in the dark, cinnamon-scented room where the man treated his patients. Thui, lying on a narrow cot with needles bristling from various parts of her wasted body, would close her eyes and drowse. Back in her room, Carmen would help Thui into bed, prepare her a pipe of opium, and, as she saw her sinking into the oblivion of the drug, take Dai to get ice cream. Toward the end, when Thui could not get out of bed, Dai moved into the warehouse, where he shared the large Chinese bed with his new mother. Galupi hired a woman to look after the dying Thui and drove the acupuncturist to her each day for treatment. With growing impatience Thui Nguyen asked about progress on the adoption papers; she wanted to be sure that Dai would reach his father's homeland safely, and every delay was a new torment.

One Sunday Carmen and Galupi took the boy to say goodbye to his mother. The last obstacles had been surmounted; Dai was now legally the son of Carmen Morales. He had a passport with the proper visa, and on Monday they were to begin their journey to America, where Dai would put down new roots. They left Thui alone with the boy for a few moments. He sat on the bed with the sense, even then, that this was a turning point in his life; many years later, when he was a prodigy in mathematics and being interviewed by scientific journals, he told me that his only real memory of childhood in Vietnam was of a pale woman with burning eyes who kissed him and handed him a yellow package. He showed me what had been in it, a faded photograph album wrapped in a silk muffler. Carmen and Galupi waited outside the door until the dying woman called them. They found her lying back on her pillow, peaceful and smiling. She kissed her son for the last time and gestured Galupi to take him away. Carmen sat beside her and took her hand, hot tears coursing down her cheeks.

"Thank you, Thui. You are giving me what I have wanted all my life. You mustn't worry; I will be as good a mother to Dai as you, I promise you."

"We do what we can," Thui said softly.

A few days later, while the Morales family was celebrating Dai's arrival in America, Leo Galupi was attending a simple funeral service for Thui Nguyen. Those eleven weeks had changed the destinies of several people, including the hustler from Chicago, who for days had been feeling a dull pain in his breast where once there had been fickleness and bluster.

Dai was a gale-force wind that revitalized the life of Carmen Morales, who forgot earlier rejections in love, penury, loneliness, and uncertainty. The future was as clear before her eyes as if she were viewing it on a screen: she would devote herself to Dai, help him grow up, hold his hand to keep him from stumbling, and protect him from any suffering she could, including homesickness and sadness.

"I suppose the first thing we should do is christen this little Chinese heathen, so he'll be one of ours," the aged Padre Larraguibel commented at the welcome-home party, cuddling the child with all the tenderness that had lain hidden in his huge Basque peasant's body but as a young priest he had not dared express. Carmen, nevertheless, postponed the ceremony; she did not want to torment Dai with so many new things at once, and besides, she thought Buddhism was a respectable enough religion, maybe even more tolerable than Christianity.

The new mother fulfilled the obligatory family ceremonies: she introduced her son to relatives and friends in the barrio, one by one, and patiently attempted to teach him the unpronounceable names of his new grandparents and throngs of cousins, but Dai seemed frightened and did not try to speak; he merely observed everything with those black eyes, never letting go of Carmen's hand. Carmen also took Dai to the jail to visit Olga, who was charged with practicing black magic, to see whether she had any ideas about getting the child to eat. Dai's only nourishment since leaving Vietnam had been fruit juices; he was losing weight and looked as if he might vanish on the air like a sigh. Carmen and Inmaculada were beside themselves; they had taken Dai to a doctor, who gave him a meticulous examination, declared him in good health, and prescribed vitamins. The adoptive grandmother went to great pains to prepare Mexican dishes with an Asian flavor and insisted in making Dai swallow the same cod-liver oil with which she had tortured her own six infants—but none of this had any results.

"He misses his mother," said Olga the minute she saw him through the bars in the visitors' room.

"I was notified yesterday: his mother is dead."

"Tell the little thing that she is beside him, even though he can't see her."

"He's so small he wouldn't understand that; children can't capture abstract concepts at this age. Besides, I don't want to put any superstitious ideas in his head."

"Ah, child, child, you don't know anything about anything." The healer sighed. "The dead go hand in hand with the living."

Olga had made a nest in her jail cell as easily as she had years before every time their home-on-wheels had stopped for the night—as if she were going to be there forever. Imprisonment did not affect her good spirits in any way; it was merely a minor inconvenience, and the only thing that stirred her ire was that the charges against her were false. She had never dabbled in black magic, because it was not good business; she earned much more helping her clients than she did putting curses on their enemies. She was not worried about her reputation—to the contrary, this unjust imprisonment would undoubtedly increase her fame—she was worried about her cats, which she had entrusted to a neighbor. Gregory Reeves assured her that no jury would believe that a few witchcraft rituals could do harm but that she must at any cost prevent the true nature of her business from coming to light: if that happens, he said, the law is intractable. Olga resigned herself to serving her sentence discreetly, without any uproar, but restraint was not her principal virtue, and in less than a week she had turned her cell into an extension of her extraordinary home consulting room. She did not lack for clients. The other prisoners paid her for messages of hope, therapeutic massages, calming hypnosis, powerful talismans, and for telling fortunes, and soon the guards were consulting her as well. She made arrangements to have her medicinal herbs brought to her a few at a time, her flasks of magnetized water, her tarot cards, and the Buddha of gilded plaster. From her cell, now converted into a bazaar, she practiced her beneficial sorcery and extended the subtle tentacles of her power. She not only became the most respected person in the jail; she also had the most visitors: the entire Mexican barrio filed through to consult her.

Fearing that Dai would die from lack of nourishment, Carmen decided she must try Olga's advice, and so in a mixture of English, Vietnamese, and pantomime, she told the child that his mother had gone to a different plane where her body was no longer useful to her; now she had the form of a tiny translucent fairy, constantly fluttering above his head to watch over him. Carmen was borrowing a page from Padre Larraguibel, who had always described angels in that way. According to him, each person has a devil to his left and an angel to his right, and the latter measures exactly thirty-three centimeters, the number of Christ's years on earth; the angel is naked, and it is absolutely false that it has wings: it flies by a kind of jet propulsion, a divine system of navigation less elegant but much more logical than the birds' wings described in sacred texts. This splendid man had become more eccentric with age, and the vision of his famous third eye had grown sharper; there was irrefutable proof that he could see in the dark as well as see what went on behind his back—which was why no one whispered during his mass. With inarguable moral authority he described devils and angels in precise detail, and no one, not even Inmaculada Morales, who was very conservative in religious matters, dared question his word. To compensate for the limitations of language, Carmen drew a picture in which Dai appeared in the foreground, while around him circled a small figure—preceded by a helix and trailed by a cloud of smoke—that had the unmistakable black almond-shaped eyes of Thui Nguyen. The child looked at it for a long time, then carefully folded it and placed it in the photo album containing the snapshots Leo Galupi had falsified of his parents, arm in arm in places where they had never been. Immediately thereupon, he ate his first American hamburger.

At the end of an intense week with her family, Carmen took

her son back to Berkeley, where she had organized a new life. Before leaving to collect Dai she had rented an apartment and prepared a room with white furniture and a profusion of toys. There were only two rooms, one for Dai and another that served as both workroom and bedroom for Carmen. She sold her pieces in shops now, not on street corners, although the old temptations were too strong to ignore completely. On weekends they drove to outlying towns, where she set up a stall at local craft fairs. She had done that for years without thinking of the discomfort, working eighteen hours without a rest, eating nothing but peanuts and chocolate, sleeping in her car, and not bathing, but Dai's presence demanded some adjustments. She sold the pockmarked yellow Cadillac and bought a strong, roomy van in which she could roll out a couple of sleeping bags at night when rooms were not available. Dai and Carmen were always together, like partners. Dai helped carry her things and set up the table, then played by himself or sat and waited for clients. When he got bored he wandered around the fair, or if he was tired he lay down for a nap on the ground at his mother's feet. As the same craftspeople always gathered at each locale, everyone knew Tamar's son; nowhere was he as safe as at those carnivals swarming with thieves, drunks, and drug addicts. On weekdays Carmen worked at home, always in the child's company. She taught him English, showed him the world in borrowed library books, drove around the city, and took him to swimming pools and public parks. Once Dai felt more secure in his new country, Carmen planned to send him to nursery school so he could play with children his own age, but for now the idea of being separated from him, even for a few hours, was torture. She poured upon the boy all the tenderness she had accumulated in years of secretly mourning her barrenness. She had no idea how to raise a child and lacked the patience to consult manuals, but she was not worried. She and the boy established an indestructible bond based on mutual acceptance and good humor. Dai became so splendidly adept at sharing space that he could build a castle of plastic blocks on the same table where Carmen was working on delicate gold earrings with tiny pre-Columbian ceramic beads. About midnight, Dai would crawl into Carmen's bed, and morning would find them with their arms around each other. After a year, Dai began to smile, timidly, but on the rare occasions they were separated, the blank mask again covered his face. Carmen talked to him constantly, not at all concerned that he had never spoken a word. How could the poor child be talking when he doesn't know English yet and has forgotten his own language? Carmen would argue during her Monday telephone call with Gregory; he's in the limbo of deaf-mutes now, but when he has something to say, he'll say it. She was right. When Dai was four and there was little expectation that he would ever express himself, Carmen yielded to general pressure and grudgingly took Dai to a specialist. The doctor gave the child a long and extremely thorough going-over, during which he did not elicit a single articulated sound, and then corroborated what Carmen already knew: her son was not deaf. Carmen took Dai by the hand and walked with him to the park. She chose a bench beside the duck pond, sat down, and explained that if she had to pay a therapist to help him learn to talk, their vacation for that year would be shot to hell because she didn't have enough money for both.

"You and I don't need words, Dai, but if you're going to get along in the world you have to communicate. Drawings aren't enough. Try to talk a little so we can go on vacation; otherwise we'll both be screwed."

"I didn't like that doctor, Mama; he smelled of soy sauce," the boy replied in perfect English. He would never be garrulous, but any question of his being mute had been settled.

Free time came to be Carmen's greatest luxury. She stopped seeing her friends and refused invitations from the very suitors she had only recently found so attractive. Until then, love had produced more suffering than good memories; according to Gregory, she chose terrible candidates, as if she could fall in love only with men who mistreated her. She was convinced that her run of bad luck had ended, but to be on the safe side decided to be cautious. For years Inmaculada Morales had been making vows to San Antonio de Padua, hoping that the patron saint of unmarried

women would take charge of finding a husband for her outlandish daughter, who was over thirty and still showed no sign of
settling down. Finding the perfect companion had also been an
unspoken obsession of Carmen's in the past. When she was without a man her dreams were peopled with ghosts of sexually
appealing men: she needed a strong arm, a warm body close to
hers, manly hands at her waist, a hoarse voice whispering in her
ear. Now, however, companionship was not the only consideration; her lover would also need to be the perfect father for Dai.
She thought about the men she had had, and for the first time
realized the extent of her rage against them. She wondered
whether she would have allowed herself to be battered in front of
the boy, or resigned herself to bathing Dai in someone's left-over
cold bathwater, and was frightened by her own submissiveness.
She reviewed recent lovers, but none passed her severe scrutiny;
she and Dai were better off alone. Maternity was calming for her
soul, and for the demands of the flesh she decided to follow Gregory's example and be satisfied with interim lovers. She also questioned why she had lacked the courage to have her baby ten years
ago, why she allowed herself to be defeated by fear and the pressure of meaningless traditions; it was not so difficult to be an
unmarried mother, after all. Her new responsibilities kept her
energy at the boiling point: her desire to work intensified, and
more and more original ideas flowed from her hands; ideas and
exotic materials from remote regions of the world came to life
beneath her jeweler's scriber, torch, and pliers. She would wake
up early in the morning with the detailed vision of a design in
mind and lie in bed a few minutes, wrapped in the warmth and
scent of her son; then she would get out of bed, don the embroidered robe Leo Galupi had given her, boil water for mango tea,
turn on the Victorian lamps over her worktable, and pick up her
tools with happy determination. From time to time she glanced at
her sleeping child and smiled. My life is complete, she thought. I
have never been so happy.

PART FOUR

PART FOUR

Be careful what you ask of Heaven; it might be granted, was one of Inmaculada Morales's sayings, and in the case of Gregory Reeves it came true in deadly earnest. In the following years he carried out the plans he had so enthusiastically proposed for himself, but all the while his dissatisfaction was building like steam in a pressure cooker. He could not stay still for a minute; as long as he was busy he could ignore the demands of his soul, but if he had a few quiet minutes to himself he felt a fire consuming him, a fire so powerful he was sure it did not originate with him but had been fed by his tempestuous father and, before him, his grandfather the horse thief, and before that who knows how many great-grandfathers branded by the same stigma of restlessness. It was his fate to roast on embers fanned by a thousand generations. That heat drove him forward; he assumed his victorious image just as the bucolic detachment and eternal innocence of the hippies were being ground to bits in the gears of the system's implacable machinery. No one could censure his ambition, because an impending era of unbridled greed was already gestating throughout the nation. The unsuccessful war had left a feeling of shame in the air, a collective desire to find vindication in other ways. No one spoke of the war; more than ten years would go by before history and art could begin to exorcise the demons unleashed by the disaster. Carmen watched the street where she and her best friends had earned their living slowly decay; she bid farewell to many craftsmen displaced by competition from dealers in tawdry products from Taiwan, and one by one she saw harmless mental incompetents disappear, having either died or drifted elsewhere when they were no longer fed. Other disturbed people, much worse off, took their place, war veterans who had succumbed to the horrors of their memories. Revolution in the streets was replaced by the plague of conformism, infecting even the student population. Criminals and the poor multiplied; beggars, drunks, whores, drug dealers, thieves were everywhere. The world is coming apart at the seams, Carmen lamented. Gregory Reeves, who had never at any time shared the ingenuous dreams of those trumpeting the Age of Aquarius, that era of supposed brotherhood and peace, had offered in response the time-honored figure of the pendulum swinging from one extreme to the other. He was unaffected by the change because he had thrown himself into his wild pursuit of the good life well in advance of the explosion of materialism that would mark the decade of the eighties. He boasted of his triumphs, while his colleagues wondered how he obtained the best cases and where he found the money to party constantly, spend a week whirling around the Mediterranean, and wear custom-made silk shirts. No one knew about the exorbitant bank loans or the bold juggling of credit cards. Reeves preferred not to dwell on the fact that sooner or later he would have to pay his bills; when his funds ran out he asked his banker for another loan, arguing that if he were bankrupt or in jail he certainly could not meet his payments, and that money attracts money like a magnet. He never worried about the future; he was too busy trying to shape the present. He said he was without scruple and had never felt so strong or so liberated; he could not, then, understand the urge to escape that plagued him night and day. He was a bachelor

THE INFINITE PLAN · 281

again and had no cross to bear but that of his own heart. He lived
a half hour from his daughter but saw her only the two times a
year he came to pick her up in his sporty car and take her out, as if
he could give her in four hours what had been lacking for six
months. At the end of each visit she was returned, sick from a sur-
feit of ice cream and cake and with a carload of gifts more appropriate for a seductive woman than for a schoolgirl. He had never
succeeded in convincing Margaret to call him Daddy; she had
decided that "Gregory" was more fitting for that almost unknown
man who sped through her life twice a year like a Santa Claus on
the loose. Nor did she call Samantha Mother. Margaret's teacher
made an appointment with Samantha to ask whether it was true
that they had adopted Margaret after her real parents had been
brutally murdered by a gang of thrill killers. She recommended
consultation with a child psychologist, but they went to only one
session because the time interfered with Samantha's yoga class. I
don't need anyone to tell me who you are, I know that perfectly
well, but it's fun to confuse that stupid teacher of mine, Margaret
explained with characteristic calm and composure. Her parents
concluded that she had a prodigious imagination and a remarkable sense of humor. They were similarly undisturbed that she wet
her bed at night like a baby but insisted on dressing like a grown
woman, that she wore lipstick and painted her fingernails, or that
instead of playing with other little girls she postured like a practiced tart. Aside from the inconvenience of diapering her at night
at an age when she was old enough to begin her first classes in sex
education, she gave them no headaches; she was mysterious, an
almost incorporeal creature whose most appreciated virtue was
that of passing unnoticed. It was so easy to forget she existed that
more than once her father joked about Olga's necklaces for invisibility being just the thing for his daughter.

During the first seven years Gregory Reeves practiced law, he
acquired the tools and the vices of his profession. His boss favored
him among the other attorneys in the firm and personally took
charge of teaching Gregory the tricks of the trade. He was one of
those meticulous and obsessive persons who need to control every

last detail, an unbearable man but a magnificent lawyer. Nothing escaped his scrutiny; he had a nose like a bloodhound for sniffing out the key to every legal problem and a mesmerizing eloquence when it came to swaying a jury. He taught Gregory to study cases in minute detail, search out apparently insignificant cracks in the structure, and plan his strategy like a general.

"It's a chess game, and the person who anticipates the most moves wins. You have to have the pugnaciousness of a pit bull but at the same time keep a cool head. If you get rattled, it's all over; you must learn to control your emotions, or you will never be one of the best, Reeves," he would say. "You have a good disposition, but in a fight you're too prone to throw punches blindly."

"That's exactly what Padre Larraguibel used to tell me in the courtyard of Our Lady of Lourdes."

"Who?"

"My boxing teacher."

Reeves was tenacious, untiring, difficult to bend, impossible to break, and ferocious in confrontations, but he was undermined by his own passions. The old man liked his energy; he himself had had energy to spare in his youth and still had a good reserve and could therefore appreciate it in others. He also celebrated Reeves's ambition because it was a good motivator: you put a carrot in front of Reeves's nose, and he ran like a rabbit. If at any moment he was aware of the younger man's maneuvering to appropriate his knowledge and use it as a trampoline to leapfrog over others in the firm, he should not have been surprised. He had done the same when he was beginning, with the difference that for him there had been no astute employer to hold him in check. He considered himself a good judge of character; he was sure he could keep Reeves bottled up and exploit him for his own benefit for an indefinite period. It was like breaking a horse: you had to give him his head, let him run, wear him down, and the minute he began to take the bit between his teeth rein him in so he would know who was in charge. This was not the first time he had tried it, and he had always had good results. In rare moments of weakness he was tempted to lean on the arm of that young lawyer so like himself; Reeves could be the son he never had. He had built a small empire, and now, approaching eighty, he wondered who would inherit it. He had few pleasures left; his body no longer responded to the spur of imagination, and he could not savor a fine meal without paying the consequences with a bellyache—to say nothing of women, a subject too painful to contemplate. He observed Reeves with a mixture of envy and paternal understanding, but he was neither a sentimental old fool nor inclined to relinquish the least shred of power to him. He was proud of having been born with a hard heart, as he was fond of telling anyone who came to him for a favor. The long habit of selfishness and the invincible armor of his avarice were strong enough to quell any glimmer of sympathy. He was the perfect master for a laborious apprenticeship in greed.

Timothy Duane never forgave his father for having brought him into the world, nor for continuing to thwart his heart's desires with his good health and bad humor. To defy him, Duane committed every known atrocity, always making sure his father knew about it, and so wasted fifty years in a festering hatred that cost him his peace and well-being. Sometimes his contrariness worked to his advantage, as when he decided to avoid military service because his father supported the war—not so much out of patriotism as because of financial interests in armaments—but usually his rebellion circled back to blow up in his face. He decided not to marry or have children, even on the few occasions when he was in love, in order to destroy his father's ambition to establish a dynasty. The family name he so detested would die with him— except for a branch of the Duanes in Ireland no one wanted to acknowledge because they reminded them of their humble origins. Cultured and refined, with the natural elegance of one born between monogrammed sheets, Timothy had a passionate interest in the arts and a congeniality that won him droves of friends, but before his father he somehow managed to hide these virtues and behave like a clod, for the sole purpose of annoying him. If the Duane patriarch was entertaining at a dinner for the cream of society, Timothy would appear without being invited and with a slut on his arm, eager to violate all rules of civility. While his father fumed that he never wanted to see his son again as long as he lived, Timothy's mother openly defended him, even when it meant a confrontation with her husband. You must see a psychiatrist, son, she often suggested, and get help with your problems; you can overcome the flaws in your character; but Timothy's response was that without the flaws he would not have any character left. In the meantime, he lived a miserable life, not for lack of means but because of his bent for self-torture. He had an apartment in the most expensive section of the city, an entire floor in an old building, decorated with modern furniture and strategically placed mirrors, and an income for the remainder of his lifetime, his grandfather's ultimate gift. Since he had never wanted for anything, he placed no importance on money and ridiculed the many foundations his father had invented, less to evade taxes than to deprive Timothy of his inheritance. His demons harassed him relentlessly, pushing him to vices he found repellent but indulged in to torment his father, even if it meant killing himself in the process. He spent his days in his pathology laboratory, sickened by human frailty and the infinite permutations of pain and putrefaction but also awed by the possibilities of science. He never admitted it, but the laboratory was the only place where he found a certain peace. He could lose himself in the painstaking analysis of a diseased cell, and when he emerged from among X-rays, test tubes, and laser beams, generally very late at night, the muscles of his neck and back might ache, but he was content. That sensation would last until he reached the street and started his car, but when he realized he had nowhere to go and no one waiting for him, he would sink back into self-hatred. He patronized the sleaziest bars, where he drank until he forgot even his name; he got into brawls with sailors and ended up in hospital emergency rooms; he spewed insults in homosexual bathhouses and only by a hair escaped the violence he detested; he picked up whores to buy an unwholesome gratification seasoned by the danger of lethal contagion. He would hurtle down a precipitous slope, experiencing a mixture of fear and pleasure, cursing God and invoking death, but, after a week or two of such defilement, suffer a crisis of guilt and stop short, shivering at the brink of the chasm opening at his feet. He would swear never again to swallow a drop of alcohol, shut himself in his apartment like an anchorite to read his favorite authors and listen to jazz into the early hours, and have his blood tested for evidence of the curse that in his heart he desired as punishment for his sins. A period of tranquillity would begin, during which he attended concerts and plays, visited his mother like a good son, and asked out girls who patiently waited with the everlasting hope of reforming him. He went on long solitary excursions into the mountains to listen to the voice of God calling to him on the wind. The only person he saw in both good and bad times was his friend Gregory Reeves, who rescued him from assorted predicaments and helped him get back on his feet. Duane made no mystery of his wastrel existence; on the contrary, he enjoyed exaggerating his infamy in order to cultivate his reputation as a lost soul. There was a side of his character, nevertheless, jealously hidden, that few suspected. While sneering with defiant cynicism at the mention of any high-minded cause, he surreptitiously contributed to those same projects, taking great care that his name be kept in strictest secrecy. He set aside part of his income for helping the needy within his sphere and for sustaining good works in distant lands—from starving children to political prisoners. Contrary to what he had expected when he chose his field of specialization, his work among cadavers increased his compassion for the living; all human suffering concerned him, but he had little emotional reserve to expend on endangered animals, vanishing forests, or polluted waters. He made fierce jokes about those campaigns, just as he railed on the subject of race, religion, and women—in part because such causes were in vogue and his greatest delight lay in creating a scandal. He was intolerant of the false virtue of people who were horrified by the thought of a dolphin trapped in a tuna net but indifferently passed homeless beggars on the street, pretending not to see them. His favorite expression was What a shitty world we live in!

"What you need is a woman who's all sugar on the outside but firm as steel underneath, someone who will take you by the ear and save you from yourself. I'm going to introduce you to Carmen Morales," Gregory Reeves told Timothy once he had resigned himself to loving Carmen like a brother, after realizing that she was beyond his reach.

"It's too late, Greg. I'm not good for anything but whores," Timothy Duane replied, for once without sarcasm.

Shannon blew into Reeves's life like a breath of fresh air. He had been climbing the ladder for years but despite his successes felt he was not getting anywhere, like the feeling of running in a nightmare. With a magician's legerdemain he was juggling debts, whirlwind trips, outrageous partying, an insane schedule, and a stable of women, with the sense, renewed every day, that at the slightest distraction everything would come tumbling down with earthquake force. He had more legal cases than he could manage, more debts than he could pay, and more lovers than he could satisfy. His good memory helped in remembering all the loose threads in that tangle; his good luck in not slipping into careless error; and his good health in not dying of exhaustion like an ox driven beyond endurance. Shannon arrived one Monday morning dressed in bridal white and smelling of flowers, with the sunniest smile ever seen in his firm's steel-and-glass building. She was twenty-two years old, but her girlish mannerisms and winsome personality made her seem younger. It was her first job as a receptionist; previously she had worked as a clerk in several shops, as a waitress, and as an amateur singer, but as she said with the voice of a beguiling adolescent, there was no future in those jobs. Gregory, dazzled by her radiance and intrigued by the variety of jobs held by someone so young, asked her what advantages she saw in answering the telephone behind a marble desk, and she enigmatically replied that there she would at least meet the right people. Reeves at once wrote her name in his address book and before the week was out had asked her to go dancing. She accepted with the calm confidence of a lioness in repose. I like older men, she remarked with a smile. Reeves did not really know what to say, because he was used to going out with young girls and had not considered the difference in their ages to be significant. Soon he would confront the generational abyss that separated them, but by then it would be too late to turn back. Shannon was a girl of her time. Escaping a violent father and a mother who covered the marks of her husband's beatings with makeup, she had set out on foot from the backwater Georgia town where she was born. A couple of miles out of town she hitched a ride with the first truck-driver who spotted her, a fantastic apparition standing by the end-less ribbon of highway, and after miscellaneous adventures reached San Francisco. The combination of ingenuousness and self-confidence fascinated everyone who met her and helped her rise above sordid realities; doors flew open before her advance, and obstacles evaporated. The invitation in her verdant eyes dis-armed women and seduced men. She gave the impression of being totally unaware of her power; she breezed through life like a celestial sprite, eternally surprised when everything turned out well. Her fickle nature caused her to flit from one situation to the next, always cheerful, with never a thought for the struggles and pain of other mortals. She did not concern herself about the pres-ent, much less the future. Through conscious amnesia, she sup-pressed the squalid scenes of her childhood, the poverty of adoles-cence, the betrayals of lovers who used her and left her, and the incontestable fact that she hadn't a cent to her name. Incapable of keeping two pennies to rub together, she survived with briefly held jobs where she earned barely enough to live, but she did not think of herself as poor because whenever she wanted something, all she had to do was ask: a few enthralled suitors were always at hand, eager to satisfy her whims. She did not use men maliciously or perversely; it merely seemed to her that there was no other rea-son for their being. She was innocent of the pain of love or any other meaningful emotion. She was fleetingly enthusiastic about each new lover—as long as the newness lasted—but soon she tired of him and moved on, with no sympathy for the person she left behind. She was unaware that she damned several lovers to the martyrdom of jealousy and hopeless dejection, because she herself was impervious to that kind of suffering; if it was she who was abandoned, she changed course without a regret—after all, the world held an inexhaustible supply of available men. Two years after they met, while bandaging the knuckles he had bloodied punching one of her conquests in the face, Shannon told Gregory Reeves in all seriousness: You have to forgive me, you know; I'm like an artichoke: a leaf here, a leaf there, but the heart is for you. From their first date it was obvious who was the stronger. Reeves was defeated on his own turf; all his experience and arrogant Don Juaning were no help now. He fell for the new receptionist the minute he saw her, not just for her physical charms—he had known more than one as beautiful as she—but also for her ready laugh and evident candor. That night, with true concern, he asked himself what he might do to save that splendid creature: he imagined her exposed to all sorts of dangers and difficulties and took upon himself the responsibility for protecting her.

"Fate led her to me for some reason," he told Carmen. "According to my father's *Infinite Plan,* nothing happens by chance. This girl needs me."

Carmen missed her opportunity to warn him because her intuitive antennae were tuned toward Dai; she was busily sewing him a costume to wear as one of the Three Wise Men in a Christmas play at school. With the telephone clamped between her ear and her shoulder, she was gluing feathers onto an emerald-colored turban before her son's attentive eyes.

"I just hope this one's not a vegetarian," she commented distractedly.

She was not. Shannon savored her new lover's culinary treats with contagious enthusiasm and insatiable appetite; it was truly miraculous that she could devour such quantities of food and still keep her figure. She could also drink like a sailor. With the second drink her eyes took on a feverish shine, as the angelic child was transformed into the sensual woman. At that stage, Reeves never knew which of the two personalities was more appealing: the artless receptionist in a starched white blouse who reported every Monday to sit behind the marble desk or Sunday's stormy naked bacchante. She was a fascinating woman, and he the geographer charting new territories. They saw each other every day at work, where they feigned an indifference that was suspicious given one's reputation as a womanizer and the other's intrinsic flirtatiousness. Several nights a week they met in marathon encounters they confused with love, and even at the office they sometimes darted into a room, closed the door, and, ignoring the risk of being discovered, writhed and gyrated with adolescent urgency. Reeves was more in love than he had ever been, which may also have been true of Shannon—though in her case that was not saying much. Gregory began to relive that portion of his youth when the volcanic eruption of his hormones had sent him in hot pursuit of any girl who crossed his path, except that now all that charged passion was focused upon a single objective. He could not get Shannon out of his mind; he kept rising from his desk to look at her, even from a distance, tormented by jealousy of men in general and his officemates in particular, including the old man of the orchids, who also made frequent stops at the young receptionist's desk, tempted perhaps by the thought of one last trophy but arrested by his sense of the ridiculous and his awareness of the limitations of age. No one passed through the reception area without being struck by the lightning of Shannon's dazzling smile. If she was not free to go out in the evening, Gregory Reeves inevitably imagined her in another's arms, and the mere suspicion set him mad. He showered her with absurd presents, hoping to impress her, unaware that she did not appreciate hand-painted Russian boxes, bonsai trees, or pearls for her ears but would have preferred a pair of leather jeans to wear with biker friends her age. With a lover's passion to share everything with the beloved, he tried to warm her to his interests. When he took her to the opera she was fascinated with the audience's elegant clothes, but when the curtain rose she thought they were watching a farce. She contained herself until the third act, but when the fat woman dressed as a geisha plunged a knife into her own belly while her son waved a Japanese flag in one hand and an American flag in the other, her laughter roared above the orchestra and they had to flee the hall.

In August Gregory took Shannon to Italy. She had worked for the firm for less than a year and was not entitled to vacation time, but that created no problem since she had handed in her resignation, to take a job with a modeling agency. Gregory spent the trip suffering in anticipation; he hated the idea of seeing her exposed to everyone's eyes in the pages of a magazine but did not dare voice his concern for fear of appearing hopelessly old-fashioned. He also refrained from mentioning his objections to Carmen, because he knew she would rib him unmercifully. As he walked down a flower-lined path on the shores of Lake Como, blinded by Shannon's incomparable charms to the misty mirror of the water and the ocher-toned villas clinging to the hillsides, it occurred to him how he might keep her by his side. He proposed that if Shannon came to live with him she would not have to work and could enroll in the university to study for a career. She was intelligent and creative; wasn't there something she would like to study? No, not at the moment, Shannon replied, with the easy laugh that came after several glasses of wine, but she would think of something. That night Reeves picked up the telephone to tell Carmen, on the other side of the ocean, his news, but could not reach her. She and Dai had left on a trip to the Far East.

Bel Benedict did not know her exact age, nor did she want to find out. The years had slightly rusted her bones and darkened her burnt-sugar skin to a tone nearer chocolate, but nothing had altered the topaz glitter of her wide eyes or entirely quenched the fires in her loins. Some nights she dreamed hotly of the only man she had loved in her life and waked moist with pleasure. I must be the only randy old woman in history—sweet Jesus, forgive me, she thought, secretly more prideful than ashamed. Shame is what she felt when she looked in the mirror and saw that the body once sleek as a young mare's now sagged like an old nag's; if my husband could see me now, she thought, he'd be frightened away. She

never rationalized that were he alive, he too would have suffered
the passing of the years and not be the lithe, joyful, and lusty man
who had seduced her when she was fifteen. But Bel could neither
allow herself the luxury of lying in bed remembering the past nor
stand before the mirror lamenting her decline; every morning she
rose at dawn to go to work, except on Sundays, when she went to
church and to market. During the last year she had not had a
spare minute, because when she finished work she had to hurry
home and look after her son. She had started calling him Baby
again, as she had when she held him to her breast and sang him
lullabies. Don't call me that, Mama, my friends will tease me, he
protested, but in fact he no longer had any friends; he had lost
them all, along with his job, his wife, his children, and his memory. Poor Baby, Bel Benedict sighed, but she did not feel sorry for
him; she actually envied him a little. She did not intend to die for
many years to come, and as long as she was alive he would be safe.
Step by step, one day at a time, was her philosophy; it was no good
worrying about a tomorrow that might never come. Her grandfather, a Mississippi slave, had told her that we have our past before
us: the past's the only real thing we have, and we can learn a lot
about living from it. The present is nothing but an illusion; as fast
as you blink your eye it's already part of the past. And the future?
The future's a dark hole no one can see; it may not even be there,
because while we're talking, death can come and carry us away.
Bel had worked for Timothy's parents so many years that it was
difficult to imagine the house without her. When she was hired,
she was already a woman of legend, one of those narrow-waisted
black women who move as if they are swimming underwater.

"Marry me," Timothy would say in the kitchen when she
treated him to pancakes, her one skill in cooking. "You're so beautiful you should be a movie star instead of my mother's maid."

"The only blacks in the movies are whites in blackface," she
would say, laughing.

When she was very young, a black vagabond with an uproarious laugh had wandered down the road looking for a patch of
shade where he could sit and rest. They had fallen in love at first

sight, with a passion so torrid it could alter the weather and change the course of time. That love engendered King Benedict, who was to live two lives, just as Olga had foretold that day during the Second World War when the truck bearing the sign of *The Infinite Plan* had picked him up on a dusty country road. A few days after King was born, Bel had forgotten the nine months of carrying her son's weight beneath her heart and the anguish of giving birth and was again chasing her man around every corner of the farm. They made love in a pool of blood beside the cows in the stable, the birds in the cornfields, and the scorpions in the barn. When the young King began to take his first hesitant steps, his father, exhausted by love and fearful of losing his soul and his manhood between the legs of that insatiable voluptuary, ran off, taking as a souvenir a lock of Bel's hair, cut while she slept. In the turbulence of their rutting, Bel had turned a deaf ear to the insistence of the pastor of the Baptist church that they contract holy matrimony in the eyes of the Lord. For Bel, a signature in the church records had little bearing; she considered herself married. For the rest of her life, she used her lover's name and told the many men who sought repose in her bosom that her husband was out of town on a trip. She said it so many times that she came to believe it, which was why she was enraged when she saw herself naked: If you don't hurry back you're not going to find nothing but a bag of bones, she scolded the memory of her absent lover.

One January morning half a century later, when the city was swept by a strong wind from the sea, Bel Benedict put on her turquoise-colored dress, hat, shoes, and gloves, her Sunday and party best. She had noticed that Queen Elizabeth always wore a monotone ensemble and could not rest until she had a similar outfit. Timothy Duane was waiting for her in front of the modest building where she lived.

"You won't live forever, Bel. What will happen to your son when you're gone?" Timothy had asked.

"King won't be the first fourteen-year-old boy who has to make it on his own."

"But he isn't fourteen; he's fifty-three."

"For all practical purposes, he's fourteen."

"That's just what I mean. He'll always be a kid."

"Maybe not; maybe he'll grow up. . . ."

"If you had some money put aside, things would be a little easier. Don't be stubborn, woman."

"I've already told you, Tim. There's nothing I can do. The lawyer for the insurance company told us straight out that we don't have a claim. Just to be nice, they're going to give us ten thousand dollars. But not yet; there's lots of papers to fill out."

"I don't understand these things, but I have a friend who can give us good advice."

Gregory Reeves welcomed them in the jungle of greenery in his office. Bel made her triumphal entry, dressed like a queen, sat on the long-suffering leather sofa, and proceeded to tell the strange story of her son, King Benedict. Reeves listened attentively, while he searched his infallible memory for the source of that name, which resonated with a distant echo of the past. It's impossible to forget a name like that; I wonder where it was I heard it. King was a good Christian, the woman was saying, but God has not granted him an easy life. They had always been poor, and in the early years they had moved from place to place as she looked for work, bidding new friends goodbye and putting King in yet another school. He had grown up fearing that his mother might run off with one of her boyfriends and leave him alone in a room in some nameless town. He was a melancholy, shy boy, and two years of the war in the South Pacific had not helped erase his insecurity. After the war he married, had two children, and earned a living as a construction worker. Then his marriage went bad, his wife threatened to leave him, and his own children felt sorry for him. Bel noticed that he was tense and sad, and she was afraid he would begin drinking again, as he had in previous crises; things went from bad to worse and finally culminated in his accident. He had been working at the second-story level, when the scaffolding collapsed and he fell to the ground. The shock knocked him out for a few seconds, but he got to his feet, apparently with only a few bruises. As a precaution, he was taken to the hospital but dismissed after a routine examination. As soon as his headache passed, however, and he began to speak, it was obvious that he did not recognize his family or know where he was; he thought he was a teenager again. His mother soon ascertained that his memory stopped at the age of fourteen; from that year on there was a void as deep as the ocean. He was given every test known and questioned for weeks; his orifices were probed, his brain was wired, he was hypnotized and X-rayed down to his soul—all without a logical reason being discovered for such a dramatic memory loss. Medical science could detect no physical trauma. King began to act like a manipulative child, inventing clumsy lies to trick his children—whom he treated like playmates—and to evade the watchful eye of his wife—whom he confused with his mother. He did not recognize Bel Benedict because he remembered her as a young and beautiful woman. Stranger that she was, however, he clung to that old woman like a limpet; she was his only security in a world of confusion. Relatives and friends doubted his amnesia; they thought it might be hysteria and soon tired of prying into the corners of his mind for a sign of recognition. The insurance company, too, was unconvinced; they suspected that King was perpetrating a hoax to collect disability; in their eyes he was a charlatan who would spend the rest of his life drawing an invalid's pension for a bump on the head. Every time his wife left the house, King felt abandoned, and when she started bringing her lover to the house to spend the night, Bel Benedict decided the moment had come to intervene and took her son home to live with her. For months she had carefully observed him without detecting the slightest thread of memory following his fourteenth year. Gradually King had settled down; he was good company, and his mother was happy to have him with her. The only irrational aspect of his behavior was that he claimed to hear voices and see angels; although the doctors discounted them entirely, mother and son became accustomed to the presence of the phantoms of his imagination. Timothy Duane had brought copies of the hospital records and letters from the insurance company lawyers. Reeves barely glanced at them, feeling the familiar fire of battle race through him, the street fighter's fervent anticipation, the thing he liked best about his profession: he thrived on complicated cases, difficult challenges, the actual skirmishes.

"If you decide to take this to court, you'll have to do it soon, because the statute of limitations is one year from the time of the accident."

"But then they won't give me my ten thousand dollars!"

"This case may be worth a great deal more than that, Mrs. Benedict. They may have offered you money to gain time, time in which you lose your right to file a claim."

Although fearful, Bel agreed to file; ten thousand dollars was more than she had saved in a lifetime of working, but Reeves inspired her confidence and Timothy Duane was right: she must do something to protect her son from an uncertain future. That evening Reeves presented the case to his boss, so excited he could scarcely get the words out, recounting the story of the handsome black woman and her grown son who had reverted to childhood because of a fall. Just imagine, if we win, we'll change these poor people's lives. . . . But he was met with diabolic eyebrows raised to the hairline and an ironic gaze. Don't waste time on such foolishness, Gregory. We don't want to open up that can of worms. He explained that the chances of winning were slim, that it would require years of investigation, dozens of experts, many hours of work, and possibly zero results, because unless they found a cerebral lesion that justified the loss of memory, no jury would accept the amnesia story. Reeves felt a rising wave of frustration. He had obeyed others' decisions long enough; every day he was more restless and more disillusioned with his work, and he saw no promise of being able to proceed independently. He clung to that sense of rebellion as he delivered to the old man of the orchids the farewell speech he had so often rehearsed in private. When he went home that night he found Shannon lying on the living room floor, watching television; he kissed her with a blend of pride and anxiety.

"I just resigned. From now on I'll be on my own."

"That's something to celebrate!" she exclaimed. "And while we're at it, Greg, let's drink a toast to the baby."

"What baby?"

"The one we're expecting." Shannon smiled, pouring a drink from the bottle by her side.

When she divorced her second husband, Judy Reeves kept all the children, including her husband's by his first wife. Over the years the marriage had become a nightmare of bitterness and quarrels in which the man usually came out the loser. When the time came for them to part, there was not even a thought that the father would take his offspring: the affection between Judy and the two dark-skinned youngsters was so solid and so warm that no one remembered they were not hers. She remained unmarried for only a few months. One hot Saturday she took her brood to the beach, where she met a husky veterinarian from northern California who was vacationing in a van with his three children and a dog. The animal's hindquarters had been paralyzed after it had been hit by a car; rather than dispatch it to a better life, however, as was indicated by his professional experience, the vet had improvised a harness so that the animal could get around with the help of the children, who took turns supporting her rear while she ran on her front legs. The spectacle of the crippled beast playing in the waves and yelping with glee caught the attention of Judy's four. That was how they met. Judy was overflowing the seams of a striped bathing suit and downing one ice cream after another. The doctor stood watching, horrified and fascinated by such quantities of naked flesh, but after exchanging a few words they struck up a friendship; he forgot how she looked and by sundown invited her to eat. The two families ended the day devouring pizzas and hamburgers.

The veterinarian took his crew back home to the Napa Valley and Judy remained behind, summoning him with her thoughts. Since her days with Jim Morgan, her first husband, she had not met anyone who was her match in bed or in a good fight. Jim Morgan had been granted early release for good behavior, and even though Judy was then married to the small Mexican with the mustache, Morgan had called to say that not one day had gone by in prison without his remembering her with affection. By then, however, Judy was embarked on a different course. Furthermore, Morgan had been converted to a sect of Christian fundamentalism whose fanaticism was incomprehensible to someone who had absorbed from her mother the legacy of the tolerant Bahai faith; for those reasons, she had chosen not to see him once she was single again. Judy's mental messages crossed mountains and vast vineyards, and soon afterward the veterinarian came to visit her. They spent a week's honeymoon with all the children and Nora, the grandmother, who by then was totally dependent on Judy. The cabin Charles Reeves had bought thirty years before had fallen back into its original disrepair. Termites, dust, and the passage of time had worked their slow labor on the wood walls, and Nora had done nothing to save the house from ruin. One evening when Judy and her second husband arrived for a visit, they found the old woman sitting in the wicker rocking chair beneath the willow tree because the roof of the porch had collapsed onto its rotted columns.

"All right, ma'am. You're coming to live with us," her son-in-law announced.

"Thank you, son, but I can't do that. Imagine how upset the Doctor in Divine Sciences will be if he doesn't find me here on Thursday."

"What is your mother talking about?"

"She thinks my father's ghost comes to visit on Thursdays; that's why she's never wanted to leave the house," Judy clarified.

"That's no problem, ma'am. We'll leave a note for your husband with the new address."

No one had thought of such a simple solution. Nora got up, wrote the note in her perfect schoolmarm's hand, collected the pearl necklace that had survived so many crises of poverty, a box with yellowed photographs, and a couple of her husband's paintings, and calmly took a seat in her daughter's automobile. Judy threw the wicker chair into the trunk, in case her mother should need it, padlocked the door, and they drove away without a backward look. Charles Reeves must have found the message, just as

he found others every time his widow moved, because he never
missed a single Thursday of his posthumous appointments, and
Nora never lost sight of the thread of the orange that joined her to
the other world. The year Gregory married Shannon, his sister
was living with the veterinarian, her mother, and a swarm of children of various ages, colors, and surnames; she was expecting her
eighth child and confessed to being in love. Her life was not easy;
half the house was given over to the animal clinic, she had to con-
tend with a constant parade of ailing pets, the air reeked of cre-
osote, the children fought like tigers, and Nora Reeves had sunk
into the merciful world of her imagination and at an age when
other old women were knitting booties for their great-grandchil-
dren had harked back to her girlhood. Judy, however, was happy
for the first time; finally she had found a life's companion, and she
did not have to work outside her home. Her husband cooked
monumental amounts of food on the grill to feed his tribe and
bought chocolate cookies wholesale. Despite pregnancy, the good
food, and her enormous appetite, Judy slowly began to lose
weight, and a few months after giving birth weighed what she
had as a girl. On the arm of her third husband, she attended her
brother's wedding wearing light voile and a delicate straw hat; she
had one babe in her arms and was trailed by seven children in
Sunday-go-to-meeting clothes, her mother, dressed like a schoolgirl, and a paralytic dog that, despite its clumsy harness, wore the
smile of contented animals.

"Say hello to your aunt Judy and grandmother Nora," Gregory told Margaret, who at eleven was small for her age but totally
adult in her behavior. She had never heard of that plump woman
or the distracted little old lady with a ribbon in her hair and
thought the whole circus was some kind of joke. She did not
appreciate her father's sense of humor.

The bridegroom hired a mariachi band from the Mission district to give a Latin flavor to his wedding; the food was provided
by one of Gregory's former lovers, a beautiful woman named
Rosemary, who was not bitter about his wedding because she had
never wanted to marry him. She had written several cookbooks

and made a career of catering banquets; with her team of wait-resses she could serve a Mexican fiesta, a brunch for Asian executives, or a French dinner with equal ease. Shannon, the center of attention, looking beautiful in an innocent dress of white organdy, danced paso dobles, boleros, and corridos until the drinks went to her head and she had to retire. The rest of the night, Gregory Reeves and Timothy Duane danced with Carmen, as in the old days of jitterbug and rock 'n' roll, while Dai, with no little astonishment, observed this new side of his mother's personality.

"That boy is just like Juan José," Gregory said.

"No," Carmen replied. "He's just like me."

Carmen had returned from her journey to Thailand, Bali, and India with a cargo of materials and a head seething with new ideas. She could not keep up with demands for her work and had rented space for a workshop and hired a pair of Vietnamese refugees, whom she trained as her helpers. During the hours Dai was in school, she took advantage of the calm and silence to design the jewelry her helpers then executed. She told Gregory she planned to open her own shop as soon as she could save enough to get started.

"That's not how it works. You have a peon's mentality. You should ask for a loan. Businesses are opened on credit, Carmen."

"How many times do I have to ask you to call me Tamar?"

"I'll introduce you to my banker."

"I don't want to end up in your shoes, Gregory. You couldn't pay off everything you owe in a hundred years."

It was true. Gregory's banker friend had to provide another loan before Gregory could open his law office, but he did not complain because that year interest rates had shot to record levels. He needed borrowers like Gregory Reeves, because very few were able to meet their payments. That situation could not last much longer; experts were predicting that economic uncertainty would lose the election for the President, a good man criticized for being weak and overly liberal—two unpardonable sins in that place and at that time.

· · ·

Gregory Reeves rented an office above a Chinese restaurant and had his name and title painted in large gold letters on the windows, as he had seen in old detective movies: GREGORY REEVES, ATTORNEY-AT-LAW. That sign symbolized his triumph. That's the low class coming out in you, man; I've never seen anything more vulgar, was Timothy Duane's comment, but Carmen liked the idea and decided to copy it for her shop, except that she wanted hers in script. The office occupied one roomy floor in the very center of San Francisco, with its own elevator and an emergency exit that would prove to be useful on more than one occasion. The same day Reeves moved into the building, the owner of the restaurant, a native of Hong Kong, came up to proffer his greetings. He was accompanied by his son, a small, myopic young man with gentle manners; by profession, he was a geologist, but he hadn't the least affinity for minerals and rocks: his true love was numbers. His name was Mike Tong, and he had been brought to this country at a very early age, when his father moved the entire family to their new home. Mike inquired whether the esteemed lawyer had any need for an accountant; Gregory explained that at the moment he had only one client and could not pay him a salary, but he would be happy to hire him a few hours a week. Reeves could not suspect that Mike Tong would become his most faithful guardian and would save him from despair and bankruptcy. By then the Latino work force had greatly multiplied. Within thirty years, predicted Timothy Duane, we whites will be the minority in this country. Reeves meant to take advantage of the experience he had gained in his native barrio, and of his command of Spanish, to seek a clientele among that segment of the population, because elsewhere the competition was ferocious: three fourths of all the lawyers in the world practice in the United States—one lawyer for every three hundred seventy persons. The most important reason, however, was that he had fallen in love with the idea of helping the most humble; he better than anyone could understand the agony of Latin immigrants, because he, too, had been treated like a wetback. He would have to have a secretary able to conduct business in both languages, and Carmen put him in touch with a woman named Tina Faibich, who had all the necessary qualifications. The applicant appeared in the office before the furniture had arrived. There was nothing but the English leather sofa, Reeves's accomplice in so many conquests, and dozens of potted plants; records and files were scattered everywhere on the floor. The woman had to pick her way through the debris and perch on a box of books. Gregory saw before him a sweet, placid woman who spoke perfect Spanish and regarded him with an indecipherable expression in her pleasant, bovine eyes. Gregory felt comfortable with her; she radiated the serenity he was lacking. He barely looked at her, did not read her recommendations, and posed only a minimum of questions—he trusted his instinct. As she said goodbye, she removed her glasses and smiled. Don't you recognize me? she asked timidly. Gregory looked again, observing her more closely. It was Ernestina Pereda, the mischievous kitten of the doctor-and-nurse games in the school bathroom, the sexy vixen who had rescued him from the torment of lust when he was drowning in the caldron of teenage hormones, Ernestina of the hasty coitus and tears of repentance, sainted Ernestina, now a respectable matron. After all the one-night stands, she had married, fully adult, an employee of the telephone company; she had no children and did not need them, she said; her husband was sufficient. She showed Gregory a photograph of Mr. Faibich, a man so ordinary you would not remember his face one minute after seeing it. Gregory Reeves stood with the snapshot in his hand and his eyes on the floor, not knowing what to say.

"I'm a good secretary," she murmured, blushing.

"This might be embarrassing for both of us, Ernestina."

"You won't have any complaint about me, Mr. Reeves."

"I'm Gregory."

"No. It's better if we start from the beginning. The past doesn't count now," and she told Gregory Reeves how her life had changed after she met her husband, a quiet man in appearance only; in private he was wildly passionate, a tireless and faithful lover who successfully satisfied her sexual hungers. She had nothing but a blurred memory of the past, largely because she had no interest in what had happened before; her present happiness was what mattered.

"I never forgot you, though, because you were the only one who never promised me something he didn't intend to deliver."

"I'll expect you at eight tomorrow morning, Tina," and Gregory smiled, shaking her hand.

"That's a fine joke you played on me," Gregory protested when he called Carmen, but she, who had known about the stealthy and guilty encounters between her old friend and Ernestina Pereda, assured him that she had not meant it as a joke, that she honestly believed Tina was the ideal secretary for him. She was not mistaken; Tina Faibich and Mike Tong would be the sole reliable pillars in the fragile edifice of Gregory Reeves's law firm. It was also Carmen's idea to attract Latin clients with ads on the Spanish television channel during the hours of the soap operas; she remembered her mother sitting hypnotized before the set, more upset about the fate of those fictional characters than about her own family. Neither of the two anticipated the impact of the advertisement. At each commercial break, a blue-eyed Gregory Reeves appeared in his well-cut suit, the image of a respectable Anglo-Saxon professional, but when he opened his mouth to offer his services he spoke in the resonant Spanish of the barrio, with the idioms and unmistakable accent borrowed from the Hispanics who observed him from the other side of the screen. We can trust him, potential clients decided, he's one of us; he's just a different color. Soon he was recognized by waiters in restaurants, by taxi drivers and construction workers, and by every warm-skinned laborer he ran into. When his office opened its doors, King Benedict was his only case; after a month he had so many he needed to look for a partner.

"Associates, yes; partners, never," was the recommendation of Mike Tong, who spent all day in the office even though he was hired for only a few hours a week.

Two years later, six lawyers, a receptionist, and three secretaries were employed in the firm. Reeves argued cases throughout

California and spent more time on airplanes than on the ground, earning money by the handful and spending much more than he brought in. By then, Mike Tong was investing the greater part of his life amid the disorder of his warren, crowded among files, papers, accounting ledgers, bank statements, and the photocopying machine, in addition to a coffeemaker, brooms, bathroom supplies, and paper cups, all of which he husbanded with the diligence of a magpie. Everyone made jokes about how tight the bookkeeper was, swearing that at night he sneaked back to fish the paper cups from the wastebaskets, wash them, and return them to the holder, to be used the next day. Mike Tong, however, was unruffled by their jokes; he was too busy toting up accounts on his abacus.

The everyday routine and the obligations of monogamy were anathema to Shannon from the beginning. She had the suffocating sensation that she was plodding through a desert of endless sand dunes, leaving behind a bit of her youth with every step. The chiming laughter that was one of her principal attractions lost some of its ring, and her natural indolence came to the fore. She was abjectly bored, tied to a husband for the sake of security, an idea suggested by her mother, who also had intimated that the best way to catch Gregory Reeves was with a well-timed pregnancy. She really wanted to marry him, Shannon told her mother, not for ignominious reasons but because she was fond of the man. He made her feel protected for the first time in her life. I'm happy to hear that, child, because soon Reeves will be rich—that is, if he isn't already, which is what I've heard, her mother replied. Shannon was not calculating and evidenced no specific interest in money, in spite of family advice to catch a big fish who could provide the queenly treatment her beauty deserved. There was another incentive: she was tired of earning her own living, keeping office hours, living within her salary; she had tried and learned it was not for her. A prosperous husband would solve all her problems, but she had not considered the price she would have to pay. Now she was a prisoner in her own home, a slave to the baby growing in her womb. For a few weeks she fought boredom by sunbathing on the dock beside the ghostly sailboat, but soon convinced Gregory that they should move; the task of looking for the mansion of her dreams helped pass the time. She could not find the house she was looking for and did not have enough energy to redecorate the one they had with any care; she hastily ordered furniture and accessories from a catalog and, when they came, arranged them any which way. She wandered through the crowded rooms and entertained herself talking to friends on the telephone; as a joke she would call old lovers at inopportune times and whisper obscenities that excited them, and herself, to the verge of madness. Deprived of an outlet for her natural flirtatiousness, she became surly, just as she did when denied alcohol. From pure boredom, she began drinking more and ended up with a serious drinking problem, like her father. She might never have noticed Mike Tong, except that he was immune to her spell; he treated her with the distant courtesy reserved for someone's grandmother, behavior that greatly annoyed her and was aggravated by the fact that he restricted the use of her credit cards and counseled caution to his boss when he was about to spend a lot of money to please her. Neither was Timothy Duane a favorite of hers; she had invited him to lunch one day, using the pretext of discussing a birthday party for Gregory, but he showed up with the Austrian tourist he was squiring that week and gave no sign of perceiving how much more beautiful Shannon herself was. The next day Duane warned Gregory to keep an eye on his wife, which sent him rushing home to ask for an explanation; he did not get one, however, because he found Shannon passed out on the kitchen floor, and when he tried to move her she vomited on him. It's morning sickness, she said, but she smelled of alcohol. Gregory helped her to bed and then stood watching her, asleep between her pink sheets, looking so young and naive that he thought Duane, biased by his cynicism, must have misinterpreted an innocent invitation. He would not be able to continue deceiving himself for long, however; in the following months he saw signs that the relationship was deteriorating, much as it had with Samantha, but he had faith that he had much more in common with Shannon than with his first wife, and clung to that knowledge to ward off depression. *At least we share a taste for food and for great love-making.* Like him, too, Shannon was restless and adventurous; she loved trips, buying sprees, and parties. *You two will come to no good; your wife has all your worst traits,* Carmen warned Gregory, but he did not see it that way. Perhaps from their similarities they could weave the foundation for a true marital relationship, but the passion of their first months quickly cooled, and raking through the coals of the once blazing fires, they found no love. Gregory was still enchanted with Shannon's youth and joy and beauty, but he was so busy with his practice that he did not have much time for family. In the meantime, Shannon was burning with impatience and acting more and more like a spoiled child. Neither of them invested much effort in keeping afloat the boat in which they were sailing, so it was strange that when it finally capsized they were so bitter about each other.

Even though Gregory's enthusiasm for Shannon was quickly waning, he failed to notice; during the months when she was pregnant, his disillusion was overshadowed by a tenderness compounded of compassion and delight. He was with her when the baby was born, holding her, wiping away the perspiration, talking to her to calm her, while the doctor worked busily beneath the blinding lights of the delivery room. The smell of blood brought back memories of the war, and he saw the boy from Kansas again, as he had so many times in his dreams, begging him not to leave him alone. Shannon clung to him as she bore down to expel the infant, and in those moments Gregory truly believed he loved her. He liked children and was pleased with the idea of being a father again. *It would be different this time,* he promised himself; *I will be closer to this baby than I was to Margaret.* He wanted to be the first to welcome it to life, and the moment the head appeared, he reached out to receive it. He held the baby up to show to Shannon, so choked with emotion he could not speak. Later he would recall that instant as the only true happiness he had shared with Shannon, but even that spark of joy faded within a matter of days.

Shannon was not interested in the duties of motherhood any more than in the role of wife or mistress of the house, and as soon as she could squeeze into the tight blue jeans of her single days, she tried to escape the trap of matrimony. Meanwhile, David, the baby, was fidgeting in a playpen, so fretful and bad-tempered that not even his mother wanted to be with him.

One day a mortified Tina reported to her boss that she had seen one of the young lawyers in the firm kissing Shannon in the parking lot. Forgive me for sticking my nose into this, Mr. Reeves, but it's my obligation to tell you, she concluded in a trembling voice. Gregory saw red; he grabbed the offender by the lapel and began punching him. His victim tried to escape by rushing into the elevator, but Gregory ran down the service stairway and trapped the miscreant in the street, creating such a scene that the police were summoned and everyone ended up having to make a statement at the police station, including Mike Tong, who returned from the post office just in time to become a witness to the end of the fight: the defeated Lothario lying on the sidewalk with a bloody nose. That night Shannon blamed what had happened on a few drinks too many and tried to convince Gregory that such incidents were utterly trivial and that he was the only one she loved. Gregory wanted to know what the hell she was up to in the parking lot, and she swore it was nothing more than a casual meeting and a friendly kiss.

"Your age is showing, Gregory; you're really out of it," was her summation.

"It seems I was born to wear the horns!" Reeves bellowed, and slammed the door.

He stayed in a motel until Shannon located him and begged him to come back, swearing her love and sobbing that she felt secure and protected when she was with him and lost when he was gone. Secretly, Gregory was waiting for her call. He had lain awake all night, tormented by jealousy, inventing futile reprisals and impossible resolutions. He feigned a rage he no longer felt, just for the satisfaction of humiliating her, but he went back to her, as he would every time he left during the months to come.

THE INFINITE PLAN · 307

When she was thirteen, Margaret disappeared from home. Samantha waited two days before she called me, because she thought Margaret had no place to go and soon would be back. She was sure it was just a little escapade: All kids her age do silly things, it's nothing to worry about, you know Margaret never causes any problems, she's a very good girl. Samantha's ability to ignore reality is like my mother's; it never ceases to amaze me. I immediately advised the police, who organized a massive search; we placed ads in every city around the bay area and made appeals on radio and television. When I went to her school, they told me they had not seen her in months; they had given up sending notices to her mother and leaving telephone messages. My daughter was a terrible student; she had no friends, played no sports, missed too many classes, and finally stopped going altogether. I questioned her classmates, but they knew very little about her, or at least did not want to tell me. I sensed they did not like her very much. One girl described her as being aggressive and vulgar, two adjectives I found impossible to associate with Margaret, who always behaved like an elegant little old lady in a tearoom. Then I talked with the neighbors and found that they had seen her going out at all hours of the night; sometimes a fellow on a motorcycle came for her, but she almost always came back in different cars. Samantha said she was sure that this was just nasty gossip; she had not noticed anything strange. Why should you be aware of your daughter's absence, I said, if you don't even notice her when she's there? In the photograph that appeared on television, Margaret looked beautiful and innocent, but I remembered seeing her mimic provocative gestures and imagined the worst. The world is filled with perverts, a police officer had told me once when I lost track of one of the children I was looking after in the park. I went through days of pure torture, checking all the police stations and hospitals and newspapers.

When I went to Timothy Duane's laboratory, needing a friend, he looked me straight in the eye and said, "This is a case for Saint Jude, the patron saint of lost causes. You must go to the Church of the Dominicans, put twenty dollars in the saint's collection box, and light a candle to him."

"You're nuts, Tim."

"Yes, but that isn't the point. The only thing that stuck with me from twelve years of school with the priests is a sense of guilt and an unconditional faith in Saint Jude. You've got nothing to lose by trying."

"Dr. Duane is right; you have nothing to lose by trying. I'll go with you," my secretary offered quietly when she heard, and so, along with the unfailing Ernestina Pereda, I found myself on my knees in a church, lighting candles, something I hadn't done since my days as Padre Larraguibel's altar boy.

That night someone called to tell me he had seen a person in a bar who looked like Margaret, except considerably older. We went there with two policemen and found Margaret passing herself off as a grown woman, wearing falsies, high heels, tight pants, and a mask of makeup painted over her baby face. When she saw me she started to run, and when we caught her she threw her arms around me, crying and calling me Daddy for the first time I can remember. A medical examination revealed needle marks on her arms and a venereal infection. When I tried to talk with her in the room of the private clinic where we had taken her, she pushed me away and in a deep voice spit out a string of curses, several of which I had never heard, not even in the barrio where I grew up or during my days in the army. She had torn the intravenous needle from her arm and with her lipstick had written terrible obscenities on the walls of her room; she had shredded her pillow and thrown everything within reach on the floor. It took three nurses to hold her while they administered a tranquilizer. The next morning I went with Samantha to see her and found her lying in bed, calm and smiling, her face scrubbed and a ribbon in her hair, surrounded by the bouquets of flowers, boxes of chocolates, and stuffed animals sent by people in my office. Of the devil-possessed girl of the previous day, no trace remained. When I asked her why she had done such a terrible thing, she began crying, apparently repentant. She didn't know what had happened to her, she said, she had never done such a thing before, she had fallen in with a bad crowd, but we mustn't worry, she realized the danger and would not see those people again. The injections were just experimentation, and she would never do it again, she swore.

"I'm fine. The only thing I need is a tape player so I can listen to music," she told us.

"What kind of music do you want?" her mother asked, arranging her pillows.

"A friend brought me my favorite tapes," she replied drowsily. "I want to sleep now; I'm a little tired."

As we left she asked us to bring her some cigarettes—no filter, please. I was surprised that she smoked, but then remembered that at her age I had made myself a pipe, and anyway, compared with her other problems, a little nicotine seemed pretty mild. I didn't think it was a particularly opportune time to discuss the effect of smoke on the lungs when she could have died of an overdose of heroin. When I went back that afternoon, she was gone. She had tricked the nurse, put on the whorish clothes she was wearing when she was admitted, and run away. When they cleaned the room they discovered a disposable syringe, a tape of rock music, and the stub of a lipstick beneath the pillow. I had lost Margaret— since that day I have seen her only in jail or in a hospital bed—I just didn't know it yet. It took me nine years to let her go, nine years of frustrated hopes, useless searching, phony regrets, endless thefts, betrayals, vulgarity, suspicion, and humiliation, until finally I admitted in my heart of hearts that I couldn't help her.

The first Tamar shop opened on a street in the heart of Berkeley, between a bookstore and a beauty shop: a thousand square feet with a small showcase and a narrow door that would have passed unperceived among other businesses in the neighborhood had Carmen not decided to apply Olga's decorating principles—in reverse. The healer's house was as embellished and gaudily painted as an operetta pagoda and so stood out against the sterile gray architecture of the Latin barrio. Carmen's Tamar was located among colorful shops: Chinese and Mexican restaurants with identifying wrathful dragons and plaster cactuses, Indian bazaars, stalls with tourist souvenirs, and flourishing pornography marts where neon signs depicted naked couples in improbable positions. It was not easy to attract a clientele amid such competition, but Carmen painted everything white, installed a white awning above the door and tracks of strong lights to accentuate the laboratory starkness of her shop. She displayed her jewelry on simple trays filled with sand and transparent slices of quartz that offered a stunning contrast to the elaborate design and rich materials. In one corner she hung gypsy skirts like the ones she had worn for years, the only warm notes in all that snowy whiteness. The air was filled with the delicate aroma of spices and the monotone chords of a sitar. "Soon I'm going to add belts, handbags, and shawls," Carmen explained to Gregory, as she proudly showed off her creations at the opening celebration. "There won't be a wide variety, but the pieces can all be combined, so that with one visit clients can come to my shop and leave dressed from head to toe." "I don't think you're going to find many takers for those getups." Gregory laughed, convinced that a woman would have to be sick in the head to wear Carmen's creations, but only minutes later he had to swallow his words when Shannon begged him to buy her several pairs of the "ethnic" earrings he had thought unreasonably expensive and saw his friend Joan, on Balcescu's arm, parading in one of the wildly colored gypsy skirts. Women are a mystery to me, he mumbled.

Carmen Morales conducted her business with the prudence of a peasant. She did her accounts every week, putting aside one part for production, another for taxes, and the rest for modest personal expenses and additions to her savings. She depended on her Vietnamese helpers to execute her designs and Mexican women in the barrio, following her precise instructions, to sew the clothes in their homes and mail them to her. She herself chose all the materials and once a year, during the summer, made a shopping tour of Asia or North Africa, hazardous journeys that would have terrified a less confident woman. She was indifferent to danger because she could not imagine that anyone would harm her. She could travel only during Dai's school vacations, and he grew accustomed to safaris by train, jeep, burro, and on foot through remote villages in the jungles of Thailand, nomadic shepherds' camps in the Atlas Mountains, and wretched slums in the populous cities of India. His slim, dark-skinned body unprotestingly endured all kinds of food, contaminated water, mosquito bites, fatigue, and sweltering heat; he had a fakir's tolerance for discomfort. He was a calm child who learned arithmetic playing with beads for necklaces and before he was ten had discovered various mathematical laws he tried vainly to explain to his mother and schoolteacher. Later, when his extraordinary talent for numbers was recognized and he was examined by university professors, his ideas turned out to be principles of trigonometry. He had a small metal chessboard with magnetized playing pieces, and on swaying trains, crushed among passengers, animal coops, shabby cardboard suitcases, and baskets of food, Dai calmly played chess against himself, never cheating. They did not always stay in hotels or in the huts of friendly natives; at times they traveled in small caravans or hired a guide and camped in the middle of nowhere.

On a straw mat on the ground or in a hammock beneath an improvised mosquito netting, listening to the menacing sounds of night birds and stealthy paws padding by, saturated by the disturbing odor of magnolia and decaying vegetation, Dai felt completely safe beside the warmth of his mother's body: he thought she was invulnerable. With her he lived many adventures, and the few times he saw her frightened, he, too, felt a stab of fear; in those rare moments he remembered his other mother, the one with the eyes like black almonds, who jetted in circles around his head, protecting him from all evil. In a bazaar in Morocco, as they pushed their way through the teeming crowd, Dai dropped Carmen's hand to stop and admire some curved knives with sheaths of tooled leather. The owner of the stall, a large, thuggish man in voluminous robes, grabbed Dai by the collar, lifted him from the ground, and cuffed him hard, but before he could strike a second blow he was attacked by a wild beast, clawing, growling, and biting like a tigress. Dai saw his mother rolling on the ground with the Arab in a whirl of torn skirts, overturned baskets, scattered merchandise, and the jeers of other men in the market. The man's fist struck Carmen in the face, and for a few seconds she lay stunned, but with the strength of desperation, before anyone could anticipate it, she had one of the unsheathed knives in her hand. At that moment the police broke through the crowd, disarmed her, and saved the merchant from a certain knifing, while the men gathered in the circle celebrated the blow struck against the stranger, denouncing her with cries and insults. Carmen and Dai ended up in jail alongside unsavory types who had second thoughts about molesting them when they saw murder in the woman's eyes. The American consul came to their rescue, and later, as he bade them goodbye, advised them never to return. We'll see you next year, Carmen replied, but could not smile because her face was swollen and she had a deep cut on her lip. They returned from those explorations with boxes filled with a variety of beads, pieces of coral, glass, antique metals, semi-precious stones, tiny bone carvings, perfect shells, claws and teeth of unidentified beasts, petrified leaves, and scarabs from the ice age. She also brought embroidered cloth and embossed leathers to use as details on a belt or handbag, time-faded ribbons for skirts, buttons and buckles discovered in forgotten cubbyholes. By then, Carmen was not working in her home. Her treasures were stored in transparent plastic boxes in her workshop, arranged by material and color; it was there she closeted herself for hours to create each design, adding and removing beads, scribing metal, cutting and polishing, in a patient exercise of imagination. It was she who started the vogues for astrological motifs of moon and stars, crystals for good luck, jewelry of African inspiration, different earrings for each ear, and a single ring in one ear with a cascade of stones and bits of silver, all of which would be copied to the point of excess. Carmen had grown more confident with the years and had refined her look slightly, but her happy disposition had not diminished, nor her taste for adventure. She ran her business like an expert, but she had such a good time doing it that she never considered it work. She was incapable of taking herself seriously. She saw no difference between her current prosperous enterprise and the days when she was making crafts in her parents' house to sell in the barrio, or dressing in colorful kerchiefs to juggle in Pershing Square. It was all part of a continuous lifetime hobby, and the fact that the zeros increased on her bank accounts did not affect her sense that work was play. She was the first to be surprised by her success; she could scarcely believe that people were willing to pay so much for ornaments she invented in a fit of inspiration to entertain herself. Life's responsibilities and the pitfalls of success did nothing to change her likable nature; she was still open, confident, and generous. Her journeys had revealed to her the endless misery and pain borne by humanity, and when she compared herself with others she felt extremely fortunate. For her, there was no conflict between a good eye for business and compassion; from the beginning she made it a point to offer employment at optimum conditions to those lowest on the social scale, and later, as her operation expanded, she hired so many poor Latins, Asian and Central American refugees, and physically disabled, as well as the two mentally handicapped men she put in charge of plants and gardens, that Gregory called his friend's business "Tamar's Hospice." She invested time and money in exhaustive training and English classes for her workers, who almost inevitably had arrived in this country after unbelievable hardships. Her spontaneous charity turned out to be a visionary managerial strategy—as were free meals, required recreation, restful music, comfortable chairs, gymnastic and relaxation classes for muscles cramped by concentration on setting stones—because her personnel responded with astounding loyalty and efficiency.

On her trips Carmen had also learned that the world is not white and never will be, and she proudly flaunted her brown skin and Latin features. Her arrogant bearing was deceptive; she gave the impression of being taller and younger than she was and presented herself with such aplomb, enveloped in her gypsy attire and tinkling bracelets, that no one took note of her heavy breasts and guitar-shaped body, or of her first wrinkles and gray hair. At school recess, Dai won a competition among his classmates for having the most beautiful mother.

"Aren't you ever going to marry, Mama?" he asked her.

"Yes; when you grow up I'm going to marry you."

"When I grow up you will be very old," Dai patiently explained; for him, numbers could not be refuted.

"Then I'll have to look for a husband as decrepit as I am." Carmen laughed and in a flash of memory saw the face of Leo Galupi, just as she had remembered him through the years and as she had first seen him, half hidden behind a fading bouquet, waiting for her in the Saigon airport. Now she wondered whether he remembered her, and she determined that one day she would have to find out, because Dai was rapidly growing up and soon might not need her. She was also weary of brief affairs; she chose younger men because she needed harmony and beauty about her, but she was beginning to feel the emotional void.

While her friend Gregory was living like a wealthy man, accumulating debts and headaches, Carmen was living like a worker, amassing money and praise. Soon the name of Tamar had become a symbol of originality and impeccable quality. Without intending it, she found herself directing style shows and giving lectures like an expert—always aware that her "expertise" was a joke. Someday they'll catch on that I don't know anything about anything. I manage to fool the world with pure blather, she told Gregory when she was featured in women's and art magazines, or in business journals as an example of a rapidly developing enterprise. A few years later, when she had Tamar branches in several capitals and almost two hundred people working for her—not including salesmen on several continents offering her merchandise to the most luxurious shops—and when her accounting department occupied an entire floor of her factory, she was still traveling on muleback through jungles and on camelback across deserts, shopping for materials and living modestly with her son, not because she was tightfisted but because she did not know there was an easier life.

· · ·

King Benedict wanted nothing in this world so much as an electric train to set up in his mother's living room. He had already built to scale a station, a town of small wooden houses, pasteboard trees, and a landscape of hills and tunnels that stretched from wall to wall, making it difficult to walk through the room. All he needed was the train; Bel had promised him that when they received the money from the insurance settlement, the train would be their first purchase. He felt disabled and clung to that woman with the long neck and yellow eyes who said she was his mother, and who was his compass in a storm of uncertainty. Since his accident, his memory was nothing but fog—forty years erased in the instant his head struck the ground. He remembered his mother as being young and beautiful; how had she become that old woman worn down by hard work and time? Who is this Bel anyway? I wish she would buy me the train. He understood that he was really too old for children's toys, but he was not interested in things that obsessed grown men. He spent hours, semicomatose, before the television set, a fantastic invention that was completely new to him, and as he watched passionate love scenes felt a vague anxiety, something throbbing in the pit of his belly, which fortunately did not last long. The catalog of electric trains was much more interesting to him than the magazine with naked women the man at the corner newspaper stand tried to offer him. Sometimes he saw himself from afar, as if he were at the movies, watching his own face in a relentless drama. He did not recognize himself. His mother had explained the accident, and his amnesia, and he was not stupid; he knew that he was not fourteen years old. He stared at himself in the mirror, unable to recognize the grandfatherly figure looking back at him; he enumerated all the changes he saw and wondered exactly when they had occurred, why he showed so many signs of wear and tear. He did not know how he had lost his hair, or when he gained weight, where the wrinkles came from, where two of his teeth had gone, why his bones ached when he threw a ball, why he was short of breath when he tried to run up stairs, and why he could not read without glasses. He did not remember buying those glasses. Now he found himself at a large table in an office filled with plants and books, sitting between two men who peppered him with questions sometimes impossible to answer, while a secretary recorded each word on a machine. Who was President in the year you were married? His mother made him go every day to the library to read old newspapers, to learn what had happened in the world during the forty years he had lost. Abstract dates became more comprehensible than articles of everyday use, like the microwave oven and other fascinating and mysterious mechanisms. King was familiar with the names of the Presidents, who won the World Series, moon shots, wars, the assassinations of John Kennedy and Martin Luther King, but he hadn't the least idea where he was when those events took place, and could have sworn he had never married. His mother instructed him every evening, telling him facts about his own life to see whether constant repetition would sweep away the mists of oblivion, but King found those obligatory exercises of memory an interminable and boring calvary. He could not believe that his life had been so insignificant, that he had done nothing important, that he had realized none of his youthful goals. He was tortured by the time he had wasted on that string of meaningless routines but by the same token grateful for a second chance in this world. His future was not a black hole behind him, as his mother told him, but a blank book before him. He could fill it with whatever he wanted to, replay the years already lived. He could have adventures, find treasures, perform heroic deeds, go to Africa in search of his roots, and never marry or grow old. If only he could remember his mistakes and successes.... He had always wanted an electric train; it was not a caprice of the moment but his oldest desire, a childhood dream. When he told Reeves about it, Reeves had smiled with his blue eyes and confessed that a train had also been his greatest wish but he had never owned one. He's lying; if he can pay for this office with gold letters on the windows, he can buy a train—two if he wanted, King Benedict grumbled to himself, but to be polite, he did not say so. And what caused his mother to choose a white lawyer anyway? Hadn't she herself told him many times to distrust whites on principle? Now the other man was placing rows of photographs on the table, and he was supposed to recognize them, but he didn't know a single one except the beautiful woman sitting in an open window with half her face in the light and the other half in shadow: his mother, of course, although very different from the old woman she was now. Then they showed him pictures from magazines and asked him to identify cities and places, almost all of them strange to him. What about these? What was that cotton plantation, and that truck? He couldn't quite remember, but he was sure he had been in a place similar to it. Where is it, Mama? but before he could get the words out, pain was stabbing his temples, and he felt dizzy. He put his arms over his head and tried to stand, but fell to the floor on his knees.

"Mr. Benedict! Do you feel all right, Mr. Benedict?" The voice came to him from a great distance. Then he felt his mother's hand on his forehead and turned toward her to put his arms around her waist and bury his head in her bosom, tortured by the pounding in his brain and the wave of nausea that filled his mouth with saliva and made him tremble all over.

It was a year before Gregory Reeves accepted the fact that there was no reason to go on fighting for a marriage that was never going to work out, and another before he decided to separate: he hated to leave David, and it pained him to admit a second failure.

"The problem isn't Shannon; it's you," Carmen diagnosed. "No woman can solve your problems for you, Greg. You still don't know what it is you're looking for. If you can't love yourself, how can you love someone else?"

"Is this the voice of experience?" Gregory joked.

"At least I haven't been married twice!"

"This will cost a fortune," Mike Tong lamented when he learned that his boss was planning a second divorce.

Reeves moved in temporarily with Timothy Duane. After a rip-roaring scene in which they shouted insults at each other and

Shannon threw a bottle at his head, Gregory packed two suitcases and left, swearing that this time he would not be back. He reached his friend's apartment as Duane was in the midst of a formal dinner with other doctors and their wives. Gregory burst into the dining room and with a dramatic gesture dropped his luggage to the floor.

"This is all that remains of Gregory Reeves," he announced.

"We're having mushroom soup," Timothy replied imperturbably. Later, when they were alone, he offered Gregory the guest room and commented that it was about time he left that accursed woman. "Besides, I was needing someone to party with," he added.

"Don't count on me; I don't have any luck with women."

"That's crazy, Greg. We're living in paradise. Not only are the women beautiful here; we don't have any competition. You and I must be the last heterosexual bachelors in San Francisco."

"That's a statistic that hasn't done much for me up till now. . . ."

Shannon was given custody of their son and soon moved into a house on a hill overlooking the bay. Gregory returned to his house, now without furniture but with the wine barrels of roses. He did not bother to replace what he had lost, because as things deteriorated his indignation at being betrayed grew, and the empty rooms seemed an appropriate setting for his state of mind. When resentment against his wife turned into a desire for revenge, he tried to find consolation in lovers, as he had done before, but discovered that instead of alleviating his problem, his "solution" complicated his schedule and fed his rage. He buried himself in work and, lacking either time or inclination, limited housework to keeping his plants alive.

Shannon was not much better; the movers unloaded everything into the living room of the new house, and there it sat: she had barely enough energy to set up beds and unpack a few cooking utensils, while the disarray and confusion mounted around her. She was not up to coping with David, a job that demanded superhuman strength; more than a nursemaid, he needed a wild-animal trainer. He had been born hyperactive and lived like a savage. When they tried to enroll him in various nursery schools for a few hours a day, the schools refused to keep him. His behavior was so barbaric that Shannon had to be constantly alert; a moment's carelessness could end in catastrophe. Early on, the child learned to get attention by holding his breath, and perfected the technique: his eyes rolled back in his head and he frothed at the mouth and collapsed in convulsions anytime he was denied some whim. He refused to brush his teeth, comb his hair, or eat with a spoon; he ate on the floor, licking up his food. He could not be left with other children because he bit them, nor with adults because he had a shrill scream that ground down the nerves of the hardiest among them. Shannon had admitted her defeat about the time David began to crawl—a period coinciding with her worst fights with her husband—and sought relief in gin. While his father worked himself into a stupor, traveling much of the time, and his mother drowned herself in liquor and frivolity, each grimly waging the war of irreconcilable enmity, David was storing up the mute rage of forgotten children. The divorce at least relieved the atrocity of daily pitched battles that left the entire family numb, including the Mexican maid who came every day to clean and look after the boy and who finally preferred the hazards of the street to that insane asylum. Shannon was more devastated by her departure than by her husband's. She felt forsaken and gave up any attempt at order, letting her home and her life gather dust and chaos; dirty clothing and plates, unpaid bills, broken appliances, and debts she tried to ignore piled higher and higher. She began her life as a divorcée in that same state of disrepair and gave up any pretense of looking after her child or her house. She was defeated before she began, with barely enough spirit to save herself from going down with the ship, escaping first for stolen moments, then for hours, and finally forever.

Reeves stayed in his empty house, with the boat rotting at the dock and rosebushes languishing in the wine barrels. It was not a practical solution for a single man, as everyone pointed out, but he felt like a prisoner in an apartment; he needed room to stretch and let off steam. He worked sixteen hours a day, slept less than five hours a night, and drank a bottle of wine at each meal. At least you don't smoke, so you're not going to die of lung cancer, Timothy Duane consoled him. The office gave the appearance of being a money-making factory, but in fact its existence hung in the balance as the Chinese accountant worked miracles to pay the most pressing bills. In vain, Mike Tong tried to lay out the basic principles of fiscal responsibility to his employer; he wanted him to see for himself the bleeding debit columns, see how his bookkeeper was dancing blindfolded on a tightrope. Don't worry, my friend, it will all work out, Reeves would say soothingly. This isn't China: we always come out ahead here; this is the land of the bold, not the prudent. Reeves could look around him and see that he was not the only one in his predicament; the entire nation was on a spending binge, deep in a bacchanal of conspicuous consumption and noisy patriotism directed at recovering the pride lost in the humiliating defeat of Vietnam. Gregory was marching to the drum of his epoch, but to do so he had to silence the voices of Cyrus, with his intellectual's mane and his clandestine encyclopedias, his father with his tame boa, soldiers bathed in blood and terror, and a host of questioning spirits. The world hasn't seen such selfishness, corruption, and arrogance since the fall of the Roman Empire, Timothy Duane often said. When Carmen warned Gregory about the pitfalls of greed, he reminded her that it was she who had taught him his first lesson in capitalism, when they were young and she led him outside the barrio to make money in the bourgeois world. Thanks to you, I crossed the street and discovered the advantages of being on the other side. It's much better to be rich, but if I can't be rich I'm at least going to live as if I were, he said. She could not reconcile this bravado with the other aspects of her friend's life that he unintentionally revealed in their long Monday telephone conversations, such as his growing tendency to defend only the poorest of the poor, never businesses or insurance companies, where he would have made substantial profits without nearly the risk.

"You're not making sense, Greg. You talk about making money, but only poor people troop through your office."

"Latins are always poor; you know that as well as I."

"That's what I mean. You'll never get rich with that kind of client. But I'm glad you are the same sentimental fool you always were: that's why I love you. You always look after others; I don't know where you find the strength."

That facet of his character had not been apparent when he was just one cog in the complicated machinery of a large firm; it had emerged when he became his own boss. He could not close the door to anyone who asked him for help—in either his office or his private life. He was knee-deep in people with problems, so many he could scarcely look after them all. Ernestina Pereda worked miracles to stretch the hours of his calendar. Often his clients became his friends, and more than once he had someone living with him who had nowhere else to go. A look of gratitude seemed sufficient reward, but he often had rude awakenings. He did not have a good eye for identifying scoundrels in good hour, and by the time he tried to get rid of them it was too late: they turned on him like vipers, accusing him of every vice of his profession. Be careful you don't get us into a malpractice suit, Mike Tong warned his boss when he saw him placing too much trust in his clients, among whom were con artists who made a living by abusing the legal system and had a history of lawsuits behind them. They would work a few months, do something to get fired, and then file suit for discrimination; others faked injuries in order to collect the insurance. Reeves also made mistakes in hiring. Most of his employees had problems with alcohol, one with gambling—he bet not only his own money but anything he could filch from the office—and one suffered chronic depression and twice slit his wrists in the washroom. It was years before Reeves realized that he attracted neurotics. His secretaries could not handle such high drama, and few lasted more than a month or two. Mike Tong and Tina Faibich were the only normal people in that circus of misfits. In Carmen's eyes, the fact that her friend had not gone under was irrefutable proof of his fortitude, but Timothy Duane called that miracle pure and simple luck.

· · ·

He entered his office by the service door, as he often did to avoid clients in the waiting room. His desk was a mountain of papers, and the floor was covered with stacks of documents and reference books; a sweater lay on the sofa beside several boxes of glass bells and reindeer. The growing clutter threatened to engulf him. As he took off his raincoat, he checked the health of his plants, particularly concerned about the funereal droop of the ferns. Before he could ring, Tina was waiting with the day's agenda in hand.

"We have to do something about the heating; it's killing my plants."

"You have a deposition at eleven, and remember that this afternoon you must be in court. Can I help a little here? This place looks like the dump, if you'll forgive my saying so, Mr. Reeves."

"All right, but don't touch Benedict's file; I'm working on that. Write the Christmas Club again not to send me any more of this junk. And can you bring me an aspirin, please?"

"I think you're going to need two. Your sister Judy has called several times; it's urgent," Tina announced, and left the room.

Reeves picked up the telephone and called his sister, who told him with little elaboration that Shannon had come by early that morning to leave David with her while she went away on a trip, destination unknown.

"Come get your son right away. I have enough with my children and my mother; I can't be responsible for this monster. Who is wearing diapers, by the way. Did you know that?"

"David?"

"Mother. I see you don't know anything about your own son."

"You'll have to put her in a nursing home, Judy."

"Right, that's the easy solution: throw her away like an old shoe. That's what you would do, no doubt, but not me. She looked after me when I was a little girl, she helped me raise my children, and she's stood by me in moments of need. How can you think I'd put her in a home! To you, she's nothing but a useless old woman, but I love her and I hope she dies in my arms, not cast aside like a stray dog. You have one hour to come get your son."

"I can't, Judy; I have three clients waiting."

"Then I'll turn him over to the police. In the short time he's been here in my house, he's put the cat in the clothes dryer and hacked off his grandmother's hair," Judy said, trying to contain the hysteria in her voice.

"Shannon didn't say when she'd be back?"

"No. She said she has a right to live her life, or something like that. I could smell the booze, and she was very edgy, almost desperate. I'm not blaming her: that poor woman doesn't have any control over her life; how could she have any over her son?"

"So what are we going to do now?"

"I don't know what you're going to do. You should have thought about this a long time ago; I don't know why you bring kids into the world if you don't mean to look after them. You already have a daughter who's a drug addict. Isn't that enough? Do you want David to follow his sister's example? If you're not here in exactly one hour, go to the police; you'll find your son there," and she hung up the telephone.

Reeves buzzed Tina to tell her to cancel his appointments for the day. She caught up with him at the door, pulling on her coat and carrying her umbrella, certain her employer needed her in a crisis of this magnitude.

"What do you think of a woman who abandons her four-year-old son, Tina?" Reeves asked his secretary halfway to Judy's house.

"The same thing I think of a father who abandons him when he's three," she replied, in a tone she had never used before.

"OK, I am going to take care of this soon, but I have to initiate a custody battle," said Gregory, putting an end to any conversation. The rest of the drive they were silent, listening to a concerto on the radio and trying to curb their worst imaginings. With David, anything could happen.

Judy was waiting at the door with her nephew's belongings,

while the boy, dressed in a soldier suit, raced through the yard, throwing rocks at the crippled dog. Tina opened her enormous umbrella and twirled it like a Ferris wheel, bringing David to an abrupt halt. His father went toward him with the intention of taking his hand, but the boy threw a rock at him and rushed toward the street. He did not get there. With the grace of an illusionist, Tina collapsed the umbrella, hooked the handle around one of David's legs, tripped him up, caught him by the tail of his shirt, lifted him off his feet, and shoved him into the car, all without losing her habitual smile. She was able to keep him immobilized all the way back to the city. That afternoon Gregory Reeves appeared in court with more than his usual zest for a battle, while his invincible secretary waited outside, subduing David with stories, french fries, and now and again a little swat.

Thus began Gregory's life with his son. He was not prepared for an emergency of this kind and had no time in his routine for a child, much less one as difficult as his own. David was so insecure that he could not be alone for a minute; at night he crawled into his father's bed to sleep, clinging to his hand. At first Gregory had to take David with him everywhere; there was no question of his staying alone, and Gregory could not find anyone to take charge, not even Judy, despite her natural love for children and the large sum of money he offered her. If in a few minutes he managed to cut off my mother's hair, the next thing would be her head, was Judy's response. Reeves's house and car were overflowing with toys, stale food, chewed chewing gum, and piles of dirty clothes. Short of any other solution, Gregory took David to the office, where employees tried at first to ingratiate themselves with Reeves's son but quickly gave up, honestly acknowledging that they loathed him. David ran across the tops of the desks, nearly choked on paper clips and then spit them out on the documents, unplugged the computers, flooded the washrooms, yanked out the telephone lines, and rode up and down in the elevator until it stalled. At Tina's suggestion, Gregory hired an illegal Salvadoran immigrant to watch David, but she lasted only four days. She was the first of a long line of nursemaids who filed through the house, leaving scarcely a trace. To hell with traumas, I'd give him a good spanking, Carmen recommended by telephone, although she had never had reason to spank Dai. Instead, Gregory consulted a child psychiatrist, who counseled a special school for children with problem behavior, prescribed pills to calm him and immediate treatment, because, as he explained, the emotional wounds of early childhood leave ineradicable scars.

"And in passing, I suggest that you enter therapy yourself; you need it more than David. If you don't correct your own problems, you won't be able to help your son," but Reeves discarded that idea without a second thought. He had been brought up in an atmosphere in which psychiatry was not in the vocabulary, and he still believed that men should solve their own problems.

Gregory and Shannon went to court to fight for the custody of their son. At the beginning she wouldn't even discuss giving up the child, but in the mediation sessions she realized that a trial would hurt David even more and every detail of her personal life would come out. Finally she relented and turned him over to his father.

That was a difficult year for Gregory Reeves. This is the height of your bad fortune; you don't have to worry now because the future will be much easier, Olga assured him later, as she was trying to convince him of the efficacy of crystals in counteracting bad luck. Calamity followed calamity, as the fragile equilibrium of his reality crumbled. One morning a distraught Mike Tong came into his office to tell him that he owed the bank more than he could possibly pay, that interest payments were strangling the firm, and that the expenditures for his divorce were still outstanding. The women Reeves had taken out for years were disappearing one by one as it became their turn to know David; none had the strength of character to share Gregory with his unruly offspring. It was not the first time Reeves had been besieged by adversity, but now he had the added burden of caring for his son. He woke early in order to pick up the house, prepare breakfast, listen to the news, plan dinner, and dress the boy; he left David at school once the prescribed sedatives had taken effect; then he drove to the city. Those forty minutes of commuting were his only peaceful time during the day. As he drove between the proud towers of the Golden Gate Bridge, which looked like tall, lacquer-red Chinese bell towers, with the dark mirror of the bay crisscrossed by pleasure and fishing boats on one side and the elegant skyline of San Francisco before him, he remembered his father. The most beautiful place in the world, he had called the city. Reeves gave his attention to the music on the radio, trying to keep his mind a blank, seldom successfully because of the interminable list of pending responsibilities. Tina made all his appointments early in the day so he could pick up David at four; he took documents home, intending to work on them in the evening, but never had the time; he could not have imagined that a child could occupy so much space, make so much noise, or need so much attention. For the first time, he felt sorry for Shannon. Besides David, there were his pets, and it was the father's job to wash out the fish tank, feed the mice, clean the parakeets' cage, and walk the yellow sheep dog they had named Oliver in memory of Gregory's first friend.

"You were stupid to let this happen. You shouldn't have bought this zoo in the first place," Carmen said.

"You could have warned me earlier; there's nothing I can do now."

"Yes there is; give away the dog, let the birds and mice loose, and throw the fish in the toilet. Everyone will be the winner."

Papers piled up on the boxes that served as bed tables. Reeves had to abandon his travels and delegate cases in other cities to his associates, who were not always sober or sane and who made costly errors. The business lunches ended, the golf games, the opera, the evenings out dancing with women in his black book, the drinking bouts with Timothy Duane; he did not even go to the movies, because David could not be left alone. Videos were no solution, because David would watch only movies with monsters or extreme violence, the bloodier the better. Sickened by so much death and torture and zombies and wolf-men and extraterrestrial treachery, Gregory tried to introduce David to musical comedies and animated cartoons, but he was totally bored by both. It was impossible to invite friends to the house; David accepted no one, thought that anyone who came near his father was a threat, and had jealous kicking fits that invariably precipitated the flight of the guest. Occasionally, if he was going to a party or had a date with an interesting conquest, Gregory got someone to watch the boy for a few hours, but he always returned to a house leveled by a hurricane and a baby-sitter on the verge of nervous collapse. The only person with enough patience and endurance was King Benedict, who turned out to have a gift for baby-sitting and who himself enjoyed the video games and horror movies. He lived a long distance away, however, and after all was as disabled as his ward. Gregory was always uneasy when he left the two alone, and hurried home, imagining the infinite disasters that could befall them in his absence. Weekends were devoted entirely to his son, to cleaning the house, marketing, making repairs, changing the straw for the mice, and scooping out the fish he tended to find floating on the top of the tank because David threw whatever was at hand into the water. Even when he was asleep, Gregory was pursued by unpaid debts, back taxes, and the possibility of finding himself in a devastating lawsuit; he lacked confidence in his associates, and he himself had been negligent with some of his clients. As the last straw, he had to cancel his legal insurance because he could not make the payments; this horrified Mike Tong, who prophesied financial catastrophe and argued that practicing without insurance protection was suicidal. Reeves was running out of money, strength, and time. He was exhausted and longed for a little solitude and silence; at the least he needed a week at the beach, but it was impossible to travel with David. Donate him to a laboratory, they always need children for their experiments, suggested Timothy Duane, who refused to come to his friend's house for fear of encountering the child. Gregory's head was jangling with noise, as during the worst days of the war; calamity stalked him from every side. He began to drink too much and was constantly plagued by his allergies, gasping as if his lungs were filled with cotton. Alcohol produced a brief euphoria and then plunged him into lingering melancholy; the next morning he awakened with flushed skin, a buzzing in his ears, and swollen eyes. For the first time in his life he felt that his body was betraying him; until then he had made fun of the California fanaticism for keeping fit. To Reeves, health was like the color of your skin, something permanently allocated at birth and therefore not worth discussing. He had never worried about cholesterol, refined sugar, or saturated fats; he was as indifferent to the digestive tract and fiber as to the mania for tanning oil or jogging—unless you had to get somewhere in a hurry. He was convinced that he would never have time to get sick and would die of a sudden attack, not old age.

For the first time, his interest in women flagged; this caused some concern, but at the same time he felt relieved: on the one hand he feared the loss of his virility, but, on the other, he knew his life would have been easier without that obsession. He had fewer and fewer rendezvous; they were reduced to hasty encounters during the day, because in the evenings he had to be home with David. Sexuality, like hunger or sleep, became a necessity that was to be immediately satisfied; he was not a man for long preambles, and his desire had a certain tone of desperation.

"I'm getting fussy. It must be age," he commented to Carmen one day.

"It's about time. I don't understand how a man who is so selective in his clothes and music and books, who takes pleasure in a good restaurant, buys the best wines, travels first class, and stays at luxury hotels, can run around with such turkeys."

"Don't exaggerate; some of them aren't so bad," he replied, but deep down he knew Carmen was right: he still had much to learn about women. The only pleasure in which he took his time, consciously prolonging the experience, was music. During the night, when he could not sleep and was too impatient to read, he lay on the bed staring into the darkness and listening to a sonata.

At the end of March, Nora Reeves died of pneumonia. Or it may have been that she had been dying little by little for more than forty years and no one had noticed. In recent years her mind wandered along winding spiritual paths, and so she would not

THE INFINITE PLAN · 329

lose her way she carried the invisible orange of *The Infinite Plan* everywhere she went. Judy asked her not to carry it when they left the house; she didn't want people to think her mother had her hand out to beg. Nora thought she was seventeen years old and living in a white palace where she was visited by her sweetheart, Charles Reeves, who appeared every teatime wearing a cowboy hat; he brought with him a tame serpent and a bag of tools to repair the world's imperfections. These visits were as regular as those he had paid every Thursday since the day long ago when the ambulance took him away to the other world. Nora's last illness began with an intermittent fever, and when she passed into a twilight world, Judy and her husband took her to the hospital. She was there two weeks, so frail she seemed nearly to have evaporated, but Gregory insisted his mother was not dying. He installed a sound system in her room so she could listen to her opera records, observed her feet moving slightly to the rhythm, and saw something like a baby's involuntary smile on her lips: conclusive proof that she did not mean to go.

"If she's still moved by the music, she's not dying."

"Don't get your hopes up, Greg. She's not eating, she's not speaking, she's barely breathing," Judy replied.

"She's being difficult. You'll see, she'll be better tomorrow," he said, clinging to the memory of a youthful mother.

But one early morning they called him from the hospital, and as dawn broke he was standing with his sister beside a bed containing the thistledown body of an ageless woman. His mother was nearly eighty, but she had bid farewell to life long before, abandoning herself to a benign madness that helped her circumvent the pain of existence without in any way affecting her good manners or delicate spirit. As she grew more infirm, Nora Reeves had regressed to another time and space, until even forgetfulness was forgotten. At the end, she thought she was a princess of the Urals, roaming the alabaster rooms of an enchanted palace and singing arias. For a long time she had recognized no one but Judy, who, incidentally, she confused with her own mother and spoke to in Russian. She returned to an imaginary youth where there were no obligations and no suffering, only the tranquil diversions of music and books. She read for the pleasure of reconfirming the infinite variation of twenty-six printed signs, but she could not remember the subject or form of what she read; she leafed through a classic novel or an instruction manual for electrical appliances with equal interest. Over the years she had shrunk to the size of a transparent doll, but with the miraculous cosmetics of her fantasy, or perhaps simply with the innocence of dying, she recovered the freshness lost in so many years of living and in death was just as Gregory remembered her looking when he was a boy, as she pointed out constellations in the night sky. Nothing, not weeks of fever and lost appetite, not the hair hacked off by her grandson's scissors and never regrown, could destroy the illusion of beauty. Her soul departed with characteristic gentleness and shyness, as she was holding her daughter's hand. She was buried without fuss or tears on a rainy day. Judy packed what little remained of her presence in a case: two worn dresses, a tin box holding the few documents that proved her passage through this world, two paintings by Charles Reeves, and her pearl necklace, yellowed with wear. Gregory took only a pair of photographs.

That night, after he bathed David and battled to get him to bed, Gregory fed the pets, threw the dirty clothes in the washing machine, picked up the scattered toys and tossed them into a closet, carried the garbage to the garage, cleaned the kitchen, reshelved the books his son had used to build a fort, and finally was alone in his bedroom with a briefcase stuffed with documents he must study for the next day. He put a Mahler symphony on the record player, poured himself a glass of white wine, and sat on the bed, the only piece of furniture in the room. It was already midnight, and he needed at least an hour or two to untangle the case at hand, but he could not summon the strength to begin. He gulped down the wine in two swallows, poured another, and then another, until he finished the bottle. He started the water for his bath, took off his clothes, and examined himself in the mirror: bull neck, broad shoulders, firm legs. Being so accustomed to having his body respond like a well-tuned engine, he could not imagine

illness. The only times in his life he had been sick in bed were
when he ruptured the veins in his leg and when he was hospital-
ized in Hawaii, but those episodes were nearly forgotten. He stubbornly ignored warning alarm bells: allergies, headaches, fatigue,
and insomnia. He ran his hands through his hair and was saddened that not only was it turning white; it was falling out. He
remembered King Benedict, who painted his skull with shoe
black to disguise the baldness he found so disturbing; after all, he
still thought of himself as a boy. Reeves observed his reflection,
searching for traces of his mother, and saw them in his long fingers and narrow feet; everything else was the solid legacy of his
father. Margaret took after her grandmother: the kitten face with
high cheekbones, angelic eyes, gentle movements. What would
become of her? The last time he had seen her, she was in jail.
From the street to jail, from jail to the street, from one senseless
act to another: that had been her life since she first ran away from
home. She was still young, but she had traveled through all the
circles of hell and had the terrifying look of a cobra poised to
strike. He tried to imagine, against all evidence, that beneath the
shell of her vices there were still traces of purity. If Nora Reeves
had been transfigured in death, Margaret might be saved from
depravity and by a miracle be reborn from her ashes. His mother
had vegetated for several decades, untouched by the world's tra-
vails, and, he was sure, would turn to mist inside her coffin,
spared the working of diligent worms. His daughter might be
saved in the same way; perhaps the long calvary that had led her
so far down the road of degradation had not yet destroyed her
essential beauty, and all that was needed was one of Olga's prodigious purges and a good scrub with soap and brush and she would
be clean, without stain—no needle marks, scratches, bruises, or
sores, her skin newly luminous, her teeth gleaming, her hair shining, and her heart forever washed clean of sin.

He felt a little dizzy, and his vision was blurred. He climbed
into the tub and sank into the comfort of the hot water, trying to
clear his mind and relax limbs cramped with tension, but the day's
events rushed to the fore: the formalities at the hospital, the brief

religious service, the lonely funeral in which the only touch of color flared from the huge arrangements of red carnations he had bought to silence his conscience for so many years of neglect. He remembered the rain, Judy's obdurate and tearless silence, and his own discomfort, as if death were some kind of indiscretion, Nora Reeves's one offense against the norms of courtesy and good manners. All through the drive to the cemetery he had kept thinking of the work piled up in the office, how he must settle King Benedict's case or take it to trial, with the risk of losing everything; he had pursued every clue, however insignificant, like a bloodhound, but he had nothing concrete to cling to. He felt a special affection for this client; Benedict reminded him of a well-behaved boy in the anachronistic skin of a man over fifty, but he particularly admired Bel Benedict, a remarkable woman who deserved to be freed from the yoke of poverty. For her sake, he must anticipate the maneuvers of the other lawyers and beat them at their own game; the first lesson he had learned from the old man of the orchids was that it is not the person in the right who wins but the one who puts up the best fight. He hated himself for thinking of business before his mother's corpse had grown cold. He remembered Nora Reeves in her last years, a woman reduced to the level of a helpless child, one more added to Judy's tribe of eight, cared for with the same brusque and impatient solicitude. At least his sister had been there with his mother, while he kept finding excuses not to go near her, as his contribution paying the bills when necessary and making a brief visit a couple of times a year. He was heartsick that his mother had not recognized him, that her mind did not register the existence of a son named Gregory; he had felt he was being punished by his mother's senility, as if her forgetfulness were but another way to erase him from her heart. He had always suspected she did not love him and that her attempt to rid herself of him by placing him in the orphanage and with the farmers was motivated by indifference, not poverty. The water was too hot; his skin was burning and his head was throbbing. Maybe another drink would not be a bad idea, and he stepped from the tub, wrapped a towel around his waist, and went to the kitchen to get a new bottle—on the way, turning off the heat because he was suffocating. He looked into David's room and found him fast asleep in the opening to his Indian tepee. Gregory poured another glass of white wine and went back to his bedroom; the record had finished playing, and he could hear silence, a rare luxury since he'd lived with his son. His mother returned, a dogged memory; she was whispering to him, trying to tell him something, and he realized he did not know her, she was a stranger. He had adored her when he was young, but they had grown apart, and sometimes he thought he hated her, especially in those difficult years when she sat in her wicker chair, resigned to poverty and helplessness, while he scrounged a living in the streets. He looked at the old photographs, yellowed scraps from another's past that was, in a way, also his, and tried to fit together the puzzle of the gentle and obedient old woman. He could not visualize her as old but saw her as a young woman in her dress with the lace collar and her hair pulled back in a bun, standing on the outskirts of a dusty town, and he also saw himself, a thin child with precise features, blue eyes, and large mouth; behind him two men were grappling with a small black girl. He screamed, and the men laughed at him, but the girl freed herself from their terrible embrace and came to stand beside Nora Reeves, who handed her a pamphlet detailing *The Infinite Plan*. Then he saw his mother walking with long strides along a lonely road; she was leading, and he was trying to catch up, but the faster he ran, the wider the distance between them became, and the figure he was pursuing grew smaller and more indistinct against the horizon. The asphalt was soft and burning hot and stuck to his feet; he would never have the strength to overcome his fatigue, he could not go a step farther, he fell, he crawled, the heat was so stifling he couldn't breathe. He felt an overwhelming compassion for that boy, for himself. Mother. . . . He called her first with his thoughts and then with a wrenching cry, and the vague images grew clearer, the hazy lines became strong brush strokes, and Nora Reeves appeared before him, real and present, and held out her hands to him, smiling. He tried to stand and put his arms around her, as he had always longed to, but could not move and sat repeating, Mama, Mama, as the room filled with blazing light and other presences materialized in the room: Cyrus, Juan José Morales holding the hand of Thui Nguyen, the boy from Kansas who had died in his arms, accompanied by other pallid soldiers, Martínez, with no trace of his former insolence but still wearing his *pachuco* garb, and many more, silently filling the room. Gregory Reeves was bathed in Nora's smile, the smile he so desperately needed as a boy and had vainly sought as a man. Time stood still, and he sat motionless in the tranquil silence, as one by one the long line of the dead disappeared. The last to go was his mother, who floated backward and faded into the wall, leaving him the certainty of an affection she had always felt but had been unable to express in life.

When he was again alone, something burst in his heart, a terrible pain deep in his chest, spreading into waves through the rest of his body, scalding, slicing, separating flesh from bone; he lost any ability to hold himself together; he was not himself but that unbearable suffering, that tortured jellyfish spreading across the room, seeping into every corner, one single open wound. He tried to get up from the bed but could not move his arms; he collapsed to his knees, unable to breathe, impaled on the lance thrust through his rib cage. For several minutes he lay panting on the floor, gasping for air, with a loud drumming in his temples. One lucid part of his brain registered what had happened and knew that he must get help or die on the spot, but he could not reach the telephone or cry out; he curled up like a fetus, trembling, trying to remember everything he knew about heart attacks. He wondered how long it would take to die, and for an instant was terrified by the idea but then imagined the peace of not existing, of not having to roll in the dust, battling shadows, of not dragging down a road behind that woman disappearing into the distance, and as he had in his youth when he hid with his dog in the foxes' den, he yielded to the temptation to let go and die. Slowly, the pain passed through him, taking with it part of his incomparable fatigue. He had the impression that he had lived this moment before. He could breathe again and felt his chest to see if something was still beating inside—no, his heart had not burst. He broke into tears, weeping as he had not wept since the war, a visceral wail that came from the most remote past, perhaps before his birth, a spring fed by tears repressed in later years, a rushing torrent. He wept for neglect in his childhood, for battles and defeats he had vainly hoped to transform into victories, for unpaid debts and the betrayals of a lifetime, for the loss of his mother and his tardy recognition of her affection. He saw Margaret falling down a cliff and tried to hold her, but she slipped from his grasp. He murmured David's name—David, so vulnerable, so hurt—asking himself why his children were singled out for the stigma of woe, why life was so difficult for them both, whether he had transmitted a curse in his genes, whether they were paying for his sins. He wept for the sum of his errors and for the perfect love he dreamed of but believed impossible to find, for his father, dead for so many centuries, and for his sister, Judy, trapped in her terrible memories, for Olga, fraudulently inventing the future with her marked cards, and for his clients, not the good-for-nothings and crooks, but the victims like King Benedict and his many unfortunate brethren, the blacks, Latins, and illegal immigrants, poor, deprived, and humble, who came to seek help in the Court of Miracles his office had become, and the tears still poured, now for memories of the war, his brothers in body bags, Juan José Morales, the twelve-year-old girl sold to soldiers, the hundred dead on the mountain. And when he realized that in fact he was crying for himself, he opened his eyes and at last faced the beast, looked at its face and thus learned that the animal always crouching behind him, that breath he had felt on the back of his neck his whole life, was the tenacious fear of being alone that had afflicted him since as a trembling boy he had hidden in the shed. Anguish wrapped him in its fatidic embrace, crept into his mouth, his ears, his eyes, his pores, filling his body as he lay murmuring, I want to live, I want to live. . . .

At that moment his trance was shattered by a persistent ringing. It took an eternity to recognize the sound, to realize where he was and see himself on the floor, naked, wet with urine, vomit, and tears, drunk and terrified. The telephone was ringing like an urgent summons from another dimension, and finally he was able to drag himself to it and pick up the receiver.

"Greg? This is Tamar. You didn't call me today ... it's Monday."

"Come, Carmen, please come," he stammered.

A half hour later Carmen was by his side, after breaking the speed limit from Berkeley. He opened the door to her, still in his towel, disoriented, and embraced her, trying to explain in a flood of words where it hurt: here, his chest, his head, his back, everywhere. Carmen draped a bathrobe around him, collected David, half asleep, got the two into her car, and raced to the nearest hospital, where within a few minutes Gregory Reeves was on a stretcher, connected to a monitor and an oxygen mask.

"Is my daddy going to die?" David asked.

"Yes, if you don't go to sleep," Carmen replied fiercely.

She sat in the waiting room beside the sleeping child until morning, when the cardiologist informed her that there was no danger; there was nothing wrong with Reeves's heart: he had suffered an anxiety attack. The patient could be released, but he should see his doctor and undergo a series of tests, and, he said, he highly recommended consulting a psychiatrist, because this man was close to a breakdown. Once home, Carmen helped Gregory shower and get into bed, brewed coffee, dressed David, gave him breakfast, and took him to school. She called Tina Faibich to tell her that her boss was in no condition to work, returned to her friend, and sat beside him on the bed. Gregory was drained, and dazed with tranquilizers, but he could breathe without pain and was even slightly hungry.

"What happened?" Carmen wanted to know.

"My mother died."

"But you didn't tell me!"

"It happened very quickly, and I didn't want to bother anyone; besides, there was nothing you could do." And he began telling her everything that happened, without rhyme or reason, a river of unfinished sentences, memories, images, and terrors, a lifetime of hurdles and loneliness—all the time holding the hand of this woman who was more than his sister, who was his oldest and most lasting love, his friend, his comrade, a vital part of himself, so close and so different from him: dark-skinned, essential Carmen, brave, wise Carmen, with five hundred years of Indian and Spanish tradition in her blood and a solid Anglo-Saxon common sense that had helped her move through the world without stumbling.

"Do you remember when we were kids and I ran in front of the train? That cured me of my obsession with death, and I went years and years without thinking of it, but now that same fixation has come back, and I'm afraid. I'm boxed in: I can never repay my loans, my daughter is a hopeless addict, and for the next fifteen years I'll be battling with David. My life is a disaster. I'm a failure."

"There are no such things as failure and success, Greg; those are gringo inventions. You just live, that's all, the best you can, a little every day; it's like a journey without a destination: it's the getting there that counts. It's time for you to slow down. What's the rush? My grandmother always said, We don't have to be slaves to the clock."

"Your grandmother was balmy, Carmen."

"Not always; sometimes she was the sanest person in the house."

"I'm sunk, and all alone."

"You have to hit bottom, then you'll push off and rise to the surface again. Crises are good for us; they're the only way we grow and change."

"Just look at me—that's who I am. I haven't done anything right, beginning with my children. I'm like the Tower of Pisa, Carmen: my axis is off true, and that's why everything comes out twisted."

"Who told you life was easy? No one is free of pain and struggle. You'll have to right your axis yourself, if that's what it takes. Look at you, Greg: you're a dishrag. Stop feeling sorry for yourself and put your shoulders back. You've been living on the run, but

338 · Isabel Allende

you can't run forever; at some moment you have to stop and face yourself. However far you run, you're always inside the same skin."

Gregory's nomadic father passed through his mind: moving on, crossing frontiers, trying to reach the horizon, to find the end of the rainbow and, in the beyond, something denied him on earth. This country offers great open spaces in which to escape, to bury the past, to leave everything behind and begin anew as many times as you need, with no burden of guilt or nostalgia. You can always dig up your roots and start over; tomorrow is a blank page. This was Gregory's story too: never still, ever a transient, but the result of all his activity had been loneliness.

"I told you before, Carmen, I'm getting old."

"That happens to us all. I like my wrinkles."

He looked at Carmen, for the first time with true objectivity, and saw she was not a girl anymore; he was happy she did not try to disguise the lines in her face—the signs of life's voyage—or the gray hairs that lighted her dark hair. The weight of her breasts bowed her shoulders, and true to her style, she was wearing a full skirt, sandals, earrings, and bracelets—everything that made her Carmen/Tamar. He imagined that naked she might look like a wet cat and still seem pretty, much more attractive than when she was a plump and mischievous young girl with braces on her teeth, or the most desirable girl in high school, or even the fully developed woman strolling with a Japanese lover through the Gothic section of Barcelona. He smiled at her, and she returned his smile; their eyes were filled with mutual sympathy, with the complicity they had shared since childhood. Gregory took Carmen's shoulders and kissed her softly on the lips.

"I love you," he murmured, aware that the words sounded banal but could not be more true. "Do you think we'll end up together?"

"No."

"Do you want to make love with me?"

"I don't think so. I must have a personality problem." She laughed. "Rest now, and try to sleep. Mike Tong will pick up

David at school and come stay with you for a few days. I'll be back tonight, I have a surprise for you."

The surprise was Daisy, two hundred pounds of beautiful, cheerful black womanhood, pure gleaming chocolate, a native of the Dominican Republic who had walked through half of Mexico and then crossed the border with eighteen other refugees in the false bottom of a truckload of melons, prepared to earn a living in the north. Daisy would change Gregory and David's lives. She took charge of the boy without complaint or distaste, with the same stoicism that had allowed her to survive the adversity of her past. She did not speak a word of English, and her employer had to act as interpreter. Daisy's method for raising children bore fruit with David, although the credit may not have been exclusively hers, since David was also in the hands of an expensive team of teachers, physicians, and psychologists. Daisy had no faith in modern science and never even learned to say the word "hyperactive" in Spanish. She was convinced that the reason for all the confusion was simpler than that: the child was possessed of the devil, a common enough occurrence, she said. She personally knew many people who had suffered the same ill, and it was easier to cure than the common cold; any good Christian could do it. From the first day, she set about expelling the demons from David's body, using a combination of voodoo, prayers to her personal saints, delicious Caribbean dishes, a great deal of affection, and a few stout smacks administered behind the father's back and not reported by the victim because the prospect of life without Daisy was intolerable. With praiseworthy patience the woman took on the task of domesticating her charge. If he seemed prickly as a porcupine and ready to climb the wall, she wrapped him in her great dark arms, cuddled him against her motherly breast, and scratched his head, crooning to him in her sun-filled language until he grew calm. The tranquilizing presence of Daisy, with her aroma of pineapple and sugar, her ever-ready laughter, her musical Spanish, and her endless store of tales about saints and witches, which David could not understand but whose rhythm lulled him to sleep, finally brought the long-awaited security. Because of this improvement in his basic routine, Gregory Reeves was able to begin the slow and painful voyage into himself.

Every night for a year Gregory Reeves believed he was dying. As his son lay sleeping and calm fell over the house and he was alone, he could feel the presence of death. Because he did not want to frighten David if he waked, Gregory locked the door to his bedroom so the child could not walk in on him, and then he abandoned himself to his suffering without offering up any resistance. It was very different from his earlier vague anguish, to which he was more or less accustomed. During the day, he functioned normally, he felt strong and active, he made decisions, managed his office and his household, looked after his son, and for brief moments had the illusion that things were going well; as soon as he was alone at night, however, he was overcome by irrational fear. He felt as if he were a prisoner in a padded room, a cell for lunatics, where it was useless to scream or beat the walls: there was no echo, no knocking in return, nothing but an enveloping void. He did not know the name for that nightmare composed of uncertainty, restlessness, guilt, a sense of abandonment, and profound loneliness, so he simply named it the Beast. He had been trying for more than forty years to elude his Beast, but finally he understood that it would never leave him in peace unless he met it head-on. To grit his teeth and bear it, as he had that night on the mountain, seemed the only effective strategy against the implacable enemy that tormented him with a crushing grip on his chest, a hammering in his temples, the fire of live coals in his stomach, and a craving to race toward the horizon and disappear forever where no one and nothing could ever reach him—least of all his own memories. Sometimes dawn came and he was still sitting huddled like a cornered animal; other nights he fell asleep exhausted after several hours of mute battle and woke dripping with sweat from a flurry of dreams he could not recall. Once or twice the grenade exploded in his chest again, taking his breath away, but now he knew the symptoms and merely waited for them to recede, trying to contain his terror lest he die from fright alone. He had lived his life deceiving himself with sleight of hand; now the moment had come to pay the piper, with the hope that he would cross the threshold and one morning wake up whole. That hope gave him strength to go on; the tunnel did have an ending; it was merely a question of enduring the forced march that would bring him out the other end.

He gave up the crutch of alcohol because his intuition told him that any consolation would delay the hardheaded remedy he had imposed upon himself. When he reached the limits of his strength, he invoked the vision of his mother as she had appeared to him after her death, holding out her arms to him with a welcoming smile; it soothed him even though he knew he was clinging to an illusion: that affectionate mother was the creation of his own imagination. He stopped chasing women, although he was not totally celibate; once in a while he met someone willing to take the initiative, and for at least an hour or two he could relax. He did not fall back into the trap of romantic fantasies; he had learned that no one else could save him, he had to save himself. Rosemary, the former lover who wrote cookbooks, used to invite him over to try her new recipes and sometimes caressed him, more from goodness than desire, and they ended up making love without passion but with sincere goodwill. Mike Tong, still addicted to his unlikely abacus despite a brand-new system of computers in the office, had not fully succeeded in explaining to his boss all the mysteries of the red scribbles in his large books, but at least he had sown the first seeds of financial prudence. You must balance these accounts or we'll all be up to our asses in shit, his Chinese book-keeper would plead, with his immutable smile and courteous bow, nervously wringing his hands. Because of his affection for his boss and his limited English, Tong had adopted Reeves's vocabulary. Tong was right; Reeves needed to get his finances in order, along with the rest of his life, which seemed on the brink of foundering. His ship was taking on water in so many places that he did not have enough fingers to plug all the holes. Reeves learned the value of the friendship of Timothy Duane and Carmen Morales, who put up with his stubborn silences for hours and never let a week go by without calling him or trying to see him, even though he was not very entertaining company. You're unbearable, I can't get you to go anywhere, what is it with you? you're a real bore, Timothy Duane complained, but even he began to tire of his chaotic life. He had abused his robust Irish constitution for so long that his body could not stand the bacchanals that once had filled his weekends with sin and remorse. In view of the fact that Reeves did not talk about his problems, partly because not even he knew what the hell was wrong with him, Duane was struck by an inspired idea: to take him, even if it required force, to consult with Dr. Ming O'Brien—but only after Gregory swore not to try to seduce her. Duane had met the psychiatrist at a lecture on mummies; he had attended to see whether there was any relationship between ancient Egyptian embalming and modern pathology, and she in order to see what kind of nuts might be interested in such a subject. They met in the coffee line during a break. She glanced out of the corner of her eye at the battered Parthenon statue lighting a pipe three paces away from a sign that said NO SMOKING; Duane, in turn, was thinking that the tiny woman with black hair and intelligent eyes must have Chinese blood in her veins. In fact, her parents were from Taiwan. When she was fourteen they had shipped her off to America to stay with compatriots they barely knew, with a tourist visa and precise instructions to study, get ahead, and never complain, because anything that might happen to her there was far preferable to the fate of a woman in her native land. A year after she arrived, Ming had adapted so well to American ways that she conceived the idea of writing a letter to a congressman, enumerating the advantages of living in America and, in passing, asking him for a resident visa. By one of life's absurd coincidences, the politician collected Ming porcelain, and because the girl's name immediately caught his attention, in a moment of sympathy he arranged for her to receive resident status. She acquired the surname O'Brien from a husband in her youth with whom she lived ten months before moving out and swearing never to marry again. At a closer look, Duane was struck by the doctor's quiet beauty, and when they stopped talking about mum-

mies and began to explore other subjects, he discovered that for
the first time in many years he had found a woman who truly fascinated him. They did not stay to the end of the lecture but left to
go to a restaurant on the wharf, where, after the first bottle of
wine, Timothy Duane found himself reciting a monologue from
Brecht. The psychiatrist spoke very little and observed a great
deal. When Timothy wanted to take her to his apartment, Ming
amiably refused, and she continued to refuse during the months
that followed, a situation that kept the tormented suitor's curiosity
vividly alive. By the time they finally decided to live together,
Timothy Duane would be totally smitten.

"I have never known a woman with such grace; she's like an
ivory figurine, and she's entertaining besides; I never get tired of
listening to her. I think she likes me, and I don't understand why
she keeps putting me off."

"I thought you could only do it with whores."

"With her it would be different, I know."

"You ask how I put up with him, Greg?" Ming O'Brien would
respond years later to Reeves. "With Chinese patience. . . . Besides,
I like neurotics, and Tim is the worst case of my career," and with
an impish wink, Ming returned to grating cheese in the kitchen of
the apartment she shared with Duane. But that was much later.

After a great deal of hesitation, I overcame the notion that
men don't talk about their weaknesses or their problems, a prejudice instilled during my youth in the barrio, where that premise is
one of the basic tenets of manhood. And so I found myself sitting
in an office where everything contributed to a sense of harmony:
paintings, colors, and one perfect rose in a crystal vase. I supposed
that the setting was meant to invite repose and confidences, but I
felt uncomfortable and after only a few minutes my shirt was
wringing wet; I kept asking myself why the hell I had followed
Timothy's advice. I had always thought that it was stupid to pay a
professional who charges by the hour, especially when you can't
measure the results. Circumstances had forced me to do just that
with David, who could not function without such help, but I had

never intended to do it for myself. Besides, my first impression of Ming O'Brien was that she belonged to another constellation and that we had nothing at all in common; I was deceived by her China-doll face and leapt to conclusions that today make me feel ashamed. I thought her incapable of even imagining the typhoons fate had blown my way. What could she know about surviving in a sordid barrio, about my unhappy Margaret, about the countless problems suffered by David, plugged for all eternity into a high-voltage line, about my debts, my ex-wives, the series of casual lovers, about my hassles with abusive clients and the lawyers in my firm, about the pain in my chest, my insomnia, my nightly fear of dying. She could know even less about the war. For years I had avoided therapy groups for 'Nam veterans; it disturbed me to share the curse of my memories and fear of the future. It didn't seem necessary to talk about that part of my past. I had never talked about it with men; I sure wasn't going to do it now with this imperturbable woman.

"Tell me one of your recurrent dreams," Ming O'Brien requested.

Fuck it. What I need is a Freud in skirts, I thought, but after an overly long pause, during which I calculated how much each minute of silence was costing me, and in lieu of something more interesting, it occurred to me to tell the dream about the mountain. I know that I began in an ironic tone, sitting with my legs up, evaluating my interrogator with an eye trained to judge women; I've seen plenty, and in those days I was still assigning them a grade on a scale of one to ten. The doc's not bad, I decided; she rates a seven, give or take a little. Nevertheless, as I recounted the nightmare, I began to feel the same terrible anguish I felt when I dreamed it. I saw my enemies, all in black, advancing toward me, hundreds of them, soundless, threatening, transparent, my fallen comrades like crimson brush strokes against the oppressive gray of the landscape, fleet fireflies of bullets passing through the attackers without stopping them, and sweat began to run down my face; my hands trembled from gripping my weapon, tears came to my eyes from the effort of aiming through that dense fog, and I was panting because the air was turning to sand. Ming O'Brien's hands on my shoulders brought me to my senses, and I found myself in a peaceful room facing a woman with Oriental features and a firm, intelligent gaze that bored into my soul.

"Look at the enemy, Gregory. Look at their faces and describe them to me."

I tried to obey, but I couldn't see anything through the mist, nothing but shadows. She insisted, and then gradually the shapes became more precise and I could see the nearest man and to my amazement saw I was looking at myself in a mirror.

"My God! One of them looks like me!"

"And the others? Look at the others! What are they like?"

"They look like me too ... they're all alike ... they all have my face!"

An eternal minute passed, in which I had time to wipe away the sweat and recover my composure. The doctor's black eyes bored into me, two deep chasms that swallowed the terror in my own eyes.

"You have seen the face of your enemy; now you can identify him: you know who he is and where he is. You will never be tortured by that nightmare again, because now your battle will be a conscious one," she said with such authority that I had no doubt at all it was true.

A little later I walked from her consulting room, feeling slightly ridiculous because I couldn't control the trembling in my legs or summon up the voice to tell her goodbye. I went back a month later, after I had time to know I wasn't going to dream the nightmare again and to acknowledge that I did need her help. She was waiting for me.

"I don't know of any magical cures. I will be by your side to help you remove the weightiest obstacles, but you have to do the work yourself. It is a very long road, it can take several years; many begin, but not very many reach the end, because it is so painful. There are no quick or permanent solutions; you can change things only through hard work and patience."

In the next five years Ming O'Brien accomplished what she

promised; she was there every Tuesday, serene and wise among her delicate paintings and fresh flowers, waiting to listen to me. Every time I tried to slip down some side street, she forced me to back up and check the map. When I came upon an insurmountable barrier, she showed me how to dismantle it piece by piece until I could pass. Using the same technique, she taught me to battle back against my old demons, one by one. She went with me every step of the journey toward the past, so far back that I experienced the terror of birth and accepted the loneliness to which I had been destined from the instant that Olga's shears separated me from my mother. She helped me bear the burden of the many forms of abandonment I had suffered, from the early death of my father—the one fortress of my early years—and the hopeless escapism of my poor mother—so soon defeated by reality and lost along improbable paths I could not follow—to the more recent betrayals by Samantha, Shannon, and many others. Ming O'Brien pointed out my mistakes, a script often replayed throughout my life, and warned that I must stay on the alert because crises have a way of stubbornly repeating themselves. With her, finally, I was able to name my pain, to understand it and deal with it, aware it would always be present in one form or another because pain is a part of life, and once that idea took root, my anguish decreased miraculously. My mortal nighttime terror evaporated; I could be alone without shaking with fear. In due course, I discovered how pleasant it is to come home, play with my son, cook for the two of us, and at night, when everything grows quiet, to read and listen to music. For the first time I could welcome silence and appreciate the privilege of solitude. Ming O'Brien supported me as I rose from my knees, took an inventory of my weaknesses and limitations, celebrated my strengths, and learned to cast off the stones I carried in a sack over one shoulder. It's not all your fault, she said once, and I began to laugh because Carmen had told me the same thing: it seems I have a tendency to feel guilty. I wasn't the one who gave Margaret drugs, it was her own decision, and there was nothing to be gained from begging her, insulting her, bailing her out of jail, locking her up in a psychiatric hospital, or sending the police after her, as I had done so many times: my daughter had chosen that hell, and she was beyond the reach of my care and affection. I was to help David grow up, Ming O'Brien said, but not devote my entire life to him or give in to his every whim to make up for the love I hadn't given Margaret, because I was creating a monster. Together we went through my infamous little black book, line by line, and to my embarrassment I realized that almost all my lovers from that long period in my life were cut of the same cloth: dependent women unable to return affection. I also saw clearly that with women who were different, like Carmen or Rosemary, I had not been able to establish a healthy relationship because I didn't know how to give of myself or to accept their surrender; I didn't have a hint what communion was in love. Olga had taught me that sex is the instrument and love the music, but I didn't learn the lesson until now, as I near the half-century mark—but I suppose it's better late than never. I discovered I had no resentment toward my mother, as I had believed, and could remember her with the goodwill that neither of us was able to express while she was alive. I no longer had to invent a Nora Reeves that suited my needs, and anyway, we shape our own past and build memories of many fantasies. I came to believe that her invincible spirit was always with me, just as Thui Nguyen's jet-stream angel is always with her son, Dai, and that gave me a certain security. I stopped blaming Samantha and Shannon for our failures; for good or for ill, I had chosen them, so the problem basically was mine, born of the deepest layers of my psyche, where the seeds of my earliest abandonment lie hidden. One by one I examined all my relationships—children, friends, employees— and on one of those Tuesdays experienced a true epiphany: all my life I had surrounded myself with weak persons in the unspoken hope that in exchange for looking after them I would receive a little affection, or at least gratitude. The results had been disastrous: the more I gave, the more resentment I received in return. Only my strong friends were fond of me: Carmen, Timothy, Mike, and Tina.

"No one is grateful for being made an invalid," Ming O'Brien explained. "You can't carry the responsibility for another person forever; a moment comes when you grow weary and you let them fall; they feel betrayed and, naturally, detest you. That's what happened with your wives, with some of your friends, some of your clients, and nearly all your employees, and you're on the way to letting it happen with David."

The first changes were the most difficult, because as soon as the foundation of the twisted edifice of my life began to crumble, the entire structure was compromised and everything came tumbling down.

Tina Faibich took the call that Thursday afternoon; her employer was in conference with two of the lawyers representing the insurance company in the King Benedict case and did not want to be interrupted, but there was such urgency in the stranger's voice that she felt she could not handle the call herself. She made a wise decision, and she saved Margaret's life—at least for a time. Come quick, the man said; he gave the address of a motel in Richmond and hung up without identifying himself. King Benedict was reading a comic book in the waiting room when he saw Gregory Reeves rush out, and while Reeves was waiting for the elevator, was able to ask him where he was going in such a hurry.

"That's not a place you should go alone, especially in a car like the one you drive," Benedict assured him, and without waiting for a response followed closely on his heels. Forty-five minutes later they were parking in front of a row of shabby motel rooms in a garbage-strewn alley. As they had driven deeper and deeper into the poorest neighborhoods in the city, it was clear that Benedict was right; there wasn't a white man to be seen. In open doorways, in front of bars, on corners, stood groups of idle youths who made threatening gestures and shouted obscenities as they drove past. Some streets had no identifying signs, and Reeves began to circle aimlessly, not wanting to roll down the window and ask for directions for fear of being spit on, or stoned, but King Benedict had no such problem. He made Reeves stop, calmly got out of the car, asked a couple of people directions, and returned, giving a slow wave to the crowd of young boys who had flocked around the car, jeering and kicking the fenders. They found Margaret. They knocked on the door of room number 9 of a wretched motel, and a huge black man opened the door; his head was shaved, and five safety pins were fastened through one ear. He was the last person Reeves would have wished to find with his daughter, but he had little time to think about that because the man seized his arm with a hand like a ham and led him toward the bed, where the girl lay.

"Looks to me like she's dying," he said.

He was just a chance client, her first of the day, who for a few dollars had bought some time with the unkempt girl everyone in the neighborhood knew and left alone despite her color because she was immune to ordinary aggression, she had crossed to the farthest shore of affliction. As he had stripped off her dress and pushed her back onto the bed, he found he was holding a broken puppet, a shocking skeleton burning with fever. He shook her a little, with the idea of rousing her from her drugged stupor, but her head lolled heavily on her thin neck; her eyes were turned back, and a string of yellowish saliva dribbled from her mouth. Shit! the man muttered. His first impulse was to leave her lying there and get the hell out before someone saw him and later accused him of killing her, but when he let go she seemed so pathetic lying there that pity had got the better of him, and in a surge of generosity carved from the violence of his own life he bent over her, calling her, trying to get her to swallow some water, feeling her everywhere to see if she was injured, but finding only that her body was in flames. Margaret was temporarily living in that grimy room; empty bottles were scattered around the floor, cigarette butts, syringes, remnants of a stale pizza, and more filth than can be imagined. On the table, beside open containers of makeup, was a plastic handbag; he turned it upside down, not knowing what he was looking for, and found a key, a pack of cigarettes, heroin, and a billfold containing three dollars and a lawyer's business card. It never crossed his mind to call the police, but he thought that she must have a reason for carrying the card in her purse; he ran to the public telephone on the corner and called Reeves, not dreaming he was talking to the father of a miserable prostitute lying near death on a bare mattress. Once he sounded the alarm, he walked to a liquor store to buy a beer, ready to forget the whole incident and make a fast exit if the police showed up, but in some deep corner of his heart he felt the girl calling him; no one wanted to die alone, he didn't have anything to lose by staying with her a few more minutes and maybe in the process pocketing the money and the drugs—she wasn't going to need them anymore. He went back to room number 9 carrying another beer and a paper cup filled with ice, and between trying to get her to drink something, rubbing the ice on her forehead, and keeping a T-shirt wet to cool her body, he forgot, during the time it had taken Reeves to find the motel, to empty her wallet.

"OK," he said, "I'm out of here," uneasy at the sight of the white man wearing a gray suit and tie—a kind of joke in that place—but out of curiosity he lingered in the doorway.

"What happened? Where's a telephone? Who are you?" Reeves asked as he removed his jacket to cover his naked daughter.

"I don't have nothing to do with this; I don't even know the girl. And hey, who are you?"

"Her father. Thanks for calling me—" And Reeves's voice broke.

"Shit. . . . Holy shit . . . Let me help you."

The black man lifted Margaret as if she were a baby and carried her to the car, where King Benedict was waiting to prevent its being stolen. Reeves sped off in the direction of a hospital, weaving through traffic and a mist of tears; his daughter, scarcely breathing, was curled into a little ball on King's lap, and he was crooning one of the timeless spirituals his mother had sung when she rocked him to sleep. Reeves strode into the emergency room, carrying Margaret in his arms. Two hours later they allowed him to see her for a few minutes in one corner of the intensive care unit, where she lay spread-eagled on a bed, connected to a respirator and various monitors. The resident gave him a preliminary assessment: a generalized infection had attacked her heart. The prognosis was grim, he said; they might be able to save her with massive doses of antibiotics, but she would have to change her life radically. Subsequent examinations revealed that Margaret's body was that of an old woman: her internal organs were wasted from drugs, her veins were collapsed from shooting up, her teeth were loose in her gums, her skin was like scales, and her hair was falling out by the handful. She was bleeding badly because of successive abortions and venereal infections. Even with that list of afflictions, the prostrate girl lying unconscious in the shadowy room looked like a sleeping angel, with no outward sign of shame, her innocence intact. The illusion was short-lived, however, and her father soon learned just how deep was the cesspool she had fallen into. The hospital staff tried to cut off her drugs, but she was shaken by spasms of agony. They prescribed methadone and gave her nicotine chewing gum, but had to place her in restraints to keep her from drinking the rubbing alcohol or stealing barbiturates. During all this, Gregory Reeves could not locate Samantha, who was somewhere in India, following her guru. Desperate, he went to Ming O'Brien, pleading for her help, although in truth he had lost any hope of wresting Margaret from the claws of damnation. As soon as the sick girl had emerged from the worst crisis, Dr. O'Brien visited her regularly, staying to talk for hours. Gregory Reeves came in the afternoons, where he found his daughter torn with self-pity, with the face of a madwoman and an uncontrollable trembling in her hands. He would sit by the bed, wanting to hug her but not daring to touch her, silently listening to an endless string of accusations and bloodcurdling confessions. It was then that he learned the extent of the black martyrdom his daughter had borne. He tried to ascertain what had led to her Golgotha, what unshakable rage and what dark loneliness had warped her life to that degree, but she herself did not know. At times she told him, sobbing, I love you, Papa, but an instant later she railed against him, howling with visceral loathing, blaming him for all her misery.

"Look at me, you goddam sonofabitch, look at me," and with one sweep of her hand she threw back the sheets and spread her legs, pointing to her sex, weeping and laughing with the ferocity of madness. "You want to know how I earn my living while you go gallivanting around Europe buying jewels for your lovers and while my mother sits meditating in the lotus position? Do you want to know exactly what the drunks and beggars and addicts do to me? Oh, but I don't need to tell you, because you're an expert in whores; you pay us to do all the shit no woman would do without being paid. . . ."

Ming O'Brien tried to help Margaret confront her reality, to help her accept the fact that she could not save herself on her own, that her treatment would take a very long time, but it was a game of illusions played before a fun-house mirror. The girl pretended to listen and said she was sick of her life of excess but, as soon as she could walk, slipped down the hall to the telephone to ask her contacts to bring heroin to her in the hospital. Other times she was totally dispirited, horrified by her own condition; she would begin telling the details of her long descent into depravity and then silently sink into a slough of remorse. Her father offered to pay for her rehabilitation in a private clinic, and finally she accepted, apparently resigned. Ming spent the morning pulling strings to have her admitted, and Gregory left to buy tickets for a flight to southern California the next morning. That night Margaret stole another patient's clothes and escaped without a trace.

"Her infection isn't cured; we merely contained the most alarming symptoms. If she doesn't continue the antibiotics, she will obviously die," the doctor said in an unemotional voice. He was hardened to every kind of emergency and had little sympathy for drug addicts.

"Don't look for her, Gregory," Ming O'Brien advised the stricken father. "At some moment you must accept the fact that there's nothing more you can do for your daughter. You have to let go. It's her life."

Meanwhile, the date for King Benedict's trial was approaching. The insurance company had stood firm in refusing to pay compensation for the accident, arguing that the alleged amnesia

THE INFINITE PLAN · 353

was a hoax. They had subjected Benedict to humiliating medical and psychiatric examinations to prove that no physical injury was attributable to the fall. For weeks they questioned him about every insignificant event that happened between the time he was a teenager and the current year. They wanted him to identify old baseball teams, they asked him what dances people were dancing in 1941 and what day war broke out in Europe. They also hired detectives, who followed him for months hoping to catch him out in some deception. Benedict tried with good faith to answer their interminable questioning, because he did not want to be considered ignorant; except for some facts he remembered from his daily stint in the library, however, everything else lay hidden in the serene haze of things yet to come. We don't know anything about the future, whether it even exists, all we can see in our mind is the past, his mother had told him many times, but he could not get a grasp on his past; it was a slippery shadow that had eaten up forty years of his time on earth. Gregory Reeves, who lived tormented by a too perfect memory, found his client's tragedy fascinating. He, too, questioned him, not to trap him in a lie but to learn how a man feels when he has the chance to wipe out his life and begin all over again. He had known King four years and during that time listened to his boyish fantasies and dreams of greatness, but he had also watched him retrace, step by step, the road already traveled, like a somnambulist trapped in a recurrent dream. King did nothing significantly different; it was as if he were placing each foot in tracks from an earlier time: he went to night classes to finish high school, received the same bad grades he had as a boy, and finally dropped out; a couple of years later, about the time he would have been sixteen, he presented himself at several recruiting offices to try to sign up with a branch of the armed forces but was rejected at each. He had seen a lot of movies about the war, and his head was filled with military glory; as consolation, he bought himself a uniform.

"In a couple of years now, he'll marry a no-good like his former wife and father two kids like my useless grandchildren," Bel Benedict complained bitterly.

"It's hard for me to believe you can trip twice over the same exact stone," replied Gregory Reeves, who had begun his silent journey into his past and often wondered what would have happened had he made different choices along the way.

"You can't live two lives or two different fates. Life doesn't come with an eraser," Bel said.

"Surely we can, Mrs. Benedict; I'm certainly trying. You can alter your story and correct the rough draft."

"No. What's been lived can't be changed. We can do better in what lies before us, but the past is the past."

"You mean we can't undo our mistakes? Isn't there any hope, for instance, for my daughter, Margaret? She's not even twenty yet."

"There's hope, but the twenty years she lost she can never get back."

"That's a terrifying idea. It means that with every step we cement a piece of our history; we carry all our desires and thoughts and actions with us forever. If that's true, we *are* our past. My father used to preach about the consequences of every act we commit and our responsibilities within the spiritual order of the universe; he said that everything we do comes back to us, and that sooner or later we pay for the evil and benefit from the good."

"He was a wise man."

"He was out of his mind, mad as a hatter when he died. His theories were a lot of tangled threads I could never unravel."

"Well, he had his values right, it seems."

"He didn't preach by example, though, Bel. My sister tells me he was an alcoholic and a pervert, that he was obsessive about controlling things and ruined our lives—at least hers. But he was a strong man, and I felt good when I was with him; my memories of him are happy ones."

"Seems like he taught you to walk a straight path."

"He tried, but he died before he could finish. My road hasn't been too straight."

Later, when he was discussing this conversation with Ming O'Brien, Reeves started telling her about his client, and Ming, who usually listened attentively and rarely opened her mouth to offer an opinion, now interrupted to ask more details. Had King Benedict been subject to unusual pressure? What kind of childhood had he had? Was he a calm and balanced person, or would Reeves say he was unstable? Her final comment was that his type of amnesia was rare, but there were documented cases. She pulled a book from a shelf and handed it to Gregory.

"You might want to look at this. It's probable that in his adolescence your client suffered a severe emotional shock or a blow similar to the one he received in the accident. When the experience was repeated, the impact of the past was intolerable, and he blocked out the memory."

"I don't think there was anything like that."

"But there must have been something very painful or threatening that he doesn't want to remember. Ask his mother."

Gregory Reeves spent the night reading, and by breakfast time he had a clear idea of what Ming O'Brien had suggested. He remembered the time King Benedict had fainted in his office while being asked to identify photographs from a magazine, and he remembered Bel's strange reaction. She was waiting outside during the deposition and when she heard the uproar had run into the library, seen her son on the floor, and bent over to help him; at that moment the open magazine on the table had caught her eye, and impulsively she had put her hand over King's mouth. She had refused to let the questioning continue, had taken King home in a taxi, and from that day had insisted on being present at all the interviews. Reeves attributed her behavior to concern for her son's health, but now he had doubts. Excited about this chink through which he could glimpse a glimmer of light, Reeves drove directly to Timothy Duane's parents' house to talk with King's mother. Bel was in the kitchen cleaning silver when the butler announced Reeves's visit, but before she could come to meet him, Gregory burst into the kitchen. We have to talk, he said, taking her by the arm, not giving her time to remove her apron or wash her hands. Alone with her in his office, he explained that very soon he would be staking her son's future on the turn of a card, and winning depended on his ability to convince the jury that King was not feigning amnesia. Until yesterday he hadn't seen how that was possible, but with her help today they might change the outcome of the case. He repeated Ming O'Brien's theory and begged her to tell him what had happened to King Benedict when he was young.

"How do you expect me to remember something that happened so long ago?"

"I'm sure you won't have to think very hard to remember, Mrs. Benedict, because you have never forgotten, not even for a minute," Reeves replied, opening his briefcase and removing the magazine that had triggered her son's attack. "What does this ranch mean to you?"

"Nothing."

"Were King and you ever in a place like this?"

"We've been a lot of places; we moved all the time while I looked for work. We picked cotton at several places like that."

"When King was fourteen?"

"Maybe; I don't remember."

"Please, don't make things more difficult for me, because we don't have much time. I want to help you. We're playing on the same team, Bel; I'm not your enemy."

Bel Benedict was silent, looking at the photograph with an expression of obdurate dignity, while Gregory Reeves watched admiringly, thinking what a beauty she must have been as a young woman and that had she been born in a different time or under different circumstances she could have married a powerful man who would have sported his sleek pantheress on his arm and no one would have dared object to her race.

"All right, Mr. Reeves, I'm backed into a corner," she said at last, sighing. "If I keep my mouth shut, like I have for forty years, my baby will end up a helpless old man without a cent to his name, and if I tell what happened, I'll go to jail and my boy will be all alone."

"There may be still another way. If you consult me as your lawyer, anything you say will be confidential and won't go beyond these four walls, I promise you."

"You mean you can't report me?"

"No, I can't."

"Then I want you to be my lawyer; I'm going to need one anyway," she decided after another long pause. "It was self-defense, as they call it, but who's going to believe me? I was a poor black woman passing through the most racist part of Texas. My son and I worked our way from farm to farm, earning a living at any job I could find; all I had was one suitcase of clothes and two arms to work. I had terrible headaches in those days. I didn't want to, but I kept getting into fights. I attracted trouble like flypaper draws flies. I never lasted anywhere very long; something always happened to make us move on. I was surprised when this big-time farmer gave me a job; all the rest of his workers were *braceros*, Latino men, but it was the season for picking cotton, and I thought he was hard up for help. I couldn't stay where the men lived, so he gave Baby and me a dirty old cabin on the far side of his land, a long ways away, where a truck came to pick us up in the morning and took us back at the end of the day. It was a good job, but the boss had his eye on me. I knew we were headed for trouble, but I was willing to put up with a lot; I promise you, I couldn't be that picky. I had my priorities in order, and putting food in my son's mouth always came first. Why did it matter if I had to go to bed with some man? Ten or twenty minutes and it was all over and you could put it right out of your mind. But he was one of those men who can't do it like everyone else; he liked to use his fists, and if he didn't draw blood, he couldn't do what he came for. Who would have suspected? He seemed like such a good man, his workers respected him, he paid a fair wage, he went to church every Sunday—he was a model boss. I let him rough me up a couple of times and call me a filthy nigger and worse. He wasn't the first; you kind of get used to it . . . and what woman hasn't taken her licks? That Sunday Baby was off playing baseball when the man drove up in his truck. I was alone, and I could see in his face what he was looking for; besides, I could smell the liquor on him. I'm not real sure what happened, Mr. Reeves, but I know he had pulled off his belt and was going at me hot and heavy, and I think I screamed, and that's when Baby came in and got between us and the man hit him hard with his fist. Baby hit the back of his head against the corner of the table. I saw my boy lying senseless on the floor, and I didn't even have to think.... I picked up his baseball bat and swung at the man's head. Just one swing with all my heart ... and I killed him. When Baby came to, I washed off his wound; he had a real bad gash, but I couldn't take him to a hospital, where they would ask a lot of questions; I stopped the blood with cold water and some clean rags. I got the boss's body into his truck, covered it over with gunnysacks, and hid the truck away from the house. I waited till dark, drove twenty miles away from the farm, and ran the truck into a ravine. Nobody knew. Then I walked the five hours back to the cabin. I remember I slept with a clean conscience the rest of the night and the next morning was at the door waiting to be picked up for work, as if nothing had happened. My son and I never talked about any of it. The police found the body and thought the man had had too much to drink and run his truck off the road. They questioned the *braceros,* but if anyone had seen anything they didn't tell it, and that's as far as it went. A little later Baby and I left that place and never set foot in Texas again. Isn't that life for you, Mr. Reeves? That forty years later that ghost would come back to haunt me?"

"Has it weighed on your conscience?" Reeves asked, thinking of the deaths he carried on his.

"Never, may the good Lord forgive me. That man was looking to be killed."

"My friend Carmen, who has more common sense than anyone I know, told me once that we don't need to confess what no one asks to know."

"But it will come out in the trial, Mr. Reeves."

"Does King still have that scar on his head?"

"Yes; it was a bad one, because we couldn't get stitches."

"We'll show that when he was fourteen he hit his head when he fell against a table, but if we're lucky we won't have to tell the rest of the story. If I can find an expert who will connect the first fall with the accident on the construction site, maybe we can settle the case without going to court, Mrs. Benedict."

At the pretrial deposition, Ming O'Brien testified that King Benedict's profile fit that for psychogenic amnesia, and given the lack of improvement to date, he would probably never recover. She explained that the record of his injuries corresponded with the normal causes for that disorder: King had a difficult childhood and youth and suffered a severe blow to the head during adolescence; before the accident he was under great pressure, and he was a depressive by temperament. When he fell from the scaffold he suffered a trauma similar to the earlier injury, and he had regressed and taken refuge in amnesia as a defense against the problems he was facing. The insurance company lawyers did everything they could to discredit the diagnosis but were brought up short by the quiet conviction of the doctor, who produced a large stack of volumes with references to similar cases. In addition, the detectives hired to shadow Benedict had nothing but photographs of the suspect playing with an electric train, reading adventure stories, and playing war in a soldier's uniform. The judge, a matronly woman as upright as Ming O'Brien, summoned the defense lawyers to her chambers and suggested that it would be to their benefit to make payment without further delay, because if the case went to trial they could lose much more. Judging from my considerable experience, she said, the members of any jury will be generous with this poor man and his long-suffering mother, as I would be if I were one of them. After two days of arguing back and forth, the insurance lawyers conceded. Gregory Reeves celebrated their victory by taking Bel, King, and David to Disneyland, where they lost themselves in a fantastic world of animals that talk, lights that turn night to day, and machines that defy the laws of physics and the mysteries of time. Upon their return, Reeves helped Bel purchase a modest house in the country and invest the remainder of the insurance money so that she and King could count on a pension for the rest of their days.

When Dai lost interest in his computer and began to use after-shave lotion and peer at himself in the mirror with a desolate air, Carmen Morales invited him out to dinner for a talk, following their custom of making dates when they wanted to discuss something important. Their lives had become more complicated, and with the years they had lost some portion of the affectionate intimacy that earlier united them, but they were still very close. Dai as a teenager looked like his Latino father, though he was more intense and somber. He had inherited none of Juan José's spirit for adventure nor any of Carmen's explosive personality; he was an introverted and rather solemn boy, too serious for his age. When he was four or five he had begun to show an extraordinary aptitude for mathematics, and from then on had been treated like a prodigy by everyone except his adoptive mother. His teachers showed him off on television programs and in contests, where he solved complex equations in his head. He had won a number of prizes, including a motorcycle before he was old enough to ride. His inherent pride was in danger of becoming arrogance, but Carmen kept him in line by putting him to work in her factory during vacations so he would have contact with working people and know from the time he was a boy how hard it is to earn a living. She also stimulated his curiosity and opened his mind to other cultures. At fifteen, Dai had traveled in Asia, Africa, and several countries of South America; he spoke some Spanish and a little Vietnamese, he had the financial end of his mother's business at his fingertips, he had a savings account, and several universities had offered him scholarships for the future. While the entire nation was debating the crisis of values among young people and the disastrous educational system that had created a generation of lazy ignoramuses, Dai was studying hard, working, and in his free time exploring the library and playing with his computer. In his room he had a small altar with the photograph Leo Galupi had faked of his mother and father, along with a wooden cross, a small clay Buddha, and a magazine clipping of the earth seen from a space shuttle. He was not sociable, he preferred being alone, and had always considered Carmen his sole and dearest companion. This likable boy, satisfied with his life and comfortable with being a lone wolf, changed abruptly toward the end of the spring. He spent hours getting ready to go out, began to dress, talk, and move like a rock singer, left the house at strange hours, and made massive efforts to be accepted by schoolmates whose company he once scorned. He renounced his passion for mathematics because he wanted to be one of the crowd and mathematics made him different from his friends. When his mother saw him painfully trying to plaster down his stubborn hair with styling gel, dabbing toothpaste on his pimples, and pacing back and forth by the telephone, she knew the time of idyllic complicity with her son was at an end and suffered a fit of jealousy she did not dare confess even to Gregory Reeves during their Monday conversations. Carmen now had Tamar shops throughout the world and counted on an efficient team of employees to manage her business while she designed new lines and promoted the company's image. She had bought a frame house in the midst of huge trees in the Berkeley hills, where she lived with her son and her mother. Pedro Morales had been dead for several years. When he knew he was going to die, he refused to go to the hospital; he did not want his life to be prolonged by artificial means and was afraid the medical bills would ruin his family and his wife would be out in the street. He had worked a lifetime to provide for his small tribe and refused to allow what he had won to be wiped out at the end. He was very proud of his family, especially Carmen and his grandson Dai, in whom he saw the reincarnation of his son Juan José. He departed this world without leaving behind any loose ends and with a sense of having fulfilled his destiny in his own good time. Inmaculada was by her husband's side in his last days and then consoled her grieving sons and daughters, son- and daughters-in-law, and many grandchildren. After the patriarch died, the family did not drift apart, because Inmaculada made sure the bonds of affection and mutual assistance never slackened. After the burial, she decided to stay with Carmen for a while, and within a few weeks divided her belongings and sold the house. For years she had put her heart into acquiring furniture and decorations, testimony to their prosperity, but when she lost her husband, material possessions no longer held any meaning. You spend the first part of your life collecting things, she said, and the second half getting rid of them. She kept only the bed she had shared with Pedro Morales for half a century, because she wanted to die in it one day. She had changed very little, as if frozen at an indeterminate age; the strength of her Indian ancestry seemed to protect her from the wasting of body and the waning of memory. She had never been more lucid; she was a steadfast, diligent old woman impervious to fatigue, weakness, or bad health. She took charge of Carmen's domestic arrangements with militant fervor; she had brought up six children in hard times in a barrio, and this house filled with comforts offered no challenges to her. It was difficult to keep her from breaking her back washing clothes or beating eggs; she was one for keeping busy. Idleness breeds illness, she always said to justify herself if she was caught on a ladder washing windows or on her knees setting traps for the raccoons forming a colony in the foundations of the house. She continued to cook Mexican dishes that only Dai and she enjoyed because Carmen was always on a diet. She rose early in the morning to water her vegetable and herb gardens, to clean and cook and wash, and she was the last to go to bed, after telephoning her children in different cities in the country—a part, she thought, of her responsibility for keeping tabs on all her descendants. The habit of doing for others was too deeply rooted to change in her old age, but she was the first to denigrate her domesticity. Years before, she had secretly applauded Carmen when she returned from her travels a "liberated gringa," as Pedro Morales grumblingly called her. And it was one of her most heartfelt delights that Carmen earned a better living than her brothers, compensation for Inmaculada's own lifetime of deferring to men. Carmen forced her mother to use modern appliances and buy tortillas in plastic bags, and opened an account for her in the bank, to which Inmaculada accorded the same devotion she reserved for her prayerbook. Inmaculada was the first to notice that Dai had entered a phase of unrequited love, and she transmitted that knowledge to her daughter.

"Tell me everything," Carmen commanded when she and Dai were seated in the restaurant.

Dai tried to deny that anything was wrong but was betrayed by his forsaken air and his blushing: embarrassment turned his dark skin beet red. His mother gave no quarter, and by dessert he had no choice but to confess—dazed with chocolate cake and squirming in his chair—that he couldn't sleep or study or think or live; the hours dragged by as he sat by the telephone, waiting for a call that never came. What can I do, Mama? I know she looks down on me because I'm not white and I don't play football. Why was I born? Why did you come get me in Vietnam and bring me up so different from everyone else? I don't know the names of the rock bands, and I'm the only moron who calls Orientals Asiatics and blacks Afro-Americans, or worries about holes in the ozone layer or beggars in the street or the war against Nicaragua—I'm the only politically correct person in the whole blessed school. No one gives a good god*damn* about those things, Mama; life is pure shit, and if Karen doesn't call me today I swear I'm going to climb on my motorcycle and drive it off a cliff, because I can't live without her. Carmen Morales interrupted his monologue with a slap on the face that resounded like a slammed door through the esoteric peace of the vegetarian restaurant. She had never struck him before. Dai put his hand to his cheek, so surprised that the litany of laments froze on his lips.

"Don't ever say that again, about killing yourself, you hear me?"

"It's just a manner of speaking, Mama!"

"I don't want to hear it, even joking. You're going to live out your life, no matter how much it hurts. And now tell me, who is this wretched girl who thinks she's too good for my son?"

Karen, it turned out, was a classmate who like every other girl in the school was in love with the captain of the football team, with whom Dai could not compete even in his dreams. The next day Carmen drove her son to school to get a look at the girl; she saw a baby-faced, washed-out blonde, half hidden behind a bubble-gum bubble. She sighed with relief, sure that Dai would recover from his lovesickness and quickly find someone more interesting, and also sure that even if he didn't, there was nothing she could do—she could no longer protect him from his own experiences and suffering, as she had tried to do when he was small. Later Carmen realized that her feeling of relief was occasioned by more than the sight of the insipid girl and her own certainty that Dai would not suffer over her forever. She was beginning to sense that there were advantages to her son's living his own life. For the first time in the thirteen years they had been together, she could think of herself as a separate and individual person. Until then Dai had been an extension of her being and she of his: Siamese twins joined at the heart, Inmaculada always said. That evening her mother found her sitting in the kitchen before a cup of mango tea, staring at the dark shadows of the trees in the last light of day.

"Do you think I look old, Mama?"

"Older than last year, but younger than next, may it please God," Inmaculada replied.

"Do you know I could be a grandmother? My life is flying by."

"At your age it goes quickly, daughter; you think you're going to live forever. At my age days dissolve like salt in water; the day's gone and I don't even know what I've done with the hours."

"Do you think someone could still fall in love with me?"

"You should ask instead if you yourself can fall in love. Happiness comes from love that's given."

"I don't have any doubt that I have love to give."

"I'm happy to hear that, because one of these days now I'll die, and Dai will be gone too; it's the normal way of things. You shouldn't be alone. I'm getting tired of saying you should get married."

"To whom, Mama?"

"To Gregory. That boy is nicer than anyone I've seen you with, which isn't saying a whole lot, of course. Where did you ever get such bad judgment in men!"

"Gregory is my brother; we'd be committing incest."

"What a shame. Then look for someone your own age. I don't know why you run around with those boys younger than you."

"That's not a bad idea, Mama," Carmen replied, with a reflective smile that made her mother a little uneasy.

Three weeks later Carmen announced at home that she was flying to Rome to look for a husband. Through a private investigator she had pinpointed Leo Galupi's whereabouts in the vast universe, a task that was not too difficult, given that his name was in large print in the Chicago telephone directory. At the end of the war he had returned home, as poor as he left; he had lost all the money he had earned in his bizarre business dealings, but was rich in experience. His years of trading in Asia had refined his taste, he knew a lot about art and had good contacts, and so had launched the venture of his dreams. He opened a gallery specializing in Oriental objets d'art, and it was so successful that after ten years he had a second gallery in New York and one in Rome, where he lived much of the year. The detective informed Carmen that Galupi had never married, and delivered a series of photographs taken with a telephoto lens in which he was seen, in white from head to toe, walking down a street, climbing into an automobile, and eating ice cream on the Spanish Steps, at the very spot where she had often sat when she went to Rome to check on her Tamar shops. When she saw him her heart gave a leap. She had forgotten his precise features—in fact, she had not thought much about him at all, but looking at those slightly blurred images, she was awash in a wave of nostalgia. She discovered that his memory had been safely stored in a secret compartment of her mind. I'd better get going, she decided; I have a lot to do. Those were nerve-racking days, preparing for a trip very different from others she had made; in a certain way, this was a life-or-death mission, as she told her mother when Inmaculada found her with the contents of her closets strewn about the floor, impatiently trying on clothes to find which were most flattering. Once arrangements at the factory and at home were complete, she had a physical exam, tinted her hair, and bought silk lingerie. She appraised herself with a pitiless eye in the full-length bathroom mirror, counted her wrinkles, and regretted the years of not exercising and of cheating on her diet. She pinched her arms and legs, confirming her worst suspicions about muscle tone, tried to suck in her stomach but was foiled by a rebellious fold, inspected her work-ravaged hands, and finally regarded breasts that had always weighed like a load she was toting for someone else. She did not have the figure she had had when she met Leo Galupi, but she decided that, overall, the inventory wasn't too bad—at least there were no telltale varicose veins or stretch marks from her pregnancy, she told herself, forgetting she was not Dai's birth mother. With all the details well in hand, Carmen went to lunch with Gregory Reeves; she had not wanted to inform him earlier about her plans, for fear he would think she was demented. Timidly at first, and then with more enthusiasm, she told him what she had found out about Leo Galupi and showed him the photographs. She received a surprise in return; Gregory accepted as perfectly natural her sudden impulse to make a pilgrimage to Europe to propose marriage to a man she hadn't seen for more than ten years and with whom the subject of love had never arisen. The plan seemed so typical of Carmen that Gregory asked her why she hadn't done it before.

"I was too busy raising Dai, but my son is growing up and doesn't need me as much now."

"You may be in for a disappointment."

"I'll check everything out very carefully before I sign anything. I'm not worried about that . . . but maybe he won't like me, Greg; I'm a hell of a lot older."

"Look at the pictures, woman. He's added a few years himself," Reeves said, spreading the snapshots in front of her, and she noticed for the first time that indeed Leo Galupi was lighter in hair and heavier in pounds. She laughed happily and decided that instead of writing or calling to announce her visit, as she had intended, she would simply go see him—thus preventing her imagination from working overtime—and learn immediately whether her wild project had a chance.

Three days later Carmen Morales appeared at the door of

Galupi's gallery in Rome; she had come directly from the airport, and her suitcases were waiting in the taxi. She was praying that she would find him in, and for once her prayers had the hoped-for result. When she walked in, Leo Galupi, who was wearing a wrinkled linen shirt and slacks and no socks, was discussing the details of the next catalog with a young man whose clothes were as unironed as his. Among the Indian tapestries, Chinese ivories, wood carvings from Nepal, porcelains and bronzes from Japan, and a plenitude of exotic art, Carmen, with her swirling gypsy skirts and faint tinkling of antique silver jewelry, seemed part of the exhibition. When Galupi saw her, the catalog fell from his hands and he stood looking at her as if seeing an oft-invoked ghost. Carmen's thought was that, as she had feared, her unwonted swain had not recognized her.

"I'm Tamar. . . . Do you remember me?" and she walked toward him hesitantly.

"How could I forget!" Galupi took her hand and shook it for several seconds, until he realized the absurdity of such a welcome and took her in his arms.

"I came to ask if you want to marry me," Carmen blurted in a nearly inaudible voice, because this was not how she had planned to do it, and even as she spoke she was silently cursing herself for having blown her chances with her first words.

"I don't know," was all Galupi could think to say, once he could speak, and they stood staring at each other in wonder, as the young man of the catalog disappeared without a sound.

"Are you in l-love with anyone?" she stammered, feeling more and more idiotic but unable to remember the strategy she had planned down to the last detail.

"I don't think so; not right now."

"Are you gay?"

"No."

"Can we get a cup of coffee? I'm a little tired; it was a long trip. . . ."

Leo Galupi led her outside, where the radiant summer sun and the sounds of people and traffic brought them back to the present. In the gallery, time had dissolved to Saigon, where they were again in the Chinese-empress room Galupi had prepared for her and where he often stood to watch through a chink in the screen as she lay sleeping. When they said goodbye, Galupi had felt the sting of loneliness for the first time in all his world travels, but he did not like to admit it and had cured himself with stubborn indifference, immersing himself in the rush of business and travel. With time, he lost the temptation to write her and grew used to the bittersweet emotion he felt when he thought of her. Her memory served as protection against the spur of other loves, a kind of insurance against romantic entanglements. When he was very young, Galupi had decided not to tie himself to anything or anyone; he was not a family man, nor one for long commitments, but thought of himself as a loner incapable of enduring the tedium of routine or the demands of life with another individual. More than once, he escaped from an overly intense relationship by explaining to his indignant sweetheart that he could not love her because in his destiny there was room only for love of a woman named Tamar. That alibi, often repeated, became a kind of tragic truth. He had not examined his deepest feelings because he enjoyed his freedom and Tamar was merely a useful ghost he called on when he needed to escape from an uncomfortable affair. And then, just when he felt he was safe from surprises of the heart, she showed up to collect on the lies he had told other women for years. He could not believe she had walked into his shop a half hour earlier and before speaking another word asked him to marry her. Now she was beside him, and he hadn't the courage to look at her, although he felt her eyes openly scrutinizing him.

"Forgive me, Leo, I don't mean to drive you into a corner; this isn't how I planned it."

"How did you plan it?"

"I meant to seduce you; I even bought a black lace nightgown."

"You don't have to go to that much trouble." Galupi laughed.

"I'll take you home so you can bathe and take a nap. You must be bushed. Then we can talk."

"Perfect; that will give you a little time to think," Carmen sighed, with no attempt at irony.

Galupi lived in an old villa that had been divided into several apartments. His flat had only one window toward the street; all the rest overlooked a small, untended garden where water sang in a fountain and vines climbed around ruined statues stained by the green patina of time. Much later, sitting on the terrace sipping a glass of white wine, admiring the garden under the light of a full moon and breathing the perfume of wild jasmine, they bared their souls to each other. They both had had countless affairs and romances; they had traveled in circles, practicing nearly all the games of deception that cause lovers to lose their way. It was refreshing to talk about themselves and their feelings with brutal honesty, with no ulterior motives or tactical considerations. They recounted the broad outlines of their lives, stated what they wanted of the future, and ascertained that the alchemy that had first attracted them to each other was still there, needing only a little goodwill to be revived.

"I hadn't thought about getting married until a couple of weeks ago, Leo."

"And why did you think of me?"

"Because I never forgot you; I like you, and I think that years ago you liked me a little too. Of all the men I've known, there are only two I would want to have with me when I'm sad."

"Who is the other?"

"Gregory Reeves, but he isn't ready for real love, and I don't have time to wait for him."

"What do you mean, 'real' love?"

"Total love; none of this halfway stuff. I'm looking for a partner who will love me very much, be faithful to me, not lie, respect my work, and make me laugh. That's asking a lot, I know, but I offer more or less the same, and for good measure, I'm ready to live wherever you want, as long as you accept my son and my mother and I can travel when I need. I'm healthy, I support myself, and I'm never depressed."

"That sounds like a contract."

"It is. Do you have children?"

"Not that I know, but I have an Italian mother. That will be a problem; she never likes the women I introduce her to."

"I don't know how to cook, and I'm fairly straightforward in bed, but in my house they say I'm pleasant to live with, probably because they don't see much of me—I spend hours on end in my workshop. I'm not much bother. . . ."

"On the other hand, I'm not very easy."

"Could you make an effort, do you think?"

They kissed for the first time, tentatively, then with curiosity, and soon with the passion stored up in years of warding off the need for love with casual liaisons. Leo Galupi led this imponderable woman to his bedroom: a high ceiling adorned with fresco nymphs, a large bed, and antique tapestry cushions. Carmen's head was swimming; she did not know whether she was giddy from the long flight or the wine, but she did not intend to find out. She abandoned herself to her languor, lacking the will to impress Leo Galupi with either her black lace nightgown or her skills learned with previous lovers. She was attracted by his healthy male smell, a clean odor without a trace of artificial fragrance, slightly pungent, like bread or wood, and she buried her nose where his neck joined his shoulder, sniffing like a hunting dog on the scent. Aromas persisted in her memory longer than any other recollection, and at that moment the image of a night in Saigon came to her mind, a night when they were so close she had registered his aura, never knowing it would stay with her all those years. She began to unbutton his shirt, but fumbled with the tiny buttonholes and impatiently asked him to do it for her. She heard the music of strings from somewhere far away, carrying the millenary sensuality of India to that room in Rome bathed in moonlight and the light fragrance of jasmine from the garden. For years she had made love with virile younger men; now her fingertips were caressing a back that was slightly stooped and stroking the fine hair at a receding hairline. She felt a gratifying tenderness for this older man and for an instant tried to imagine what roads and what women he had known, but immediately succumbed to the pleasure of loving him, leaving her mind blank. She felt his hands removing her blouse, her full skirt, her sandals, pausing, hesitantly, when he came to her bracelets. She never took them off, they were her final armor, but she thought the moment had come to be completely naked, and she sat on the edge of the bed and pulled them off, one by one. They fell noiselessly upon the rug. With exploring kisses and knowing hands, Leo Galupi began to familiarize himself with her body; his tongue moistened her still firm nipples, the shell of her ears, her inner thighs, where her skin shivered at the touch; she felt the air growing dense and panted from the effort of breathing; a glowing urgency flowed through her loins, and she ground her hips and moaned as she escaped him, until she could not wait any longer, turned him onto his back, and swung astride him like an inspired Amazon, clasping him between her knees amid a storm of pillows. Impatience or fatigue made her clumsy; she twisted and slithered like a snake, seeking, reaching, but she was wet with pleasure and summer's sweat and finally collapsed on him, laughing, crushing him with the gift of her breasts, enveloping him in a rain of unruly hair, and whispering instructions in Spanish he could not understand. They lay like that, embraced, laughing, kissing, and murmuring foolish words in a sonorous mixture of languages, until desire became too great, and at one moment in their playful tumbling Leo Galupi took the lead, without haste, steady, pausing at each station along the way to wait for her and lead her to the farthest garden, where he left her to explore alone until she felt herself slipping into a shadowy void, and a joyous explosion shook her body. Then it was his turn, as she caressed him, grateful for that absolute and effortless orgasm. Finally they slept, curled in a tangle of legs and arms. In the days to come they discovered they had fun together, that both slept on the same side, that neither smoked, that they liked the same books, films, and food and voted for the same party, that sports bored them, and that they regularly traveled to exotic places.

"I don't know how good I'd be as a husband, Tamar," Leo Galupi apologized one evening in a trattoria on the Via Veneto. "I have to have freedom to move around. I'm a vagabond."

"That's one thing I like about you; I'm the same way. But we're at an age when we could use a little calm."

"The thought frightens me."

"Love takes its time. You don't have to answer me right away—we can wait till tomorrow." She laughed.

"It's nothing personal; if ever I decide to marry, you'd be the one, I promise."

"Well, that's something anyway."

"Why wouldn't it be better to be lovers?"

"It isn't the same. I'm too old for adventures. I want a long-term commitment, I want to sleep every night beside my life companion. Do you think I came halfway around the world to ask you to be my lover? It will be great to grow old, hand in hand, you'll see," Carmen replied with finality.

"Good God almighty!" exclaimed Galupi, quite openly pale.

The opportunity to sit once a week in the quiet of Ming O'Brien's consulting room to talk about myself and mull over my actions was an experience I had never known. At first I found it difficult to relax, but she won my confidence, and little by little we opened the sealed compartments of my past. For the first time, I talked about that day in the broom closet, when Martínez raped me, and after that confession I was able to explore the most secret areas of my life. The second year was the hardest. I left each session choked with tears; Ming hadn't lied when she told me it is a painful process, and more than once I was on the verge of giving up. Fortunately, I didn't do it. As I reviewed my fate during those five years, I came to understand the scenario of my life and took the necessary steps to amend it; with time I learned to keep my impulses in check and stop short when I was on the verge of repeating old mistakes. My family life was still a nightmare, and there wasn't much I could do to improve it. Margaret was beyond my reach, but I concentrated on giving David's life as much structure as possible. Until then I had used what Ming called the slot-machine system: my son always got his way; all he had to do was keep pumping the arm of the machine, knowing that sooner or later he would hit the jackpot. He would ask for something, and I would refuse; then he would pester me unmercifully, simply wearing me down until I gave in. Setting boundaries for him wasn't easy, because I had never had them as a boy; I grew up on my own in the street, and I thought that people formed their own lives, that experience was the best teacher. But in my case I had been given discipline and values by my father while he was still alive—they say that the first five or six years are very important in our formation. Besides that, I had always looked out for myself, had always had to work. My children had grown up like savages, without care and without real love, but they had never lacked for anything material. I used money to compensate for the affection I didn't know how to give. A poor substitute.

One of the most important decisions was to lighten some of the burdens I was carrying and to reorganize my office. It was impossible to change the character of my employees, but I could replace them; it wasn't my role to cure them of their vices, pay for their shortcomings, or solve their problems. Why did I invariably surround myself with alcoholics? Why did neurotic or weak people cling to me like lint? I needed to revise that aspect of my personality and defend my own interests. It cost more to run the office than it took in; I myself was responsible for the greater part of the income, but my billfold was always empty and almost all my credit cards had been canceled. My good friend Mike Tong had put in anguishing years trying to square the numbers, and Tina had warned me to the point of exhaustion that my associates not only neglected clients but sometimes handled cases privately, without entering them in the firm's accounts; they also charged me for personal expenses—telephones, restaurant bills, trips, even gifts for lovers. I didn't listen to her; I was too busy paddling around in my personal chaos. I thought that nothing could sink me, that I could always find a way to solve my problems; I had overcome other obstacles and would not be defeated by unpaid bills and fingers in the till—but finally the burden had become more than I could carry. For a long time I debated, feeling doubt and guilt, until Mike Tong, with the precision of his abacus, and Ming O'Brien, with her perseverance, helped me dismiss the parasites one by one and close the branches of the firm in other cities. I kept on Tina, Mike, and a young, intelligent, and loyal female associate; I rented space to a couple of other professionals to reduce the overhead and defray expenses. I learned then that work on a small scale was more profitable and more enjoyable; I held all the reins in my hand and could devote my time to the challenges of my profession rather than burn my energy dealing with an oppressive succession of insignificant complaints. I also had closer contact with my clients, which is what I like best about my work. At the same time, I was making changes in my personal life that paralleled those in the office; I rid myself of many superfluous belongings and habits that bothered me; I gave up the arrogance of Spanish cigars—in fact, stopped smoking altogether—and never tasted a drop of alcohol—the only way to put an end to my allergies. My little black book with its list of ladies got lost in the back of some drawer, and I've never come across it since. Because I had less money to spend, I had no choice but to scale down the way I lived, and the nights on the town became history. I was very busy with David and with my work, and I no longer had Timothy Duane to incite me to sin. That didn't mean I began to live like an anchorite; far from it: I suppose I will always be true to my nature as a bon vivant.

"Very *good*! If you don't get married again, in three years we will pay off your debts," Mike Tong announced joyfully the first time our income surpassed our outlay.

That year I sold the house I owned at the beach and finally settled accounts with Shannon, who the minute she received the last check left town; she had no fixed plans but was eager to begin a new life as far away as possible. I visualized her traveling down

THE INFINITE PLAN · 375

the road until she vanished into thin air, the reverse of her arrival, not on foot this time but in a luxury automobile. Months later I saw her picture in a magazine, advertising cosmetics with an apple-bright smile; I had to look twice to recognize her; she looked much better than I remembered. I cut out the page and showed it to David, who pasted it on the wall of his room. He had a rather hazy image of his mother: a beautiful and cheerful creature who appeared from time to time to smother him with kisses and take him to the movies, a melodious voice on the telephone, and now a seductive face in an advertisement. With my help he had made a wooden chest for her birthday; he sent by mail drawings he had signed especially for her. For him, Shannon was the ethereal vision in fairy tales, a princess in blue jeans who whirled by from time to time like a merry breeze and then blew away. On any practical level, nevertheless, she didn't count for much; his mother was Daisy, who combed his hair with holy water to exorcise the demons and who was there when he opened his eyes every morning and when he closed them every night.

"I want to see my mother," David told me one day.

"She went away and won't be back for a while. She misses you, but because of her work she lives in another city. She's a famous model."

"Where did she go?"

"I don't know, but I'm sure she'll write soon."

"She doesn't love me; that's why she went away."

"She loves you very much, but life is very complicated, David. You won't see her for a while, that's all."

"I think my mother died and you're not telling me the truth."

"I give you my word of honor that it's the truth. Didn't you see her picture in the magazine?"

"Swear it."

"I swear."

"And swear you'll never marry again."

"I can't do that, son. I told you, life is very complicated."

For a few days he was withdrawn and silent; he sat for hours in his window, staring at the sea, something unusual for a boy who was always in a vortex of activity and noise, but soon he was distracted by the excitement of getting ready for our vacation. I had promised we'd go camping together in the mountains, and take Oliver and buy a shotgun to hunt ducks. Shannon continued to be what she had always been for her son: a gentle mirage.

The accusation of malpractice fell from the sky at the end of that same year and seemed so preposterous that I wasn't in the least disturbed. It was brought by one of my former clients, someone my firm had represented several years before. He was an alcoholic. It had all begun when he was riding an interstate bus to Oregon; he'd had too much to drink and halfway there started raving about monsters chasing him. In this deranged state, he pulled a knife and attacked the other passengers; he wounded two and missed killing a third by a miracle: the blade slashed his throat millimeters from the jugular. With the help of a few brave passengers, the driver disarmed the attacker, made him get off the bus, and then sped to the nearest hospital, where he unloaded the victims, who were bleeding copiously. The police did not apprehend the assailant, who had gone into hiding, but four days later a truck picked him up along the highway. It was winter; his feet had been frostbitten and had to be amputated. When he got out of the hospital and dealt with his criminal case, he looked for someone to represent him in a suit against the bus company for having abandoned him in open country. My firm took the case; in those days, we took anyone who knocked at the door. Three knifed passengers are good reason to put the sonofabitch off my bus; it was his bad luck that he froze his feet while he was hiding from the police, but he got what he deserved, the bus driver said in his deposition. Despite the claimant's record, we were able to settle the case for a respectable sum because the bus company found it less trouble to make payment than to go to trial. Once the man spent that money, however, he went to several lawyers and finally found one who would initiate a case against me. I had no insurance, so if I lost, it was the ball game, but I never in my wildest dream imagined such a thing could happen—no jury in the world would find in the criminal's favor. Mike Tong didn't agree; he said

THE INFINITE PLAN · 377

that if the suit had been against the bus driver, the jury would stand firm; any one of them who put himself in the place of the passengers and the victims would vote against the plaintiff, but this guy was suing *me*.

"On one side they'll see a poor cripple on crutches, and on the other a lawyer wearing a silk tie. The jury will be against you, Mr. Reeves; people hate lawyers. Besides, you'll have to hire a defense attorney, and where will we get the money for that?" My accountant sighed. For once setting aside the respect with which he had always treated me, he took me by the arm, pulled me into his cubby, and confronted me with the unquestionable reality of the books.

Mike had it right. Three months later the jury decided that the bus driver should not have ejected the man from the bus and that my firm had been negligent on the client's behalf in settling with the bus company instead of going to trial. That verdict, which produced no little amazement in the legal world, was the crowning blow. For years I had been teetering on the edge of a precipice, but this was the final push. Unless I found Sir Francis Drake's treasure buried in my patio, I hadn't a prayer of paying the amount of the judgment. I joked about it, unbelieving, when I heard the verdict, but very quickly the gravity of what had happened left no room for jokes; in a matter of hours I must take drastic measures. I called in Tina and Mike. I thanked them for their long and loyal service and explained that I would have to declare bankruptcy and close the office, but I promised that if I could somehow start again in the future, there would always be a place for them. Tina burst into inconsolable weeping, but no glimmer of emotion crossed Mike's impassive Asiatic face. You can count on us, he said, and repaired to his burrow to work on his books.

Throughout the eternity of the trial, I was beside my defense lawyer, fighting fiercely over every detail; it was a time of terrible tension, but when it was over I accepted the verdict with a sangfroid I didn't know I possessed. I had the sensation of having lived through similar situations before; yet again I was on a dead-

end street, as I had been so often in the barrio. I remembered all
the times I had run home, trailed by Martínez's gang, sure that if
they caught me they would kill me—but I was still alive. I had
emerged unscathed from skirmishes in Vietnam where others had
left their lives, and had survived that night on the mountain when
all the dice were loaded against me. The beatings I had taken in
school and the harsh lessons of the war had taught me to defend
myself, to hang on. I knew I mustn't lose my head, or my sense of
proportion; compared to past battles, this was just a blip; my life
would go on. It passed through my mind that I might take up a
different career; being a lawyer has its dark side. I questioned the
validity of living my life with a sword in one hand, eating myself
up with meaningless combativeness. I still ask myself that question but have no answer; I suppose I can't imagine a life without
struggle.

On Sunday I was resigned to closing the firm. Among other
alternatives, I contemplated the possibility of going to some Latin
American country; I have very strong ties with that part of the
world and like speaking Spanish. I also thought of moving to a
small town, where life was simpler, where I could do something
for people and be part of a community, as I had been in the village
in Vietnam; after some thought, however, that seemed a kind of
flight. Carmen and Ming are right: no matter how far you run,
you're always in the same skin. I also thought about moving to the
country. The week David and I spent camping, with little to do
but hunt ducks and fish, with no company but the dog, were very
important for me and showed me an unexpected side of my character. In the solitude of the countryside, I recaptured the silence of
my childhood, the silence the soul finds in the peace of nature,
silence I had lost when my father fell ill and we had to stay in the
city. From then on, my life had been marred by noise, far too
much noise, and I had grown so accustomed to the incessant
racket in my head that I had forgotten the blessing of true silence.
The experience of sleeping on the ground with only the stars for
light brought back the one truly happy period in my life: traveling
with my family in our truck. I regressed to my first memory of

happiness, myself at four, urinating on a hilltop beneath the orange-streaked dome of a magnificent sky at dusk. To measure the infinite vastness of the space I had regained, I shouted my name there beside the lake, and the echo from the mountains returned it to me, purified. Those days in the open air were also enormously beneficial to David. His accelerated nervous system seemed to slow to a more normal pace; we did not have a single argument, he returned to school in good humor, and two months went by without a kicking fit. We'd be much better off if we left this life where pressures can mount to such an unbearable pitch, but the truth is I still can't see myself as a farmer or forest ranger; why fool myself? Maybe later ... maybe never. I like people, I need to feel I'm of some use to others, I don't think I'd last very long tucked away like a hermit. Did you know that it was in that wild country I learned about you? Carmen had given me your second novel, and I read it during that vacation, never imagining that one day I would meet you and make this long confession. How could I suspect then that together we would go back to the barrio where I grew up? In more than four decades it had never crossed my mind to go back; if you hadn't insisted, I would never have seen the cottage again, in ruins but still standing, or the willow tree, still vigorous despite neglect and the garbage dump that had built up around it. If you hadn't taken me, I would never have found the weathered sign of *The Infinite Plan* that was lying there waiting for me, paint peeling, wood worm-eaten, but with its eloquence intact. Look how far I've come to reach this point and find there is no infinite plan, just the strife of living, I told you that day. Maybe, you answered, maybe everyone carries a plan inside, but it's a faded map that's hard to read and that's why we wander around so and sometimes get lost.

I accepted the fact that the house and the car, the only two things I owned in the world, were gone; I owed money on everything else, and we'd have to see how to manage that. In the end, that would be a problem for the auditors and lawyers; they'd be there Monday to pounce on the spoils like piranhas. The idea made me boil with rage, but it didn't frighten me. I've earned my own living since I was seven, doing all kinds of jobs, and I'm convinced I'll always find a way to make it. I was worried about the people who worked for me, though. They're my true family, but I felt sure that Mike and Tina could find another job without much difficulty, and that Carmen would take Daisy, because Doña Inmaculada is getting too old to take care of that house by herself. That night I dropped in on Timothy and Ming to tell them what was happening. Six months earlier I had finished my therapy, and now Ming and I were excellent friends, not just because of the long relationship cultivated in her office but because she was living with Tim, who was a different person ever since she walked in and set his life in order with her wisdom. Ming, it turned out, was an excellent balm for my tormented friend. During the five years of my painful self-exploration, I had come full circle, and when I finally reached the place where I had begun, Ming declared that I didn't need her help anymore. She told me I was beginning the most important part of my treatment, the part I had to do alone, that I was like an invalid who had been taught how to walk again but would regain his equilibrium and strength only with laborious practice, step after step. With much patience on her part and effort on mine, we had cleared away the volcanic confusion that had clouded the first half of my destiny. Holding her hand, I had entered the room of the badly built and unfinished machines my father had always talked about, and gradually imposed some order. I had thrown away unnecessary parts, welded pieces together, reshaped imperfections, and finished what had been left unfinished. There was still a lot to clean out, but I could do it alone. I knew that my journey through this world would always resemble a surreal tapestry, imperfect for the many loose threads, but at least now I could see the design.

"Well, I've been fucked over for sure this time. I don't have any more credit at the banks, and I can't pay my debts. I have no choice but to declare bankruptcy," I told my friends.

"Everything that really matters is safe from this crisis, Greg. You're losing material things; you'll come out with everything else intact," Ming replied, and she was right, as always.

"I guess I'll have to begin all over again," I muttered, but with a strange feeling of euphoria.

Life is irony added to irony. When I saw my family disintegrating and eliminated many other relationships from my life, I lost my terror of being alone. Then when I saw the house of cards of my law firm collapsing and was wiped out, I experienced true security for the first time. And now, just when I had stopped looking for a companion, you appeared and compelled me to plant the rosebushes in solid ground. I realized that in my heart money had never interested me as much as I wanted to believe; the acquisitive goals I set in the hospital in Hawaii were wrongheaded, and deep inside I had always suspected that. I was not deceived by my supposed triumphs; the truth is that all my life I had been pursued by a vague sensation of failure. It took me an eternity, nevertheless, to learn that the more I accumulated, the more vulnerable I was, because I live in a world where the opposite message is drummed into us. Tremendous lucidity is required—Carmen has it—not to fall into that trap. I did not have it, and I had to sink to the very bottom to obtain it. At the moment my world caved in on me, when I had nothing left, I discovered I didn't feel depressed, I felt free. I realized that the most important thing was not, as I had imagined, to survive or be successful; the most important thing was the search for my soul, which I had left behind in the quicksand of my childhood. When I found it, I learned that the power I had wasted such desperate energy to gain had always been inside me. I was reconciled with myself, I accepted myself with a touch of kindness, and then, and only then, was rewarded with my first glimpse of peace. I think that was the precise instant I became aware of who I truly am, and at last felt in control of my destiny.

Monday I arrived at the office early in order to clear up some final details. I was met with a bouquet of red roses on my desk and the complicitous smiles of Tina Faibich and Mike Tong, who were there even before me.

"We don't have Sir Francis Drake's treasure, but I did arrange some credit," my accountant announced, twisting his tie, which he always does when he's nervous.

"What do you mean, Mike?"

"I took the liberty of calling your friend Carmen Morales in Rome. She is lending us a large sum of money. And I have an uncle who is a banker, and he's agreed to give us a loan. With that to go on, we can negotiate. If we declare bankruptcy, no one will get a penny; it's to your creditor's advantage to work out terms with us and be patient."

"I don't have any collateral."

"Among Chinese, your word of honor is enough. Carmen said that you had bankrolled her since she was six years old and that she's just lending you a hand in return."

"More debts, Mike?"

"We're used to it; what's one more stripe to the tiger?"

"You mean we keep up the fight!" I smiled, aware that this time it would be on my own terms.

You know the rest, because we've lived it together. The night we met, you asked me to tell you my story. It's very long, I warned you. That's all right, I have a lot of time, you said, not suspecting what you were getting into when you walked into this infinite plan.

Insights,
Interviews
& More . . .

Isabel Allende on Destiny, Personal Tragedy, and Writing

© William Gordon

"Life is nothing but noise between two unfathomable silences." Can you describe that noise, what it is, and what it means to you?

We have very busy lives—or we make them very busy. There is noise and activity everywhere. Few people know how to be still and find a quiet place inside themselves. From that place of silence and stillness the creative forces emerge. There we find faith, hope, strength, and wisdom. Since childhood, however, we are taught to do things. Our heads are full of noise. Silence and solitude scare most of us.

You often talk and write about destiny. What is destiny for you?

We are born with a set of cards and we have the freedom to play them the best we can, but we cannot change them. I was born female in the forties into a conservative Catholic family in Chile. I was born healthy. I had my shots as a child. I received love and a proper education. All that determines who I am. The really important events in my life happened in spite of me. I had no control over them: the fact that my father left the family when I was three; the 1973 military coup in Chile that forced me into exile; meeting my husband Willie; the success of my books; the death of my daughter; and so forth. That is destiny.

> The really important events in my life happened in spite of me. I had no control over them.

Just before your daughter, Paula, went into a coma, she said, "I look everywhere for God but can't find him." Do you, can you, have faith in God after such a tragedy?

Faith has nothing to do with being happy or not. Faith is a gift. Some people receive it and some don't. I imagine that a tragedy like losing a child is more bearable if you believe in God because you can imagine that your child is in heaven.

Do you think that fiction has a moral purpose? Or can it simply be entertainment?

It can be just entertainment, but when fiction makes you think, it is much more exciting. However, beware of authors ▶

who pound their "moral messages" into you.

You have written letters all your life, most notably a daily letter to your mother. You've also worked as a journalist. Which form or experience of writing helped you most when you started writing books?

The training of writing daily is very useful. As a journalist I learned to research, to be disciplined, to meet deadlines, to be precise and direct, and to keep in mind the reader and try to grab his or her attention from the very beginning.

Does writing each book change you?

Writing is a process, a journey into memory and the soul. Why do I write only about certain themes and certain characters? Because they are part of my life, part of myself, they are aspects of me that I need to explore and understand.

You always start writing on January 8th, but when do you finish? How long does it take you to write your books?

I write approximately a book per year, but it takes me several years to research a theme. It takes me three or four months to write the first draft, then I have to correct and edit. I write in

66 Writing is a process, a journey into memory and the soul. 99

Spanish, so I also have to work closely with my English translator, Margaret Sayers Peden. And then I have to spend time on book tours, interviews, traveling, et cetera.

Do you have a favorite among your books?

I don't read my own books. As soon as I finish one I am already thinking of the next. I can hardly remember each book. I don't have a favorite, but I am grateful to my first novel, *The House of the Spirits*, which paved the way for all the others, and to *Paula*, because it saved me from depression.

You grew up in Chile but now live in the United States. Which country has had the most influence on your writing and why?

It is very easy for me to write about Chile. I don't have to think about it. The stories just flow. My roots are in Chile and most of my books have a Latin American flavor. However, I have lived in the United States for many years, I read mainly English fiction, I live in English, and certainly that influences my writing.

66 I don't read my own books. As soon as I finish one I am already thinking of the next. 99

A Conversation with Isabel Allende

Which of your male characters do you like best? Remember that Flaubert said, "Madame Bovary, c'est moi!"

Gregory Reeves, in *The Infinite Plan*. I like him so much that in real life, I married him some years ago, and not even marriage has made me stop liking him.

The Infinite Plan *is based on the life of your husband, William Gordon. How much is fiction and how much reality?*

I don't honestly know. I think all my books, with the exception of *Eva Luna* and a few stories, are much more reality than fiction. In *The Infinite Plan*, the characters are based on human models, and nearly everything that happens is real. Sometimes I needed two people to create a character, as was the case with Carmen/Tamar. The models were Carmen Alvarez, a childhood friend of Willie's, and Tabra Tunoa, my good friend, who gave me her biography to use for Tamar. Gregory Reeves was very easy, since Willie was the model. . . . I didn't have to invent the character; it was there, waiting for me. No need to exhaust my imagination.

What was Willie's reaction when he read the book? Weren't you afraid he would be horrified to find himself

66 In *The Infinite Plan*, the characters are based on human models, and nearly everything that happens is real. 99

exposed in those pages, with all his problems and faults?

My mother said it would lead to a divorce, but none of it was a surprise to him because we had discussed each chapter. When I met him and he began to tell me the story of his life, I knew I had to write it, and I think that was why I fell so quickly and deeply in love. From the very beginning, I told him what I had in mind; there was nothing hidden. I spent four years sleeping with that story, checking details, asking questions, visiting the places where events had occurred, interviewing dozens of people. When he read the book, Willie told me, he was deeply moved: "This is a map of my life; now I understand where I've been." The danger with that, of course, is that now he thinks he's Gregory Reeves and goes around worrying about who will play him in the film. He thinks Paul Newman is a little short. . . . ∽

66 When I met [Willie] and he began to tell me the story of his life, I knew I had to write it, and I think that was why I fell so quickly and deeply in love. 99

Taken from *Isabel Allende: Life and Spirits*, Celia Correas Zapata, Arte Publico Press, 2002

Excerpt: *Island Beneath the Sea*

Read on for a preview of Island Beneath the Sea, *Isabel Allende's new novel, available in hardcover in May 2010 from HarperCollins Publishers.*

Zarité

In my forty years I, Zarité Sedella, have had better luck than other slaves. I am going to have a long life and my old age will be a time of contentment because my star—*mi z'etoile*—also shines when the night is cloudy. I know the pleasure of being with the man my heart has chosen. His large hands awaken my skin. I have had four children and a grandson, and those who are living are free. My first memory of happiness, when I was just a bony, runny-nosed, tangle-haired little girl, is moving to the sound of the drums, and that is also my most recent happiness, because last night I was in the Place Congo dancing and dancing, without a thought in my head, and today my body is warm and weary. Music is a wind that blows away the years, memories, and fear, that crouching animal I carry inside me. With the drums the everyday Zarité disappears, and I am again the little girl who danced when she barely knew how to walk. I strike the ground with the soles of

> 66 Music is a wind that blows away the years, memories, and fear, that crouching animal I carry inside me. 99

my feet and life rises up my legs, spreads up my skeleton, takes possession of me, drives away distress and sweetens my memory. The world trembles. Rhythm is born on the island beneath the sea; it shakes the earth, it cuts through me like a lighting bolt and rises toward the sky, carrying with it my sorrows so that Papa Bondye can chew them, swallow them, and leave me clean and happy. The drums conquer fear. The drums are the heritage of my mother, the strength of Guinea that is in my blood. No one can harm me when I am with the drums, I become as overpowering as Erzulie, loa of love, and swifter than the bullwhip. The shells on my wrists and ankles click in time, the gourds ask questions, the djembe drums answer in the voice of the jungle and the timbales with their tin tones. The djun djuns that know how to speak make the invitation, and the big maman roars when they beat her to summon the loas. The drums are sacred, the loas speak through them.

In the house where I spent my earliest years the drums were silent in the room we shared with Honoré, the other slave, but they were often taken out. Madame Delphine, my mistress then, did not want to hear the blacks' noise, only the melancholy laments of her clavichord. Mondays and Tuesdays she gave classes to girls of color, and the rest of the week she taught in the mansions of the grand blancs, where the mademoiselles had their own instruments because they could not use the ones the mulatta ▶

> " The drums conquer fear. The drums are the heritage of my mother, the strength of Guinea that is in my blood. No one can harm me when I am with the drums . . . "

girls touched. I learned to clean the keys with lemon juice, but I could not make music because Madame forbade us to go near her clavichord. We didn't need it. Honoré could draw music from a cookpot; anything in his hands had beat, melody, rhythm, and voice. He carried sounds inside his body; he had brought them from Dahomey. My toy was a hollowed gourd we made to rattle; later he taught me to caress his drums, slowly. And from the beginning, when he was still carrying me around in his arms, he took me to dances and voodoo services, where he marked the rhythm with his drum, the principal drum, for others to follow. This is how I remember it. Honoré seemed very old to me because his bones had frozen stiff, even though at the time he was no older than I am now. He drank taffia in order to endure the pain of moving, but more than that harsh rum, music was the best remedy. His moans turned to laughter with the sound of the drums. Honoré barely could peel sweet potatoes for the mistress's meal, his hands were so deformed, but playing the drum he never got tired, and when it came to dancing no one lifted his knees higher, or swung his head with more force, or shook his behind with more pleasure. Before I knew how to walk, he had me dance sitting down, and when I could just balance myself on two legs he

66 His moans turned to laughter with the sound of the drums. 99

invited me to lose myself in the music, the way you do in a dream. "Dance, dance, Zarité, the slave who dances is free . . . while he is dancing," he told me. I have always danced. ❧

Have You Read?
More by Isabel Allende

DAUGHTER OF FORTUNE

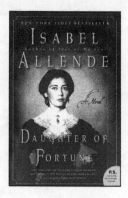

An orphan raised in Valparaíso, Chile, by a Victorian spinster and her rigid brother, young, vivacious Eliza Sommers follows her lover to California during the Gold Rush of 1849. Entering a rough-and-tumble world of new arrivals driven mad by gold fever, Eliza moves in a society of single men and prostitutes with the help of her good friend and savior, the Chinese doctor Tao Chi'en. California opens the door to a new life of freedom and independence for the young Chilean, and her search for her elusive lover gradually turns into another kind of journey. By the time she finally hears news of him, Eliza must decide who her true love really is.

"An extravagant tale by a gifted storyteller whose spell brings to life the nineteenth-century world. . . . Entertaining and well paced . . . compelling."   —*Los Angeles Times*

"A rich cast of characters . . . a pleasurable story. . . . In *Daughter of Fortune*, Allende has continued her obsession with passion and violence."
      —*New York Times Book Review*

PORTRAIT IN SEPIA

As a young girl Aurora del Valle suffered a brutal trauma that shaped her character and erased from her mind all recollection of the first five years of her life. Raised by her ambitious grandmother, the regal and commanding Paulina del Valle, she grows up in a privileged environment. Aurora is free of the limitations that circumscribed the lives of women at that time, but is tormented by terrible nightmares. When she finds herself alone at the end of an unhappy love affair, she decides to explore the mystery of her past and to discover exactly what it was all those years ago that had such a devastating effect on her young life. Richly detailed and epic in scope, this engrossing story of the dark power of hidden secrets is intimate in its probing of human character and thrilling in the way it illuminates the complexity of family ties.

"Rich with color and emotion and packed with intriguing characters."
— *San Francisco Chronicle*

13

ZORRO

Born in southern California late in the eighteenth century, Diego de la Vega is a child of two worlds. His father is an aristocratic Spanish military man turned landowner; his mother a Shoshone warrior. Diego learns from his maternal grandmother, White Owl, the ways of her tribe, while receiving from his father lessons in the art of fencing and in cattle branding. It is here, during a childhood filled with mischief and adventure, that Diego witnesses the brutal injustices dealt Native Americans by European settlers and first feels the inner conflict of his heritage.

At the age of sixteen, Diego is sent to Barcelona for a European education. In a country chafing under the corruption of Napoleonic rule, Diego follows the example of his celebrated fencing master and joins La Justicia, a secret underground resistance movement devoted to helping the powerless and the poor. With this tumultuous period as a backdrop, Diego falls in love, saves the persecuted, and confronts for the first time a great rival who emerges from the world of privilege.

Between California and Barcelona, the New World and the Old, the persona of Zorro is formed, a great hero is born, and the legend begins. After many adventures—duels at dawn, fierce battles with pirates at sea, and impossible rescues—Diego de la Vega, a.k.a. Zorro, returns to America to reclaim the hacienda on which he was raised and to seek justice for all who cannot fight for it themselves.

"Allende's discreetly subversive talent really shows. . . . You turn the pages, cheering on the masked man."
—*Los Angeles Times*

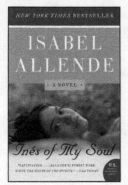

INÉS OF MY SOUL

This magisterial work of historical fiction recounts the astonishing life of Inés Suarez, a daring Spanish conquistadora who toiled to build the nation of Chile—and whose vital role has too often been neglected by history.

It is the beginning of the Spanish conquest of the Americas, and when Inés's shiftless husband disappears to the New World, she uses the opportunity to search for him as an excuse to flee her stifling homeland and seek adventure. After a treacherous journey to Peru, she learns of his death in battle. She meets and begins a passionate love affair with a man who seeks only honor and glory: Pedro Valdivia, war hero and field marshal to the famed Francisco Pizarro. Together, Inés and Valdivia will build the new city of Santiago and wage a ruthless war against the indigenous Chileans. The horrific struggle will change them forever, pulling them toward separate destinies.

Inés of My Soul is a work of breathtaking scope, written with the narrative brilliance and passion readers have come to expect from Isabel Allende.

"Riveting . . . it simply captivates. . . . A colorful and clear-eyed portrait of a woman and a country."
                                                    —*Chicago Sun-Times*

APHRODITE: A MEMOIR OF THE SENSES

Under the aegis of the Goddess of Love, Isabel Allende uses her storytelling skills brilliantly in *Aphrodite* to evoke the delights of food and sex. After considerable research and study she has become an authority on aphrodisiacs, which include everything from food and drink to stories and, of course, love. Readers will find here recipes from Allende's mother, poems, stories from ancient and foreign literature, paintings, personal anecdotes, fascinating tidbits on the sensual art of food and its effect on amorous performance, tips on how to attract your mate and revive flagging virility, passages on the effect of smell on libido, a history of alcoholic beverages, and much more.

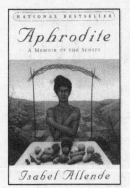

"Allende turns the joyous preparation and consumption of fine food into an erotic catalyst."
                    —*New York Times Book Review*

PAULA: A MEMOIR

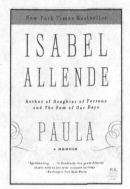

With an enchanting blend of magic realism, politics, and romance reminiscent of her classic bestseller *The House of the Spirits,* Isabel Allende presents a soul-baring memoir that seizes the reader like a novel of suspense.

Written for her daughter, Paula, when she became ill and slipped into a coma, *Paula* is the colorful story of Allende's life—from her early years in her native Chile, through the turbulent military coup of 1973, to the subsequent dictatorship and her family's years of exile. In the telling, bizarre ancestors reveal themselves, delightful and bitter childhood memories surface, enthralling anecdotes of youthful years are narrated, and intimate secrets are softly whispered.

In an exorcism of death and a celebration of life, Isabel Allende explores the past and questions the gods. She creates a magical book that carries the reader from tears to laughter, and from terror through sensuality to wisdom. In *Paula,* readers will come to understand that the miraculous world of her novels is the world Isabel Allende inhabits—it is her enchanted reality.

"Spellbinding. . . . In flawlessly rich prose, [Allende] shares with us her most intimate feelings."
                —*Washington Post Book World*

MY INVENTED COUNTRY: A MEMOIR

Isabel Allende evokes the magnificent landscapes of her country, a charming, idiosyncratic Chilean people with a violent history and an indomitable spirit, and the politics, religion, myth, and magic of a homeland that she carries with her even today. The book circles around two life-changing moments. The assassination of her uncle Salvador Allende Gossens on September 11, 1973, sent her into exile and transformed her into a literary writer. And the terrorist attacks against her adopted homeland the United States on September 11, 2001, brought forth an overdue acknowledgment that Allende had indeed left home. *My Invented Country,* mimicking the workings of memory itself, ranges back and forth across that distance between past and present lives. It speaks compellingly to immigrants and to all of us who try to retain a coherent inner life in a world full of contradictions.

"The book gets my undivided attention when it expounds on the relationship of the author to that country of hers, invented, imaginary, fictional, to the story of her family, which is itself invented memory, and to her vocation as a narrator."

—*Los Angeles Times*

THE SUM OF OUR DAYS

In *The Sum of Our Days*, internationally acclaimed author Isabel Allende reconstructs the painful reality of her own life in the wake of the tragic death of her daughter, Paula. Narrated with warmth, humor, exceptional candor, and wisdom, this remarkable memoir is as exuberant and full of life as its creator. Allende bares her soul as she shares her thoughts on love, marriage, motherhood, spirituality and religion, infidelity, addiction, and memory—and recounts stories of the wildly eccentric, strong-minded, and eclectic tribe she gathers around her and lovingly embraces as a new kind of family.

"Terrific. . . . Funny, insightful, moving, and filled with Allende's unique voice."
—*USA Today*

Don't miss the next book by your favorite author. Sign up now for AuthorTracker by visiting www.AuthorTracker.com.